Fredrika Bremer, Mary Botham Howitt

The four Sisters

A Tale of social and domestic Life in Sweden

Fredrika Bremer, Mary Botham Howitt

The four Sisters
A Tale of social and domestic Life in Sweden

ISBN/EAN: 9783337082444

Printed in Europe, USA, Canada, Australia, Japan

Cover: Foto ©Andreas Hilbeck / pixelio.de

More available books at **www.hansebooks.com**

A TALE OF

Social and Domestic Life in Sweden.

BY

FREDRIKA BREMER.

AUTHOR OF

"THE NEIGHBOURS," "NINA," "THE PRESIDENT'S DAUGHTERS," "THE H—— FAMILY,"
"THE HOME," "HOMES IN THE NEW WORLD," ETC., ETC.

TRANSLATED BY

MARY HOWITT.

Authorized American Edition, with the Author's Dedication.

Philadelphia:
T. B. PETERSON AND BROTHERS,
306 CHESTNUT STREET.

DEDICATION FOR THE AMERICAN EDITION.

TO THE

Blessed Memory of

A. J. DOWNING,

THIS BOOK IS DEDICATED IN LOVE AND GRATEFUL REMEM-
BRANCE BY THE AUTHOR.

"THE women must regenerate us socially," was a favorite saying of yours, my friend, a saying precious to me as coming from a spirit so just, so observing, and discriminating as your's; and as it seemed to me to express a feeling inherent, though only half conscious, in the people of your country—the great New World, the land of promise and of hope to millions of hearts in Europe.

It also corresponded deeply to the faith of my own heart. But if woman shall be able to accomplish the great work which we believe intrusted to her by the great Author of life, our laws and customs, institutions and education, must not counteract the normal development of her noblest faculties, of her will and aspirations; they must rather be to her the very soil and sun in which the tree of her life can grow, and develop its branches, and bear its fruits, in full correspondence to its inward essence.

(xix)

You will certainly assent to this, my friend, you, whose skillful hand loved to raise plants of every kind so as to propitiate their full growth and God-given beauty or grace. But is it so with regard to human institutions, for the growth of woman's mind, and the full development of her God-given gifts?

You know, my friend, that it is not so; you observed it already on earth, and must know it better still in that blessed society where men and women commune as angels before the face of God. Even in your native land, which a friend and countryman of mine calls, "The promised land of woman, and of the child," and where the women are indulged and left fancy-free certainly more than in any other country on earth, it is not so. There, even there, indulgence has not yet become justice, and the love for women not reverence to her mission, so as to command a training for her mind, and opportunities for its development corresponding to that mission—training and opportunities which alone can make her acquire her full worth. Nor has she yet been propitiated so far in any country on earth, though superior natures have, in almost all countries, shown the worth and influence she is capable of.

Of her situation in my own land, with reference to our laws and social customs, I have drawn a picture in the work under the name of "The Four Sisters," and which I dedicate to you; then by men such as you, and to you congenial, I should wish my work to be judged. Its bitter parts must be excused on the score of bitter pain, not of a selfish kind. The patriarchal bonds which keep back the growth of woman's mind and social life in Sweden, and which sometimes amounts to the most crushing tyranny, I have shadowed forth in these pages, often with a heavy heart.

But I have done it for love for the moral growth and worth of my people, in strong faith and hope that when its noble spirit came to look facts in the face, and know the suffering and debasement, or the bitterness of spirit arising from this state of things, it will rise and carry out in the liberation of woman, the noble motto of our present King, "*Truth and Justice.*"

My people was the first among the Scandinavian nations to liberate its slaves, when the blessed voice of the Redeemer was heard in the North, proclaiming the brotherhood of all men and the freedom in the *father* God. Certainly it cannot long be one of the last to liberate the loving companion of man, *woman*, from a state of tutelage and bondage, which other Christian countries have already shaken off for her. More than this liberation, I do not at present hope for. But when the day will come, when the sons of the earth will better know their true welfare, they will give much more still to her who is to be the Mother and first teacher: in fact, the inspiring Egeria of the future generations, the coming Man! From your heavenly home, my friend, methinks I see you smiling down, " Amen."

Since we parted on American shores, the homes of my country have drawn nearer to those of your land in sympathy and love for their noble hearts, their beautiful life; and I am happy to know that I have some part in this, though only as the well who gives back the images of the flowers and stars looking down in her mirror.

Your noblest poets and prose-writers have begun to be translated in my native tongue. "Uncle Tom's Cabin," has been read passionately by rich and poor, in the palaces and cabins of my land; Longfellow's poems are translated by a graceful Swedish muse; and Washington Irving's " Wolfert's Roost," is now read in our daily papers throughout the land, with that peculiar pleasure and charm awakened by this delightful writer, ever young, ever pure, writing as no other, romantic interest with classical purity and elegance, beloved by all classes, read in all lands.

Even your books, my friend, are spreading in my country, and are, this moment, helping my brother-in-law to build a house and plant a garden for his summer residence.

At my parting with you, I promised to give the right of publication in America of a work of mine to a friend of yours, whose generous spirit even I had learned to know and to appreciate. In now giving my " Four Sisters" in the hands of the Publisher, I am conscious that I intrust to him the work, which, of all my writings, has the deepest root in my own life and consciousness—a work which sacred duty commanded me to write. And I am happy to fulfill my engagement to him, and a wish of yours.

FREDRIKA BREMER.

THE FOUR SISTERS.

AN EVENING PARTY.

"Nowhere," says the proverb, "do things happen more oddly than in this world." And nowhere in the world did things happen more oddly than on a certain evening in our good town of Kungsköping; for there was a great party there, and people were heard talking in this style:

"Now, ladies and gentlemen, we must set to and arrange everything! Every group in order! Camellias, mignonettes, and roses, you all stand in that corner: good fairies and hobgoblins in the opposite one. Gods and goddesses, stand forward—Olympus to the right, Valhalla to the left!—Jupiter, Colonel Jupiter, where is he?—'Pon my honor, standing and shaking hands with Odin. Colonel Jupiter, do you hear? What have you to do with Valhalla? You belong to the Olympian division. Mrs. Frigga, be so good as to take charge of Odin and his people. We must keep order in the world."

"Yes, certainly: only don't forget that Odin must dance with Juno, and I with Jupiter."

"Of course, in the grand Polonaise. But now every one must go to his own post. Colonel Jupiter, be so good and stand here beside your worthy offspring, Mars and Vulcan, Apollo and Bacchus! General Odin, march forward!—if I may be so bold. Lieutenant Thor—superb! Assessor

Balder; very good! Miss Iduna, be so obliging!—Iron-master Brage—where the deuce is he gone to? Ha! ha! he stands bowing to the graces of Olympus. Do you hear, my good sir, leave all that till the great polska. Your place, for the present, is in Valhalla, and on this side. The Parcæ here; the Nornor there; that is as it should be. Good fairies and goblins, let me see you in your own region! No deserters now. It is enough to turn one's head. Apropos of head, where have we a Mimer's head? Where can we get a Mimer?"

"Professor Methodius!"

"Our one-eyed uncle! Splendid. But where is he?"

"There! standing with his forefinger to his nose, demonstrating his system to the Countess P. He is, no doubt, at this very moment amid the creation of the world. I can see it in his face."

And that was true enough. The Professor, called Methodius, was really standing before the Countess P., and replying to her somewhat mischievous inquiry of "how the system was going on?"

"Thank you for the inquiry; oh yes, it rocks to and fro like the seaman aground in his vessel." And the Professor laughed heartily at his own conceit. "The fact is, that as yet I cannot get it rightly in order, cannot set it to work, as they say. Nevertheless I have got part way. And if one is only sure of the foundation, one may feel quite safe in building up the house and putting the roof on. In the same way, if one will improve the state of the world one must know something about the beginning of the world, and therefore must begin at the beginning. One must go methodically to work. Suppose now that we imagine the beginning, I mean the creation. Imagine then, my gracious Countess, a —movement, yes, just a movement, as of an immense mass of meal porridge, which fills all space; and the whole of this mass moves and moves and seethes, just as one sees porridge heaving and seething in a big pot. But through all this heaving and this seething, the grains (the atoms, as the learned call them, but we will express ourselves in a popular manner) collect or mass themselves together into small lumps and clumps, and these again lump themselves together into still larger and larger lumps and masses—and so it goes on till—till at last all the porridge-grains have adhered in one great lump or mass, which we call the earth. Now it is ready ; now there it lies, like a great ball, and now it gets a good sound blow or bang on its side, which sends it spinning round and round into infinite space, till——"

"But, my dear Professor, who gave it the blow ?" inquired the Countess.

"Blow here and bang there !" exclaimed Major von Post, the lively *maître des plaisirs* of both the town and the present company, interrupting at this point the history of creation ; "pardon, good uncle, but since you helped our Lord in the creation of the world, be so good as to help us a little in bringing our Valhalla into order, and lend us your head for Mimer's head."

The good Professor seemed at the first moment somewhat confounded by this unexpected proposal, but immediately replied with a good-tempered smile :

"Most willingly, if I can only be sure about what is going to happen to my head. For as I remember, Mimer's head had to undergo some extraordinary operations, such as being cut off, being boiled, and——"

"Ah, dear papa, there is no danger. I'll be answerable for your head," interrupted, laughing, an elegantly attired lady, over whose full, but still youthful countenance, such a sun-shine of joy and kindliness was diffused, that it seemed as though it could never have any wrinkles ; and while Minmi Svanberg endeavored with her white and soft hand to smoothe down the Professor's disorderly grey-streaked locks, she continued ; " we assume here many dissimilar shapes, but always remain ourselves nevertheless. I am going to be, one after another, first a witch, then a goddess, and lastly Pax Domestica, with a whole train of sweeping-brooms and dust-pans ;—papa, be a splendid Mimer !"

"Well, just as you like, my dear Mimmi; but——"

"Everybody must come; one go after another. Let us begin, let us begin, ladies and gentlemen, or we shall never be ready!" exclaimed the Major.

"One moment; just one moment more, my dear Major," besought the lady of the house; "let us first have tea. It is just ready. And everything will go on with so much more spirit when people have had some refreshment."

We hope that by this time we have corrected the suspicion which our readers at the beginning might have entertained, namely, that they were in a company of fools. They are now aware most likely that they are in company with very rational people, assembled to amuse themselves with a merry scheme. The company have this evening met in Merchant Dufva's large drawing-room, for the rehearsal of a great fancy-ball, which was to take place a few days later in the splendid new Assembly Rooms of the town, and which was to be the crowning festivity of all the festive occasions of the present winter; "altogether most exquisitely, most divinely amusing," said the young girls.

People had enjoyed this winter many public festivities in the good town of Kungsköping, which, although not properly belonging to the small towns, yet, nevertheless, under ordinary circumstances, participated in the ordinary mode of life peculiar to small Swedish towns, which has been described by a lady residing in a small town as follows:—"One day is so terribly like another that people don't know how to distinguish one from another." For this reason many an inhabitant of a little town, that he may not drop fast asleep from sheer weariness, endeavors to keep himself awake by drinking punch, playing at cards, and many other such pastimes, which have the result of making the purse light, and the heart heavy. The ladies again, when they do not partake of the gentlemen's pastime—which sometimes happens—generally endeavor to amuse themselves with coffee-parties, novel-reading, and petty scandal, by way of a little spice to the thin, spiritual soup of daily life. And this especially dur-

ing our long northern winters. But this winter in Kungsköping formed a brilliant exception to ordinary winters. The
railroad, which was being laid down just outside the town,
had brought to its social circles a number of young engineers,
for the most part lively and intelligent men, who had given a
new spring to every pleasure, and people had especially afforded them opportunities for cheerful exercise at their balls, and
their suppers, which had taken the character of balls. In short,
nobody could remember there ever having been so gay a
winter before at Kungsköping.

People talked also about three marriage engagements which
were on foot, besides one which was a settled thing. This
last was between the eldest daughter of the house where the
company were now assembled, and the rich ironmaster, Tackjern, "a very good match," said everybody, because Eva
Dufva would have her own house, her own carriage—to
say nothing of having a very respectable man for her husband.

Eva Dufva, however, looked pale, and not very happy.
But she was one of many sisters of a family not rich, though
tolerably well to do—and they all, parents and sisters, had
been delighted with this wealthy offer. She would be able to
make them all happy; could invite her parents to dinner, and
her sisters out into the country to visit her at her country-
house. Eva Dufva said *yes* to the iron-master Tackjern, who
offered her all this. The wedding was therefore to take place
in May, upon the silver wedding-day of her parents, and the
golden wedding-day of the old grand-parents; and in preparation for this great occasion Mr. Alderman Dufva repaired,
added to, and put in order his house, and the approaching
three-fold marriage festival cheered the house and the minds
of all with every kind of happy preparation. Mrs. Dufva
herself, a handsome woman, who loved to do everything on a
magnificent scale, appeared to be the moving soul in everything, arranging and determining all with the utmost pleasure;
only now and then she cast a stolen and troubled glance at
the pale and grave bride elect, her daughter. But thought

she to herself, "when she is married, and sees herself possessed of everything so splendid and good, then———"

And so thinks many a mother.

Now whilst tea and other refreshments are carried round, and the gods and goddesses, good fairies and goblins, seat themselves in window-nooks and at little tables, and enjoy themselves and talk together, we will avail ourselves of the opportunity to become more intimately acquainted with some persons and groups of the party, and listen to the conversation which is going on amongst them.

We will first approach a married couple, who look particularly comfortable, because we love comfortable people and married couples, and we can see plainly enough that they are such; that little clergyman, with his somewhat undersized figure; his broad chest, his almost child-like, round, and open countenance, and that little lady whose appearance gives us a foreknowledge that she unites in her own person both Mary and Martha, and who now, laying her hand so confidentially on the pastor's shoulder, says in a low voice:

"Now, my little old man! Now I think it is a good opportunity for you to bring forward your proposal."

"Now? How so?" sighed the little pastor, with a comic expression of terror, "my dear little old woman, let me strengthen myself first; let me get a little power and courage by the help of this good tea, and these good biscuits, and— and—a little glass of rum! Do you see—this is a subject which it is not so easy to introduce. Do you see—Here comes Mimmi Svanberg; only don't talk about that proposal. Sit down and drink tea with us. What would you like? what would you have? A pair of old boots? I would very willingly keep them for myself. Mother, don't you forget that Mimmi is to have my old boots—*nota bene*—only I must wear them out first."

"Ah, what is it that you good people are laughing at?" asked a lady with a singularly dark and mournful physiognomy, as she advanced towards the trio. This was the widow Ulrika Uggla.

Mrs. Uggla and Mimmi Svanberg are the greatest contrasts in the world. The latter smiles, and is always endeavoring to make life more easy for herself and others; the former sighs over everything, and sees everywhere only that which is painful and unsightly.

"I do not know," continued she, "how people can be so merry when there is so much sorrow and vexation in the world."

"For that very reason," replied Mimmi Svanberg, "one must endeavor to make it more cheerful. Besides, there is also a great deal which is very good, and which makes one very happy."

"Yes, so it seems to you; but to those who think a little more seriously on things in general—in this very house, for instance, it seems to me that all this joy is really sorrow in disguise."

"In this house! But where, in all the world, can one find a more comfortable home,—a more agreeable family,—a more beautiful understanding between parents and children,—more amiable young girls?

"Yes, those seven Miss Dufvas!—it is really a cheerful prospect to have so many girls; poor girls to be got rid of; what is to become of them all?"

"Oh, time enough for that yet; such nice girls as they are. Besides, one of them is already engaged."

"Yes, but how does she look? As if she were ready to make away with herself. Nothing but sorrow will come out of that marriage, that I can foresee; and all the other girls— they will, all of them, be like superfluous cards."

"There are no longer any such cards in the world," said Mimmi Svanberg, laughing; "now-a-days all people are needed for the well-being of the public, and may each one take his proper place and help the others in private or public societies."

"Psha! with your public societies; they are the most troublesome things that I know, and, if I have my will, Ingeborg shall have nothing to do with them. They are all downright nonsense, and good-for-nothing schemes.   Girls can make fools enough of themselves in the world without adding these public societies to their folly!"

Mrs. Uggla's doleful countenance, and mode of expressing herself, seemed so absurd to Mimmi Svanberg, that she burst into an uncontrollable fit of laughter: the clergyman, however, took up the subject more seriously, and replied:

"I do not think so.   If girls make fools of themselves in the world, it is their own fault and the fault of their mothers. Would to God that I had twice as many daughters as Mrs. Dufva; I should find ways and means and employment for them all, partly at home and partly from home, precisely in some of those excellent societies for the well-being of the community, which offer to all and every one an opportunity of being useful, and serving our Lord, each one according to his several talents and turn of mind."

"It is all talk!" said Mrs. Uggla, with an angry expression; "a girl ought to get married and have her own family and domestic affairs to look after.   And that Ingeborg might have had, if she had not in her youth been a romantic simpleton, and refused a good offer, merely because she was not in love with the man.   For that reason she now sits there like a piece of furniture, and is red-nosed, and old, and never will be anything but an old maid.   It is altogether nothing but stupidity and vexation."

She, of whom these hard words were spoken, was a young woman of about thirty, or somewhat more, and whose appearance and manner betrayed a painful consciousness of a youth which was passed, and a restless endeavor still to retain it. She had handsome teeth, and therefore she oftentimes smiled, although her smile was deficient in gladness, while her dress was more youthful than became her age and her appearance. When her mother's restless and gloomy eye was fixed upon her, she might especially be seen to assume a gaiety and liveliness which evidently did not proceed from the heart.   Hence it followed that she appeared affected, and was considered to be so.

Mimmi Svanberg, who understood and valued Ingeborg Uggla better than her splenetic mother did, said:

"Ingeborg is not a common character, and may yet marry well if she likes. In the meantime I think that she showed her good taste, and her noble, right feeling, by remaining rather in her mother's house than marry a man whom she could not like."

With these words Mimmi Svanberg, as if afraid of further contention on the subject, rose up to speak with some other persons in the room, calling forth, for the most part, wherever she came, cheerful conversation and laughter.

We will now listen to what that group of young men are saying.

A. "It is dreadfully slow here. There won't be a single card-table this evening."

B. "I doubt it. Let's make the best of a bad business. I'll go and talk with the ladies."

A. "The deuce you will! It is such hard work making polite speeches. No, I'll be off to my club, smoke a cigar and have a bowl of punch, which you're very welcome to empty with me."

B. "Not a bad idea; but—I'll just have a little talk first with little Miss D. She is a very nice little girl, and is said to have in expectation her fifty thousand banko."

C. "Introduce me to her, my good fellow! Be so good as to introduce me; but stay, tell me first, for I am only just come to this place, which are the richest girls here this evening."

B. "I can't exactly say—not precisely; let's look round. First there are the young ladies of the house; my friend Von Tackjern is betrothed to one of them, but the other six or seven are yet to be had."

C. "The sweet little doves! but are they worth anything? you understand me!"

B. "Not much to speak of, I fancy, except handsome feathers—a good outfit."

C. "Well, we'll let them fly. There are two very pretty girls sitting there, as much alike as if they were sisters."

B. "The Miss Roses; the Roses, as they are generally called : most charming girls ; they are very accomplished——"

C. "Yes, but have they any money as well ?"

B. "They have nothing but hearts and roses."

C. "Well, we'll leave them sitting there, then. Now let's go on in the fair."

B. "Beside them sits Miss Uggla ; not exactly poor, and rather a niceish sort of girl ; but she's getting old now ; has been at balls for I don't know how many years, so that she is quite faded and passée."

C. "Pass her by then and go on to somebody else. Who is that who sits beside her, dressed in black ? she has a fine figure, but she looks so cursedly positive."

B. "Be on your guard against her, for she has a sharp tongue ! She is nevertheless worth her twenty thousand banko, that is to say, when papa, old Falk, is dead ; because, so long as he is alive, he won't part with a single stiver, that's a certainty."

C. "Twenty thousand banko ! nay, that is too low a figure for me to put myself under the petticoat government of such a ruler. Such bondage as that must be pretty well gilded."

B. "Here comes the bridegroom elect, the future son-in-law of the house, my friend Von Tackjern, a rich and capital fellow —coming to speak to me."

C. "Introduce me to him, my good fellow ; I am only just come to the place, and should like to become acquainted with the respectable——"

The introduction took place. Mr. Von Tackjern was a formal, substantial gentleman, who liked evidently that people should bow down before him, but was not very much inclined to bow to others. He looked as if an iron poker were run through him from head to foot. To the congratulations of his friend on his betrothal with so amiable a young lady, he replied coldly :

"She is a good girl, and will, I hope, be an excellent wife, and make me happy. I look for the reality in happiness as well as in life."

B. "A very right and prudent way of thinking; it would be well if every one thought as rationally."

Von Tackjern. "Yes, people would render themselves and their country better service in that way than by giving themselves up to every kind of fantastic and philanthropic whim. That philanthropy, with all its societies and collections, it totally ruins——"

B. "Don't speak so loud, for here comes a lady very formidable on this score, one of our fellow citizenesses——"

"Say formidable, because she is irresistible by her good heart and her good temper, this tutelar saint of the poor," said a young man who stood near the speakers, "and one cannot possibly say no to anything which she desires."

"It is one of my principles never to put my name down to any subscriptions," said Von Tackjern, and buttoned up his coat.

"And it is one of mine always to do so," said the former speaker, "when they are promoted by persons whom I know to be really the friends of the poor, as is the case with my cousin Mimmi Svanberg."

Mimmi Svanberg came up to the last speaker at this very moment and asked in a merry and low voice:

"My good Yngve, your father was a warm friend of his country, and you are his worthy son, and—you have no doubt an old pair of boots! I want a pair this week."

"They shall stand before your door to-morrow morning, my dear cousin; because if I have not any, some of my friends have, which will be quite at your service. Whose old legs are you going to make happy with them?—though it is all one to me. But do you not want two pair? Go and ask our rich ironmaster here——"

"No thank you; I shall take care not to do so. I know to whom I go. Thank you, dear Yngve. But I have not done with you yet; I want to turn this evening to good account; and you must help me to do so. I want the price of the tickets to be applied to the benefit of our infant school. Cannot you propose it, Yngve? We must speak to our good

2

pastor about it and endeavor to interest Mrs. Tupplander in the subject. Where is she ?"

Mrs. Tupplander sate in the middle of the sofa, glittering in full feather and pomp of attire, enthroned like a queen, or rather as one who would enact the queen. Mrs. Tupplander would in fact be very willingly queen-regent of the town, the greatest chicken in the hen-coop, as the saying is, the first lady in company, and as yet no one has contested the place with her, because she is a rich widow, who gives liberal alms, and extremely good dinners, to which her housekeeping companion, a lady of good family, the Honorable Miss Krusbjörn, greatly contributes. Miss Krusbjörn has a genius in this line, and manages Mrs. Tupplander's house both in a clever and splendid manner, which is precisely according to Mrs. Tupplauder's notions. Mrs. Tupplander and Miss Krusbjörn divide the rule of the family, as in a constitutional government, into the upper and lower house; but in case of difference of opinion, which frequently occurs, the lower house generally carries its own point. Mrs. Tupplander bears the name, but Miss Krusbjörn has the power. Yet Mrs. Tupplander and Miss Krusbjörn could not live without each other. But enough for the present about these ladies.

Mimmi Svanberg, who saw the weaknesses of her fellow creatures, and smiled at them rather than let them annoy her, was nevertheless sometimes annoyed by Mrs. Tupplander, though she always kept up a good understanding with her for the sake of her poor neighbors; and therefore she listened with great patience to the description of a dinner which Mrs. Tupplander was about to give, and of all the delicate dishes and wines, the whole sprinkled with the praises of Miss Krusbjörn and her talents. When, however, Mrs. Tupplander approached the end of her dinner details, Mimmi Svanberg attacked her on her weak side, as the friend and patroness of the poor, and obtained the promise of her help on behalf of a needy family, as well as her advocacy and co-operation in a plan which would be brought forward that very evening. In this way compelled to a certain degree, Mrs. Tupplander gave her consent, but added with a little pepper, as it were, on the tip of her tongue:

"I cannot for my part imagine, dear Mimmi, how you can undertake and have so many things on hand at once; your father, on the contrary, never seems to be ready with anything which he is about."

"The reason is," replied Mimmi gaily, "because papa lives for eternity and I merely for the moment."

Mimmi Svanberg had in fact a mode of speaking and acting very unlike that of her father. It might at the first glance appear to be of that kind which many ladies are well versed in, and which may be called the hand-over-head method. But if all those who made use of this method were guided by so good a heart and so clear an understanding as Mimmi Svanberg, then they would, in their hand-over-head proceedings, always manage to say and to do the very wisest and best things.

As a matter of course Mimmi Svanberg, with these warm impulses and this disposition, was a favorite in the town both with rich and poor, nor would it amaze any one to find that she had a great number of uncles and aunts, above forty cousins, and an almost incalculable number of good friends and acquaintances who looked up to her for counsel and help in joy as well as in sorrow. Much more amazing was it to many people, and to myself among the rest, that Mimmi Svanberg, warm-hearted, universally beloved, and good-looking, should not have fixed her heart steadfastly upon some one, instead of moving about in an element of human love and beneficence, like a bird in the air or a fish in the water, finding enough for herself there without desiring anything besides. Perhaps there might lie behind some concealed cause,——which we may discover on some future day.

We will now accompany her light step to a group of ladies, to whom we, a few moments ago, saw the eyes of two gentlemen directed, assaying their worth. It was thus that some young girls talked of the party at which they were assembled.

"Ah, how gay it will be here! Quite charmingly gay. But

don't you think that the bride elect looks very grave, and her lover very stupid?"

"Yes; this match is, on her side, a mere money match. There was another whom she liked much better; but Von Tackjern is rich, and she has accepted him to please her family."

"Poor girl! If I had been in her case I would have had Lieutenant M. He is so handsome, and so agreeable."

"Excepting when he is a little—tipsy, which he is sometimes."

"Oh, but then he is so very charming to ladies. He is so very nice! It really becomes him to be a little 'half-seas-over.'"

"I would not thank you for a husband half-seas-over, let him be ever so charming. No, much rather Von Tackjern for me; less charming but more sober. That will certainly be no life half-seas-over, but neither will there be any ruin. I know nothing in the world worse than ruin."

"There are in the world many kinds of ruin. But what does Hertha say about it?"

The young lady now appealed to was the same that we heard spoken of before, "with the fine figure, but who looked so deucedly positive." A remarkably noble person and rich golden hair were, in fact, the only things which agreeably distinguished her. A cloud seemed to envelope her whole being, and gave a sort of cloudy and unpleasant air to her otherwise regular features. She sate silent and indifferent, immovable almost as a statue, and apparently lifeless. If roses had ever bloomed upon her cheeks they had already faded, together with the spring-time of youth; a grey monotonous tint lay on her whole countenance; the eyelashes drooped heavily over the dark, inanimate eyes. Her dress was distinguished by its simplicity and homeliness. It bore not, the slightest superfluous ornament, yet it fitted her exquisite form with the nicest exactitude.

At the words, "What does Hertha think about it?" she slightly turned her head, and said coldly:

"I think it is a miserable state of things where a good and charming girl cannot have any other choice than to marry a man half-seas-over, or a man without a heart, and who evidently does not trouble himself much about her."

The young girls laughed, and said in a low voice:

"Hertha speaks plain enough! She is not afraid of saying what she thinks."

"Afraid!" exclaimed Hertha; "no, I am not afraid—not now, at least."

"But, my dear Hertha," said, anxiously, a little elderly lady, who was incessantly twiddling her fingers as if she were winding yarn, or unravelling a tangled skein, "one must think a little, though, about what people may say. Besides, just remember! Eva Dufva has no fortune, and will be so well provided for all her days."

"I think," said Hertha, with the same cold indifference as before, "that it is humiliating for a girl to marry merely to be well provided for. Much more honorable would it be for her to help to provide for those whom she loves. That it seems to me is far preferable, is an honor."

"Ah," returned the little old lady, whose countenance and whole person had a resemblance to a ravelled skein, "now Hertha is again coming out with her odd ideas."

"She is quite right," said a lady in the circle; "marriage is frequently unhappy because girls don't marry themselves to souls, or hearts, but to—purses."

"No, no," sighed a pale young woman, "not to purses, but to dreams, and that is not much better, at least for the happiness of the heart. One sees so much that is beautiful in him one loves; one sees in him the ideal about which one has dreamed, and which is to elevate one to the good and the great. One fancies that one shall find a God, and one finds—" here she suddenly checked herself, while a faint crimson suffused her pale countenance, and she merely added—"and one finds that which one did not expect."

"But, my dear Emily," said the elder lady, smiling, "if we do not find gods in our husbands, neither do they, indeed, find goddesses in us.　And men are, in a general way, much better informed, and much more thoroughly educated than women,—that even you must concede, Hertha."

"They know much more, perhaps," replied Hertha, "but it is not the fault of the women that there are few things which they can learn, and even those few so seldom thoroughly. But even then, are men more just, more reasonable, more high-minded than women?　Do they think and act more from the innermost of life?　In a word, have they more true human culture?"

"But do women in a general way possess this?" asked one of the ladies, in a depreciating tone.

"They would possess this, and might even impart it," replied Hertha, "if their feeling for the innermost of life obtained—life, truth.　But it is not developed, and therefore both sexes remain alike trammelled and fundamentally uncultured."

"Nay then, Hertha has a regular frenzy to-day, quite first rate!" said the young girls, smiling.　"Only think, if the gentlemen heard you!—You will certainly never be married, Hertha."

"Well, and what then?" said Hertha, bluntly, but at the same time half smiling.　"Is marriage, in a general way, so happy in this world, that the highest happiness may be considered as being found in marriage?"

"Ah, no," said the pale young lady, with a sigh, "but it makes us mothers, and in that way it gives us a rich and deep experience of life, which can never be the lot of an unmarried, childless woman."

The young girls were quite silent, as if struck by the truth of these words.

Hertha said, "All married women have not children.　And is there not a peculiar, rich experience, a deep insight into life, which can alone be the portion of the unmarried woman?"

Hertha's voice betrayed an inward emotion, as she continued :—

"If our education were not so utterly miserable, and the

object of our lives so utterly poverty-stricken and circumscribed; if we were early instructed, instead of seeking for support out of ourselves, to seek for it in our own breasts, in our own powers; if we were able to devote life and life's energies to great and noble purposes; if we were permitted to listen to the inner voice, and follow its inspirations rather than all kinds of opinions around us; if we were allowed to do the work which we should love to do,—then I am certain that we should become noble and even happy, should be lawgivers to ourselves and even others."

"Good gracious! my dear Hertha, do you wish that ladies should be lawyers, or perhaps attorney-generals, and sit on the high seat of justice?" said the little old lady, working with her fingers more nervously than ever, and evidently very uneasy.

"Not exactly so," replied Hertha, half smiling; "but rather—more than that."

"What more? what more?" asked many ladies in the group, smiling and inquisitive.

Hertha was silent for a moment, and then said, whilst a faint crimson lighted up her cheek, though the melodious voice continued calm as a tranquilly heaving wave:

"In the old times it was believed that something great and deep was indwelling in woman, which could not be fully developed unless she remained *alone*, alone with the Divinity. Then even women were priestesses in the service of the holy, of the divine. This belief is now lost. Now people merely wish that young girls should be 'sweet girls,' accomplished' and so on, that they may get married as soon as possible, it matters little with whom, so that he can but provide well for his wife. This is a miserable view of life and of the destiny of woman, degrading to women and perhaps still more so to men. For the blame of it lies very much in womanly cowardice, but still more in the want of justice and high-mindedness of man; and he lowers himself in the same proportion as he lowers us."

"Nay, you are now going too far, dear Hertha!" exclaimed

the little old lady, writhing in agony: "consider what you are saying. Things don't go on in this world as in *le palais de la Verité.* You will make yourself detested both by gentlemen and ladies."

"I know it," said Hertha, with her hands crossed, and the calmness as of a sybil.

"And only think if any of the gentlemen here heard you! they would be so angry at you! you would never be invited to the balls. You'll be getting into the newspapers; you'll have, like me, a lawsuit on your shoulders. It does not answer, speaking one's mind so freely—you'll make yourself and all of us unhappy."

"Have you, then, so bad an opinion of us as to believe that we could not bear to hear a little keen truth?" inquired a mild and manly voice; and a young man, who, leaning against the window-frame, concealed from the group of ladies by the thick curtains, had heard the conversation, now came forward, took a chair, and seated himself in the circle just opposite Hertha. His handsome person, the manly, frank, and generous expression of his youthful countenance, the ease and calmness of his bearing, which betrayed a certain modest assurance, or rather certainty of not displeasing; all these, combined with the melodious voice, won for him immediately the cheerful attention of the whole group.

He continued, addressing his remarks to Hertha :

"You are perfectly right. We men are in many ways deficient in the deeper human culture; but it is incumbent on the ladies to give us this; for they have, incontestably, an inborn deeper sense of the innermost of life than we. The latest work of the Creator obtained this as her dower."

"But our legislators think quite otherwise," replied Hertha. "They regard women, at least in our country, as beings who are still in their tutelage; and, precisely as a consequence of this, they frequently become weak, vaciliating souls, that never can attain to years of discretion, lacking faith in themselves. I don't mean," continued she, her cheek again tinged with a faint crimson, "the faith which is the offspring to blind self-love; many have too much of that; I mean the faith which comes from confidence in the truth of our own being, in God's light and voice within us."

"True, very true," again said the young man. "Ladies often rule more through feminine caprice and weakness, or by their outward attractions, than by their nobler powers. The greater number never imagine how they would become a thousand times more powerful if they had a pleasure in becoming true, high-minded women seeking only the highest. Then would they elevate us with themselves. If there were now-a-days women such as the priestesses of antiquity, female judges, vestal virgins, it is at their feet that I would sit, to their words that I would listen, as to oracles from the holiest depths of life. And for my best knowledge and most valuable attainments, I have to thank women of this self-illuminating, guiding class."

A light, as of the rosy dawn above the cloudy east, lit up Hertha's cheek at these words, and her eyes flashed like diamonds, catching the rays of light. It brightened her whole countenance, whilst the little lady at her side looked utterly amazed and confounded.

Drawn on, probably as much by the bold candor and the purport of Hertha's expression, as well as by the effect which it was evident his words had upon her, the young man continued to address his conversation principally to her. He had for several years resided in foreign countries and different parts of the world, and he related various things to show the position of woman, and her influence upon different races of mankind; for, singularly enough, he appeared to have devoted his particular attention to this subject. Every one within the circle of ladies listened attentively, and each word which he uttered was a question eliciting fresh light on a subject which in so many ways interested all. Hertha alone said nothing; but the narrator seemed nevertheless to speak more especially for her.

When soon afterwards he was suddenly called away from the circle, and this broke up, a whispering chorus was heard of,

"Who is that agreeable young man? Most amiable; interesting! charming!   I am regularly in love with him!   (N. B. It was an elderly lady who said that.)   Who is he? Where does he come from?   How happens it that nobody has seen him before, or even heard speak of him?"

"It happens in this way," said one of the elder gentlemen, enlightening them, "that he never before was in our neighborhood.   His father was the proprietor of mines in Norrland, and he is now appointed as engineer to our new railroad.   I don't know a more excellent or more promising young man than Yngve Nordin.   And he is generally much liked by the ladies.   But take care of your hearts, young ladies, for he is said to be what is called a great ladies' man, but somewhat fickle in his fancies."

"I would willingly have him for my son!" said one of the ladies.

The Roses smiled and whispered to Hertha: "Well, stern Sybilla, what have you to say against this young man?   I fancy that he has found grace in your eyes!"

Hertha smiled with an air of indifference, and said: "He was polite to us."

She now prepared, in company with the little, fidgety old lady, to leave the party, and her countenance again began to assume its gloomy, dissatisfied expression.

Candles were lighted in the drawing-room, but it was deep twilight in the little parlor where Hertha and her companion attired themselves.

"Don't forget to put your shawl on the wrong side out, Hertha," said the little old lady; "both your shawl and collar, for it will be damp out of doors.   We have stayed a very long time.   Heaven grant that papa is not angry!   Shawl on the wrong side, Hertha!   Oh, that you should have such odd notions, and talk so!   If you could but be like other people! Shawl on the wrong side—mind that!"

Whilst Hertha silently and mechanically followed the directions which were thus given to her, she felt her hand kissed and wetted by a hot tear by some one whom she in the darkness could not distinguish.

"Who is it?" said she softly, "that has kissed my hand?"

"It is somebody who admires you," replied, softly, a sweet feminine voice, "and who wishes she had your courage!"

"My courage!" said Hertha. "Oh, God keep you, Eva, from ever experiencing that which makes me courageous enough to—shock human beings."

She kissed the young girl and hastened into the hall, as if afraid of saying more, whilst little aunt Petronilla fumbled after her things, muttering, "Hertha! Hertha! now she will certainly forget her gloves. Hertha, where is my green bag and the tea-cake for little Martha's nameday! Oh that she should be so unguarded! No, see, I have my bag on my arm and the tea-cake is in it! But which way is Hertha gone? I must always take charge of her!"

The signal for breaking off the conversation, and which also seemed to have occasioned the departure of Hertha and aunt Nella, was an exclamation from Major Von Post, which again summoned gods and goddesses, good fairies and goblins, to a general rehearsal of the groups and scenes of the fancy ball.

"Now you must make haste with what you have to say, my little old man, or you will be too late;" whispered eagerly the wife of the clergyman to her husband; "I long to be going; I someway don't feel quite in spirits; I don't rightly know why."

The good pastor now started up and said in a strong, deep voice: "Ladies and gentlemen, divinities of Olympus and Valhalla! will you allow a poor mortal to say a few words to you before you begin your sports, and before I take my departure? Have I permission to speak?"

The universally beloved pastor was always willingly listened to, and "Speak," "Speak," was heard on all sides.

"Ladies and gentlemen," continued the speaker, with a mixture of mirth and seriousness, which sometimes was changed to deep feeling, and then the voice became husky and faltering, as if it struggled against emotion, and a sudden paleness overspread the otherwise child-like, joyous, and open countenance: "Ladies and gentlemen! we are now assembled here to arrange a something which it is believed will be very entertaining, and I believe it will be so too. I believe also that King Solomon was right when he said that there was a time for every thing, and that mirth has its time and is good in itself. But if one could at the same time both amuse oneself and do good, then there would be a twofold advantage. I believe that this may now be done. Allow me to tell you how. But in the first place I must give a little introduction."

"Now in the name of common sense what's coming? Some Magdalen institution, or society for the encouragement of criminals!" muttered Mr. Von Tackjern, between his teeth, and buttoned still closer his breast pocket.

"It is both pitiable and laughable at the same time!" sighed Mrs. Uggla; and Mrs. Von Tupplander shook her feather-adorned head, and said half-audibly, "Ah, so tiresome!"

The speaker continued: "Whilst we are here amusing ourselves by playing at gods and goddesses, and ordering gallons of punch and champagne for our Olympian feast, dozens of poor ragged and sometimes half-famished little children, without care-takers either for body or soul,—for many of them have wretched, some of them no parents at all,—are running about our town, in our streets, under our very windows. These children need guardianship, instruction; they need mothers and schools. My wife and a few other ladies have long wished, and even labored, to establish an infant ragged school into which such poor little children as these could be received; and they have succeeded so far as to bring about a beginning, but ah! so small a beginning, that it is literally but an infant school, and not sufficient to receive one-third part of the children which require care. We want a locale, we want funds to enlarge the place and to enable us to give the poorest of the children their dinners at the school. Many of our good and considerate ladies here know of a certainty how great need there is to establish some superintendence over the poor children and their homes, as well within as without the town, and they will therefore unquestionably consider that the proposition which I am now about to make is not ill-timed, nay rather that this is just the proper time and season in which to bring it forward. I propose therefore that all the Goddesses and Graces, that is to say, all the ladies here present, should form themselves into a *Ladies' Society* to visit the homes of the poor, look after the children, and take charge of and use all their means to support the infant school; and I further propose that for the obtaining of the necessary funds for this purpose, the entrance-tickets for the approaching festivity may be made chargeable with a sort of impost for the benefit of the Ladies' Society and its Infant schools.

"Ladies and gentlemen!" continued the speaker with earnestness, "many of you are perhaps not aware that at no great distance from our Olympian company, here in the town, there stands in a lane an old house, or rather a barrack, called the Great Quarter; there, for many years, has been assembled together more misery and wretchedness than many of you have even seen during the whole of your lives, and that amidst these dregs, this scum of our town's population, live children—little children, ladies and gentlemen,—whom any mother's heart, here in this room, might thank God to call her own, and yet which are in the Great Quarter cast down into every kind of wretchedness. I say to you, ladies and gentlemen, that this is a state of things which we ought not to tolerate, but that we must cleanse out this quarter of hell, or at least rescue the children from it, and let them come into God's light and life. It is our Christian duty! My wife has often urged me to speak to you on this subject, and now I have done it,—and I am glad that I have!"

The little clergyman wiped the perspiration from his brow, and then continued with a smile.

"It may seem a little bold to request the Muses and the Graces to cleanse out the Great Quarter, but since the day when—a God washed on earth the feet of the poor, the Olympian sisters have not regarded it as below their dignity to help in obtaining shoes and stockings for poor children. We have a good proverb, which says, 'A quick beginning is half the winning.'   Let us therefore begin the work this very day, this very moment.   Let us here at once form a Ladies' Society."

"I am intending to write a book against Ladies' Societies!" said the Protocol Secretary, N. B.   "I have already collected the material."

"Yes, it is these philanthropic undertakings and societies which are the ruin of us!" said Mr. Von Tackjern, whilst he buttoned yet another of his coat-buttons.

"We are never going on right; we shall become a poor-house and a hospital!" sighed Mrs. Uggla, shaking her whole body.

"He might have waited till my dinner, then I could have drawn out of the thing," thought Mrs. Von Tupplander, with displeasure, shaking her head.

Various gentlemen, in the meantime, both elderly and young, had, at the mention of "a fund for a good purpose," immediately put their hands in their breast-pockets to feel for their memorandum-books; and the Countess P., who had lately come to the place, where her husband had bought a large property, and who, on account of her goodness and unassuming manners, made the world forgive her beauty, rank, and wealth, hastened, together with Mimmi Svanberg and a few other ladies, to the good pastor, thanked him, and begged him to "reckon upon them."

The prevailing tone of the company, however, remained hesitating and doubtful.   People were heard to say: "It is not now the time."—"One must think about the thing."—"After the fancy-ball one should have time to attend to the question."—"Now one must think about Olympus and Valhalla, and the costumes."

Yngve Nordin raised his voice to ask the decision of the company respecting the sale of the tickets, and the appropriation of the money to the before-mentioned fund.

It was agreed to with acclamation; discussion of the main subject itself was deferred till another time, and Major Von Post's voice was again heard summoning gods and goddesses to take their places, and the arrangement of the merry divinities came into full swing.

"Let us go now, my little old man," whispered the wife of the pastor to her husband, who was again wiping his hot forehead. "We have at all events obtained something, and I want to go home."

"How? Are you ill?"

"No, not exactly so. But I feel an anxiety, an oppression! You know that I feel so sometimes. It is to me as if the very floor were burning under my feet. By all means let us go!"

"Directly, directly! Let us merely take leave of the hostess!" And the good married couple soon disappeared from the scene of action, where all was now in a state of merry confusion.

HERE AND THERE ON THE WAY HOME.

"In a minute or two I will be with you again, but I must now accompany papa home!" said Mimmi Svanberg to her friends, as she prepared to accompany her aged father.

In the hall she found Ingeborg Uggla, waiting with her usual patience for her ill-tempered grumbling mother, who was detaining Dr. Hedermann, the principal physician of the town; a man both beloved and feared; beloved for his skill and his benevolence, feared for his epigrammatic wit, especially by the ladies, to whose deceit and vanity he ascribed the degenerate state of the present generation, and whom he therefore continually attacked by his sarcasm. Mrs. Uggla had seized upon the doctor just as he left the company, and having described her cramps to him for the thirtieth time, and received a promise of some drops, now proceeded to unburden her heart.

"Is it not both pitiable and laughable at the same time with all these schemes?"

"What schemes, my gracious lady?"

"Oh, the fancy-ball and ladies' society!"

"The ladies' society!" exclaimed the doctor: "the most rational proposition in the world, only it has something serious about it. But it will come to nothing. It will be mere playwork. Ladies have not time for such things. They have more serious business to attend to; their dress, their pleasures; their worsted-work, their housekeeping also. I believe—nothing will come of it—nothing, merely amusement, believe me. Good-night, ladies! Much pleasure at the fancy-ball, and—many catarrhs and pleurisies after it;—for that's generally the way! Good-night!——"

Mimmi Svanberg laughed. "The good doctor," she said, "he has his fixed idea! I wish we could cure him."

"He hates women," said Ingeborg, with a sigh, the depth of which, together with the expression of her eye, and her paleness, were remarked by Mimmi Svanberg, and strengthened her in the idea which she had long entertained, that a deep, but unrequited sentiment attached Ingeborg to the eccentric, though really amiable and universally esteemed physician.

"He is a rational man," said Mrs. Uggla, "because he believes that everything in the world gets worse and worse."

"But we, with our societies, think of making everything better and better!" said Mimmi cheerfully; "and I calculate upon Ingeborg as a member of that which we are about to establish."

"Then she will certainly never get married," sighed Mrs. Uggla. "These public societies, or unions, are altogether direct hindrances to private unions."

"I don't believe so," said Mimmi; "but if they should help us to become more active and happy human beings than hitherto without marriage, then, really, there would be nothing to complain of. What do you say, Ingeborg?"

"I acknowledge," said Ingeborg, not without emotion, "that I consider a happy marriage as the happiest of all unions, and the greatest happiness upon earth; but, if this cannot be obtained, it is then desirable to employ one's life and one's energies in another direction. And in this way ladies' societies may be very useful to those, who, like myself, are too bashful or are not active enough to undertake anything upon their own responsibility. Social life," added she, in a lower voice, as she stealthily wiped away a tear, "seems emptier and emptier the older one grows; one laughs and chatters and looks as if one were amused, but—sorrow often sits at the heart. Happy they who have a good home, and some one there to live for!"

"Oh, yes!" said Mimmi, with a glance of tenderness at her old father; and then, with heartfelt sympathy, she watched Ingeborg enter her own room with her mother, whose last

3

mutterings were heard to be something about "stupid schemes," and "Sodom and Gomorrah."

"Ingeborg must come to see us; it must be made pleasanter for Ingeborg," whispered Mimmi silently to herself. "But, how is this?" continued she aloud; "are not our old pastor and his wife standing there on the bridge and looking at the house where we have been this evening, as if they had left something behind them? Good evening, my friends, what is going on now? What are you contemplating in the new moon?"

"I am looking back to the home of my childhood, to the Dufvas' house," said the pastor's wife. "I know not why, but it seems to me as if I should never more behold it. Just here, on this bridge, there came such an extraordinary uneasiness over me, and I could not help turning round. How splendid and gay it looks, with lights in all the windows."

"If it does not befal our dear lady as it befel Lot's wife!" said Mimmi, jokingly. "We now go part of the way home together, and our road lies past the Great Quarter, where I have business with little Mina's mother. I cannot tell you, sir," said she, addressing the clergyman, "how glad I should be to get that child out of that Great Rubbish Quarter. What do you say? shall we all go and pay a visit there this evening, in this beautiful moonlight?"

"But, my dear Mimmi," said the pastor, somewhat alarmed, "you don't remember that it is late, and that, in the moonlight, one may happen to see things in the Great Rubbish Quarter, which are not the most edifying in the world!"

"Oh, nothing that we need trouble ourselves about; at all events, not in the room which Mrs. Granberg inhabits," answered Mimmi, laughing; "and besides, we are a large party altogether. I should just like to see how the Great Quarter looks in the moonlight. Perhaps we shall not have many opportunities of seeing it much longer, as it is condemned by the public. But where in the world are all the old drunken women to go to, and where many of the sober ones too, who live there with their children? We must, dear pastor, build some comfortable dwellings for the more respec-table classes of the poor!"

"Yes, yes! everything in regular course; if we can only do it! You are so terribly energetic, dear Mimmi, and my convenience, you see, requires time!"

"Your convenience," said Mimmi, laughing, "may take its time if we only may make a beginning. And in the first place, begin with sweeping clean the Rubbish Quarter. It was a good idea, just this very evening, to propose the Ladies' Society! When people have settled down again quietly after the fancy-ball they will have time enough to think of more serious things. I hope we shall be able to get some good fellow-laborers. I have been speaking to Ingeborg Uggla, and have hopes of Hertha Falk. What a pity it is that she was not in the groups this evening, she would have made such a magnificent Norna or Valkyria!"

"Yes," said the pastor's wife, "only too gloomy. It is wonderful how that girl of late has grown dark and plain. I fancied that when she grew up she would be good-looking. But now she always looks as if she were in an ill-humor. The second sister we never see now in company. It is said that she is greatly out of health. At one time there was a talk about her being married; but the father, people say, was opposed to the match."

"Poor girls!" said Mimmi, now quite seriously, "they are certainly not happy at home. Their aunt was very severe to them while she lived, and the old man, people say, is both avaricious and cross. Ever since that affair in the family they have almost entirely ceased to have intercourse with other people. The girls, nevertheless, are noble and good, espe-cially Hertha, although she is a little peculiar, a little odd; but one seldom sees them, and they are very much attached to each other. They have also a relation, a young man who lives in the family, and who is, I fancy, a little insane. In a word, there is a plentiful growth of wormwood in that house."

"But now, see, we are at the Great Quarter. Now light your lanthorn, good Jacob, because the moon does not light the steps of the Quarter, and we must not break our legs if we can help it!"

The clergyman's servant, the respectable Jacob, who attended his master and mistress, did as he was desired, and they ascended the steps, Professor Methodius endeavoring the while to initiate the clergyman into the first principles of his system for the improvement of society, to which the latter listened without replying a word.

The narrow wooden steps led to a landing, on which were several doors. Mimmi opened one of these, as an old acquaintance, and the party entered into a large, long room, in which no less than six families resided, one in each corner, and two in the middle. The room was lighted by the moon and one single small tallow candle, before which a middle-aged woman sat on a broken stool, mending old clothes; upon a bench near her sat two children busy sorting rags. The boy was a handsome, well-grown child; the girl, whom Mimmi called Mina, had nothing remarkable about her, except a pair of bright blue eyes, which seemed to look lovingly and gladly forth from a sickly, pale, and meagre countenance. No one could have imagined, from her expression, that her legs and feet were withered, and that she was compelled always to remain in one place, or to move herself along upon her knees.

"That is our best little girl in the infant school," said Mimmi Svanberg, in an under tone to the clergyman; "and she has a voice which makes it a joy to hear her. Besides, she is such a good and contented child. When any of the other poor children have food in the school she never begs any of it, her large eyes only look so beseechingly that it really goes to my heart when there is not sufficient for her to have some, or when it is not her turn, for it is a certainty that she gets no dinner at home. The mother——Good evening, Mrs. Granberg, you see that I have not forgotten you, and you shall have the boots either to-morrow morning or the morning after, so that you

can then sit out in the market to sell your things without your
feet being frozen; thank you, thank you, Mrs. Granberg.
Here is our pastor come to see you, and would like to know
how you manage to provide for yourself and your children.
Just tell him how you contrive."

Poor Mrs. Granberg, whose eyes sparkled with gratitude in
her pale, emaciated countenance, said humbly,—"How good
you are to inquire after a poor creature like me!"

She seemed embarrassed, and it was only after she had heard
the familiar remarks of the pastor's wife about health and sickness, &c., that she by degrees became more communicative.

"Ah," said she, then, "how fortunate they are who do not
know what sickness is, and how it deprives one of one's power!
Many a time have I cried because I was not able to work and
earn a bit of bread for me and my children, as I used formerly; but that has not been the case for some years. One trouble I have that I shall carry with me to the grave, and that I
got before the girl was born. It was in the depth of winter,
and we lived outside the town. It was a bitterly cold and
snowy winter, and we suffered great want. Granberg had
been away for fourteen days, and I did not know where he was.
For three whole days we had not had a morsel of bread nor a
bit of meat inside the house. The child cried; I spun, and
when I got very hungry and weak I laid me down to sleep.
Anxiety and hunger soon woke me again. But I would not
weep nor yet give in, because of the child to which I should
soon give birth, and for its sake I determined to keep in as
good heart as I could. I sate down again to my spinning-
wheel. At length I could bear up no longer; I took my
homespun jacket, the only thing I had left belonging to better
days, and went to Petter's Anna, and asked her to take it to
Stenbom's to put it in pawn, and bring me back something to
eat, for we could not go on famishing any longer.

"Stina went, and soon came back again, with two cakes of
bread, six-pennyworth of meal, and a herring. And we
cooked, and we ate, and how good they were. But Stina had
met Granberg as she was going out, and told him how badly

off I was at home; and he knew it well enough, and that was just the very reason that he kept away; he knew that there was nothing to be had.

"Some days afterwards we heard that Granberg had sold the jacket at a public-house for eight rix-dollars. But I knew nothing about it of a certainty before he came one day drunk into the room, and threw upon the floor a sack which held half a bushel of peas, and exclaimed, 'See, there you have your jacket!' I then understood the whole thing, there was a noise in my head, a rending pain in my body, and I fainted away. After that little Mina was born—a poor little creature, such as she is now, and I have never since then had a day free from pain."

"Poor Mrs. Granberg!" said the pastor's wife compassionately, but in an undervoice, as she sighed, "My God! my God!"

She and her husband then turned to the little girl with the bright, cheerful eyes. They asked her, if it were not wearisome to be always sitting.

"Oh, yes," replied the child, "it would be a deal nicer if I could run and jump about, like the other children; but I can always amuse myself, as it is!"

"She is always so cheerful," said her mother, with a melancholy smile, "she has been sitting to-day for a little while at the top of the stairs, and heard the lark sing; and then her geranium's coming into flower. She has always something to be pleased about. She would sing all day long like a bird, if only, poor child, I could feed her better. But since she has gone to the infant school she is, for all that, very happy!"

"The Almighty has blessed the child for your sake, and he will bless you through the child!" said the pastor with emotion.

Whilst the good couple were talking with Mrs. Granberg, Mimmi Svanberg had silently stolen away into a corner, where a poor woman suffering from cancer lay upon a straw mattress. She had helped to lay her on her bed, and to dress her sore. She had for some time attended her thus as a nurse.

In the meantime the other inhabitants of the room were
all in movement, thronging around the pastor and his wife,
some of them with pitiful stories, and some of them evidently
in a state of liquor.

"Now let us go," said Mimmi Svanberg to her friends;
"you must talk another time with the pastor, good people.
You can very well understand that it is now too late. We
must all go to bed. Good night! good night!"

Once more in the street, she said,—

"Take care now, dear pastor, that Granberg has some help
from the guardian of the poor. She is well deserving of it, is
she not?"

"You artful Mimmi!" said the pastor, jokingly threatening her with his cane. "I'll lay any wager that you had
that design in your head all the time, and fooled me up those
steps, where I was very near losing my balance and falling
backwards, just on purpose to accomplish it! Ay, you are an
excellent one! Confess, now, that you did it on speculation!"

"Yes, that I did!" said Mimmi, laughing heartily; "I
knew that my good pastor could not resist, if he saw the thing
brought before his own eyes; and the guardians of the poor do
well to go among them a little."

"Get along with you! Yes, if he have anything to give.
You don't know, not you, how he is beset; and of a truth I
cannot see the bottom of this increasing misery, nor tell what
will be the end of it, if active ladies do not come to our rescue,
and take charge of poor families and children, so that there
may be some order and improvement, and if they do not make
us better acquainted with the people so that we can separate
the goats from the sheep."

"Yes, that is indeed exactly what we will do with our
Ladies-societies," said Mimmi Svanberg gaily, "we will separate between Mrs. Granberg, who is an invalid and a good
woman and mother, and Mrs. Bergström, who is a wretched
ditto, and teaches her children to beg and to steal; we will
endeavor to raise up the one, and look after the other and her
children. But then comes the Protocols-secretary, N.B., and

writes a book against Ladies' societies, and makes a dead-set at us."

"He will not do it," said the pastor, "or else I will write a sermon against him and the Philistines."

"Let him write, and let us act," said the pastor's wife, "that will be the best. Don't forget, dear Mimmi, that you promised to come and help me to dress the bride in the morning. It will be about noon, and you will stay and dine with us."

"Yes, if I may only go away in the afternoon, for I promised to help the Dahlströms with the funeral, and after that I am to be god-mother at Palmstjernas; they have got such a nice little boy—a great joy in the family."

"And now see, we are at home. I shall bring with me a flowering myrtle-branch for the bride. Good night! Don't forget, dear pastor, poor Granberg and little Mina."

Ten minutes later, Mimmi Svanberg was with her father, who, wrapped in his large, flowery dressing-gown, seated in his easy chair, at his writing-table, absorbed in the labyrinth of his system, and involved in a cloud of Havanna ambrosia, was as happy as any professor possibly could be, who saw an amended and a happier world shining through its fragrant and transparent haze. Happy in his way, he kissed his daughter, and said from the depths of his heart, "You are my own child, that you are—you take after your father—you desire to make your fellow-creatures happy. If you had only a method. But you are deficient in method, my child. Well, well, every bird sings according to his bill, and every one has his own way."

"And all ways lead to Rome," said Mimmi, laughing. "And there we shall certainly meet, papa, dear, if not before. And now I must return for a short time to the Dufvas' to make my appearance as Pax Domestica, with a great broom in my hand, to endanger people's domestic peace. That will make a sensation! But I shall see papa yet again before morning."

We must now go back an hour of time in the evening, and accompany Hertha and Aunt Petronella, or Nella, on their way home from the evening party; Aunt Nella keeping up an incessant patter of small talk in this style:

“To think that you will never learn to be prudent and to act and talk like other people!”

“I don’t wish to be like other people,” said Hertha.

“Yes, that is just the misfortune. What can be the use of being different to everybody else? What can be the advantage of saying everything that one thinks, as if one was in *le Palais de la Vérité?* It only vexes people and leads to anger. You’ll be getting a lawsuit on your shoulders, just as I have for my honesty’s sake; I wish that you would take warning by my example. Then you might escape all the entanglement that I am involved in, and that everlasting waiting, like me, for a summons.” Here Aunt Nella stopped, because Hertha stopped as she said,

“I must go up to Amalia for a moment.”

“To Amalia!” exclaimed Aunt Nella, horrified, “and you know that the Director has forbidden any of us to have intercourse with her!”

“Nevertheless, I must see her this evening; I have some work for her, and she needs it. Go quietly onward, dear aunt, I will soon overtake you.”

“No, ah, no; that I dare not—dare not go along the street alone at this time of night, no. I would rather than that go up with you to her, if you must go; but——”

Hertha had already gone into the house and knocked softly upon the door of a room, within which a faint light had been seen in the street, shining through a curtained window. After knocking she said softly, “It is I, Amalia; open the door.”

“I’ll not go in,” said Aunt Petronella, angrily; “I’ll neither compromise nor involve myself, by going to such—”

The door opened, and Hertha entered. It was a young woman of fine figure, and even of an agreeable appearance, who opened the door; but her eyes seemed heavy and red, and a bitter expression gloomed the whole countenance.

“You come, nevertheless, Hertha,” said she, with emotion. “You do not forget me.”

“No, never; see, there is some work, Amalia, at least for a week; you will be well paid. It is for Eva Dufva; and there is some bread and some cake. It was given me; it is mine, and you can take it without hesitation. You have certainly had nothing to eat to-day."

"No; but that does not matter. I have had food for the poor little fellow; it would have been harder to have been without work. Then one's heart gets so heavy, and one is so sad. But now—God bless you, Hertha!"

It was a little poverty-stricken room in which this conversation took place. All within it, however, was neat and well kept; beside the bed stood a cradle, in which lay a sleeping child. Hertha approached the cradle, whilst she said,

"If I could do all for you that I would, Amalia, you should never either want work or bread; but I am able to do so little."

"God bless you for your good-will, and for never upbraiding or despising me, as others do. Oh! it is so bitter; so very, very bitter, to be despised, and to know that one deserves it. When I think of what I was, and what I might have been, it almost drives me mad."

"Your fault is small, Amalia, in comparison with his, who misled you and deceived you. You loved him, but he did not love you."

"Yes, if I had loved him *much*, Hertha, then I would have excused myself more; but I only loved him sufficiently to be easily——weak; if I had only had somebody or something to strengthen me! It was levity, curiosity, youthful impulses which made me unfortunate; it was the want of something better to fix my feelings, my thoughts upon. My heart was full, my life so poor, my brain and my future so empty; I wished to experience the feelings of life, if only for a moment; —Ah, I little thought that I should have afterwards to drink its dregs during the whole remainder of my days! And if you had not sustained me, I could not have borne it!"

"You must bear it, Amalia," said Hertha, with sorrowful earnestness, "you are a mother: you must live and work for your child's sake; and you will do it, I know, and I love you for it!"

"Yes, Hertha! For this child have I worked and starved, and starved and worked; and my only consolation is that I stand before God and man such as I am; that I have concealed nothing, evaded nothing, either responsibility or penalty. Yes," she continued, rising and directing a fixed gaze on her sleeping child, "I will be a *mother*, I will live and work, so that no want and no neglect may be the lot of my child; but ——I feel myself weaker of late, and—if I should die!"

"Then is your child *mine!*" said Hertha, seizing Amalia's hand; "and so long as I live and can work, it shall want for nothing. Of that, be certain, Amalia; and if the world casts stones at you, I will defend you, and say that you were a good mother; that you were worthy of esteem, because you had the courage to bear the scorn and contempt of society by keeping your child with you and living for it, like a true mother; and I have not words to tell you how I despise those who depreciate and condemn you. I honor you for it, Amalia; and if I were free and could——"

"I know, I know; and don't say any more. I cannot tell you how it consoles, how it strengthens me, that you approve of my conduct in this respect. It will give me new courage to live and suffer and to resist temptations; for oh, this solitude and want of occupation are terrible! Hertha, do not forsake me!"

"Never!" replied Hertha, and pressed Amalia's hand as she added, "I will come again very soon; but I must go now. I hear aunt coughing, and my father expects me. But, Amalia, expect me soon again!"

Hertha found Aunt Nella, who was waiting in the passage, in a very excited state.

"You will compromise both yourself and me," said she, angrily, "what will people think, what will people believe, from such visits, at this time of night? It will bring me into a thousand difficulties. Besides, it has kept us so long, and the Director will be so very cross! And Heaven knows what new accusations my enemies may advance against me when the cause comes to be heard! Oh! oh!"

Thus talked and sighed the poor lady the whole way. Hertha answered not a word, and by her expression no one would have suspected that she heard a single syllable ; and the truth is, that the talk about the enigmatical lawsuit brought about by one or more mysterious enemies—all gentlemen— and the incessant danger in which Aunt Nella stood, by reason of its protracted hearing, had so often sounded in Hertha's ears, that she was accustomed to listen to it, as one listens to the dissonance of a barrel-organ for ever playing the same piece, with a certain submissive suffering, in expectation of its some time ceasing.

It was an evening towards the end of March, and the heavens shone bright with stars above the grey ice-clad earth. Hertha's glance was raised with a gloomy expression to this brilliant heaven, and then it fell upon the frozen ground on which she was walking with a weary, heavy step. She seemed to be drawing a comparison between the two, and to be think-ing with the poet Henrik Wergeland :

> Stars ! if ye could only see
> All earth's silent misery,
> Oh ! then in the heavens nightly
> Ye could not shine forth so brightly !

Her steps and Aunt Nella's tongue stopped at the same moment. They had now reached—

THE OLD HOUSE.

READER, has it not sometimes happened to thee, as thou wert wandering in our towns, to cast thine eyes upon a house from which they were involuntarily repelled with an unpleasant impression, unless they became riveted upon it with that kind of interest which is produced by dark mysteries? The house may be well-built, with its two or three stories, and yet have a certain dark and ruinous appearance. It is flecked and blotched with grey, and a sickly yellow-green, wherever the plaster has fallen off, or is damp-stricken. No flowering plants are to be seen in the windows, from all of which seems to look forth a something dark and brooding. The tiles of the roof are also dark, some broken and decayed, others moss-grown. The steps look as if nobody gave themselves the trouble to sweep them or keep them clean. Whichever way you turn your eyes, they are met by some ill-conditioned feature. There is a something dead, a something divested of beauty and of life, about the place.

You may·be certain that many silent sighs are breathed forth daily in such a house; many bitter unseen tears are shed, and tortured hearts beat, beat as though they would burst the dark, imprisoning walls, in vain! The old house stands there, like a dark mystery closing its walls around the burning strife and agony of the living soul from one ten years' end to another, hiding them from the eye of the world. The profound drama of human life goes on within it; the child is born, brought up, developed, loves, yearns, longs, suffers, and withers away. The old house speaks not a word about it. It silently conceals the mysteries of family life from the cradle to the coffin, with all its unspeakable bitterness, its corroding rust, which eats into the heart, as the old song says, and the world around has no idea of it. It merely has an idea that "wormwood grows in that house."

At times, however, these internal corroding disorganizations, these secret agonies, the measure of which has been heaped up to over-flowing, burst forth, and then something terrible occurs. Husband is murdered by wife, or wife by husband, or child by the parent, or an incendiary fire takes place which destroys the old house, and spreads desolation far around; and these reveal, now and then, the dark mysteries of the old house to the world. Tattling tongues are thrust forth from every window; the walls talk for the first and perhaps for the last time. There is then an end of the old house; that which remains is a ruin.

Sometimes the house still remains, but shunned of all who would choose for themselves a dwelling. For such houses are said to be haunted. Some uneasy ghost walks there. But long before it arrives at that stage, the old house stands from one ten years' end to another, silent and dark, as a moss-grown graveyard, whilst living hearts slowly bleed to death within it.

There are many such houses in the world, though not many with such good cause as the old house before which we are now standing.

In the lobby, Aunt Nella made a hesitating pause, and said:

"If—perhaps—if I might escape going up to my brother-in-law!—I am quite sure that we have stopped over our time, and he will certainly be so angry!—If you would say——"

"I shall say that you were tired, and obliged to rest!" said Hertha. "Go to my sisters, aunt dear, and give my love to them. I will give a kind greeting to papa from aunt!"

And with these words Hertha sprung up-stairs.

"Well, if you think you can manage it so; then—but where is she?—Well, well, if she ever is plagued with a law-suit, as I am, she will not be so nimble-footed!"

And sighing and twiddling the strings of her reticule, Aunt Nella trotted across the court to another part of the house.

Hertha was very soon obliged to moderate her pace, because there was no light on the stairs, and it was very dark. On the second flight of stairs she was met by a youth carrying a candle, and who advanced towards her with agitated haste.

"Hertha—cousin—what a long time you have been?" and the light of the small candle, which was stuck crookedly into an old brass candlestick, fell upon the figure of a tall, but not strong youth, the mass of whose dark hair had a disordered appearance, whilst his eyes, deep-seated under a broad but low forehead, glanced forth with an unsteady, uncertain gaze. There was something gloomy and bewildered in the whole appearance of the youth, and his voice was rough, as if breaking, although he seemed to be about twenty years of age.

"Have I been so very long, dear Rudolph?" said Hertha kindly and calmly. "What o'clock is it?"

"Certainly twenty minutes past eight. Uncle sits with his watch in his hand——"

"Give me the candle, Rudolph; you drop the tallow on the stairs. Let us go in. Has it been a very tedious evening?"

"Most dreadfully tedious!"

"It is my fault. I ought not to have stayed so long.— Help me!—Thank you, I'll take off my over-shoes myself; but my cloak—thank you, Rudolph! I'll keep my shawl on. It is so cold here!—"

They stood in a large desolate room, lighted merely by the thin candle crookedly placed in the brass candlestick. Hertha shuddered involuntarily as she cast a long glance round the gloomy room in which fire seldom burned.

"Let us go in together!" continued she, and advanced resolutely towards a door on the left, in the large room. As she put her hand on the lock, she involuntarily paused a moment whilst she drew a deep breatl ; she then opened the door and went in.

Here, in a frugally-furnished room, was merely one person, and that a man. He sat on a sofa just opposite the door, with a table before him, on which two candles were burning. His feet were wrapped in flannel, and he held a gold watch in his hand. There was was no possibility of mistaking who he was. He was the master of the house and the bugbear of the family.

He was a slender and rather small man ; his features were regular and well-defined ; his hair, steel-grey and bristly, stood straight up from his high and commanding forehead ; and beneath the dark, bushy eye-brows lay a pair of large, dark-grey eyes, whose stern and angry glance was now fixed upon Hertha.

"You've stayed over your time !" said Director Falk, in a fierce voice, to his daughter. "It is twenty-two minutes past eight by my watch. What made you stop so long ?"

"I did not know what time it was ;—I forgot !" replied Hertha coldly.

"Forgot !" burst forth the Director, "forgot ! Is that any excuse ? Ought people to forget their duty ? That, perhaps, you think nothing of ; or think, perhaps, that it is beautiful, noble, independent ! That I know is according to those modern theories of which you are so fond ; according to the laws of female emancipation, I suppose, by which you will emancipate yourself from obedience to parents ? Forgot, indeed ! One of these fine days you'll be forgetting that you have a father, or that you have any duties at all to perform towards him. Forgot !—and you tell me so in that obstinate way, as if you had a right to demand whatever you liked, and in whatever way you choose, without any reference to me. But I will be master in my own house ! I will have obedience there and subordination ! I'll be d——d a thousand times, if I will bear to have my people one time after another disregarding my orders, and forgetting the time which I fix for them. I know what I will, and I will have my will ! And I will have my own will to be law in my own house ! I won't endure to have people forgetting what I have said to them above a hundred times. And more than a hundred times have I said that I would have the gate locked at eight o'clock in the evening, and I would not, on any pretence, have it open after eight; and, therefore, you ought to be at home at eight precisely every evening: before eight, or at eight precisely! Have you heard that before now, or not?"

"I have heard it!" replied Hertha, as before.

"Very well; then be so good as to act accordingly, or I will have the gate locked and barred every afternoon, and you shall not so easily get out to any of your pleasure parties, which make you forget your duties at home."

"But why must it be precisely eight o'clock?" asked the young man in a grunting, ill-tempered voice.

"Why? you scoundrel! Because *I will* have it so, and that to the minute. That is enough, I hope, or what next? Bah! What must you be mumbling for? Keep your foolish tongue within your teeth, till people speak to you! Don't you be meddling in that which is no business of yours. You've nothing to say on the subject! If you had not been my nephew, I would long since have turned you out of doors, you good-for-nothing, you! Write and count a little you can, and that little you have learned of me; but sense you have none, and that neither I nor anybody else could ever drive into you! You are, and will remain to be, a clown all your days, and fit for nothing but to eat the bread of charity! And if ever you mix yourself up again in things that don't concern you, I'll—give you a good dressing! My feet are cursedly weak, but my hands, thank God, are active enough, and that you shall have some experience of! Be silent! I have not talked to you, but to Hertha!"

"Rudolph is a good lad!" said Hertha, with a flashing glance, "and will some day be a clever man; and able to provide for himself, without being obliged to eat the bread of charity. Even now, he is very useful in the counting-house!"

"To whom are you saying that!" shouted the Director

4

turning to his daughter; "are you going to teach me? Do
you understand such things better than I do? Now, really
the pretension of young women is going too far. One thing,
however, I will advise you, and that is, to keep to your spin-
ning-wheel and your housekeeping affairs; for more than that
neither you nor any other woman in the universe understands.
Thank God, if they can understand what is before them.
Shoemaker, stick to your last! I won't allow any one to encroach upon my rights. But now-a-days women will mix
themselves up in everything, and therefore everything goes
wrong. There's such a deal of talk about this genius! and
this genius! and this must be an artist, and that a book-keep-
er, and that an author, or a professor, or some other great
thing! Cursed talk, altogether! I wish that they were real
kitchen-geniuses! then they would at least do something useful in the world. But now they are too grand for that—Hea-
en help us!—must live for a higher object, be fellow-citizen-
esses, or some folly or other! It provokes me only to think
of it: and so long as I live, and am master in my own house,
my daughters shall not make a spectacle of themselves to the
whole world with any such stupidity, but shall attend properly each one to her own business. I will not tolerate any
modern notions about freedom and emancipation in my
house."

Thus the Director continued to scold, turning towards his
daughter, who, from the moment when he again addressed
her, stood quite silent, pale and immovable, her dark eyes riv
eted upon him with an expression of deep inward suffering
which sometimes seemed transformed into hatred and defiance. But not a syllable passed her pale lips. Rudolph again
sat down by the wall, with his head drooped upon his breast,
his usual attitude, and his now darkly gleaming eyes fixed
alternately upon the Director and Hertha.

This painful scene was interrupted by the old servant,
Anna, who came in to say that supper was ready.

Aunt Nella now made her appearance, together with two
quite young girls of twelve or thirteen years of age. Aunt

Nella made her salutation in an embarrassed manner, and busily twisted and twirled her reticule-strings. The girls made their curtseys very diffidently, and did not advance beyond the door, when they saw their father's angry and excited appearance.

He in the meantime called them up to him, and seemed to become somewhat mollified whilst he looked at them; asked them some questions, filliped their noses, and called them names, which made them blush up to their ears, and filled the eyes of one of them with tears.

Then they were called " simpleton" and " fool," and " cry-baby," which caused the fountain of tears, so plenteous and so easily excited at their age, to overflow, which provoked a fresh ebullition of sneers—" What's the meaning of this? Cursed sentimentality. I'll have nothing of that sort: I won't allow it. If you can do nothing but cry, you may go your way and amuse yourselves the best you can. Can't your aunt teach you something better than crying? Can't she teach you to be rational girls and not simpletons?

"They are yet so young, so sensitive," stammered Aunt Nella.

" Oh, bah, sensitive!" said the Director. " The devil take your feelings and your sensibility, which is nothing but cursed nonsense! It is so beautiful and so affecting to be so sensitive, and to sit and sigh and read novels, and cry and pout at everything, and be displeased with the whole world, and make themselves unhappy about nothing. But I will not have my daughters brought up in this way. I will have them made useful and practical human beings, and not to live in dreams and nonsense. I will have nothing to do with any such thing. Do you hear me? Mind, then, that we have no more grimaces. Now come and sit down to table."

Old Anna had just said that dishes were at the table.

The Director, supported upon the arm of the faithfu. old servant, and by a stick, limped out into the dining-room, followed by the others in silence. Two tallow candles, standing upon the table, dimly lighted the large dark room.

"How pleasant it is to have light here!" whispered Rudolph to Hertha.

"What's that?—What are you saying?" asked the Director, turning upon him a pair of threatening eyes. Rudolph cowered before them, as it were, and was silent.

"I believe that you'll be lively enough!" said the Director; "and—there's that for you! Be less nimble with your tongue, and have more sense another time."

And Rudolph received a blow on the cheek, which made a buzzing in his ears. Hertha's eyes flashed fire at this, and Aunt Nella began to cry.

"Come, come, no nonsense!" said the Director; "sit down to table. Where is Alma, why does not she come up?"

"She is not well; she is gone to bed," replied Aunt Nella, who tried to swallow her tears in a glass of beer posset.

"Cursed nonsense!" mumbled the Director again; but as when the thunderbolt has fallen the storm gradually abates, so now the Director's ill-humor seemed to have discharged itself, and a certain depression took its place. He seemed as if he wished to dissipate it by talking on indifferent subjects, but he received either monosyllabic replies, or no reply at all, if his remarks were not put in the form of questions. The frugal meal was very soon ended; no one seemed to have enjoyed it, excepting Rudolph, who ate ravenously, and the Director, who seemed to take his usual basin of wine-gruel with his usual appetite.

When they all rose from table, the Director said a short "Good night" to Aunt Nella, who curtsied, twisting the while the strings of her reticule, and to the little girls, who went forward and kissed their father's hand, while they "thanked him for a good meal," and said "good night." His glance rested gloomily and joylessly upon the children, who seemed to wish to get away.

"Oh, how unbearable it is here," whispered the spirited little Martha to her sister Maria; "I would positively marry at night if I were only sure of waking a widow the next morning."

"Hush! hush! don't talk so," admonished Aunt Nella, as she prepared to leave the room with the children. Hertha and Rudolph had already accompanied the Director.

"Set out the table and give me the cards," said he.

Rudolph brought a round table which he placed before the sofa, and Hertha laid upon it a well-worn pack of cards, and they sat down to a three-handed game. A more lifeless and joyless card party could hardly be conceived. Hertha played mechanically; she was very pale, and spoke coldly and with constraint the words which the game required. Rudolph, again, made continual mistakes, which gave the Director occasion to be almost continually scolding him. Excepting in this way, not a word was spoken. They did not play for money. The Director seemed pleased with winning the game, which he almost always did, because the others played ill or without interest. Thus were spent two hours. The Director then looked at his watch and said, "It is now eleven, we may close."

Rudolph and Hertha silently pushed away their chairs, carried away the table, and put the cards aside.

"Good night, Rudolph; you can go to bed," said the Director coldly. "Hertha, stay, I wish to speak to you."

Rudolph bowed sullenly and left the room, after he had cast a lingering glance at Hertha.

Father and daughter were now alone; there was a deep silence, each seemed to wait for the other to speak first. At length the Director said :—

"Hertha, you have failed in duty to your father. Do you not think you should beg his pardon ? "

Hertha made no reply. Her heart was full of stormy feelings and bitter words. She was afraid of speaking lest she should say too much. The Director continued in a milder voice :

"I desire nothing but the best interests of my children. I fulfil my duty to them, and I desire only that they should fulfil theirs towards me—should show me obedience and gratitude."

Again there was no reply. Astonished at Hertha's silence, the Director looked inquiringly at her, endeavoring to interpret the peculiar expression of her countenance, in the same way that we puzzle over a difficult riddle. Many thoughts and feelings seemed to be working there; some seemed wishful to find expression, but were opposed by others, which said, "It is not worth while; he cannot, he will not understand." In the meantime there was something in the milder voice and countenance of her father, together with his suffering state, which seemed to touch her deeply, and she merely said with melancholy seriousness, as she bowed her head,

"Good night, my father."

The Director looked at her and extended his hand for her to kiss, for it was the custom in his house, morning, noon, and evening, for the children to kiss the hand of their father. For some years, however, this old usage of childish reverence had become oppressive to Hertha, because her heart was not in it, and this evening it was an impossibility to her. She repeated merely in a constrained voice, "Good night," bowed her head as a parting salutation, and went out, saying, "I will send in Anna."

The outstretched hand remained thus for a moment, then it was clenched convulsively; a dark, angry red flushed the pale countenance of the Director, and he exclaimed :—

"The devil take their notions of emancipation."

He sat silently staring with the expression of an enraged beast until the faithful old servant, Anna, came in to help her master to his bed.

She had lived in the family more then twenty years, was accustomed to speak her thoughts, and the Director listened to her more than to any one else in the house ; he was in the habit of speaking more confidentially with her than with any other being in the world. Now, therefore, from the necessity of unburdening his heart after the scene which had just .occurred, he began :—

"Things are getting madder and madder than ever .in this world."

"Yes, yes; but—" said Anna, who was somewhat of a misanthrope, "the older people get, the worse they get."

"That I don't know," said the Director angrily, "but this I do know, that young girls get more and more unreasonable in their demands, and more and more disobedient and ungrateful to their fathers."

"Yes, yes, but, poor things,—their lives are not so very amusing either."

"Amusing!—Why should they be amusing? It is better for young girls that their lives should be dull than amusing. It teaches them to be serious, industrious, and domestic."

"Yes, but I don't think it would do any great harm if they had a little amusement at the same time. I don't mean any giddy sort of amusement, but something pleasant to think about and wish for, and which would enliven them, and give them a sort of outlet. For life is very heavy, and very narrow sometimes for us women."

"Oh, nonsense. What do you want? What do my daughters want? Have they not everything which they require—whether of clothing or of food?"

"Yes, certainly—yes, certainly. But look you, Director, this is my way of thinking,—young people must have something to live for; something which is their own, and which they can improve; yes, something certainly to think about and occupy themselves with for the future. Look you, I am only a poor woman-servant, but I have my own certain occupation for every day, and my own certain wages for every year, which I can do just as I like with; some of it I can put every year into the Savings' Bank for my old age, or else to help a friend. And I believe that every human being ought to have his own, and liberty to do with it as he likes; because that leads to peace and contentment."

"You are right, inasmuch as it applies to those who have attained to mature years, and can properly take care of themselves, and that which belongs to them," said the Director. "But young girls cannot do that. They are mere children. If they had anything of their own, and liberty to do what they liked with it, there would soon be an end of it. Precisely because I wish my girls to have some time something to manage, and live upon, and not be dependent on others when they get old, precisely for this reason must I manage and save for them. And so I shall continue to do even if they are ungrateful. I know, however, that one day they will be thankful to me."

"Yes, but Director, I still think that Mamsell Alma and Mamsell Hertha are old enough and sensible enough to be able to manage for themselves."

"You don't understand it. I know better. Alma is a good girl, but too weak to be able to take care of herself. And Hertha is a headstrong, self-willed girl, who needs to remain under guardianship all her days."

"Nay, look now, I say that the Director does her a great injustice!" exclaimed Anna, with the boldness of a faithful old servant; "and her deceased ladyship Hård did not understand her any better. But this I say, that though she has a head and a will of her own, yet that she is really an uncommonly clever young lady, and does not deserve injustice, and could manage both a town and a nation, if it came to that. She has not been at all like anybody else ever since she was a child, and may be a little peculiar and proud, but so good-hearted and so noble-minded, so reasonable—"

"It was you and her mother who spoiled her with talking in that way," interrupted the Director. "She is stubborn and self-willed, I say, and needs discipline. It does not do for girls to have their own will or to be their own advisers. And it is now, as it has been, my will that my daughters shall direct themselves according to my will, and not say or do anything which is contrary to it. I am master of my own house, I hope, and they are my children, and that's positive! If my daughters are wise they will find it best to obey their father."

"But if they should die?"

"What do you mean?—What are you talking about?" said the Director violently, "why should they die?"

"Ay, I believe, that—Mamsell Alma will not be very long

in this world. I believe that sorrow has taken very deep hold upon her."

"It is your foolish fancy and superstition," said the Director, as before. "What is amiss with her? Is she not in every day to dinner, the one day like another? I see no change in her."

"But she does not come up in the evenings any longer, and she looks so deathly of late. And I know that she has got no sleep the greater part of the night, ever since——"

"Stupid stuff! stupid fancies!" again interrupted the Director angrily. "She has been somewhat complaining for some time. But the doctor sees her twice in the week, and she will soon be better. But if any of the girls complain you think directly that they are in the agonies of death. It is nothing but stupid superstition! Now then, help me into bed, and give me over that little chest."

Old Anna was affronted by the often repeated accusation of "stupidity," and said not another word, doing only, as a machine, that which her master desired her. He now therefore dismissed her, saying coldly:

"Good night! see that the fire is carefully taken down in the kitchen, and don't leave till it is all black on the hearth. Do you hear?"

When the Director was left alone, he opened, half sitting-up in bed, the little chest or cash-box, and his wrinkled angry countenance grew brighter, as he opened, examined with the candle, and again folded together various small strips of paper. After that he smiled with satisfaction, and said half aloud to himself:

"Not so bad! not so bad! Old Falk is a well-to-do man; a well-to-do man, a substantial fellow, a rich man. Ay, ay; nobody shall look down upon him! People shall take their hats off to him—a rich man!"

And so saying he laid the chest under the pillow, extinguished the lamp, and turned himself to sleep, whilst his thoughts repeated to him, like a lullaby, "A rich man! A rich man!"

And no warning voice whispered in his ear, "Thou fool! this night shall thy soul be required from thee!"

THE SISTERS.

When Hertha left her father's chamber, she found Rudolph in the dining-room, who stood as if waiting there, with the now nearly burnt-down candle in his hand. He advanced towards her, flourishing the candle as he said:—

"Hertha, will you—will you? Say only a word; I will do whatever you wish!"

"What do you mean?" asked Hertha astonished.

"It is so cold here! Don't you think that it is very cold now?—cold! I saw you shiver. Do you know, I believe, that it never will get any better!"

"Go to bed, Rudolph, you'll be warm there. Go to bed, poor Rudolph, and sleep, and dream and forget. Good night, dear Rudolph!"

"I will light you down, Hertha."

"Not this evening, Rudolph. I will light myself. Give me your candle for to-night and let the moon be your lanthorn into your garret, thus you can oblige me, Rudolph."

"I'll go with you for all that," said Rudolph, "because something might happen to you on the stairs!" And he attempted to put his arm round her waist.

Hertha pushed him gently away, and said in a determined manner, "I will go alone, Rudolph. I can light and help myself. Good night, Rudolph."

She went, locking the door behind her.

Rudolph stood a moment silent and moody, muttering to himself—

"Well, well, she'll have to fly to me for help some time—before she thinks!" and passed through another door from the dining-room, which led by a winding staircase up to his own chamber in the attics.

Hertha went down two flights of stairs, to the lower story, and into the court. The Director's chamber faced the street and was at the other end of the house.

Hertha entered a little stone passage, upon either side of which was a door. She knocked softly upon the one to the left. It was opened by Aunt Petronella.

"Are my little sisters still awake?" asked Hertha softly.

"Hertha, Hertha, is it you?" cried the young fresh voices from the inner room. "Ah, come, come, and tell us something about the ball and the costumes, Hertha."

"Not this evening, but in the morning, my darlings," said Hertha, as she bent over her sisters' beds, whilst her neck was clasped by their young arms. "I am come to say good night to you, and give you a few sweetmeats from the great entertainment at the Dufvas'."

"Thanks, thanks, you dear, naughty Hertha! Good night; now dream some wonderful dream that you can tell us to-morrow morning at breakfast!"

Hertha's dreams were celebrated in the family, and had constituted for some years the most remarkable incidents in this secluded family, nay, even their principal pleasures.

Hertha promised to pay particular attention to her dreams this night. Aunt Nella had sat, before Hertha's entrance into the room, deeply absorbed over a large portfolio, and, amid a mass of letters, scraps of newspapers, patterns of collars and needlework, verses, and every variety of paper-article lying together in the utmost confusion, was endeavoring to catch hold of and bring together the ravelled thread of that threatening, mysterious lawsuit which was hanging over her head. The endeavor seemed hopeless to uninitiated eyes, but Aunt Nella, who had all her days found an exquisite pleasure in unravelling tangled skeins, seemed not to have any doubt about being able to accomplish it, and yet fully to bring to light the mysteriously intriguing enemy, who most frequently showed himself as an indefinite, but prejudiced and offended gentleman, whom Aunt Nella in her youth had had the misfortune to stumble against.   A yarringles stood near her, upon which was a tangled skein of yarn, the threads from which had become entangled among the papers of the portfolio ; all seemed to become more and more perplexed ; the old lady, however, comforted herself by the entanglement on the yarringles, in the hope, as she said silently to herself, that the one ravel might help the other.

Nor was it a bad idea either: Aunt Nella's countenance and her law-prospects brightened considerably, as she, with admirable patience and even skill, opened a way for the thread through all the knots and the labyrinths of the skein ; and still, as more and more the whole was subdued into order, and the winding went on uninterruptedly, and the skein diminished on the yarringles, lighter and brighter became her state of mind, and more and more hopeful her thoughts of the ultimate issue of the impending lawsuit.   When Hertha, therefore, came in from her sisters', the old lady having laid aside her portfolio for the tangled yarn-skein, and her state of mind having begun to brighten with the decreasing entanglement, she said quite kindly to Hertha :

"I am winding now to spole for your weaving, my dear Hertha ; and if you were but as industrious as I am, it would soon be ready."

Hertha only replied " Good night," with an unhappy expression of countenance, and crossed the passage to the second door.   Of this she had the key.   She opened it and went in. It was a large room, in which might be perceived the smell both of smoke and damp.   Ceiling, walls, fire-place, all showed evident want of repair.   There was but little furniture, and that of the most homely character ; although in this, as in other things, the careful hand of woman was observable.   A loom and two spinning-wheels stood in the room.   Its only ornament was a little book-case and a few pictures, the work of Hertha.   In a deep recess on the left hand ;—but before we proceed to this we will say a few words about the two sisters themselves, who had spent together here the best part of their youth, who had here together laughed, and together wept, loved, and comforted each other; spent their days in hard work, and often lain awake through the night to read together the old heroic songs or history, Hertha's favorite reading, or novels, which were Alma's; together became enthusiastic about grand ideas, laid out grand schemes, nay even poured out their warm feelings both in prose and verse (but merely for each other, because they possessed no other public), and then seen their youthful dreams grow dim, and their life change into—that which it was now.

Their mother died in giving birth to the youngest of her daughters. The two eldest were then much younger. The mother's illness, occasioned in great measure from want of happiness in her marriage, had gloomed the childhood of her daughters. After her death their father's sister came to take charge of the household. The difference between the influence of the former mistress of the family and the present, was like that between a soft, rainy summer, and a severe winter. Mrs. Hård was a lady who exalted herself for her love of truth and justice, nor will we deny her these qualities; but she had not love, and therefore her view of things was never entirely true; she could never see the whole truth in any object which she condemned, and her judgment was, therefore, neither just nor enlightened by the beneficent light of reason.

Hertha was thirteen years old when this lady came to live in the family; she was at that critical age, when the child awakes from her slumber and looks around her with opened eyes upon the world; and when all the necessities and questionings of the soul burst forth thirsting for the light of day. The unusual, and therefore restless temperament and faculties of the child were misunderstood and misconstrued by Mrs. Hård. She saw dangerous or altogether improper tendencies in everything, and she considered that truth and justice required her to represent to her father every fault or deficiency in its blackest color, which she called "its true color," that the young girl might be punished in the severest manner. Mrs. Hård believed that she acted in this respect as a model of conscientiousness and justice. The deeply sensitive and enthusiastic girl, who saw her least mistake represented as something monstrous; her most innocent actions suspected; her best intentions often misconstrued to the very opposite; all her questionings about deeper subjects of life repulsed as " needless inquiries," and every expression of her young, aspiring soul sternly repelled, became at first miserably unhappy, almost driven to despair, and cast into a state of perfectly chaotic darkness as regarded herself, her fellow-creatures, life, truth—everything. The necessity which there was in her own soul to pour forth love and reverence, and which instinctively turned towards those who were her natural guardians, was received by them only with injudicious severity, and in a spirit of worldly wisdom. She thought at first that they must be right, and she herself wrong. But she saw her sister, the gentle, and, according to her judgment, the almost saintly Alma, condemned and severely treated also. At this, her naturally strong mind released itself out of the slavish depression which was otherwise gaining the mastery over her, and she overcame it through love to her sister. " That light," of which the Gospel speaks, " which lights every man who comes into the world," diffused its illuminating beams through her own conscience, to judge and condemn those who could unjustly judge and act towards that angelic sister. The light within her own conscience was strengthened and awoke to a still higher life, by means of the religious instruction which she at this time, together with her sister and the young people in the community where she dwelt, received. And although this might be imperfect, and fettered by the mere literal interpretation, as is generally the case, and although even here her inquiries respecting difficult dogmas were repulsed by the teacher with the remark that, " People must not ask questions; that Reason must be subdued under the obedience of Faith;" still, nevertheless, her naturally powerful instincts towards the highest justice and the highest good, obtained by this means new words and an increased strength. Armed with these, she now turned herself towards those who had endeavored to curb her and her sister. She demanded a higher standard of truth and of justice than theirs. They did not understand her. But, nevertheless, there were moments when Mrs. Hård trembled before the young girl, whom she wished to rule, so threatening was her glance, so commanding was her whole being at the slightest unjust word or treatment where Alma was concerned. Mrs. Hård did not venture any longer to treat Alma with severity. But all the more from this very cause, did she describe Hertha to her father as of a factious and self-willed disposition; and every word which she spoke, and all her actions, were retailed and represented to him from this point of view. And as she carried to the father the most exaggerated reports of his daughters, so did she likewise report to the daughters every word of his and all his denunciations with exaggerated severity, at the very time that she declared herself to be endeavoring to mollify him, and to be a peacemaker between them; and, probably, she really believed herself to be so, because a great many people are struck with an extraordinary blindness as regards themselves. By these means Mrs. Hård produced a gradually increasing bitter misunderstanding between father and daughters.

We have drawn a dark picture of family relationships. Would to God that it were of rare occurrence!

That which, also, still more clearly showed Hertha the want of true insight and justice in the aunt, as regarded herself and her sister, was her perfect weakness and blindness towards her own daughter Amalia, a gay and handsome, but self-willed young girl, who was very much addicted to pleasure. The mother approved and allowed her to follow her own whims and fancies; let her amuse herself at parties out of the house, where her little triumphs were flattering both to her own and her mother's vanity; whilst the daughters of the house were compelled to hard work for the benefit of the family. But it was not the work, in the meantime, that they complained of; it was the want of light, as it were, in the doing of it, the want of enjoyment, and any future advantage from it. They did not, however, complain aloud; for they knew if they did so it would merely lead to reproof and sermonizing.

Under such a régime, spring up in young energetic natures, amid the best circumstances, a great revolutionary taste, warm sympathies for the Poles, the Hungarians, and for all oppressed nations, together with the wish to fight for them; in more doubtful circumstances, many dark wishes for which people bitterly reproach themselves, but of which they cannot prevent the recurrence; as, for instance, the death of certain near relations; a fire or some other violent accident, or for anything, in fact, which should interrupt the murderous compulsion and monotony of daily life.

Fewer heavenly rays of light penetrate into such a hell of domestic life than into any other shadowy region of the earth. The negroes of the Slave States of America have their religious festivals, when they can give full play to their souls in sermons and in songs, and drink in new life from the light which flows from the life and doctrine of the Saviour, when they enjoy together their blissful communions and festivals. But in loveless homes of the north, a young woman lives a more fettered and gloomy life than that of the serf and the slave. It is not clothing and food that is wanting, neither is it always enjoyments of a common, empty, and short-lived kind; that which is wanting is an atmosphere of life, is freedom, and a future, the bread and the wine which give pleasure to life.

In the first place arises in young girls, under such circumstances, the longing to become free, in the only way which opens itself to them, through marriage.

"I will get married, even to the devil himself!" said Hertha, in her younger days; "if only to deliver you, my Alma, from this intolerable home!"

Alma, of a gentler feminine character than Hertha, would not marry any one, and least of all "the devil," but———.

Both Alma and Hertha were charming enough to attract the attention and fancy of men; but they went very seldom into company, very seldom saw strangers at home, and never young men. An exception, however, was made on behalf of one young man, a relative of the family, and of more than ordinarily interesting character. He supplied the young girls with books, conversed with them on subjects which deeply interested them, disputed with Hertha, and soon became sincerely attached to Alma, as was she to him. He was very modest, and, according to the old Swedish usage, first asked the father's permission before he declared his affection for the daughter. But he was rejected by the father, who considered his worldly prospects not sufficiently promising, and who would not give up Alma's share of her mother's property, her just inheritance, into the hands of another.

The severity with which the young man's offer was rejected, without reference to Alma's feelings, led him to suppose that she had no liking for him. Without any explanation with her, therefore, he left the family, and even his country.

This took place about three years before.

At the same time an event occurred which rendered the domestic circumstances still more difficult. The handsome and gay Amalia, gladly escaping from her dull home, paid frequent visits in the country to young friends gay and lively as herself. The levity of her behavior here attracted attention, and Mrs. Hård was warned; she received these warnings with proud disdain, yet nevertheless recalled her daughter home—but too late. The thoughtless girl was—a fallen woman: she acknowledged it, but obstinately refused to mention the name of him who had brought her to shame, and reproached her mother for having, through the education she had given her, been the cause of her misfortune. This, together with the sorrow and disgrace, were more than the proud, yet at the same time morally weak, woman could bear. It broke her down at once, and she did not long survive it. Amalia had, in the meantime, removed to a distance, and it was not until two years afterwards that she returned, under an assumed name, and in the deepest poverty, to the town where she spent a portion of her giddy youth.

Mrs. Hård's death freed the young daughters of the house from an incessant oversight in which there was no love; but,

5

as their father's temper after this occurrence became extremely irritable and suspicious, his daughters' lives were, in some respects, still more wretched than before. He seemed to become every day more and more niggardly and petulant, and more and more opposed to all freedom and cheerfulness within the family. Aunt Nella had always been what the Director himself called her, a cypher in the house, as regarded everything excepting the care which she took of the younger children. She had taken charge of them from the time when they were born, and had always been to them a good motherly caretaker and teacher of the first rudiments. But she became more timid and childish as years went on, and also more occupied by her one idea—the impending great lawsuit.

Such was the state of affairs in the family at the time when the great fancy-ball was to take place in the town, and when Hertha, at her sisters' earnest desire, accepted—"in order to enliven herself and them a little "—an invitation to the rehearsal, which she had received. We now return to the moment when Hertha, returned from this rehearsal party, entered Alma's chamber.

In a deep recess on the left hand stood the sisters' bed, on which now, half reclining on high pillows, lay the elder of the two sisters—herself still young. She wore a fine white nightdress; the light of a small uncostly nightlamp, on a table by the bed, lit up a mild pale countenance, which was beautiful rather from the expression of soul than from the beauty of the features, and in which at this moment, so much patience, yet at the same time so much sorrow, was expressed, that no one could have seen it without being affected by it. She held an open Bible before her, and had been reading in the book of Job—that deep voice from a remote antiquity, which has been through all ages, and still remains to be, the most faithful interpreter of the groans and cries of the agonized soul. She who now read it held a lead-pencil in her hand, with which she had marked the following passages :—

"My breath is corrupt, my days are extinct, the grave is ready for me."

"He hath destroyed me on every side, and I am gone; and mine hope hath he removed like a tree."

"Wilt thou break a leaf driven to and fro, wilt thou pursue the dry stubble?"

When Hertha entered, her sister closed the book, and a faint smile lighted up the mild pale countenance.

Hertha threw off her cloak, and hastening to the bed, fell upon her knees, and took one of her sister's hands, which she covered with kisses. Torrents of tender tears now streamed from those eyes, lately so cold and stern, and the voice which was lately constrained now exclaimed, in the most sweet and melodious tones—

"Alma, my Alma! Sister, dear sister!"

And burning tears wetted the hand which she, with inexpressible love, laid upon her face.

"Hertha, my dear heart, why are you so excited?" asked the sick girl, as she bent her head down to her sister's forehead, and laid her other arm round her neck.

"Ah!" replied Hertha, "from a thousand causes; because I love you so much and hate others, and because I am afraid that you are going away—away from me, my Alma! I have been very wicked this evening, but that is nothing to what I shall be when you are gone—you, my good angel! I shall become stern and full of hatred, because both God and man are alike unjust and severe."

"Don't say so! certainly, things are very strange in this world, and there is a great deal which might be otherwise; but—some time—some time it will all be clear, all good!"

"I don't know that, I don't believe that, as you do. If God can some time and somewhere let the good have the victory, why not now and here?"

"Yes, why? That we don't know. But this we do know, that the impersonation of the highest love died upon the cross, and arose from the grave and spoke of peace and joy beyond it!"

"Yes, He! He was good and great. But He lived and

died for a great purpose ; and we, and many besides us, seem merely to live to pine away slowly and die, without any object !"

" Yes," said Alma, sadly, " that is the worst of it. The long, bitter agonies !"

Hertha arose from her knees and wrung her hands as she wept bitterly. At length she said :

" You see what it is which embitters me so much against the author of our life. You so good, so angelic, so loving that you would never let even a worm suffer, who never did anything but what was good, why should you be so plagued ? When we were children, and our mother was alive, and we were happy in her embrace, then it seemed to me that I had a sense of God and could love Him. But since then it has become so dark. I cannot any longer love God ; I do not love—I do not understand this dark terrible power, which has called you and me, and so many others, out of our nothingness, saying, 'Awake—love, yearn, suffer !' And then we awoke ; we tasted of life's bitterness, we loved and suffered, and had a sense of the gloriousness of life, merely to know that we must forsake it ; then again this power seizes upon us, saying, ' It is enough ; lie down and suffer and die ; go down into thy grave. Thou hast lived enough !' No, I cannot love a God who acts thus towards us. I do not love the God which I see in the government of the world ; nor the God which the Bible talks of ; he is not a good, not a just power !"

" My sweet Hertha, do not talk so ! There is so very much which we are not able to understand."

" There is, however, a great deal which we do understand, Alma !—a great deal which our conscience tells us, and which stands written there in ineffaceable characters. To this I must and will adhere ; indistinct and insufficient though it be, it is still the only light which now lights me in this dark world, the only spot which is still green and fresh, which belongs to me, and where I feel myself at home. If there be a good God he talks to me there, in my own conscience, because it loves the good, it hates the wicked, it desires **that** which is just. If I were no longer to trust to this light, no longer to listen to this voice, then I do not know what I should become or what I should do.

"I have held my peace so long, I have left unspoken so much that stirs my whole being, Alma! With you alone can I give vent to my feelings. You only can read my heart. I feel as if your glance had a healing power. Lay your hand there; let it rest there for a moment; perhaps it may allay this bitterness, which I now feel towards them who gave us life, against them whom we call our father in Heaven, and our father on earth. Bitterness against one's father is a frightful feeling! Oh, Alma! when I think that it is our father's fault that you are lying here heart-broken; that you might have been the happy wife of the man who loved you if our father's obstinacy and covetousness had not separated you!"

"Do not speak of it, Hertha!" interrupted Alma, whilst a death-like paleness overspread her countenance; "do not touch upon that subject."

"Forgive me, beloved! But I know that it is *that* which is killing you. Ever since then have I seen you fade and waste away, as by some secret malady; your eyes become larger; your cheeks emaciated, and you—oh, Alma, sweet Alma! I feel I shall hate him!"

"Do not hate him. Pity him rather. Believe me, he is not happy. He has not always been as he is now. Ever since our mother's death, Anna says that his temper has become gloomy and morbid; and our aunt made him more morose than he otherwise would have been."

"But he is also unjust and severe! Had he given us our right, then you would not have been as you now are. Why does he withhold from us our mother's property? Why does he render us no account of what we possess, or of what we ought to have?"

"We have, in fact, no right to desire it. We are, according to the laws of our country, still minors, and he is our lawful guardian."

" And we shall always continue to be minors, if we do not go to law with our father, because it is his will that we should ever be dependent upon him, and the laws of our country forbid us to act as if we were rational, independent beings! Look, Alma, it is this injustice towards us, as women, which provokes me, not merely with my father, but with the men who make these my country's unjust laws, and with all who contrary to reason and justice maintain them, and in so doing contribute to keep us in our fettered condition. We have property which we inherit from our mother ; yet can we not dispose of one single farthing of it. We are old enough to know what we desire, and to be able to take care of ourselves and others, yet at the same time we are kept as children under our father and guardian, because he chooses to consider us as such, and treat us as such. We are prohibited every action, every thought which would tend to independent activity or the opening of a future for ourselves, because our father and guardian says that we are minors, that we are children, and the law says, ' it is his right ; you have nothing to say !' "

" Yes," said Alma, " it is unjust, and harder than people think. But, nevertheless, our father means well by us ; and manages our property justly and prudently with regard to our best interests."

" And who will be the better for it ? We ? When we are old and stupid, and no more good for anything ! See, I shall soon be twenty-seven, you are twenty-nine already, and for what have we lived ?"

Alma made no reply, and Hertha continued :

" If we had even been able to learn anything thoroughly, and had had the liberty to put forth our powers, as young men have, I would not complain. Is it not extraordinary, Alma, that people always ask boys what they would like to be, what they have a fancy or taste for, and then give them the opportunity to learn, and to develope themselves according to the best of their minds, but they never do so with girls! They cannot even think or choose for themselves a pro-

fession or way of life. Ah, I would so gladly have lived upon
bread and water, and been superlatively happy, if I might but
have studied as young men study at universities, and by my
own efforts have made my own way. The arts, the sciences,
—oh, how happy are men who are able to study them; to
penetrate the mysteries of the beautiful and the sublime, and
then go forth into the world and communicate to others the
wisdom they have learned, the good they have found. How
glorious to live and labor day by day, for that which makes
the world better, more beautiful, lighter. How happy should
one feel, how good, how mild; how different that life must be
to what it is, where there seems to be no other question in
the world but, ' What shall we eat and drink, and what shall
we put on?' and where all life's solicitude seems to resolve
itself into this. Oh, Alma, are we not born into this world
for something else? How wretched!" and as if overwhelmed
by the thought, Hertha buried her face in her hands. Presently she became calmer, and continued, looking steadily
upwards :

" How dissimilar are objects in the world, as well in nature
as among mankind. The Creator has given to each and all
their different impulse and destination, which they cannot
violate without becoming unnatural, or perishing. This is
allowed to be an unquestioned law as regards the children
of nature. People do not require from the oak that it shall
be like a birch, nor from the lily that it shall resemble the
creeping cistus. With men it is the same; they are allowed
each one to grow according to his bent and his nature, and to
become that which the Creator has called them to be ; but
women, precisely they who should improve every power to
the utmost, they must become unnatural, thoughtless, submissive tools of that lot to which men have destined them. They
must all be cast in one mould and follow one line, which is
chalked out for them as if they had no souls of their own to
show them the way, and to give them an individual bent.
And yet how different are the gifts and the dispositions of
women ; what a difference there is, for instance, among us

sisters, all children of the same parents. What a clever and active practical woman will our Martha become, and Maria, on the contrary, how unusually thoughtful and pleased with study is she! You, my Alma, are made to be the angel of domestic life, and I—ah, I do not know, I cannot tell what I was created to become. I yet seek for myself; but if I had been able to develope myself in freedom, if the hunger and the thirst which I felt within me had been satisfied, then I might perhaps have become something more than ordinarily good and beneficial to my fellow-creatures. Because, though it may be bold to say or think it, I know that I might have been able to acquire the good gifts of life in order to impart them to the many; I would liberate the captive and make the oppressed soul happy; I would work, and live and die for humanity. Other objects are for me too trivial. There was a time when I believed what people and books said about home and domestic life, as woman's only object and world; when I thought that it was a duty to crush all desires after a larger horizon, or any other sphere of action; weak, stupid thoughts those, which I have long since cast behind me ! My inward eye has become clearer, my own feelings and thoughts have become too powerful for me, and I can no longer, as formerly, judge myself by others. There was a time when, above all things, I thirsted after an artist's life and freedom; but that, even that, is a selfish, circumscribed aim, if it be not sanctified by something higher. Marriage is to me a secondary thing, nay, a wretched thing, if it do not tend to a higher human development in the service of light and freedom. That which I seek for and which I desire is, a life, a sphere of labor, which makes me feel that I live fully, not merely for myself, but for the whole community, for my country, my people, for humanity, for God, yes, for God! if he be the God of justice and goodness—the father of all. Perhaps I may never attain to that which I wish for; perhaps I may sink down, buried in the inner life, which is mine and so many other women's portion in this world; but never, never will I say that it is woman's proper inheritance and lot, never will I submit, never will I cease to maintain that she has been created for something better, something more; yes, if she were able fairly and fully to develope all the noble powers which the Creator has given her, then she would make the world happier. Oh! that I could live and labor for the emancipation of these captive, struggling souls, these souls which are yearning after life and light; with what joy should I live, with what gladness should I then die, yes, even if to die were to cease for ever! I should then, nevertheless, have lived immortally!"

"How handsome you are, after all, Hertha!" exclaimed Alma, as she looked up with rapture to her sister, who looked radiant in her longings after freedom and love.

"Handsome," repeated Hertha, blushing and smiling sorrowfully. "Ah, there was a time when I know I might have become, might have been good-looking, if—but that time is gone by. Now I grow plainer every day, because my soul and mind are embittered more and more against both God and man. I have sometimes had the most extravagant thoughts of how I might deliver us from this misery. I have thought of going to Stockholm and speaking to the King!"

"To the King! Ah, Hertha!"

"Yes, to the King. They say that King Oscar is noble and just; that he does not refuse their rights to any of his subjects. I should speak to him in this manner (now you are the King and I am your subject): 'Your Majesty, I come on behalf of myself and many of my sisters. We have been kept as children, in ignorance of our human rights and duties, and held as minors, in order that we may not become mature human beings. Both our souls and our hands are in bonds, although God has bade us to be free, and although we demand nothing but that which is good and right. In other Christian countries, and even in our own sister-land, your Majesty's kingdom of Norway, her rights have been determined by law to woman at a certain age, and this the age of her best powers; but in our country, in Sweden, the law ordains, that the daughters of the country shall for all time be under bondage, and declared to be under age, unless they happen to be widows, whatever their age may be; or they must appeal to the seat of justice to demand that freedom, which still their guardians can prevent their obtaining.'"

"But now, if the King should say, 'My dear child, you and your many sisters need support and guidance. You could not manage or keep things in order for yourselves.'"

"Then would I reply, 'Your Majesty, let us be tried, and your Majesty will then see that it is quite the reverse. Many noble-minded and liberal-minded women have shown it to be so, and these might become more, might become many, if the laws of our country allowed it. Children could not learn to walk alone, if they were not released from the leading strings; they could not use their eyes unless light were allowed to enter their rooms.

"'Let us only know that we may be, that we are permitted to be our own supporters, and we shall learn to support ourselves and others. Your Majesty! grant us freedom, grant us the right over our own souls, our lives, our property, our future, and we will serve you, and our country, and all that is good, with all our heart and all our soul, and with all our powers, as only they who are free can do!'"

"Well said, my beautiful, noble Hertha!" exclaimed Alma. "I wish that the King and the estates of the realm could both see and hear you, they would then repent of having done an injustice to the Swedish woman—having been willing to depreciate her worth and limit her future."

"And that of the community at the same time," added Hertha, warmly, "because a great deal of that which is so wretched in morals and in disposition, proceeds from the want of esteem which women have for themselves, the want of fully comprehending their high vocation as human beings. Our poor Amalia, for example, and many besides her, had assuredly never fallen and become despised creatures, if they had early been able to look up and onwards to some noble and available destination for which they could live and labor every day. How dark and narrow is the space which man allots to woman in this world! and when she feels it, when the hearth becomes too narrow for her, how lonely and unprotected is she in the great world outside. Besides which, how few are the women, and how happy the circumstances must be for them, who become all that they might and ought to be, in comparison with the mass who live and die imperfect human beings not one half or quarter developed. And I, who condemn them so severely, what am I myself but an imperfect outline of a human being? and it is only my combating against the condition that causes it, nothing else, which gives me any respect for myself. Because I know it—I might be something different, something more!"

"And you will be that yet," said Alma, "because you are not of the common class, and your rich and beautiful gifts cannot be extinguished or grow rigid for want of use. I have a feeling within me, Hertha, that you have yet much that is beautiful to experience and to live for. Some time—some time I will speak to our father about you and the little girls. He wishes, after all, our best interests; he loves us in his way."

"So also does the slave-owner his slaves and serfs, and it is, ' only out of care and regard for them,' that he refuses them their freedom. I am weary, Alma, of so much and such useless talk about love and love. I wish people would say less about love and more about justice—true justice : especially that they practised it more in the world. For injustice is the root of all want of love, of all evil. Without justice there can be no true love, neither can it be preserved. There was a time, when I was a child, when I loved my father very much; when I looked up to him as to a higher being, and even now it sometimes happens, when I have seen him sitting there with his strong, handsome features, like an old, deposed king, as now when he is ill, that my heart has been drawn towards him with wonderful power,—I would give a great deal to be able to love him, and to be loved by him; but, already, whilst I was yet a child, he taught me to fear him, and since then, now that I understand his selfishness, his injustice—I have lost all faith in him, all desire to do that which he wills, and I feel at times much more likely to hate than to love him. Every day the relationship between us becomes more and more bitter."

"And yet, yet it ought to be so different. Wait, my sweet Hertha, wait yet awhile; I have an impression on my mind that a change is about to take place,—my mind is in such an extraordinary state this evening, sad, and yet cheerful!—But, Hertha, I will now speak to you about something else— beseech something from you."

"Ah, tell me what it is. Anything which you wish, and which is in my power I will do."

"I want to talk to you about Rudolph. Sweet Hertha, do not be too friendly with him. I very well understand the reason of your kindness to him, but he may mistake the motive, and fancy it proceeds from quite another cause."

"He is not very wise, poor lad; he has never seemed to me to be quite sharp; but then our father has been so severe and violent towards him. Through all the five years that he has lived in this house he has never once had a kind word, nor a kind glance, nothing but scolding and reproaches. Besides, he is always hard at work, and very seldom enjoys any leisure. One would be sick to death of such a life! And he always looks so melancholy and ready to hang himself; I have felt that he really needed a little sisterly kindness and care."

"Yes, if he would only take them in the right way. But he is evidently in love with you, and ever since the day when you rushed to him, and he saved you from the drunken man, he seems to think that he must be near you. This makes me uneasy. It looks as if he thought he had a right to be your protector."

"And that he has perfectly," replied Hertha, laughing, " when it comes to saving me from a drunken man. He is tall and strong, and on that occasion behaved stoutly and courageously. I fancy even that since that time he has been more lively and cheerful, and has seemed to have more self-reliance. Ah, it is such a good thing to win the esteem of those nearest to us, to be able to do something for them. Do not be uneasy, dear Alma, about Rudolph and me. He is like a poor plant which has grown up in the dark, and which requires light to obtain its right color and form. Let me be the light to him. We are almost brother and sister, and the poor fatherless and motherless lad has no one in all the world who cares or thinks about him. There is in him a certain raw strength which, properly developed, may make a man of him. And even if he did for a time mistake my feeling for him, the mistake cannot last long; I am neither handsome nor agreeable enough to be dangerous to any man's peace, and I become less and less so every day."

"You do not understand. You may be more dangerous than many a more beautiful woman to him, who sees you in your daily life."

"So say you, who were, and indeed still remain to be, my only beloved lover. But I will do as you say, Alma. I will be circumspect with Rudolph. Poor Rudolph!——"

"Thanks! How beautiful your hair is! there are wonderfully lovely golden rays in it when the light falls upon it sideways, as now."

"I will take great care of it, too, for your dear eyes' sake."

"My eyes thank you for doing so; it does them good. What time is it?"

"It is near twelve."

"Then I may take my opium drops; otherwise I know that I shall not sleep."

"I will give you them. Thank God for these friends, which make us forget life and its misery. This has been a bitter day to me: now I will take a sleeping draught with you, and with you wander into the land of dreams. Perhaps we may there obtain the knowledge of why we live, for we cannot do so here."

And Hertha took the same number of drops as she had given to her sister, and lay down by her side on the bed.

"Will you not undress?"

"No: what is the use of continually dressing and undressing for—no purpose whatever. I am weary with this eternally the same and the needless. Besides, I shall perhaps in my dreams wake up his Majesty, and have to make a speech for the captives; and then all at once it might occur to me that I was undressed in case—I were so. But now I am ready for whatever adventure befalls."

"Yes: dream now some really remarkable dream, which you can afterwards tell to us and to the king. Good night; but let me lay the coverlid over you. So then."

"Do you feel yourself better now?"

"Yes, much better. I fancy that I shall have a good night."

"Thank God! Kiss me. Good night, my Alma! Alma mine! Alma, thou my Alma! Pray God for me, and for us all!"

The two sisters laid their arms round each other, and soon were soundly asleep, and Hertha dreamed a remarkable dream.

HERTHA'S DREAM.*

It seemed to her that she was a soul newly born to earth. She was reposing in the granite mountain as in her cradle. She saw herself, as though the body was a transparent, ethereal form for the soul, and in the soul she saw the clear—heart, with its wonderful system of ventricles and arteries, through which the life throbbed along warm crimson paths, and far within it burned a flame, which now rose and now sank, now seemed dimmer, now clearer, but evidently striving upward, as if seeking for a freer space.

It was morning, and the sun rose brilliantly upwards. She rejoiced in the light of the sun, and drank a greeting to it from small beaker-like leaves with purple edges, which stood around her cradle filled with bright drops of dew. Her heart beat with longing for light and life. From her little nook in the bosom of the granite mountain, where she lay upon a soft bed of moss, she saw the heavens bright above her head, and the hills and valleys of the earth spreading far around. She saw a lofty, glorious, verdant tree, whose branches stretched over the whole earth, and even up to heaven; they were laden with beautiful fruit, and she heard voices singing from the tree-top in the words of the old Finlandic proverb—

> Listen to the tree-top's whispering,
> At whose root thy home is planted!

---

* The *prevision* of this dream will not fail to strike our readers as extraordinary. But who shall say that many a phantasm of a dream may not be a prophecy of the future ? Hertha's dream must, as far as it deals with events which had not then occurred, be regarded as such.

A clear fountain gushed murmuring upwards, not far from the root of the lofty tree. She saw three beautiful grave women fetch water from the fountain and water the tree, which upon this seemed to grow ever greener and fresher. Swans with brilliantly-white plumage swam, singing the while, on the waters of the fountain. Hertha saw men coming and going under the shade of the tree, plucking its fruit, and then bringing back again with exultation beautiful creations which they called their work. She saw glorious forms, proud erections, and the most exquisite ornaments proceed from their hands: she saw them rejoice over their work, and again and again derive power for fresh labor from the fruits of the magnificent tree.

With a beating heart she inquired—

"Who are these?"

A voice answered. "These are the worshippers of the Sciences and the free Arts; and they who, in the shadow of the tree of life and freedom, devote themselves to the callings which ennoble and gladden the heart of man." Many of these people seemed to pay an especial homage to woman. They delineated her form in manifold ways; they composed songs and made beautiful speeches in her honor; calling upon her to beautify the earth and to make it happy.

Hertha felt the fire in her heart burn higher and higher, and it inspired her to think, "Oh, that I, like one of these, labored in the shadow of the beautiful tree, enjoying its fruits, and gladdening the hearts of my fellow-creatures!"

With that she dreamed that she saw, looking down from heaven above her, a countenance of infinite majesty and infinite fatherly love, and involuntarily she looked upwards and besought—

"Father! let me labor and rejoice, as these my brothers!"

"Go, my daughter!" replied the glorious mild countenance, with a smile of approval.

Hertha then gladly left her nook in the bosom of the primeval rock, and wandered towards the beautiful tree. But it was more distant than she had imagined, and she encountered many hindrances by the way. But she overcame them all; hastened courageously forward, because she never ceased to hear the murmur of the fresh fountain and the whispering in the head of the mighty tree. She now saw it near at hand, but she became aware that it was inclosed by walls, which altogether prevented her from advancing farther. There were various gates in the walls, distinguished by the different names of academies and schools. These gates seemed at a distance to be open, but as soon as she approached, with the intention of passing through them, she found them closed. She knocked, and prayed for admission. But the porters replied—

"Men only have free ingress and egress here. We have no room for women in our halls of learning, nor have they anything to do there."

Hertha replied with humility: "I can learn to do beautiful and noble work as well as my brothers. I will not interfere with any one, but patiently work and learn, in order that I may be able some day to refresh the human heart. Therefore, let me also gather fruit from the large tree of the world."

She was then answered with severity: "Go, the fruit is not for you. Return to your nook in the rock, and learn to cook or to spin. That is the befitting occupation for you and your compeers. You have no part with the free."

Voices were now heard within the gates, saying, "Let the young woman in: she ought also to enjoy the fruits of the tree."

But other voices said: "No."

And there was a contention at the gates, because some wished them to be opened, but others opposed it. The latter were stronger, and therefore the gates remained barred.*

* Hertha was not always clairvoyant in this dream, as appears from the fact that she did not see that actually a certain number of female students have been admitted within the last two years into the Musical Academy of Stockholm, neither were the later endeavors of the directors of the industrial school at Stockholm for the formation of a female class revealed to her. As regards the academy of the fine arts, it has been closed against the admission of female pupils since the departure of the noble-minded Professor

Spurned but not cast down, Hertha went on, seeking for some gate by which she might enter. Anon she arrived at a portal over which was written in ornamental letters, Industrial School, beneath which was inscribed "Open to ladies." Hertha, well pleased, knocked at the gate as she thought, "at last!" But the gate was not opened. She knocked again and again. At length the porter was seen peeping from a window.

"Be so good," said Hertha, "as to open the gate for me."

"Very willingly," said the porter kindly, "if I can do so. But it is next to impossible; it sticks so fast!"

And indeed it did stick fast! The porter labored with all his might, and even called a couple of men to help him, and they all did their best to get the gate open, but in vain.

"It is set immovably fast with rust," said they. "It must be greased before it can be opened, and that cannot be done before the diet assembles."

Hertha wandered still onward, seeking for a gate through which she might enter, but was repelled from all, frequently with scorn and severity. She looked through a lofty iron gate; saw the bright fountain and the beautiful women who watched them, and besought of them:

Quarnström from his native land. It is necessary to observe that the deeply-suffering mind of Hertha reflected itself in her dream, and caused her to see every circumstance on its darkest side. Whether she saw them too dark in Sweden may be questioned. Some able men in this country seem to think not, as Bishop Agardh, for instance, in his pamphlet "On Life Insurances for Swedish Women," and a profoundly thinking anonymous writer of Göttland, whose excellent little pamphlet "On Girls' Schools, with a few Words on their Advantage, and the duty of the State to establish and support them" (published by L. J. Hierta, 1850), deserves to be universally known. The last mentioned pamphlet has for motto the following lines:—

> "I will that Woman have instruction,
> That she thereby may be accountable.
> I will that woman be accountable,
> That she thereby may share life's happiness."

We understand by this *happiness*, also, *self-knowledge*, *nobility*, and thank the author most cordially for the noble-minded word.

"Give me a draught of water, to refresh me! I am perishing of thirst."

They looked at her, those beautiful, grave women, with glances of deep compassion, and replied:

"It is forbidden to us!"

And the eldest of the Nornor added:

> A doom hath been spoken,
> A curse from the old times
> Lies on thee, O woman,
> From verdurous Munlum.
> Nor, till 'tis remitted
> Canst thou taste the waters
> From Urda the fountain,
> The fountain which giveth new life.

The stern Norna Verdandi now spoke and said:

> It is not for the feeble;
> It is only for *courage heroic*,—
> For the will that o'ercometh,—
> For him that doth honestly combat,—
> He only is worthy!

But the younger of the three looked with a glance full of **fire** on Hertha, and said:

> Blessed are they who have *seen*,
> Who combat in faith and in hope!
> They shall be welcome;
> They shall win victory!

Hertha understood not the words of the Nornor. She understood merely that she was not worthy to drink of the life-giving fountain; that they had rejected her.

Silent and with tearful eyes she turned back to her little nook in the bosom of the mountain. All was as she had left it. The small beaker-like leaves around her bed had filled themselves with tears of dew and stood sparkling, and offering her these drops of heaven's kindness. She drained them eagerly, kissed these small friends of her childhood gratefully, and thought to herself:

"I will become such as you are, and rejoice in the light and beauty of the sun for the sake of others. I will endeavor to be like one of you, and desire nothing more."

But all at once the sky grew dark: the heavens were overcast with heavy leaden-grey clouds; the sun disappeared behind them; the verdure of earth withered; the leaves fell; all beauty vanished, and a dense, frosty-cold mist veiled every object. Hertha was chilled to the bone; she felt her limbs stiffen, but still the flame burned brightly in her heart, kindling up life, as it were, still more, and calling forth a still more burning desire for light and life, even after the earth and every outward object were enveloped in the ice-cold mist. She saw, as it were, still more clearly into her own being, and knew that a powerful life animated her. She looked around her on the granite mountain, and it revealed itself to her inward sight. She beheld there a multitude of women, whom her soul called sisters, sitting as she did, in narrow cells of the rock, and spinning upon wheels (to which the epithet *humdrum* has ever been applied) which seemed to have neither end nor object, because the flax appeared never to decrease on the distaff, nor was the reel ever filled. The spinners gazed with alternately longing and stupified glances out into the misty distance, singing to a monotonous and melancholy air:

> We're spinning, we're spinning the whole day long;
> We're singing for ever the self-same song;
> The days may be weary, the prison walls strong,
> Yet we know that he comes, that he comes before long.
> Oh, sisters, the friend whom no man gainsaith,
> Our bridegroom, deliverer, Death!

Hertha felt the deepest kindness and the most cordial sympathy for these imprisoned souls. But below the mountain she saw a number of men who were called legislators, keeping watch that the captives might not escape and become free.

"What have they done then, what have we all done," asked Hertha bitterly, "that we are to be treated thus?"

She sate silent for awhile with her burning heart, in the cold unregardful world, and waited for an answer. But no answer came. And the worst of it was, she saw herself sitting like the others, spinning upon a humdrum wheel, and singing like the others:

> We're spinning, we're spinning the whole day long,
> We're singing for ever the self-same song, &c.

And she thought within herself, that rather than live in this way it would have been better never to have been born.

But she did not sit long thus. Her soul lifted itself up; she bethought herself of the words of the Nornor by the Urda fountain, that its waters were only for the heroic-hearted, and for them who combated in sincerity! And at once there dawned within her a strong desire to free herself and her captive sister-souls. She threw away from her both distaff and reel, arose and said, " I will combat in sincerity ! "

Then flamed aloft the fire within her heart, raised her from the earth, and floated her forth above the heads of the legislators through the regions of space. This feeling thrilled her with joy and hope, and she thought: "The curse on me and my sisters may then be annulled, and our portion, after all, may be among the free !"

She involuntarily turned towards the East—towards the region where she saw the ascending sun; and borne, as if upon invisible wings, she floated forth over the earth. Suddenly, however, she felt her career impeded, and a harsh voice exclaimed :

" Halt ! Who goes there ? "

" A soul," replied Hertha, " which seeks freedom, life, and happiness for herself and many sisters."

" What purpose can that serve ? " said the voice : " a soul ? and you are a woman ? Away with such talk ! Here, in this country, women have no souls. They are not reckoned in the population. You cannot go forward hither. Face about, march ! "

"Who are you?" asked Hertha, "and what right have you to command me?"

"What right?" thundered the voice. "I am the great Imperial Ukase, and stand at my post to prevent anything contraband from entering the country."

"But I am not contraband," said Hertha; "I am only a soul, who ———"

"Do not argue, but obey," interrupted the voice, "else you'll have to work in Siberia." A female soul which is seeking for liberty is the most dangerous contraband article in the world.

"Let me merely pass uninterruptedly through your country, O great Ukase; I will not tarry in it, but only proceed onward towards the East, yonder where the sun rises!" besought Hertha.

"You are a well-behaved person," said the Ukase more mildly, "and therefore, although I will not allow you to go uninterruptedly through my country, yet I will show you something, eastward, which may perhaps cure you of your fanaticism for liberty."

And with this he allowed her to look through a large telescope, which gave her a view of the East, as far as China, where not only the souls of the women, but also their feet were imprisoned; and everywhere, on the face of the earth, towards the sunrise, she beheld women oppressed and despised, excepting where they became feared as despotic and vengeful powers, which sometimes happened when they succeeded in breaking their chains by violence.

"What have they done?" inquired Hertha, "to be thus treated?"

"What's the use of pitying them?" replied the Ukase. "They are treated as well as they deserve, or as they need to be. Yes, in my holy country, very much better. Here women are outrageously well used. They are not required to pay tribute to the crown, as souls, and they are allowed to inherit one fourteenth part of all property left by their relations. By this means they can dress themselves handsomely, and talk about trifles as much as they please, provided only they are obedient and do not make undue use of their liberty. Now hear me, girl, you are good-looking, and I have taken a liking to you; remain here and you shall become the white slave of a rich Bojar. Come, you shall be very well off."

And the great Ukase seized her by the arm.

Terrified and proud, at the same time, Hertha released herself from his grasp and fled, hurling back as she did so a glance of contempt at the great Ukase. She fled northward, because she saw lights shining, and heard songs of rejoicing on the shores of the icy-sea. Here she found a wild, nomadic people, who wandered about its dreary plains and through its frozen primeval forests. They were now celebrating their fair and a wedding. Hertha saw the men knocking one another about as if they were drunk, until finally they fell upon the snow, and there slept. In the hut, the women surrounded the bride, and gave her drink, and drank themselves out of a jug amid loud laughter and noise.

"Are you free and happy?" inquired Hertha, from them.

"What is *free?*" replied they. "Is it any particular kind of brandy? If so, let us have some, that we may give it to our fathers and husbands, that they may not misuse us. Give us some, that we also may be happy. Otherwise, happy she who dies on her third night. We are born to thraldom."

The north wind roared across the ice-field, and the wedding-scene vanished in a cloud of whirling snow. After that it was calm and the Aurora-borealis danced a torch-dance around the arctic circle, so that it was as light as the brightest day; and in this light Hertha beheld crowds of men and women, who were wandering around clad in skins, with their herds of rein-deer and their dogs. But everywhere, among these wild hordes, were the women servants to the men, and their equals only in their hours of debauch and of fight. Sometimes, however, the women became witches, and were then called "wise," and were both feared and obeyed, because their power was great to do evil and to work revenge; and their glance, which was called "the evil eye," had the power of bringing down misfortune both on man and on beast.

Hertha turned away from this region and this people with a shudder, and again she was wafted over the earth; but this time towards the warm countries of the South.

She saw a sky different to the cold sky of the north; a more beautiful, more luxuriant earth, affluent with flowers and fruits. The air was delicious, as kindness itself; fountains leapt upwards; music filled the air—everything seemed to be gushing over with life and its enjoyment.

She found herself in a large garden near a large city.

"Oh," thought Hertha, "here human beings must be free, good, and happy; here I shall be able to meet with freedom for myself and my imprisoned sisters."

Scarcely had she so thought, when some solemn and magisterial looking persons approached her, and said:

"You are talking about freedom: you are a suspicious person: what are you doing here?"

She replied, "I seek for freedom for myself and my sisters."

The official gentlemen looked at one another and laughed, as if they would say, "She is out of her mind."

And they said again to her, "What is it that you wish for?"

She replied in the same words as before.

"Are you rich?" they asked.

"No," she replied; "my soul and my will are my only wealth."

"Then you are a simpleton," said they; "get married if you can, if not, go into a convent."

"No," replied Hertha, "I will live and labor in freedom and innocence for the object after which my soul longs."

"No freedom is innocent," said they, "at least among women. An old sin lies against your sex. And in any case, you are a dangerous person, because you talk about freedom, and you come from a country where freedom in the old times struck deep root and grew to a large tree, as it is said, and

where the women, more than once, have fought for the free
dom of their country; therefore you cannot be left at liberty
here."

"Oh," thought Hertha, "they do not know how little the
women of my own country can be called free." But she said
nothing, because she would not cast a slur on the laws of her
own land.

All at once she now heard a great cry: "To the convent,
to the dungeon, with the fool, with the enthusiast for
liberty!"

And a crowd of men dressed in black seized upon her, and
hurried her forward towards a large gloomy building with
small grated windows. Fear and anger gave her strength;
she wrested herself out of their hands, and fled. Again the
fire in her heart flamed aloft and bore her away and away,
until she heard no longer the threatening derisive cry.

She now paused, and looking around saw that she had
reached a large city, the smoke of which was seen ascending
from a distance. Wearied, she sat down upon a stone, but
she felt herself so solitary, so forlorn, so depressed because of
the hardness of man, and because of the curse which rested
upon her sex, that she began to weep bitterly.

With that a splendidly brilliant cloud came floating from
the near outskirts of the city, and settled down upon the
earth close to the spot where Hertha sat. It was as if woven
of fluttering gauze, spangled with silver and gold; lovely
young girls stepped forth from its brilliant depths, in airy
attire, with eyes that sparkled with joy, and garlands on their
heads. They approached her and said:

"Why do you weep?"

Hertha replied: "I weep because there lies a curse upon
me and my sex, which banishes us from free labor and from
joy."

The girls laughed and said: "Oh, what curse?—what
banishment? Don't trouble yourself about what the ill-
tempered say. Only be right merry and gay, and then you
may be as free as you will. You are too young and handsome

to cry away your life. Come along with us and do as we do. We will receive you into our company."

"And what is it that you do? And what are you?" asked Hertha, with a beating heart, half-fascinated by the appearance and the conversation of the girls, and half frightened by a something which she saw in them, but to which she could not give a name.

The young women laughed, looked at one another, and replied :

"We are called ladies of pleasure; because we live for pleasure alone. We play with the hearts of men, and we rule them. If they are sometimes cruel to us in their sport, we can be revenged on them. And if we can once succeed in getting them into our net, there is no escape for them all their days. We ensnare, and laugh at those who fancy themselves our masters."

"And what is the object of all this, and for what do you live ?" asked Hertha once more.

The girls laughed and answered: "We live for the moment. We ask for nothing more than to enjoy the day as it passes, and to amuse ourselves in the best way possible. We are the freest creatures in the world. We live freely, or at other people's expense, in all countries. We follow no laws but our own fancy ; we obey the voice of no duty. We take husbands and then leave them, just as it pleases us. We might have children like other women, but we do not bind ourselves like other women to sit and slave for them; we merely look after our own pleasures !"

"You might have children, and yet will not take charge of them?" said Hertha, astonished. "Who then does take charge of your little children ?"

"We don't exactly know," replied the girls. "The people at the Foundling Hospitals sometimes ; we have not time for such things. We will be free women."

"Oh," said Hertha, "your freedom is not of the kind which I yearn after. Your freedom is a mistake. You believe yourselves to be free, but you are slaves——"

"What, we slaves!" interrupted the girls, laughing; "come, we will show you how we are bound!"

And they drew Hertha along with them in the dancing circle; in vain she besought of them to cease; in vain to let her go; they dragged her along with them, whirling round in the dizzy bewildering circles until her senses seemed about to leave her, and anguish took possession of her heart. But the gay ladies still danced and drank wine, exclaiming the while: "Thus, thus to the end of life; thus, thus in eternity !——"

"Oh, it is horrible !" exclaimed Hertha, as she at length freed herself from their trammels. "Away ! away ! with you ! I will have no part in your freedom !"

The gay ladies laughed contemptuously.

And again they veiled themselves in the splendid cloud, which now, borne away as if on millions of butterflies' wings, was driven by the wind back to the great city. It was a splendid sight, and Hertha heard for a long time their merry voices and laughter.

Hertha looked after them with profound melancholy, and said to herself: "These think themselves free and happy; and I !——"

The fire burned in her heart, and she felt that she was born for something better than their happiness. But for what ?

"Oh," thought she now, "I will go to the learned and the wise of the earth, and ask them how the curse can be removed, under which I and my sisters, and even those giddy beings who were here just now, are all lying, and which deforms our life and our whole being. Of a certainty they will know, and of a certainty they will tell me how ; and I will then live and labor for this purpose every day and every hour of my life."

The fire in Hertha's soul again lifted her from earth and floated her away to a country and a people who were the most learned and the most deep-thinking in the world. In that country German was spoken.

Hertha arrived at the very moment when a large general assembly of learned and wise men were convened and had divided themselves into three chambers, each one of which had its own important science to attend to, and they were just now met in council.

In the first chamber they discussed an important question, viz. the beard of Thersites, because the learned interpreted in different ways the word which Homer uses on this subject; and they were now in such hot dispute, with their proofs and counterproofs, that they were very near coming to blows, all about "Thersites' beard." It was just at this moment when Hertha announced herself and prayed to have an audience granted her.

"What is she? what does she want?" asked the learned.

"She says," replied the doorkeeper, "that she is a human being who seeks the emancipation of an oppressed portion of humanity."

"What kind of idea is that?" replied the learned, shaking their heads in a gentlemanly sort of way; "what does it concern us? How dare she come with such common-place business to an assembly occupied with the subject of Thersites' beard? It is the height of audacity and thoughtlessness! Show the human-being out! She will not gain anything here!"

Thus rejected, Hertha went to the second chamber and knocked at the door. Here they were at this moment most deeply occupied on the tail of a new species of rat, as well as by the digestive process of a peculiar kind of animalcule, and they were so interested and so absorbed by these new discoveries, that they merely replied impatiently to Hertha's petition: "We have not any time for souls! Go to the legislators and statesmen."

Hertha presented herself therefore at the third chamber, where the statesmen and legislators were sitting in council. They were just then engaged on one of the four points of the Oriental question, and were skirmishing away with thousands of pens. To Hertha's petition they made answer that they were occupied with subjects of vital interest to the world, and had not time to busy themselves with ladies' affairs. They told her to lay her business before the ladies' chamber.

"Yes," thought Hertha, as she turned away from the assembly of men, "I will go to the noble and thinking women of the country. They will perhaps be better able to comprehend the importance of my business."

She proceeded, therefore, to a large assembly of venerable matrons. They were all sitting and knitting stockings.

"Oh, mothers!" said she, addressing them, "aid me, for the sake of your daughters, in removing the curse which lies upon our sex, and which prevents us from perfecting our being and attaining to the high purposes for which we would strive!"

The matrons replied: "What do you mean? We have our housekeeping to attend to; our husbands and our children to care for. Our daughters learn languages and music and ladies' work and housekeeping-business. Our sons pursue studies which will help them on in the world. We have quite enough to look after. Do not come and annoy us with your troubles!"

"Is there nobody in the whole world," said Hertha, astonished and wounded, "who can understand me and my errand, who will aid me in liberating the fettered and captive soul of woman?'

"Go to France," replied the matrons. "The French are the politest men in the world, and are fond of revolutions. Try there. But it would be much better to stop at home and knit stockings. Between-times you could go to church and attend lectures."

"Should I find justice and truth if I did so?" asked Hertha, sorrowfully, as she turned her glance from the council of matrons to the assembly of young men. Here she saw a vast number of young fellows smoking cigars and rocking themselves in rocking-chairs, whilst in a half-sleepy voice they asked, "What is truth? what is justice?" After which they blew forth such a quantity of smoke that Hertha was nearly choked.

Her thoughts and soul then sped her away, without loss of time, to Paris. But such a terrific noise and bustle prevailed there that she felt wholly bewildered. It was at the time of a great World's Exhibition, and everybody was pouring in thither. One portion of the people sang, " What shall we eat and drink, and wherewith shall we amuse ourselves?" And another portion were holding a council as to how they could best destroy one another. Nay, they had appointed a committee to distribute rewards to such as had invented new species of fire-arms, or other destructive machines, which in the shortest possible time could destroy the greatest possible number of human beings. And they were just now about to reward a person who had invented a kind of explosive giant bomb-shell, which would in a moment deprive whole battalions of grenadiers of their eyesight. People were vastly enthusiastic about this discovery, and it was intended to have a medal struck in honor of its inventor, so that he might be immortal. This assembly was in such a good humor, that they proposed to Hertha to make her a citizeness of France, on condition of her subscribing to the medal. But when Hertha mentioned her business, the gentlemen replied smiling, that that was quite another affair, and that they had not now time to attend to it. But they bowed and protested that the ladies ruled the world; that they were all powerful through their charms; and with that they rushed out to shout hurrah for Queen Victoria, who at this moment was making her entrance into Paris. And all the people of France drank the cup of brotherhood with the people of England, and shouted " Vive l'Angleterre!"

Hertha now recollected that she had always heard England mentioned as the true native land of freedom and human kindness, and her yearning and the fire in her heart carried her at once thither.

When she reached that country she felt herself invigorated and re-animated, because she perceived a powerful public spirit there, which made itself felt on all hands like a refreshing breeze, and she saw that the glorious tree of liberty, bearing its golden fruit, grew there more vigorously and to a larger size than anywhere else on the face of the earth.

And here she saw the great John Bull standing in the midst of an immense throng of people, distributing orders and work, glancing meanwhile now and then into a French dictionary, and repeating phrases from it, because having now become very good friends with the superintendant of the French, whom they called Emperor, he wished to interlard his conversation with polite phrases. John Bull looked so practical and so jovial that Hertha took courage and addressed him.

"Good sir, help me to liberate myself and my captive sisters."

"Je suis charmé!" replied John Bull. "I am a champion of freedom and a great ladies' man, but—but—but—we are now so much occupied by the war in the East, and are at this very moment doing our best to perfect a huge projectile, a gigantic projectile which, when it explodes, will poison a whole city with its stench. It is a great matter, a very great matter. This is, my good girl, a great time for humanity, and if you and your sisters will come hither and help to cast bullets, or to give lessons in the French language, then—"

"We could not do that," replied Hertha. "But help us, I beseech you, to gain our rights and our liberty as human beings; then we will serve you in another way; we will help you to establish liberty, peace, and joy upon the earth."

"Peace!" exclaimed John Bull, "I do not wish now for peace, but for war."

"War against the oppressor is a good and a right thing, and it is a glorious sight to behold free nations allied for this struggle," replied Hertha, "but *we* even amid war could extend the kingdom of peace."

"I have not now time to aid you in such undertakings," said John Bull, impatiently, "my mind is occupied by the war in the East. Besides I am not quite sure that I should approve of your notions. Woman's true sphere is domestic life. I must have my tea and my comforts, and the ladies to look after them. Woman must not be taken out of the family circle. I cannot therefore approve of your ideas and schemes of emancipation until I am assured that they will not interfere with my tea and my daily comforts. Adieu, my good girl! But, by the by, you had better go to my half-brother Jonathan, who lives yonder across the sea; he has plenty of time, and is always ready to take up wonderful inventions and crotchets. Or stop. I can give you better advice still. Go to Rome. There is at this very time a great Convocation of bishops and the clergy there. Talk with them. If they cannot give you counsel I don't know who can. They sit with their bibles before them all day and sleep upon them at night. They ought to be able to answer your questions. Good bye, madame! *Comment vous portez-vous? Très-bien, je vous remercie!*"

"Rome, eternal Rome!" thought Hertha, and the fire in her heart flamed aloft at the thought of all the greatness which once had lived there, and of all the beauty which still survived. "Yes," thought she, "I will go thither, I will fling myself at the feet of those spiritual men, and beseech of them to remove the curse which fetters me and my sisters."

She saw Alma Roma, and the great Concilium of the clergy, their proud forms and haughty glances. It was a time of great solemnity, and Hertha heard them say:

"Henceforth shall the whole of Christendom worship the Virgin Maria, as a divine, supernatural being, for this has been commanded by the Holy Ghost, through his high-priest, Pio Nono."

And a great festival was ordained in honor of the divinity, and there was a great jubilation.

Hertha heard this with astonishment, but rejoiced at the same time, and bowing with profound reverence before the venerable gentlemen, she said: "You have exalted an earthly woman high above the living and the dead; of a certainty then you will aid her sisters, women now on the earth, in the acquirement of their temporal and eternal rights. Of a certainty you will give to them equal rights with men to strive after liberty, happiness, and a sphere of labor?"

"Wait a little," exclaimed the spiritual men; "that is quite another thing. Let us see what stands written." And they began to turn over the leaves of their bibles, which lay open before them, till they found a passage which they read aloud.

It stood written: "And thou shalt be subject to thy husband, and he shall rule over thee."

With that the fire flamed upwards in Hertha's soul and inspired her to say:

"You do not give the *whole* truth; you speak only from the Old Testament. But I know there is also a New Testament, and that it there stands written that woman has been made free, and that man and woman are alike free in Christ. I know also that it there stands written, that they who are worthy of the resurrection from death, neither marry nor are given in marriage, because they are like the angels, and are the children of God. And do we not, indeed, pray daily that the will of God may be done on earth as it is done in Heaven? Why do not you, the servants and potentates of Christ, speak to me the whole truth?"

With this one of the bishops, a liberal man, raised his voice and said:

"The young woman is right, and we have all done her an injustice. She whom Christ called mother and sister, with whom he conversed familiarly, and to whom he revealed himself after his resurrection, she, of a truth, has become free thereby; her will ought not to be subject to the will of any other than that of the Most High, and she ought to be free to do all which God calls her to do. Let us enact laws more just as regards her than any hitherto enacted by human wisdom, that we may promote the advent of God's kingdom on earth as it is in Heaven."

But all the other bishops and spiritual men became angry at this, and opposed themselves to him, and called him a secret Protestant, a newsmonger, and a visionary. When the noise had again subsided, Hertha prayed to be allowed to say a few words. But the clergy exclaimed with loud and stern voices, "Let the women keep silence in the churches." And they extended their crosiers above Hertha, and bowed her to the earth.

Grief of soul and a noble indignation caused the fire to burn more hotly in her heart, and inspired her to speak a great and holy name, the name of the Saviour. At the sound of this name the crosiers, which had pressed so heavily upon her, were suddenly raised, so that she no longer felt them. She named it a second time, and an invisible hand raised her up and strengthened her as by magical power. Yet a third time she named it, and the whole imposing assembly of cardinals' and bishops' robes grew dim, and seemed to fall together like white ashes, and were seen no more.

A manly figure, full of majesty and beneficence, now seemed to move alone over the earth, raising all who were bowed down or oppressed—the slave, woman, the prisoner, the poor, and the oppressed : thus passed he onward, whilst a radiance diffused itself as from the grey robe in which he was wrapped, until he appeared to vanish in the horizon. All space seemed with that to become vacant and desolate.

"Oh!" thought Hertha, "*that* was the Saviour, the *deliverer!* Oh, that I could but find his kingdom! There would I abide and labor as the lowest of his servants!"

And her soul's yearning and love caused her again to float over the earth towards the regions where she had seen the Saviour disappear.

But below her sounded a chorus of female voices, like a low wind rising from the earth, which lamented :

"Thou wilt seek in vain for his kingdom on earth. As yet justice has nowhere opened a path for the full revelation of love. Nowhere as yet have mankind followed the doctrine of the Saviour. We must yet for a long time pray, 'Thy kingdom come!' Pray with us."

"Yes, I will pray and—die!" thought Hertha, and it seemed to her that all hope had expired within her, and that her life must end. She felt weary of living.

And now appeared before her inward eye a vision of **her** native land. She remembered those grey moss-clad mountains, that old eternally green tree of freedom, the murmur of the Urda fountain, and the warlike songs of the swans. She knew that there, in her father-land, women were more oppressed, and had less independence allowed to them, than in any other Christian country; but still it was her native land —a land rich in great memories and noble powers. An unspeakable longing seized upon her soul, and drew her hastily thither.

She again beheld them, those moss-covered primeval mountains, and heard from afar the soughing of the mighty branches of the tree of the world, and heard again the whispering voice amid it, which said :

> " Listen to the tree-top's whispering,
> At whose home thy foot is planted !"

And there, at the foot of the tree, but, ah ! so far, so very far from her, she beheld the large grave Nornor sitting by the Urda fountain, and it seemed to her that she heard their voices speaking amid the soughing of the mighty tree :

> It is for *those spirits heroic,*
> Those who have *seen,*
> For this, who have earnestly striven.
> Ask not from man.
> List to the voice of the spirit.
> Watch thou, and wait thou.
> Only be worthy,
> Strong in endurance.
> The hour is advancing.
> Who hath seen, he shall conquer

Invigorating as the wind from the mountains was the sound of these rhythmical measured words. But their true significance was concealed from Hertha, and they seemed to have reference to others rather than to herself.

Again she was seated in her little nook in the bosom of the

granite mountain; she heard the monotonous song of the spinners' all around her. The cup-like leaves stood as before round her cell, and offered her the dew-drops which they had collected in their hollows. She again found everything pre cisely as it was before, only she herself was no longer the same. She had lost the freshness of her youth and her former cheerful hope. She sate silently with but one wish, and that was to die. Days, weeks, months, years went on, but death came not. The cloudy sky hung grey and leaden above her head, and hard and cold the granite mountain inclosed her like a prison. Hertha felt her limbs becoming stiffened, but the fire within her heart neither grew chill nor dim. It burned restlessly and consumingly. Sometimes Hertha was strengthened by the words of the Nornor, which seemed to sound through infinite space above her head: sometimes her heart died within her under the depression of her monotonous existence, and she could not help sighing, "What wilt thou, oh thou restless flame of life! There are moments when thou burnest brightly; but long weary times when thou merely burnest and torturest me, revealing the darkness within and around me! Die out, poor spark! die out! Let it be night, and silent—for ever!"

"Nay, live! Live, and enjoy life as we do!" exclaimed voices at no great distance; and Hertha again beheld the brilliant cloud and the girls with their garlands of roses.

"You see," said they, "we are still near you. We are at home in all countries, and everywhere are we alike—free and alike happy. Be as we are!"

"Away!" replied Hertha. "Away, you lie! I see that your cheeks are painted, and your flowers are artificial. I see beneath your gay demeanor a secret unrest. Poor sisters! you are afraid of old age and death. Of them I am not afraid. I feel a something great within my suffering and longing heart which I do not perceive in you. And rather than live happily, according to your happiness, I will die unhappy with those who are unhappy. I weep—you smile: and yet, poor sisters! I cannot but deplore you."

With that the gay group departed in two companies. The one laughing scornfully, but from the other were heard sorrowful, lamenting voices:

"And even we were at one time as thou art. We felt something within our hearts; we sought for light and for freedom, but society barred to us the paths which led to light and to life; and we were led astray by *ignes fatui*, which promised happiness and liberty, but which burned off those very wings which had lifted us upwards. We have fallen: we know it; and that it is which makes our secret misery. Who counts our silent sighs? We might have been so different! Now it is too late. Let us drink wine and forget; for we must indeed live!"

Again the two companies united into one group. But in that same moment the rouge grew black upon their cheeks, and flames bursting forth from the earth caught their fluttering garments, and the splendid glittering cloud was changed into a heap of ashes. Hertha heard a wild cry of horror and anguish, which died away by degrees into lamenting sighs, whilst a stormy wind dispersed the ashes into space. Hertha wept over the fate of the daughters of pleasure. And anon she turned to hear their dying voices hoarsely whispering in the tempest:

"Weep for thyself. Thou art different, but thou art not better than we, and thy fate may become still more dreadful!"

And it seemed to Hertha that her soul was changed, and that the upward-striving, yearning flame within it assumed another character. It had yearned to warm and to benefit: now it would merely punish. She herself was transformed into a horrible being, which spread destruction around her. The flame in her heart extended itself through all her limbs, and everything which she touched was kindled by it. Her hand had become a flaming torch. She laid it upon her father's house, and wild flames burst forth. She saw them grow higher and higher, and spread on all sides, setting fire to other and yet other houses. She heard the bells tolling, the beat of the alarm-drum, the shouts and terrified cries of people, the grating wheels of carts and of fire-engines. The noise and the tumult increased every moment, and it seemed to be whispered into her ear—

"Fire! incendiary fire!"

An unspeakable anguish overcame her, because it seemed to her that this was her work. All at once the thought occurred, as is sometimes the case in distressing dreams, "It must be a dream!" She endeavored to wake, striving violently with the dream-spirit that held her captive; at length she conquered, and—awoke.

THE INCENDIARY FIRE.

A RED, wildly flaming glare lit up the sisters' room, which was situated within the court. The bells tolled; the alarm-drum was sounding, and amid a horrible din of human voices, one shrieking above another, the cries of "Fire! fire! Help! help! Water! throw it here! Quick! Help!—Save us!" seemed to fill the air. Hertha fancied herself still dreaming, or else delirious with the effect of the sleeping draught. But a glass of water which she hastily swallowed, and a violent blow upon the door, together with the words "Hertha! Come out! Will you be burned in your bed?" cleared away all the mists of sleep. She opened the door. Rudolph stood there, with bewildered looks. "Come!" said he, "come! I will save you!"

"Help me to save Alma first!" said Hertha, at once calm and decided.

Rudolph obeyed. Hertha hastily flung on her sister's clothes, wrapped her in a cloak, and led her, assisted by Rudolph, into the court. Here they found old Aunt Nella and the two youngest girls trembling and crying, and almost without clothes.

A quantity of furniture, bedding and household utensils, had already been thrown into the court, which was thronged with people.

Hertha removed her sisters and aunt to as great a distance from the house as was possible in the court; and desired them to wait for her there. This done, she turned towards the burning house with a determined countenance, as if considering what must next be done. The whole of the upper portion of the house was on fire, and wild tongues of flame flashed from the windows of the second story.

"My father!" exclaimed Hertha, "where is my father?"

"There!" whispered Rudolph in her ear, with a wild sort of insane joy flashing in his eyes, and pointed up to the second story of the house, "there! where the fire has just now caught! He cannot escape!"

"Wretched being! what have you done?" whispered Hertha in reply, as a horrible idea presented itself like lightning to her soul.

"Free yourself, and—me with you!" returned Rudolph. "Come! I will save you! I will carry you through a thousand fires!" And, throwing his arms round her, he held her fast as he endeavored to force her away. But Hertha thrust him from her with all her strength, as, with a flashing glance, she exclaimed, "Hence! Begone from me! Save *him*, or—I will never see you more!——"

At that moment a horrible crash was heard. A portion of the roof had fallen in, and volumes of thick smoke and whirling flame burst forth from the abyss which was thus made. A moment's silence and astonishment succeeded. Then was heard a wailing and an agonized cry for help, like that of a weak old man or of a child. It seemed to proceed from that part of the house over which the roof had fallen.

Another cry answered it from the court below; a strong cry, sounding like "Yes!" full of resolution and strength, and a young girl rushed into the burning house. It was Hertha. Rudolph was about to follow her steps, but a rafter which fell from the burning roof struck him on the head. He stumbled backwards, fell, and remained for some time without consciousness.

Old Falk had been sound asleep over his treasures, beneath his pillow, when he was awaked by the cry of fire and the tumult in the street below. The chamber in which he lay was full of a stifling smoke, which made his brain dizzy, and almost took away his breath. His first movement was to seize his cash-box, and with this in his hand, he raised himself in bed, and tried to collect his senses. He called his faithful old servant by her name, but received no answer. With difficulty he raised himself to his feet, and endeavored to reach the door which opened into the dining-room. But his brain reeled, and his feet could not support him. He fell, and crept from where he fell, on hands and knees, to the dining-room door, shoving before him his precious casket. He had now reached the door, but both head and hands refused their office, when he attempted to stand upright. He called the old servant; he called Rudolph, and terror made his voice loud and strong, but no voice replied to his, and no hand unfastened the bolted door. He fancied he could hear wild shrieks of joy and derisive laughter in the room beyond, mingled with the roar and the crackling of the fire. Every moment the heat became fiercer in the chamber, and the smoke thicker. The anguish, as of death, seized on the old man's heart—and the sweat of agony burst forth from his forehead, as in the depths of his soul he seemed to hear the words:

"Thou fool, this night shall thy soul be required from thee!"

And out of the darkness which thickened around him, he seemed to see pale countenances looking forth, gloomy and threatening; gazing upon his torments. He knew them all again. They were souls which had been intrusted to him to protect and to make happy. They seemed now to ask him how he had fulfilled his duty towards them. Smoke and flames encircled him, nearer and nearer every moment. He felt himself approaching the limits of life and beyond that he saw nothing, except a something, shapeless, indefinite, threatening, horrible, more horrible for its indefiniteness than the most horrible form which reality could present; a something unknown and yet inevitable, which approached, every moment, nearer and nearer, beyond the most terrible death.

Terror again gave him strength and consciousness sufficient to raise himself up, seize the handle of the door, and also to open it. But in the selfsame moment that the door was opened the heat smote him across the face, and a horrible crackling noise, together with a surge of smoke and flame which filled the whole apartment, caused the wretched old man to fall across the threshold, and for the first time forced a cry of lamentation and prayer out of that hard shut-up breast!

"Lord, my God! wilt thou thus suffer me to die? Lord, my God, have mercy upon me! Help, help!"

And his hands for one moment released their hold of the cash-box, that they might be clasped together in an agonized, death-agonized prayer.

Again a frightful crackling noise of burning was heard in the room. The opposite door was flung open, and there, enveloped in smoke and flame, stood, not the angel of judgment; but, like an angel of deliverance, the old man's daughter, Hertha.

He stretched towards her his trembling hands. She rushed forward to him and raised him in her arms. She never had believed herself so strong as now, nor ever had she been so. She carried her father through the burning dining-room. His trembling hands grasped convulsively the precious money-box

"There is yet time!" said Hertha, encouraging and comforting him. "Be not afraid, my father! We soon shall be out in the open air."

The flames almost choked the assurance on her tongue, and seemed as if they would bar her onward advance. They scorched her cheeks and her clothes, but she staggered not nor hesitated.

"Courage, courage, my father!" whispered she as she bore onward her precious burden through the midst of raging fire, as calmly and resolutely as if no death-peril were at hand. She knew of a certainty, she felt it within herself, that she should save her father. The flames stretched out, hissing behind her, their serpent-like tongues; soon they no longer reached her. She went steadily down the long flight of stairs; the roof of the dining-room falling in behind her.

When Hertha descended the steps from the lobby into the court, bearing her father in her arms, the people hurraed and waved their hats. Then, and not till then, her limbs failed her; she sank down upon her knees, but did not loose hold of the burden which she bore. Faithful as a mother who holds her child clasped to her breast, held she her father, with her eyes fixed only on him. He appeared almost unconscious.—She drew a deep and strong breath.

"We are saved, father," whispered she, "breathe, breathe, my father!"

People crowded round them, and conveyed them from the immediate neighborhood of the flames, to the spot where the rest of the family were assembled. The old man, by degrees, regained the use of his senses; but the violent shock which his nerves had sustained caused a tremor of the whole body, and when, not without emotion, he had pressed all his children to his heart, he sat gazing immovably, and without uttering a word, at his consuming property.

Hertha, having drunk a glass of water, appeared perfectly restored, and immediately busied herself in preparing hand-barrows and bearers, and, having made beds with mattresses and coverlets, on which to lay her father and Alma, had them conveyed from the scene of conflagration. She and the others, old Anna among the rest,—who had gone to sleep that night by the kitchen fire, instead of her own room, adjoining the chamber of her master, whence it happened that she was not within his call,—now all left the court. The fire had already caught several houses in the neighborhood, and these now also were burning with a violence which defied every attempt at extinguishing it. The inhabitants fled from all the houses in the neighborhood of this growing destruction; they threw from the windows, bedding, mirrors, earthenware, in the wildest confusion. The fire, the terror, the throng, and the tumult increased every moment.

Hertha, who observed, by the direction in which the flames were driven by the wind, that the fire would probably extend to the northern portion of the town, which consisted in great measure of wooden houses, immediately turned her steps, with those of her family, in the opposite direction, across a bridge which spanned the river Klar, to a meadow, planted with trees, outside the town, where the inhabitants amused themselves in the summer, and which was called the King's field. Many of those who were already homeless, or who feared to become so, followed her example. And they who did so, did well. Because they who removed with their rescued property to houses or to situations near to the fire, had a second time to leave their places of refuge for others more remote from the increasing conflagration. The wind unfortunately rose, and blew violently, so that the flames were driven onward, in still more terrible career, from house to house, from lane to lane. The wooden dwellings were consumed like tinder.

And now again was exhibited, both as regarded the extinguishing of the fire and the work of removing and saving the inhabitants of the burning houses, the method which on so many similar occasions has distinguished the temperament and habit of the Swedes, and which we have already spoken of and designated as " the hand-over-head-method," but which in this particular case was governed by no kind of internal harmony. The superior authorities of the town, the sheriff of the district, and the Burgomaster, could not agree as to the mode by which the fire should be extinguished. The fire-engines were found either not to be at hand or else they were out of order; many of the hose were utterly useless; water was called for, but none came; many commanded, but nobody obeyed; and perhaps could not obey because the commands were issued in the most bewildering confusion, hither and thither, now this and now that. Besides which, a great number of persons became, in the terror of that awful fire, perfectly confused in their understanding. One tall strong man was seen busily occupied in saving a doll's chest of drawers, another hurried along the streets with an empty drinking-glass in his hand, a third wheeled out of the town four bundles of fire-wood in a wheelbarrow; one old lady rushed out of her house with her bunch of keys in her hand, and a young lady, too hurried to attire herself, carried a ball-dress on her arm.

Many worthless people availed themselves of the horror

and confusion of the time to plunder and carry away the property of others. And none were found to guard against this mischief. Many good citizens, who did not lose their presence of mind, made unheard-of efforts to extinguish the fire and save both life and property from its destruction; but these were either each one for himself, or they were in detached groups, so that system and co-operation were wanting altogether.

In the meantime the fire advanced in its destructive career with the increasing wind. Before morning had dawned, every one of the lanes opening into the street in which stood the house of the Falks, as far as the large market, was a heap of smouldering ashes, and soon after, the market itself was burning at every corner. The new Assembly House, with its splendid ball-room, where the great fancy ball was to take place, the anticipation of which had made so many a young heart beat with joyful hope, took fire, and the flames danced as if with joy through the spacious apartment, devouring all the new silken curtains and furniture, melting the splendid chandelier, and turning to ashes all the gilding and the other grandeur. An hour afterwards, and the great house opposite was also burning—that very house, where, the evening before, gods and goddesses chatted so merrily together. The silver-haired golden-wedded pair, the handsome host and hostess, with their young daughters, the seven Miss Dufvas, stood houseless in the market-place, and saw their comfortable home become a prey to the flames.

In the course of the forenoon all the houses in the market-place were burning, and the fire flung itself down into the streets and lanes where the poorer portion of the town's population dwelt. Presently it had reached the Great Quarter, that great rubbish-quarter, as Mimmi Svanberg called it, and a whole mass of miserable old men and women, ragged queans with their streaming hair, and half-naked children, poured forth pell-mell, together with piles of broken furniture, halves of tables and fragments of chairs, tattered bedding, coffee-mills, dirty buckets; every three-fourths of the whole being nameless indescribable things, in chaotic confusion. The confusion among the laborers at the fire became also still greater and greater. Many grew weary of their work, when they saw that the fire only increased more and more. Many also had become pitiless, and not seldom were heard in reply to prayers for help or succor the cruel words, "It is no business of mine!" or "You may do it yourself!"

No one commanded, no one obeyed any longer. People rushed about everywhere, and saved what they could, and let the fire and fate take their own course.

"To-day it is come to pass that the gentleman and the servant are all as one. He that will work, does so; and he who will not, lets it alone!" said a working man, whose whole appearance proved how unceasingly and bravely he himself labored; "but then you see," added he, "I can't think, for my part, how anybody can let working alone!" And so saying, he again hurried out to render assistance wherever he saw that it was needed.

It was the pastor's man-servant, the respectable Jacob, who now saw the cause of his mistress's premonition, and contended resolutely against its sad reality.

The reality exhibited a surging ocean of flame, heaving in the wind and spreading on all sides; a tumultuous mass of terrified and houseless people flying with children and household stuff out of the burning town into the King's-field, where now safety from the devouring element could only be looked for.

In the midst of this press of people, and this confusion of ruin, an elderly lady, around whose person a mass of parti-colored garments fluttered like feathers, in the wind, might be seen, wildly seeking something, and hurriedly inquiring right and left:

"Have you seen my noble young lady? Can no one tell me which way my young lady, the Honorable Miss Krusbjörn, is gone?"

"Oh, she's gone straight down the fire and brimstone pit!" said a working man, who wished to be witty.

"No," said another, "I saw her posting off to heaven, right out of the fire, with outstretched arms and streaming hair, and she kept shrieking, 'My noble lady! my noble lady!' so there need be no wailing about her!"

"And I," said a third, "I saw her running out of the town, with a butter-tub under one arm and a huge cheese under the other. She must be at Stockholm by this time, so as she ran!"

"That must have been before she set off to heaven," remarked the former, "because I can swear that I saw a noble young lady, who looked the very image of a curly bear,* and who——"

"Ah! you are a parcel of good-for-nothing fellows, and you are telling lies altogether!" exclaimed Mrs. Tupplander, for it was she. "Oh, my unfortunate young lady! Where is she? where is she? Can nobody tell me where the Honorable Miss Krusbjörn is gone!"

Two ladies were now standing on the little bridge which crossed the river Klar, watching the fire. They were the pastor's wife, Mrs. Dahl, and Mimmi Svanberg.

"Ah, my presentiment!" said the former, "I felt such an evident impression last evening, that a great misfortune hung over the town. The poor, poor people!——"

A hand lightly touched the shoulder of the pastor's wife, and a gentle voice said, "This is a terrible sight, dear Mrs. Dahl. What is to be done? Could we not help the poor creatures one way or other?"

The pastor's wife turned round and recognised the young and lovely Countess P., who, dressed in a quilted petticoat, with silk shoes on her feet, and a shawl over her head, had hastened from the house, which they inhabited for a time, and was now on her way to the fire.

"Of a certainty we ought to do so," said the ever-ready Mimmi Svanberg, "at least, I, who am strong. The Countess and Mrs. Dahl I think would do best not to stand here and

* Krusbjörn.

run the risk of taking cold, but go home and order coffee and soup to be made for the poor sufferers, for I fancy there will soon be great need of it. I have ordered my Lovisa to set on the large coffee-pot—I left papa himself busy grinding."

"Ah, good heavens! have you none of you seen my noble young lady!" cried a shrill, despairing voice, and the three ladies presently beheld Mrs. Tupplander, in a costume almost as remarkable as her looks were wild, coming towards them, as if on flying feathers. "Where, where can she be gone?"

"Where was she when you saw her last, dear Mrs. Tupplander?" asked Mimmi Svanberg.

"Ah, she was in the midst of my salting-tubs," replied Mrs. Tupplander, "because, although the fire had not reached my house, yet it might do so without giving any notice, and, therefore, I resolved to get all my things into a place of safety; and I and all my people carried off what we could. But just as I thought that we had got most of the things safe, and that Miss Krusbjörn should keep watch over them, she—was nowhere to be found, and nobody can tell me where she is gone! But when I saw her last she was among the salting-tubs!——"

"Then she will come there again," said Mimmi Svanberg, consolingly; "because, if she has once safely escaped the fire, she will assuredly not run into it again."

"Yes, but who knows that?" said Mrs. Tupplander, refusing to be comforted; "the fire makes people lose their wits! Ah, my poor Krusbjörn! My poor young lady!"

"I will go and give orders for making soup," said the pastor's wife; "that is a good idea. Fortunately we have lately killed a bullock."

"And I will order both soup and coffee," said the young Countess; "but now I should like to help the poor people to save their things. Look, there are two young girls, who are carrying a bed, and almost staggering under their load. There is certainly a sick person in the bed. Let us help them!"

In the bed lay a poor, old sick woman from the Great

Rubbish Quarter. She lay crippled with rheumatism, and heard the tumult of the fire, and saw the flames thrust their fiery tongues through the cracks of the walls, and thought to herself, "I must be burned here in my bed, because nobody will think of me, poor wretch!"

But two very young girls—"young baggages," as they are called in the quarter, because their clothes were ragged, and they could not get into service for want of better clothing —they thought of the poor old creature, and one said to the other:

"Let us go and save the poor soul!"

And with that they burst open the door, carried out the bed in which was the old woman, and so through the burning streets in the direction of the King's-field; but the bed was heavy, and they were nearly sinking beneath their burden, when two ladies were seen hastening towards their aid. These were Mimmi Svanberg and the young Countess. With their help the old woman was brought into the field, in safety from the flames, and the Countess took off her own shawl to defend her from the cold, whereupon she, spite of all her protestations, was wrapped in the woollen jacket which Mimmi Svanberg wore under her cloak. After that the two hastened to help others who also were heavily laden.

Every moment increased the number of the houseless who fled to the King's-field.

And with every moment the conflagration grew; and the wind rose more and more. It was an awful and a sorrowful sight. Nevertheless, it was impossible for Mimmi Svanberg to avoid smiling, as she saw Mrs. Tupplander fluttering about in her extraordinary costume, seeking among the crowds of fugitives, and incessantly crying, "My noble young lady! Has nobody seen my noble young lady!" Sometimes she shrieked aloud in a shrill voice, "Miss Krusbjörn!" But no voice replied.

The Countess P. and Mimmi Svanberg had now met with an active fellow-worker in their Samaritan labors. This was Hertha, who had no sooner seen her own family in safety,

8

grouped at the foot of a large oak-tree, than she hastened to render all the help in her power to other homeless people.

It was noon, and no bounds were set to the destructive element, which seemed as if it might extend its ravages over the whole of the town. The mass of the people and the town authorities were now alike without courage or counsel, and scarcely any further attempts were made to stem the tide of destruction.

At the distance of six English miles from the town were working, this very morning, fifty men on the new railway, under command of Lieutenant Nordin.

"There is a fire at Kungsköping!" said he to the navvies, "and it seems to me that they are in want of a good deal of help. I have seen a tremendous smoke ever since day-break, and it appears to increase, rather than otherwise. I shall go there, and any of you lads, who like to go with me, are welcome. I should be glad to say to any such, that they should have their day's wages. But that I cannot do, because it is tolerably certain that they will have nothing for their trouble."

Every one of the fifty, immediately and without hesitation, accompanied their young and beloved overseer.

In about two hours they were on the spot. Yngve Nordin, and a couple of his acquaintances, hastily arranged a plan for preventing the progress of the fire ; and when the fifty fresh pair of arms, which Yngve had brought with him, unanimously and vigorously obeyed their commander, a new turn was soon given to the work of extinguishing the fire. It began really to abate, and its further progress seemed stayed. Nevertheless, they were met by unforeseen difficulties, partly through the failing supply of water, and partly through the want of harmony among the city authorities.

For instance, a number of young navvies had succeeded in raising a sail-cloth to the roof of a house which stood in the corner of a narrow lane, and just opposite to one which was burning furiously. They considered themselves perfectly sure of saving this house, and a whole row of others. There they sat upon the roof, pouring torrents of water over their sail-cloth, when orders came from the magistrates that the sail-cloth must be taken down, in order to be placed upon another house which was already on fire. The young fellows ventured to act in opposition to the authorities assembled in the market-place. The magistrates' messenger was sent crest-fallen away, and they still sat triumphantly on the roof. But, as a matter of course, they were the minority; the majority in the lane below were determined to have their own way; the navvies were obliged to loosen their ropes and give up their own schemes. The sail-cloth was carried off in triumph, and the end of it was, that the house itself, and many others near it, together with the sail-cloth, were all consumed.

"We must pull down that house," said Nordin, an hour later, speaking with decision to the magistrate, and pointing to a house which had not yet taken fire, but was so situated as to render such a step necessary.

"Pull it down!" exclaimed the other, almost shedding tears; "surely it is quite enough for the houses to be burnt down without our pulling them down. No, that shall never be done as long as I live!"

Ynge was obliged to restrict his operations to the well-directed use of the fire-engine tubes. He put himself at the head of this part of the business, he himself working one of the hose. But now water failed them.

"Be so good as to let us have some water here!" said he to a gentleman who stood quite calmly at a short distance from him, watching the fire, with his hands in his pockets, "we must have more water here immediately, otherwise we cannot save this house."

"It is no business of mine!" replied Mr. Von Tackjern. "I don't trouble myself about anybody's house but my own, and that stands safe yonder. That is the house I keep watch over."

"Certainly, your house is not yet in danger, and with God's help it shall not be so," said Yngve; "you can, therefore, without any risk, go and see after water."

"Go yourself, and the devil take you!" replied the surly and selfish proprietor of the unendangered house.

Yngve Nordin, as quick as lightning, gave him a box on the ear, and was just about to rush after water himself, when a voice in the crowd exclaimed:

"Stay where you are!—in a moment water shall be here!"

The voice was that of a woman; it was Hertha's. She and Mimmi Svanberg, in the course of their work of salvation, had been brought to this place, and had thus heard the altercation between the two gentlemen.

Before many minutes were over, Hertha returned with a hand-water-cart, which she herself drew.

In the meantime, Mimmi Svanberg saw Mr. Von Tackjern talking, in an under-voice, to a strong-limbed, coarse-looking working-man, to whom he gave some money. On this the man nodded assentingly, and immediately as. Nordin, who continued to direct the hose, turned round to look after the much needed water, he received so violent a blow between the eyes from this hired ruffian, that the spectacles which he wore, on account of being near-sighted, were smashed on his face. Without staggering or pausing a moment, Nordin returned him so heavy a blow on the side of his head as to knock him down, after which he slunk off, uttering imprecations. Nordin, near-sighted as he was, seemed, in the meantime, helpless, although, fortunately, his eyes were uninjured by the blow, and fortunately, also, he was not unprovided for in case of accident. With the utmost calmness, as if nothing unpleasant had occurred, he took a second pair of spectacles from his pocket, and turned himself again to work.

When, however, he was about to retake the pipe, he saw, to his surprise, that it was in the hand of a young woman, who was not for the moment directing it upon the fire, but upon the fellow who had dealt the insidious blow, and the person who had hired him. Both rushed away from the unexpected dusch-bath. Hertha laughed, and then directed the mouth of the hose against the fire. But the enraged fellow turned again, and was rushing towards her, uttering a volley of insult, when once more she directed the pipe against his mouth, and the torrent of water drowned its coarse abuse, after which it was again turned to the flames.

Yngve, who immediately recognised Hertha, stood for a few minutes the silent spectator of her deeds, and seemed to have great enjoyment in thus watching her. But when he saw the sparks of fire fall upon her beautiful plaits of hair, for the handkerchief which had been tied on her head had fallen back upon her shoulders, he took off his cap and put it on her head.

"You work well, comrade," said he, smiling, and with a tone that expressed heartfelt esteem, as he took the hose from her hand, "but your hand is not strong enough for this work; it is better suited to mine. Thank you for the help you have given."

"If I can be of any use here, say so at once," said Hertha, replacing the cap on his head, and drawing the handkerchief over her own.

"Take care, if possible, that there is no want of water here," said Yngve, "and then, with God's blessing, we shall soon put an end to the fire."

"Good! you shall not want water," said Hertha, hastening away. She talked with several of the unoccupied people among the crowd, and succeeded, by her earnest words, and her animated and resolute demeanor, in inducing them to assist her, and in this manner she had soon organized a systematic and regular line of water supply, from the Klar to that part of the conflagration where Nordin and his men were working. Already the fire began to abate. It was evident to all who were near that this was the most important point, and that if the fire could now be extinguished, any further danger of its progress was over.

"Now for it, my lads!" said Yngve. "Some of you must mount on yonder wall, in order to direct the water from that elevation upon the opposite house. If you can extinguish the fire there, all is right!"

More ready or braver-hearted people, in the hour of danger,

than the Swedish working-classes, are nowhere to be met with. In a moment the men were seen clambering up the yet burning ruins. When they had reached the top of the wall they raised an hurrah of triumph. The force of the water from this height was very great.

In half an hour the conflagration was stayed; all danger from its further extension was over. Again they hurrahed, standing on their dangerous elevation, and the next moment the wall fell, with all its array of brave laborers. An hour afterwards Yngve Nordin was borne away from the smoking ruins by his young comrades, with one knee and his left arm greatly injured by the falling wall, the last achievement of the fire. But he would not consent to be removed from the spot before he had collected all his men around him, and convinced himself that no lives were lost of those who had scaled the wall. He took counsel with the physician of the place respecting such as were injured, and having arranged everything for their comfort and well-being, allowed himself to be removed to the parsonage, outside the town, where, during the time that his works on the railway would keep him in that neighborhood, he had his home.

Night came down; the conflagration was stayed; the drum beat in joyous announcement; but more than two thousand persons, whom the fire had ruined, or rendered homeless, wandered about the town or in the fields outside.

NIGHT IN THE KING'S-FIELD.

The greater number of the fugitives were assembled in the King's-field, because it lay nearest to the portion of the town in which the fire had raged, and because its large although yet leafless trees afforded some little shelter.

Gloomy and leaden hung the sky of that March night above the still burning ruins of the town. Now and then flames were seen to leap up from amid masses of fallen houses, which flung a dreary illumination over the desolation which lay within, and the sorrowful spectacle in the field outside. There might the miserable fugitives be seen wandering about, not knowing what to do, or sitting in groups keeping watch over their rescued possessions, many with their heads tied up, or with bandaged eyes or limbs, testifying of their too close contact with the fire, and all pale, dejected, and wearied; the greater part of them hopeless and bewailing. The gloom of the night seemed only to increase the misery. They were perished with cold; children cried, and many a mother had no means of keeping her little ones warm but by clasping them to her bosom. Many a poor wretch seemed perfectly stupified by dark and gloomy despair. In vain Mimmi Svanberg and the young Countess went from one to another, offering them warm coffee and bread, and a comfortable fire-side at either of their houses; nobody was thirsty or hungry; nobody was willing or dared to leave their rescued household stuff. They thanked the kind ladies almost with indifference, and continued to sit staring on the ground, at the reeking ruins, or out into the darkness. The wailing of the children, now and then a cry of misery, and heavy sighs of deep anguish, alone broke the melancholy silence.

Here and there people were talking about the cause and origin of the fire; dark suspicions were uttered, and the words, "it was done on purpose," were whispered from one to another. Here and there also people were scheming how they best could take advantage of the darkness and the confusion; and Mimmi Svanberg heard a mother say reproachfully to her son, a lad of ten years old:

"If you were only like a fox and brought home what you could get, then you would be worth something!"

The lowest classes of the town's population, so long left neglected in their wretchedness and ignorance, had become dangerous, and the better classes, both of the poor and the rich, were afraid of them, and not without reason.

Hertha had succeeded in placing her family in a certain degree of comfort. The father and the invalid sister lay on mattresses at the foot of an old oak tree. The younger sisters were also warmly clad; and little Aunt Nella sat, not unlike a great bundle of rags, restlessly working her fingers upon the precious portfolio, in which lay the papers of the great lawsuit, and puzzling her poor brain to find out whether this fire would not deliver her from some of its involved intricacies.

Rudolph had been unwearyingly helpful to Hertha in arranging all in the best possible manner for the comfort of the whole family; and yet Hertha would not reward him with one kind word, nor even one glance. She spoke affectionately to her little sisters; she wrapped shawls around her father's feet; she warmed Alma's hands in her bosom and upon her cheeks; she looked after the comfort of Aunt Nella and old Anna with kind solicitude; for all she had words of affection and encouragement, but not for Rudolph, although he seemed to watch for her eye, as the faulty and chastised dog watches for the forgiving eye of his master.

The Director sat almost immovable, gazing towards his burned-down house, and his lips now and then muttered, as if unconsciously, the thought which most haunted his soul; "It was not insured!" He continued to tremble as if shivering with cold. Now and then he convulsively clutched at his money-box.

The darkness veiled more and more the sorrowful picture, but no sleep visited the eyes of the unfortunate fugitives Snow-flakes fell and mingled themselves with the ashes, which the night wind scattered over their heads ; dull, lamenting cries and sorrowful groans were carried by it across the field.

All at once a strong voice was lifted up, which exclaimed ; "'Come unto me, all ye that labor and are heavy laden, and I will give you rest!' thus, my afflicted friends, cried the Redeemer to you, yesterday and to-day. Listen to his message."

At this unexpected declaration all heads were raised. But the darkness at this moment was so dense that no figure could distinctly be seen, no one could discern the messenger. All the more powerful, therefore, was the impression produced by those words which resounded across the field, amid the dismal darkness of the night, from the lips of the invisible preacher, who, with a voice and power full of inspiration, conveyed the consolations and light of the Gospel to those miserably unhappy people sitting in the midst of darkness ; showing them the all-seeing eye of the Father guarding them in the gloom of night, the loving Father's heart ready to console all, to help all. Never did any sermon improvised for the moment produce a deeper effect upon its hearers. The stupor of misery, silent despair, and gloom passed away from the soul ; people spoke ; they wept ; they sobbed aloud ; but it was no longer because they were inconsolable. They were profoundly arrested, they were unspeakably affected by the thought of Him who bore with us the crown of thorns and the cross, and who bore them for our salvation. Never before had his image been presented so clearly and brightly to the minds of the listening people. They poured out their emotions, like the waves of a surging ocean, in sighs and tears, as they listened to the powerful and faithful discourse of the preacher. All at once, this was interrupted by a wild shriek of self-accusation :

"It was I; it was I who caused all this misery, I——." Here the voice was silenced, as if stifled by external violence. The darkness prevented its being known from whom the cry proceeded; but some persons who were near fancied that they saw a figure, like that of a youth, hastily raise itself, as from the ground, but which was almost as hastily dragged down again by another figure.

Darkness and silence again covered the scene. There was a moment of deep and breathless silence. All seemed to be expecting that a dark mystery was about to be revealed; that the author of the fire was about to come forward to avow his guilt, and many hands were involuntarily in motion ready to seize upon the criminal. They waited, one, two, three, four, five minutes; but all remained silent. A dull, threatening murmur, like that of approaching thunder, was then heard rising from the mass of people in the field, the murmur from a thousand breasts and lips; but above this again was raised, loud and powerful, the mild and manly voice of the first speaker, exclaiming:

"Should there be here any guilt-burdened heart which would accuse itself of causing accidentally, or by design, the misfortune under which so many are suffering, then—may God have mercy upon him! We desire not his confession! It would not be any benefit to us. It might make others more unfortunate than they already are. Let him keep silence. God will speak as a judge in the depths of his heart. And if that voice should become more terrible than he can bear, let the unhappy one remember, that the Lord our God is a forgiving God; that if our own heart accuses us, God is still greater than our own heart, and knows all things. Let us not judge one another!"

At this moment the blush of morning was kindled in the eastern horizon, on the other side of the desolated town, and its rosy light gleamed beautifully against the dark clouds. The preacher paused for a moment in order to turn the minds of his hearers from thought of the incendiary to that of the Redeemer.

"See," exclaimed he, "see the sign of the Redeemer in the sky; the sun, the light which again ascends after the dark night. Read the handwriting of fire in the Heavens! No night without a morning; no sorrow without God's mercy over it! As the light comes to the earth so comes the deliverer, the consoler to us. Behold His light! Listen to His words and His promises. My friends, let us stand up and praise him by our song, 'Blessed is he who cometh in the name of the Lord!'"

It was a profoundly affecting sight, when that great multitude of people, many of whom had lost their all in the fire; hundreds and hundreds of men and women, old people and children, still pale and bearing the traces of the misfortune which had despoiled them, all at once, as if impelled by a mighty impulse, rose like one man, and under the guidance of their spiritual teacher struck up the glorious hymn—

"Hosanna to the Son of David."

Higher and higher ascended the flames of the morning radiance, diffusing light over the whole country; and still louder and more powerful became the song, and every countenance, lately so pale and gloomy, looked now, turned towards the ascending light, and illumined by its splendor, like a choir of redeemed and thanksgiving spirits. Tears ran plentifully from many an eye, but there was no longer the pang of despair. Many a year hence will more than one of those now present testify, "For all that of which the fire deprived me, would I not have been deprived of that moment."

Among those who took no part in the universal transport of devotion was Rudolph. Hertha's evident abhorrence of him, and the sight of all the want and misery which the conflagration had caused, threw a terrible light on the dim consciousness of the young man's mind. He now felt within him, impressed, as it were, in fire and burning flame, the perception of the criminality of a deed which, according to the measure of his dull faculties, was merely intended for the liberation of himself and his beloved, as well as for the punishment of the tyrant. The words which had been spoken amid the darkness of the night, filled as it was with sighs and lamentations, awoke in him a despairing desire to acknowledge his guilt and to die. Hertha would weep over him; God would forgive him. These thoughts opened for him a door of escape from the gulf which threatened to swallow him up, and his newly-awakened feelings broke forth in a cry of self-accusation, which yet failed to reveal the dark mystery, because it was checked by the hand of Hertha, which suddenly closed his lips.

"Silence! Will you be the death of me? Silence, or I will never forgive you!"

With these words she drew him down to her on the ground, and talked earnestly to him, in an under voice, whilst the heavens tinged themselves with rosy light, and the Hosanna-song resounded above their heads. She pressed into his hand the small sum of money which she possessed, and which she had earned by her own labor, together with her only trinket, a little gold cross, which she had inherited from her mother; and, before the hymn had ceased, or the sun had arisen above the horizon, Rudolph was no longer to be seen on the King's-field.

The singing was over, and the throng of people who had risen to their feet in the inspiration of the moment, soon again sank down to earth, and to the troubles and wants of the day. Again were seen on the King's-field the three ladies, who the evening before had in vain offered refreshment; they were now attended by two girls, who bore upon a yoke on their shoulders, large baskets, containing coffee and bread. The "young baggages" had been hastily clothed, and now resembled very decent young women, as they followed, with their huge baskets of rye-bread, Mimmi Svanberg and her companions from one suffering group to another, distributing the refreshing beverage, together with consolatory and encouraging words. And seldom had Mimmi Svanberg found greater necessity for the cheering influence of her hand and tongue.

"Good morning, my dear woman. See here, drink a cup of warm coffee; it will cheer you up. Yes, it is a great misfortune; but all evil in this world passes away. Look, here is a roll to dip into your coffee. What nice little children you have! It was of God's mercy that none of them were injured in the fire. Yes, one has always something to be thankful for. But such children as these always bring joy with them. See here, little ones, you shall each have a nice wheaten cake and a drop of coffee. They are good, are they not? And beautiful weather, too, we shall have to-day. After a storm God always lets the sun shine."

"And, good Master Smithson, how are you going on? Badly enough I see. But our good, clever Doctor Hedermann will come and dress your burns, and then, when they are better, such a good, clever fellow as you are, will soon get your forge and bellows up again, and you will have a great deal of work to do when the town comes to be built up. It will be the making of you, Master Smithson; both you and your family will be three times as well off as before! Drink a cup of coffee on the strength of it, and take a roll too. Every one is the smith of his own fortune, Master Smithson, and that you'll find one of these days."

"Poor Mother Greta, with such a lot of little ones! Look, here is something nourishing both for you and them. We will, after this, have a famous large room for our Infant School, and then Mother Greta must promise to let the children go regularly to it. It won't do to let the young creatures be running about the streets, as they have done. Look, little children, there's bread and warm coffee for you. Now you'll be good children and go regularly to school; everything will be so much better when you are not in that miserable, unhealthy quarter. There is no misfortune so bad but that some good may come out of it. And we must, all of us, try to bring good out of evil."

"And now good morning to you, old mother in bed. You won't say no to a drop of coffee, I fancy. How old are you? Eighty! That is a good old age. You can do with two cups, perhaps. Drink, my good woman, and keep your heart up! It will, perhaps, be all the better for you in the end. Such a misfortune as this brings you under the notice of people.

Look you, mother, there are the girls that carried you out of the fire. They have got nice new clothes for that, and both you and they may live to see good days yet. Our Lord never forgets us, and everybody, one day or another, finds that out. At noon I shall bring you some warm soup."

"Little Mina! God bless the child! There you sit on your poor little legs! How did you come here?"

"Mother put me on her back and brought me here," replied the child.

"That was very good of mother—that it was; but she'll be glad of it some day. See, here is some breakfast for you, and for mother and little brother. It does me good, child, to see you look so cheerful, and with such bright eyes. Don't you think it is a very sad thing to be sitting here in the open meadow and shivering, without either house or home?"

"Oh, yes: it was a good deal warmer in the room; but the sun shines so bright now, and we have had such beautiful singing!"

"You are a good child! Look, there is a nice twist for you. When we once get the infant school rightly afloat, then you shall sing with the children there. Don't you be anxious about Mina, mother; she will be singing mistress in the school some day. A child with such a disposition is one of God's blessings."

In this way refreshment for the body and consolation for the heart were distributed among the most indigent of the homeless throng in the King's-field, by those three kind women, who, during the forenoon, found many fellow-laborers in their task, both gentlemen and ladies.

Another group, also of three persons, had been busied among the afflicted on the King's-field ever since sunrise, affording on all hands help and comfort. These were, the town's physician, Dr. Hedermann, attended by Hertha Falk and Ingeborg Uggla. He examined the burns and injuries of the poor sufferers, which were then treated with soothing medicaments and bound up, according to his instructions, by the two young ladies. These three moved along gravely, and speaking but few words; but the expressions of manly earnestness and compassion in the countenance of the noble physician and that of the warmest sympathetic feeling in the two ministering ladies, together with the quietness and tenderness of their movements, made them beautiful to behold. The countenances which appeared plain or old in the ball-room, here, in the light of morning, looked young and beautiful, as if in a renewed youth. More than one remarked this, and Mimmi Svanberg rejoiced silently over it, because she it was who sent her friend, the good Doctor, the two assistants, whose ability and disposition she knew.

These groups formed a refreshing contrast to the scene which the King's-field presented at daybreak. It was that of a camp, reminding the beholder of the horror and desolation of war.

During the day might be seen many pale figures wandering among the smoking ruins and the desolated places of the town, their countenances impressed with woe, seeking for what had been, or for what still remained of, their former houses.

Near to the spot where lay the ruins of their former comfortable home, stood Mrs. Christina Dufva, with her husband and their children.

"We have had," said she, "happiness and prosperity for so many years; may it then not be needful for us to be tried by some affliction? We are, however, all preserved to one another. We are in good health—we can work. Let us not lament, but rather thank God!"

"My girls! my doves!" said the father, "thank God that I have you all!"

The seven young girls gathered round their parents, like a flock of doves, caressingly, "They would work for them, they would help them, and one another."

Mrs. Tupplander also in the early morning stole to her house, which she found untouched by the flames. The first sight which met her eyes struck her with astonishment, and for the first moment with horror, for it was her noble young lady, the Honorable Miss Krusbjörn, who stood there, living as life itself, in the kitchen—eating bread and butter. We will draw a veil over the effects of the re-union and the explanations which took place.

During the day Mrs. Uggla also went abroad, bewailing herself for that which had happened, and for all that which would yet happen ; feeding her dismal imagination with the most gloomy pictures of the future and of the irremediableness of all wretchedness, and—" those seven Miss Dufvas—for them there was no longer any hope!"

The greater number of the more affluent of the houseless throng found themselves during the course of the forenoon under the shelter of a roof, either through the kindness of friends and acquaintances, or else by means of payment. The greater number of the poorer sort had to remain in the open air for more than one four-and-twenty hours, and the old woman of fourscore, three times four-and-twenty hours. In vain did the good occupants of the parsonage, Mimmi Svanberg, and several others, open their hospitable doors. The number of the sufferers was too great ; and besides, many of the townspeople who were so fortunate as to possess their substance and their spacious homes untouched, reasoned like the selfish man of property, when his help was asked, " It is no concern of mine !" and remained unmoved spectators of their brethren's want and labor.

Director Falk and his family removed to a small suburban house which they rented, and Hertha's time and thoughts were for the moment wholly occupied in settling them down here as comfortably as was possible, under existing circumstances. For the first time her powers, both of body and mind, were fully occupied, and this was very beneficial to her.

The town-authorities were fully occupied also, partly with providing for the most necessitous of the sufferers, partly with convicting and sentencing those villains who availed themselves of the public misfortune and consequent disorder to rob and steal, and the judge of the district swore a solemn oath, that none who were detected in such practices should escape his vengeance and that of the law.

CONSEQUENCES.

Husr! She is about to speak; she has something to say, the dying young woman who lies yonder on the bed. She appears to be contending with the shadows of death, in order yet to cast some glances, to speak some words, in the world which she is about to leave. Those eyes, supernaturally bright, seem at times to gaze into yet unknown infinitude, as she exclaims again and again, " How wonderful! how wonderful!" But still the shadows hold her back.

"Light! light! more light! It is indeed my wedding-day! I shall indeed be married to Arvid! Dress me in my wedding-clothes! Dress me as a bride! Arvid's bride! Place the myrtle-crown on my head! No—no—in my hand! Arvid is really away, and I am the bride of death! My father has willed it so! He banished Arvid: he was very severe; and therefore I am lying here! I should like to have lived as a happy wife. Arvid loved me so much, and I loved him! We could have worked: we should have had enough with my maternal inheritance. But my father—but don't let him know; it would grieve him. I would not willingly grieve any one. But we will not speak of the past. What have I said? Ah! I am so selfish! I cannot forget! But the moment is come when I may speak, because I am about to die. Father! father!" And with a violent effort the dying young woman raised her head, and the supernaturally bright eyes gazed searchingly among the figures of those who were in the chamber with her. He whom she called for approached her bed—falteringly. The eyes formerly so severe and unpitying are now dimmed with tears.

Oh, gentle angel of death! thou makest the weak to be

strong, and the severe thou makest weak. Alma took her father's hand and riveted upon him a penetrating glance. "My father!"

"Here I am. What wilt thou with me, my child?"

"Father! give thy children their right,—light, freedom; thou gavest them life; give them that which alone makes life valuable. They will then love—will love thee, as only the free can love. Thanks! I am going hence; God has liberated me. Hertha remains behind! Father, give her freedom; dost thou understand me, my father?"

"Yes; and I promise to do that which thou desirest."

"Thank thee! now I can die calmly. Be just to Hertha, father; greet Arvid, tell him—ah, no, forgive me. I know not rightly what I am saying——"

"Try to sleep, my child; perhaps thou wilt be better!"

"No, no! I must now look upon those whom I love!"

And Alma's glance turned from her father to her sisters, as she whispered, "My sisters, kiss me!"

They kissed her, weeping.

Alma's eyes now sought Hertha's, as she whispered, "Hertha, my beloved! my only one!"

Hertha was there; laid herself softly by her sister's side, wound her arms around her, and pressed her lips to hers. Thus rested the two young sisters, who had so long trod in company the narrow thorny path, now clasped together in a heartfelt embrace, as though they never more would separate. But it is the last time that they will ever rest thus; it is the last time that their lips have whispered to each other words heard only by themselves and God.

THE SONG OF THE BELLS.

THE bells are chiming for the dead. And never do the
Swedish bells give forth more beautiful, more cheerful, and
more animating sounds than on such occasions. 'There is in
that funeral-chime a secret anthem of joy; so cheerfully, so
freely, and exultantly peal forth those melodious tongues
through the fresh vernal atmosphere of an April evening. So
thought many a one who listened to them that day ringing
over the grave, where had just been laid a young woman,
dead in the prime of her life. Beside the grave stood one to
whom their song was more intelligible than to any beside.
She stood alone in the evening by the grave, which enclosed
the dearest friend she had on earth, and it was to her that the
bells sang:

> Oh, for the youthful!
> Hence taken early;
> Weep not, nor mourn for her.
> It is well with her!
> From days dull and cheerless,
> A pleasureless future,
> From life without life's light
> Hence is she taken.
> Never more, never more, can she be captive!
>
> Death, the great reaper,
> Thou art more merciful
> Than human hearts are,
> Or human statutes;
> They ordain thraldom,
> Thou givest freedom,
> Releasest the bound one,
> The patient, the loving,
> She can no longer, no longer be captive.

Oh, glorious freedom!
Love and truth changeless,
Fountains eternal,
In which she confided,
Towards which she pilgrimed,
You are her own now!
She is free, she is free, with the **freed ones!**

Therefore be joyous,
Be joyous and sing ye,
Sing ye, her sisters,
Rejoice for the life which
Was death to her, living,
By death is transfigured
To life everlasting!
Never more, never more can she be captive!
She is free, she is free with the freed ones,
Well is it with her!

Thus sung those melodious voices through the serene spring atmosphere, to one heart whose unspeakable anguish was wonderfully appeased by that spirit-like song, whilst torrents of tears fell upon the newly-raised turf of the grave. High above the grave carolled the larks in the deep-blue, and seemed to repeat, as in a tone of exultation,

She is free, she is free, with the freed ones!

FATHER AND DAUGHTER.

A FLOWER UPON THE GRAVE.

DIRECTOR FALK sat in his little room at Kullen, as the little suburban residence to which the family had removed after the fire was called, and saw the sun set behind the budding fruit-trees in the garden. He still sat with his feet swathed in woollen socks and suffering from gout. The expression of his countenance was less severe than formerly, but, if possible, more gloomy. Both his head and his hands had visibly a tremulous, palsied movement. His pale countenance and his firmly-closed lips showed that he had taken some resolute determination, upon which he was about to act, although it cost him a great effort to do so. He seemed to be expecting some one or something. He expected—his daughter Hertha, to whom he had sent a message that he wished to speak to her.

Three weeks had passed since the night of the fire, and one since the corpse of Alma had been borne from the house. The horrors of that night, and cold taken at the same time, had hastened the progress of her disease, and rapidly completed the work which it had begun.

How many a time had Hertha, who well knew the original cause of her sister's illness, thought in the bitterness of her heart how she would by her death-bed one day reproach her father aloud, because *he* was her executioner; had thought over before-hand the terrible words with which she would punish the hard, selfish man. The hour came, but she then saw her father bowed and broken, trembling near his victim, and she could no longer find words wherewith to reproach or punish him. She had only tears for them both.

Since that event, however, father and daughter seemed to avoid each other. Aunt Nella, or old Anna, carried question and answer from one to the other, when this was needed. Rudolph's name was never mentioned by the Director, neither did he seem to like to hear him mentioned by any one else, and the unfortunate youth was shunned by the family almost as one dead. Every one believed him guilty of originating the fire.

Hertha now, more than ever, called upon to act both for herself and others, and more than ever, therefore, in want of that liberty which had been promised her, to direct her own actions and manage her own lawful property, both wished and feared, at the same time, to have some conversation with her father. Thus things stood on that evening, when a message came which summoned her to him.

If any one has done thee a great injury and by that means called forth the demons of hatred and bitterness into thy heart—and worse injury than that can no one do to a soul—and God give thee grace to do thy injurer a great service, there arises something great within thy whole being, which makes it much easier for thee to forgive, even if thou art not besought to do so. Thou hast acted like the Highest on the earth, and His peace—which surpasses all peace and all strife—covers with its wings the bitter waters of thy mind.

When Hertha came before her father, her glance was less cold, and her demeanor less rigid than usual. She had carried him like a child in her arms and on her breast, through fire and flames. The memory of that had wonderfully mollified her heart. Yet that heart throbbed violently as she entered her father's room and advanced softly to the chair in which he sat. He looked up hastily, and motioned with his hand to a chair which stood near his, as he said:

"Sit down; I wish to speak to you."

Hertha saw that the hand trembled; it affected her.

After a moment's silence the old man began, with a voice which he endeavored to make firm.

"You have done me a great service; you have saved my

life. I wish to show you my gratitude. Tell me what you wish me to do for you?"

"Give me my liberty, father," said Hertha, with a mild but firm voice,—" and the property that I inherit from my mother. I am twenty-seven years old, and I wish to be declared as having attained my majority."

"It shall be done," replied her father, "if I can only get time to take the necessary steps. I am prepared to render an account of the property inherited from your mother; I have been a just steward, according to the best of my ability; the last misfortune does not touch it—that—that you can well understand."

Hertha bowed her head in silent acquiescence; her father continued :

"The interest of your mother's property, together with your proportion of your late sister's share, amounts to a sum sufficient to enable you to live independently wherever you would like. You have a right to do so. You are of the class of strong women who are able to be their own support, and even to support others. I have hitherto not believed in the existence of such; I have, perhaps, been unjust in this respect, at all events as regards you, as I saw at the time of the fire, and even since then. Be therefore free, my daughter; see and do that which pleases you, and, in the meantime, take this sum of money,"—and with a trembling hand he laid in that of his daughter, a roll of bills to the value of about a thousand rix-dollars banco—"they are some of my savings, you can do with them what you like; use them for a journey or whatever else you have a wish for."

Money, as reward for an act of love, which saved him from a horrible death! and yet Hertha received it with gratitude, because money is a means of much good, and of happiness to many; besides she well understood her father's really good intentions. Tears filled her eyes as she thanked him. He assumed a harsher tone :

"I know that you do not love me, and perhaps it is not altogether your own fault, because you have not understood

my affection for you; nevertheless, I know that I have wished
for and desired, the future advantage of my children." Here
he suddenly broke off and fixed his eyes upon the ground. It
was as if a pale shadow rising therefrom had whispered,
"Why do I lie here? I might have lived happily as a
wife."

Hertha was silent; the old man wiped away the sweat-
drops from his brow. His whole frame trembled. After a
moment he resumed—

"If I have made a mistake, then I am, perhaps, severely
enough punished. In the meantime, may you be free and
happy, far from a father and a home which you do not love.
The interest of your mother's property can be paid to you at
any place wherever you may be. And I desire nothing more
from you than that you should tell me where you would like
to be."

"Here!" said Hertha, as she rose up and laid her hand on
the arm of her father's chair, "here, with you, my father, if
you will allow it. Oh! you have little understood me and the
liberty which I have coveted. And you shall understand me
better, if you will promise me, what I now ask of you, and
which I know that I deserve."

"And what is that?" asked the Director, as he looked up
to his daughter with an excited glance.

"Your confidence, father!" said Hertha, mildly and
gravely. "Believe that I desire what is right and good, and
let me remain with you to prove this to you. Have confidence in me, and—be kind to me and my sisters, so that we
may love you, and endeavor to make you happy. I am no
longer a child, my father! I will be a mother to my younger
sisters, and manage your house according to my best ability.
I know that this is my duty; it will also be my pleasure, if,
father, you will only give me my freedom and your confidence,
and be kind to me for—*Alma's sake!*"

Now it was spoken out: that reproachful, bitter word,
which had so long brooded in Hertha's breast, but a loving
angel had anointed the arrow's point with a healing balsam.

It pierced the heart deeply, penetratingly, but at the same time softeningly, as with a chastising look of love.

The old man said nothing: he bowed his head, and large heavy tears rolled down the deeply-furrowed cheeks.

Then another head bent down softly to his, and a young fresh cheek, wet with tears, was laid close to his. A beautiful sorrowing memory united father and daughter in one common bitter pain. Yes — blessed are they who can thus weep together!

Gentle feelings produce profoundly beneficial effects upon stern natures. It is the spring-rain which melts the ice-covering of the earth, and causes it to open to the beams of heaven.

Old Mr. Falk felt it to be so, and he raised his head, as he said in the gentlest voice which his daughter had ever heard from her father:

"Let it be as you have said. We will endeavor to begin anew with each other. I am only afraid that—I may be quite too heavy a burden to you, for I feel that some great change is about to take place in my state of health."

He was not aware that it was precisely a presentiment of this change; the sight of that palsied hand and that tremulous head, which had moved the daughter's soul to the resolve, that her youthful strength and health should be his support.

THE SON OF THE TWILIGHT.

It was almost dusk when Hertha left her father and went down to her own room. As she approached the door, however, she involuntarily started back, perceiving a dark, almost shapeless form, lying upon the threshold, and glaring upon her with a pair of terrible eyes from beneath a thick mass of unkempt and disordered black hair. Hertha shuddered involuntarily as she said, "Rudolph!"

He continued to stare into her face, which was lighted up by the crimson of the sunset, as well as by the conversation which she had just had with her father.

"Rudolph!" repeated she, in a voice half of anger and half of terror. "Rudolph! is it you?"

"Yes," replied he; "and you? are you the angel of judgment?"

"I am Hertha, your cousin. Stand up: don't lie grovelling in that way. Stand up: be a man! I have been expecting to hear something from you for a long time."

"Don't talk sternly to me. It will do no good. I am too much used to that. And now I don't care for the whole world. Trample on me, if you like. Here will I die."

"Get up, Rudolph, and come with me into my room. I will talk with you there."

The calm determination in Hertha's voice, and the words, "in my room I will talk with you," produced a great effect upon the unfortunate young man. He rose up. She opened the door of the room, and he followed her in. She surveyed him attentively, and when she became aware of his wholly desolate, and, as it were, shipwrecked appearance, she said with heartfelt compassion:

"Poor Rudolph! Where have you been?"

"I don't exactly know. In the great woods about here."

"You have need of something to eat and drink. Wait a moment."

Hertha went out and soon returned with bread, some cold meat, and a bowl of milk.

"The fire is out in the kitchen," she said, "and I cannot now get up anything warm; but take of this—eat and drink."

"Oh, Hertha! Then you can still take some interest in me."

"Yes—yes: I shall always be your friend, Rudolph. But now, eat and drink. After that we will talk."

Rudolph ate and drank like one who had neither eaten nor drunk for several days. After awhile he said, "Thank you, I have had enough."

"Let us now have some talk, Rudolph," said Hertha, with calm resolution. "Tell me what you have thought—what you think of doing for the future. What do you wish for— what would you like?"

"To see you!"

"And after that?"

"Die—What have I to live for?"

"You must not die yet, Rudolph," said Hertha, solemnly. "You must live in order to reconcile to you those friends whom you have alienated; to make amends for injuries you have done, and to become a better man."

"How can I live? Where must I go to?"

"The world is large. You must go out into the world, into a foreign land; a long way from this place. People already suspect you here. People are making inquiries after you. If once you are seized, you will either be executed or imprisoned as a malefactor. Oh, Rudolph, you have done mischief enough already—do not make us still more unfortunate!"

"Tell me, tell me then, what shall I do?" said Rudolph, bewildered and unable to take counsel with himself. "You— you I will obey. Oh, Hertha, you have a wonderful power over me. But, when I think of that horrible night; the flames; the houseless throng, and you looking at me like the angel of judgment and punishment——"

"I shall not henceforth look at you in that way, Rudolph. I am your friend, your sister. Now listen to me, Rudolph. You must immediately go hence. Here is some money; three hundred rix-dollars; they are my own, and now they are yours. I know that you have a thorough knowledge of money. With this you must immediately go to Götheborg, and from thence to Copenhagen. You must there go to our relation Banker Falk. I have written to him, and here you have a letter to him. He will receive you; of that I am certain, and take charge of you for a time. As soon as you reach Copenhagen write to me and tell me everything that concerns you. And I will then write to you and send you more money if you require it. "

"I shall not require it!" said Rudolph, "because I am grown up, and I can write and keep books for wages. I will do everything that you bid me, Hertha, if you will only promise to think of me and write to me often. I know that I did what is very wrong that night;—a wonderful light entered my mind then—but, Hertha, do not abandon me!—You are the only, only person in the whole world who has any regard for me; the only one who asks after me; who wishes me well, the only one——"

"No, not the only one, Rudolph," interrupted Hertha, in whose soul at this moment the fountains of divine salvation opened their depths,—"Jesus came to this world to save sinners; go to Him, Rudolph, and He will be with you; He will be your friend."

"How can I go to Him?—You have never before talked to me about Him; do you believe in Him, Hertha?"

"I did not formerly understand Him, as I do now, Rudolph. My eyes have been closed. Alma knew Him better than I did. Look, here is a little book about Him; in which she often read, and in which she has marked many passages. Take it, read it, and do that which the Saviour commands, and He will lead you to God. The sin which you have hitherto committed, God will forgive, because you knew not what you did; your reason was clouded, poor Rudolph, and you had no guiding friend. But now you know that what you did was sin; and God has opened to you a way by which you can make atonement. I know that your heart is not wicked. If you follow Jesus it will become good, and you will never do otherwise than what is right. Wherever you happen to be, Rudolph, remember this: help the oppressed and the suffering, whether they be human beings or animals. But never seek vengeance for yourself, Rudolph; leave vengeance to God who sees all things. Go, and be merciful to your fellow-creatures, as Jesus has set you the example. Oh, Rudolph! there is a great deal which is dark and sorrowful and bitter upon earth, but He is light and He is goodness, and with him as your guide you will attain to light and the highest life. You have much to live for, much which can make life noble and good and divine. You have hitherto lived as a poor child of darkness, Rudolph; now you must live to become a child of light and of God!"

Hertha's tears gushed forth as she thus talked with a power and an enthusiasm which even affected herself. Rudolph listened in silence with eyes riveted upon her, whilst he many times breathed deeply, as if he felt a heavy burden lifted from his breast and inspired a new breath of life. When she ceased speaking, he lifted up his head and said:

"God has spoken to me through you, and I have rightly comprehended and understood every word you have said; and I will do as you have told me. Yes, I will be a child of God; I will follow Jesus; and you follow him also, Hertha, and thus we shall both go the same way, and in the end we shall be united?"

"Yes, Rudolph, yes, in heaven, as angels of God, if we are worthy of becoming such. But now, dear Rudolph, you must go; before morning you must be on your way to the coast. The steamboat to Götheborg sails early to-morrow from K***. You must make haste to be in time for it. Your whole future wellbeing may depend upon it. Remember what we have talked about!"

"Yes, yes; I will go. Farewell!"

He offered her his hand; she took it and went out with him into the court. It was a cold, bright night, at the close of April; hoar-frost covered the meadow. The stars shone brightly above their heads in the blue expanse of heaven. When they had reached the little lane which led from the house to the high road, Rudolph said:

"Hertha, let me have a parting kiss."

She could not refuse him at that moment; she raised her face to his; but he clasped her in burning love and pain, and covered her face with hot kisses.

With an involuntary feeling of horror and disgust Hertha tore herself from his arms, as she exclaimed, "Away, away!"

Rudolph turned and went on his way sobbing aloud. But just as he reached the end of the lane, he felt a hand touch his arm, and Hertha again stood before him with the light of hope and compassion again beaming in her countenance; she pointed to heaven and said:

"There, Rudolph, there!"

With these words, she hastened back; gathered up the hoar-frost from the grass, and washed her face with it, which seemed to her polluted by Rudolph's kisses. So doing, she listened to the sound of his footsteps, which became more and more distant on the desolate high road in the silent night. When she could no longer perceive them, she breathed more freely. And as she stood there, alone beneath the brilliant, starry heavens, in the silence of night, a joyful peace stole over her mind; an indescribably wonderful and pleasant feeling of approaching morning and spring came consolingly with the breeze of night, which refreshingly caressed her forehead, and touched her eyebrows as with a spirit's kisses. The strengthening and edifying words which she had spoken, the consolation which she had given to another, came now like good angels back to her own bosom, with the presentiment, that an ever-lasting love ruled the world, and that she might become its messenger. The feeling of a living, inward communion with a higher, holy, life-giving power, arose in her soul as a morning watch, and opened it to one of those unspeakable, almost wordless, but not the less powerful, prayers by which earth's poor children, yet enveloped in night, endeavor to reach the Lord of life and light, and which may be thus interpreted:

" O Thou, of whom I have a presentiment, Thou whom I yet do not know, whom I yearn to know and to love—God! enlighten me with thy countenance, turn thy countenance towards me, and give me thy light and thy blessing!"

The thought of Alma; the longing to experience something about her, something from her, mingled itself with inexpressible melancholy in her sigh after divine light, which she breathed forth into the silence of night. And who is there, who, having lost by death a very dear friend, does, not in every hour of deepest life and longing, speak, with inexpressible sighs in the depths of his soul, the beloved name; pray for a sign, a token, ah! merely an inward intimation that the departed is present, that he hears, that he loves us, that he enjoys the light, the blessedness of which we stand in need, and that he obtains good for us, and for them who sit in darkness, from the Father, whose ear he is nearer to than we!

So it was with Hertha, as she stretched forth her arms into empty space, and called in a low voice, " Alma! Alma!"

But no sound, no sign, no token replied to her from the desolate infinitude. She let her hands fall; dried her tears, and again entered her chamber in order to lay to rest in the arms of sleep all uneasy questionings, all the pangs of thought and of feeling. Tears soothe. It is a great relief to be able to weep. Hertha's tears calmed the agitated billows of her soul. She slept and had a dream, which afforded her great consolation.

She dreamed that it was night, and that she went into her silent chamber to go to rest. Alma was dead, and she was alone with heavy thoughts. She then saw the glimpse of a white figure by the window, which seemed as if wishful to withdraw itself behind the white window-curtain. A thought

passed like lightning through Hertha's soul, " It is a sign from
Alma ! "   And she sprang up hastily, as if to retain the fleet-
ing token ; she reached behind the curtain, she wished to
take hold of the white floating spirit-veil, but when she withdrew her hand, behold ! she held in it a bouquet of the most
beautiful flowers, such as she had never before seen ; little
bells, like lilies of the valley, Alma's favorite flowers, of the
loveliest pale pink color, which hung in little fragrant clusters
on their graceful stems. Delighted and happy, she pressed
the beautiful bouquet to her lips, to her heart, and returned
with them to her bed. On this there opened above her a
large window, and she saw the brightest deep-blue heaven
above her, and there, in the highest profound, shone—was it
a fixed star, or a beaming eye ? she knew not which, but only
that from the brilliant heavens it beamed down upon her, and
the flowers which she held in her hand, floods of a light, as
effulgent, as gentle, and as pleasant as we might imagine
would be the glance of the blessed.

In many a dark hour which succeeded, Hertha's soul was
comforted by the remembrance of that dream.

NEW SCHEMES AND UNDERTAKINGS.

SOMETHING NEW UNDER THE SUN.

Mrs. Tupplander is in all her splendor, the Honorable Miss Krusbjörn is all activity, and every maid-servant in the house as busy as a bee. There is going to be a great breakfast of chocolate and bouillon, with the necessary cakes and pastry for a great number of guests, how many is not exactly known; this only is sure, that there will be a great many. That is to say, the Ladies'-Society which had been proposed, but not organized, before the fancy-ball and the great fire, and which, since the latter occurrence, had hastily come into operation, both from external and internal necessity. The same necessity had, with equal haste, led to the formation of a society of gentlemen under the name of the Poor's-Relief Committee, to assist and provide for the poor rendered destitute by the fire; and both these societies were this day to meet at Mrs. Tupplander's to arrange their plans of procedure, and consult together as to some general means of relieving the most extreme cases of distress caused by the late calamity. Pastor Dahl was to take the chair on this occasion, and Mimmi Svanberg to act as Secretary. Protocol-Secretary N. B. was also to be there, on pretence of collecting material for the work which he intends to write on Ladies'-Societies.

Both ladies and gentlemen arrived—a great number of them. People took off their things; they shook hands; they asked one another how they did. They collected in little groups, the ladies to themselves, the gentlemen to themselves, as is so generally the custom here in the north. Each talked with his neighbor in a low voice. Chocolate and biscuits were handed round; they sipped and they dipped; they set down their cups; they seated themselves on chairs and sofas, and then there was a silence, because our little pastor stood up upon a little elevation at the end of the large drawing-room, and was about to make a speech, and, as usual, people were very glad to hear what he had to say.

But now it happened to him, as it had not unfrequently happened before, that his heart became warm, that his thoughts took an unexpected turn; in short, that he was inspired to say something quite different to that which he had prepared at his writing-table. Everybody could see that he was affected; that his mind was full of matter, that his eyes beamed as though they would light up the whole company. All at once he exclaimed:

"Ladies and gentlemen! It will not be of any use our coming together like strangers to each other—the men here, the women there! What! Are we not brothers and sisters, children of the same Father, and united here for the same purpose in his service? No: we must not break ourselves up into a Ladies'-Society and a Gentleman's-Society, we must have one Brethren-society, or a Brethren-Covenant of men and women both, divided into families of brothers and sisters, who will help one another in love to labor for the good of the general household.

"When God created the human race, He created them man and woman, and gave them to each other as helpers in life, just as people set one half to another, to make a perfect whole. And, look! He has done it for one and for all human beings, for the small and for the large world alike. Man and woman must extend to each other their hands as brethren and as married couples, not merely in the private home, but also in the great home, which we call social life. Thus was it in the early Christian community, when men and women acted together in concert, distributing bread and prayers. Thus ought it to be again, and in more affluent measure, when that parent community, which the Holy Ghost touched with his divine influence, has penetrated all peoples and all realms, and the Christian family renews its spiritual relationship in every sphere of human life, and all by that means participate in work —that is bread—and prayers. Then will the garden of Eden again open its gates to the children of Adam and Eve! Let us to-day, on our spot of earth, and in our little portion of the large field of labor, begin the work: let us unite ourselves in a more inner meaning of the word than hitherto: let us extend to each other our hands for a true fraternal bond; thus shall we accomplish the Creator's design, who intended not that man alone, or that woman alone, but that man and woman united, the perfected human-being, should have dominion over the earth!"

"That is really and truly something new under the sun!" said Mimmi Svanberg, smiling, to the pastor, as she hastily noted down the principal points of his speech. "May it only be carried out!"

Protocol-Secretary N. B. raised his voice to protest against the proposition, which, he said, was "unnecessary, and would lead to nothing but confusion." He ended by demanding a vote on the subject. It struck him with a sort of panic-terror that he himself, as now a member of the Poor's-Relief Committee, should, in case the pastor's proposition was carried, become in fact a *bond fide* member of the Ladies'-Society; and how then would it go with him and the book he was about to write? He now therefore desired, by a strong negative, to make a protest against the resolution, and hoped to find a majority on his side.

But he was deceived. During the late terrible occurrences in the town, and the consequent suffering, men and women had labored together as brothers and sisters in the common work of rescue and relief, so that the present assembly, which consisted for the most part of these very people, found them-selves extremely well disposed to adopt the resolution; and when one of the most generally esteemed men of the town, the noble old lawyer Carlson, rose to thank the speaker, and to declare that he agreed in all the views of the reverend speaker, and seconded the resolution, the company rose with almost general acclamation.   Three or four Noes were overpowered by the general Yes! and other indubitable expressions of cordial approval.   Mr. Protocol-Secretary N. B. left the room.

The company then proceeded immediately, under the direction of their spiritual teacher, to organize the new society. A main division or family, was formed, which undertook the management of the monetary affairs, as well as various other families, each taking their respective portion of labor; each being empowered to lay down its own laws or mode of procedure, although in certain questions subservient to the direction of the Head Family.   Each division or family had a father and a mother, who selected the other members of the family group.   By this means Dr. Hedermann became "father" of the family whose duty it was to attend to the health of the sufferers from the fire.   And he summoned as his children and assistants, half in joke and half in earnest, Ingeborg Uggla and Hertha Falk, who more than willingly placed themselves under his guidance.

The childless, and yet so truly the motherly, Mrs. Dahl was elected unanimously as " mother" of the family which had charge of the destitute children.   She received the appointment with tears of joy, because she saw, in her mind's eye, the Infant Asylum, the wish of her heart, the infant-school, flourishing to her heart's desire under the shelter of her wing.

Mrs. Tupplander looked a little confounded and affronted when she heard herself proposed as the mother of the " Soup-Kitchen Family," and she seemed to think that such an undertaking was below her dignity; but she suddenly brightened up when the amiable Countess P. hastened forward to offer her assistance in the Commissariat Department, and to supply the great copper with herbs, barley, and vegetables from her estate in the country.   Her husband, Count P., on this declared, laughing, that he should not separate from his wife, but should, as her brother in the soup-kitchen-family, send in two fathoms of fire wood, and have a bullock killed for the use of the family copper.

All present came by degrees into the best possible humor. The spirit of human-love, which had inspired the proposition in the first place, communicated itself to and animated all hearts. Pride and self-love vanished before a magical, gentle influence: fear and mistrust of their own or other people's powers disappeared also before a cheerful and strength-giving courage; many were affected, they knew not rightly wherefore; they joked, but with tears in their eyes; remarks were made which sounded satirical, but the point of the satire was sharpened by love: they called one another "father," "mother," "sister," "brother;" they shook hands like members of the same family. Mimmi Svanberg was a member of every family, and was at length declared to be a "free-citizeness," free to act according to her own pleasure, and to take part, either by word or deed, as it pleased her, in every circle alike.

They agreed upon their futuremeetings, whether family-wise or for general assembly, and then separated. Thus amid joke and earnest, and amid general mutual good-will, was formed the little federal union which was destined to exercise so great an influence upon the fate of many of its members, and which Mimmi Svanberg called "Something new under the sun."

Mrs. Tupplander did not exactly know what to say about the whole undertaking; whether it was a proper thing or whether it was not. She looked at the Honorable Miss Krusbjörn. But when the Honorable Miss Krusbjörn took off her wig to cool her enthusiasm, for she was really of an enthusiastic disposition, and declared that she had never seen anything like it, and that she would make soup for the society all the days of her life, for that it was to make soup for God the Father himself, and for all His family!—then was Mrs. Tupplander satisfied, and said, "That there should not be any want of soup for the poor towns-folk as long as she herself lived there."

And thus these two also accepted their allotted parts well satisfied,

HERTHA'S PART.

HERTHA'S part, as well as that of Ingeborg Uggla, was, as we have seen, decided by the share they had taken in the labors of the first morning after the great fire. Dr. Hedermann called them, with a sort of fatherly pleasure, his daughters and amanuenses, and evidently entrusted to them the care of those who had received burns and other injuries during the fire. He supplied them with medicaments, and laid down the mode of treatment, which he left the young female physicians to apply and carry out, having soon had sufficient proof of their skill in doing so, which he had witnessed, both with pleasure and a certain admiration, though he took care not to let it be noticed. His highest praise being merely:

"Very well done. Only go on as you have begun. Only persevere!"

The good doctor in fact was so occupied by the amount of sickness which followed the fire, by the colds, the catarrhs, and pleurisies, which it occasioned, that he was greatly in need of all the extraneous assistance which could be rendered him by the different members of his new family.

Most people, when they think of wounds and the dressing of them, think of something which is disagreeable and repulsive. We believe nevertheless that some there are who would understand us if we spoke of the pleasure and charm of such an occupation. Women in the old times were renowned for their skill as leeches; and from the most remote antiquity have they been distinguished as such, even in the north, and still there are some to this day amongst us who are thus remarkable.*

* I trust it will be permitted to me here to say a few words of high esteem and acknowledgment regarding the female surgeon of Stockholm,

The true female-surgeon looks upon the wound, as a mother looks upon a sick child ; and when the wound, well cleansed and washed, smiles at her with a certain fresh and calmed expression as if it would thank her for the treatment, she on her part regards it with a feeling of satisfaction and pleasure. She lays upon it the fine white lint, spread with healing ointment ; she presses softly upon it folds of fine linen ; she binds it with white bandages ; she tends it as though it were a little child, and feels involuntarily for it a tender and maternal sentiment. When she thus sees it well attired and comforted, and reads in the countenance of the patient how comforted he or she has become, and thenceforward, day by day, sees her nurse-child becoming better and better, which is the rule for these injuries, then does the healing-art appear to her lovely and agreeable, almost as one of the fine arts itself. She knows besides, that for this in reality simple art, there are wholly dissimilar gifts, and wholly dissimilar fingers, and one and all with joy, know themselves to be artists in their particular branch.

Thus was it with Hertha and Ingeborg, and the peculiar love and delicacy with which they pursued their vocations made them doubly welcome and beneficial to their patients.

Among these was Yngve Nordin. He had, as the reader may remember, been carried away after the fire was ex-

Miss Årberg, and at the same time to express the wish that some of the wealthy who occasionally send their carriages to fetch the skilful surgeoness, will some time or other take the trouble of seeing the reception which she every day gives to the poorest population of Stockholm, who come streaming in to her through open doors with their wounds and injuries. Then they would be filled with admiration, as we have been, of the unwearied patience, the cheerful temper, as well as of the liberality with which she gives her time, her skill, and her ointments to the thousands who have nothing to give her but their thanks, which sometimes even are transformed by the ignorant and depraved into abuse. They would then wish, as we have done, to provide her a better place for her benevolent activity than she now has, and the means, without too great a loss, of continuing it ; and they would perhaps, more fortunate than ourselves, be able to accompiish that which they wished.

tinguished, to the parsonage, with his left arm together with his knee greatly injured by the falling of a wall. Doctor Hedermann took Hertha with him on his visits to this patient, and taught her how to bind the injured limbs. In the beginning, when Yngve suffered also from fever, he himself visited him every day. But when he became convalescent he often sent Hertha alone to attend to the patient, and came himself only every other day, and after that only twice a week, in order to ascertain that he was properly attended to. When the young physicianess first came alone she asked the pastor's wife to go in with her to the invalid. The pastor's wife did so, but soon went out again, partly because Yngve often talked with Hertha on subjects which made her yawn, or read poetry to her in language which she did not understand, and partly because she could not remain long in the sickroom uninterrupted, being called out perpetually by many people and for many things.

"But—is it well that they are so long together—those two young folks?" said the pastor one day, a little doubtfully, to his wife; "the young girl has no mother; you ought to be that to her!"

"I would very willingly be so to her," replied the pastor's wife, "if I could only escape sitting there the whole time, while she dresses his wounds, and they talk about things which don't concern me, and he reads to her English which I don't understand, and I am obliged to sit there like a sheep. No, that is more than I can do; I must look after my house and my servants. There is no danger with those young people, you know; I think, for my part, that our Lord has them in his good care!"

Our Lord had so; and in a much higher sense than the pastor's wife thought of. Yngve's injuries were not dangerous for life or limbs; he would certainly soon be well and wholly restored, yet still they were of that kind—the injury to the knee in particular—which required much care, much time, and much patience. The young man had no remarkable share of the latter, he longed for activity. It was a severe trial to him to be compelled to bear and to wait. Hertha's society and conversation became soon, therefore, as necessary to him as her care. But his also at the same time obtained an unexpected influence over her. They had met and had stood by each other's side in the hour of danger, amid fire and flame. This, together with the similarity in thought which their first conversation had betrayed, gave them, now that they were again thrown together by fate, a feeling of friendship, a brotherly and sisterly acquaintance, which removed all embarrassment and made their intercourse easy and agreeable.

In order to occupy Yngve's thoughts and turn them to a more pleasing subject, Hertha requested him to read something aloud to her whilst she was engaged in attending to her surgical duties. He in this way made her acquainted with his favorite modern poets, and read to her in particular those of his friend the young American bard, James R. Lowell, in which all the ideas of the new world and the new time, freedom, labor, pure joy and brotherhood, a perfected life for all in the great drama of the world, found an eloquent expression, and were presented in a bewitching form. These poems gave rise to many questions and much thought. Yngve had spent two years in the United States, and had deep sympathy with the young upward-struggling life which is in agitation there, as well as in the free states of Europe, but which there found a fuller and freer expression. He loved to talk on this subject.

"And the women in the new world," inquired Hertha on one occasion, "have they poured forth no song, no lofty and large-hearted desires and aspirations as the men have done?"

Yngve told Hertha of the noble women with whom he had become acquainted; whose religious earnestness and liberal-minded fellow-citizenship had greatly influenced the development of his own mind. He made her acquainted with the movements in the Free States, which are there known under the name of "Woman's Rights Conventions," and read to her many large-minded sentiments of progress, from the lips of women during these assemblies. He justified them against

the misconceptions with which they were regarded by preja-
diced eyes, and showed that, what women on these occasions
demanded, beyond everything else, was their right to an
education and a freedom, which afforded to every one a possibility and a means of becoming that which God, by the gifts
which he has bestowed upon her, calls her to be.

Hertha's heart beat high, proudly and joyfully at the same
time, when these communications were made to her. She
felt proud on behalf of her sex, proud of the words which
women had uttered, and of the future in which they were the
pioneers; she felt humble when she thought of the great responsibility which was laid upon them, and happy when she
saw men combating for this object, as if it were their own;
and when she heard a young man, as now, advocating these
views with earnestness. Never did Hertha feel less inclined
to insist upon the dignity of the rights of her sex than now.
She only felt a strong desire to be worthy of a noble justice.
Often did the two young friends imagine together pictures of
the future which would dawn; of the beautiful and the pure
life which would exist when man and woman should become,
in a far higher degree and significance than now, each other's
helper in life, giving to each other a hand in all earthly labor,
each according to his nature and his gifts, as equals and as
friends, in want and in joy.

During such conversations it happened, as might be expected, that the two speakers looked deeply into each other's
eyes and each other's souls, and that they found each other
beautiful, as they thus beamed upon each other truth and
mutual satisfaction. It also happened sometimes, that the
minutes sped along on such rapid wings, that they never remarked the flight of time till hours were passed, and the
striking of the clock reminded Hertha that—she was " expected at home."

Once, during such a prolonged conversation, it happened
that they slid unawares into the familiar *thee* and *thou*. It
came so naturally, so entirely of itself, that though both
crimsoned, Yngve exclaimed with enthusiasm :

"Ah, let it be so; it is just as it ought to be. Are we not on the familiar *thee* and *thou* terms in our feelings, our views, our aspirations? Why then should we not be so in reality? It was not mere accident which made the little word escape our lips. It was necessity; it was truth.

"Be thou my good, my stern friend," continued he with emotion. "I have never possessed such a one, but I need it. My love, my endeavors are pure: but I do not find in myself the earnestness and the steadfastness which I wish for. I have been, to a certain degree, spoiled by prosperity, by too partial friends, by a mother who has been, perhaps, too tender and affectionate. I am too desirous of praise and easy success, too much afraid of offending or running against the prejudices of others, even for the sake of truth. I would become different, I would become a man such as you could highly esteem. Help me to be such, Hertha; always tell me the truth; never spare that which you regard as weak or as blameable in me; be always honest towards me, and thus you will become not merely my physician, but also my soul's friend and benefactor."

This pleased Hertha right well. She besought Yngve to perform the same kindness to her in return, and thus was formed a bond of friendship between them, the soul of which was to be an incessant endeavor after the highest purity and love of truth, together with the most unflinching candor.

This gave a new impulse and renewed life to their intercourse and their conversation. Hertha had long since been accustomed to a certain independent mode of speaking what she thought, without regard to its offending or exciting an antagonistic spirit in others. She had done it in bitter dissatisfaction with every-day life and people, and in the deep consciousness of her own superior power. But in Yngve Nordin she had met with a kindred soul, and if she in her expressions also treated him, as she did his sex, with a certain unsparing severity, it was because she maintained that men in general were spoiled by the weakness of women towards them, and by the laxity of public opinions which this gave rise to.

She maintained that they needed a strong purifying bath of truth, and this she, from time to time, gave to her friend in no sparing measure.

Yngve Nordin took it in good part—partly because in many respects he participated in her views, partly because he was a young man of more than ordinary nobility and excellence of character, and besides, it was very interesting to him to hear a young woman, taking her stand on pure womanliness, express herself freely on a number of subjects, which are commonly banished from the conversation between gentlemen and ladies. Besides which he heard and saw that, during her severe criticisms, she exhibited so great a love of truth and the highest excellence, and took so high a view of the destination of the human being as witness to the truth and servant of the Most High, that he felt himself, as it were, to grow in mental stature whilst listening to her. His contempt for the mean and the depraved increased, and his love for the elevated and the noble increased likewise. He often felt himself in a high degree animated by the ideal which beamed so beautifully in the soul of his stern, but noble friend, and sometimes, on the other hand, depressed, dissatisfied with, and mistrustful of himself. But never so as regarded her. He felt a deep conviction that she was a noble, large-minded woman. It, then, was not her fault, if he and others appeared to her eye, yearning as it did after perfection, to be weak, imperfect, "half human beings." And if it appeared so to her, it was right in her to say so, and it was good for him to know it.

Besides, Hertha was beautiful when she gave vent to her noble indignation against what appeared to her unworthy, either in men or in society. Her demeanor was always calm, but lightning flashed from her eyes. And however severe she might be as a judge, she was always gentle and excellent as nurse of the suffering young man, and tended his injuries with hands as skilful as they were singularly beautiful.

Yngve had, in the beginning, regarded her as a sort of moral phenomenon, which was very interesting to him as a study. But the power she exercised over his soul increased daily. He allowed himself to be, as it were, magnetised by her, and he would have suffered himself to have been taken captive by her, like a new Telemachus by a new Calypso, if her influence had not been of that kind which aroused, instead of lulling to sleep his spiritual power.

The subject of their first conversation on the occasion of their first meeting, was often resumed by the two friends, and canvassed in manifold variations, nor was Yngve always as gentle as he was then towards the weakness and frailties of her sex. Neither did Hertha attempt to defend these; still she passed a milder judgment upon them than on those of men.

" Women," she used to say, " are not yet all that they might be. Their full day is not yet come. Wait till then before you pass sentence upon them."

One day she spoke with much bitterness of the lenity with which public opinion regards the offences of men against the law of morality, in comparison with the severity with which it treats those of woman, especially if she be young, unprotected and poor,—branding her all the more if she be noble enough to bear the consequences of her false step.

Yngve perfectly agreed with her in this respect, but the subject appeared to be painful to him; he crimsoned, and turned his eye away from her. Hertha also crimsoned, and dropped the subject for the time, only to return to it on some future occasion with deeper earnestness. But this subject cast a shadow for the time over Yngve's image, which had begun to beam in her soul with unusual purity and beauty. She recalled to her mind the remark of the old lawyer, Judge Carlson, respecting him and his fickleness, on the first evening she saw him, and she thought to herself:

" After all, then, he is like the usual run of men. Even he is not blameless." This reflection grieved her, and she became more reserved and stern in her behavior towards him.

Many would have fancied that Hertha's behavior and conversation might have awoke dislike in Yngve, and made love impossible. Yes, certainly, that love which is pictured as driving in the cloud in the effeminate chariots of Venus or Freja. But there is a love of a higher character, which human beings venerate and pay homage to with justice—

> For he is a God ;
> He knows his own paths,
> And the paths which lead through the cloud.

Besides, persons of strong and independent character, like Hertha, might very easily offend fine folks, high-bred ladies and gentlemen (when they have not superior minds), and especially gentlemen of the corps diplomatique and all such as are more versed in drawing-room life than in life's most holy sanctuary ; but they exercise a powerful influence on all such characters as feel an impulse towards the morally pure and strong. When such as these meet with a soul free from human fear, loving to live in those regions where unveiled truths dwell in her sacred light, they are enchanted by it, even if it should appear under the form of a Eumenid.

The Eumenides were women, and a secret love was mingled with their chastising, scourging power.

Hertha was regarded by Yngve in this light, and he gave himself up with a sort of rapture to the sentiment of pure admiration with which she inspired him. She awoke within him, however, sentiments of another kind. Often when, with crushing invective, she gave vent to her indignation against something mean or unjust, Yngve fixed his eye upon her with a keen and penetrating expression, as if he would ask, "How is it that thou still so young hast become so bitter ?" It distressed him on her account, and awoke the desire in his heart to reconcile her with life.

Neither this glance nor this desire was unobserved by Hertha. How little need is there of words between souls which are in harmony with each other ! The magnetic spiritual currents pass through them with fulness of life. And occasion soon offered for Yngve to operate openly on Hertha's soul.

Hertha's views, both of the world and of life, were in reality very gloomy. She had only seen the darkest side, whether of life or of history. Human beings seemed to her, for the most part, either to be executioners or victims, and in both cases slaves. The former excited her hatred, the latter her compassion. Injustice and suffering, force and falsehood and darkness, seemed to her to have the world in dominion from century to century. The one age of humanity was in truth no better nor wiser than the other. Mankind discovered, indeed, new means and machines for their advantage or pleasure, or else to destroy one another in larger masses; but the individual man continues still the same, equally circumscribed, equally cruel, and equally weak, equally imperfect to-day as yesterday, and for thousands of years past. We have a presentiment of the perfection of God in our consciences; we fancy that we sometimes perceive a glimpse of his image in some great and good human being who wanders alone on the earth, for the most part misunderstood, most frequently slandered, and finally crucified by his age for the sake of his superior love. But the Great Invisible himself and his government are hidden from us, and are incomprehensible to us; they are dark mysteries, and human life on earth a dark, and to the greater number, a joyless riddle. We speak about a faith and a hope which we in reality do not possess. We wander in twilight, and know not whence we come, nor whither we shall go.

To these gloomy views, which often returned, and which exhibited the dark depths of Hertha's soul, Yngve opposed the light which he derived from theology and history, his favorite subjects, to which he had exclusively devoted himself when he had studied with the intention of becoming a minister of the Gospel. This career in life he had only abandoned from the necessity not only of providing for himself as soon as possible, but also for his tenderly-beloved mother. He selected therefore a path which would all the more rapidly conduct him to this object. Yet at the same time he did not neglect his favorite studies, but steadfastly pursued in them the development of the age and the human mind. A clear intellect and a heart open to the innermost of life enabled him to separate the gold from the dross, and in any case to possess himself of the pure ore.

He now endeavored to impart to his friend that which he himself had found and possessed, as the most precious treasure.

He endeavored to show her from the pages of history how God, in the beginning dimly perceived by the darkened conscience of man, yet entering into and brightening it by degrees, was partially comprehended at first in scattered rays, circumscribed forms, or by lightning flashes, which for the moment illumined, but often at the same time blinded the still weak, uncertain human glance; he endeavored to show her how He, spite of this, continually became more intelligible to the eye of the world, until he fully unveiled his divine countenance in the Son, and revealed in him that which he in eternity *is*, *works* and *wills*. Yngve endeavored to place human history before Hertha as a means of education with respect to self-knowledge and to God. He endeavored above all things to fix her eye upon that form in whom he has revealed to us his own being; for he maintained with the great historian, Johannes von Müller, that "from this point all the cardinal questions, whether of life or of history, may be answered; all enigmas solved, and the whole world itself, sunk in sin and sorrow as it is, be elevated and enlightened."

Yngve saw in Hertha, more than once, a full comprehension of the vision of light, which he called up before her. But it endured in her soul no longer than the lightning-flash through the night, over which the clouds again close with impenetrable darkness. She turned her sorrowful and questioning glance upon human life of yesterday and to-day. Must it remain thus, for ever?

And then Yngve showed her also, from historical data, that an augmenting flood of life and liberty is actually advancing over the earth from one century to another, extending itself still more and more. Sometimes checked—nay, even driven back for shorter intervals—it appears in the long run ever victorious, ever embracing new peoples and realms, or calling forth a higher developement in those already secured. Even as the Nile, as soon as it becomes fructified by a drop from heaven, perpetually increases and fructifies the plains of Egypt, so human life,—especially since the history of Christianity has become part of it,—has become an ever-advancing progress into light, liberty, and happiness.

"You say," continued Yngve, "that the human being of to-day is no better and no happier than his predecessor of eighteen centuries ago; that no human being is now holier than the Virgin Mary or the beloved disciple John. That may be, because the human being cannot attain to above a certain degree upon earth. But this degree may be high enough to make him worthy of the Kingdom of Heaven. And I, for my part, should be quite satisfied with a heaven peopled with beings whose life is truth and love. And from century to century, especially since the new birth-day of humanity, the number of such as attain to this degree increases; the circle of such enlarges, as we, the community of earth, obtain immunity as free citizens in heaven, and on earth obtain the privilege and the possibility of the highest human freedom and dignity. This is the explanation of God's government, and of human life on the earth. Temporal happiness or misfortune are exceptional moments. The important thing is, that the human being attains to God; every other good comes with that, sooner or later. Earthly prosperity and happiness grow as a consequence of spiritual freedom and self-government, and continually bear a proportion to them. Compare the whole popular life of the early Christian people with that of the present day; compare pagan China with the free communities of North America, and you will see it plainly; you will see that God makes known his being in humanity by means of a godly human life, and doctrine engrafted upon the tree of popular life. If our social life still exhibits so much imperfection and deficiency, it is without doubt because the conscience is still in bondage to the latter; because the Christian law of liberty is still only applicable to one-half of the members of society; because the mothers have not yet

11

become the guardians of the sacred fire upon its altar. We have yet much to do, but we shall do it. Because, God is with us.

"But the innumerable human masses, which never can enter the sphere of freedom! the millions who live like caterpillars, and who die without having seen the light of the spirit?" inquired Hertha.

"God Almighty lives!" said Yngve, with cheerful courage, "and we know that he is the supreme justice and love. That is sufficient. Such as he has revealed himself must he remain to be in all eternity, and so must he work for all things, under all circumstances, in all worlds. We know that he will that all men should attain to the knowledge of the truth, and that 'all things are possible to him.' They must all attain to it, sooner or later, on this earth, or in other worlds. The sooner or later in the calling of the individual, or of a people, to enter into the vineyard, is a subordinate thing. All must nevertheless come, all may choose and decide freely for themselves. That is the rule of God's ordination, evident already for us on earth."

"How happy you are, Yngve," said Hertha sometimes, "to have been able to learn and think so much, and to see things so clearly! One's heart and one's life may become very dark, merely through ignorance."

The conversion of the sceptic is often described as the work of a moment; as a miracle of divine grace, in which the human being's own endeavors and reason have nothing whatever to do. But we do not believe in this. The conversion of St. Paul may be reckoned as the exception to the general rule, which may be likened to the gradual but irregular breaking forth of the light from a cloudy sky. The doubt of the soul, and the gloomy facts of life and human nature are the clouds. We believe that the sun is behind them; we see it sometimes burst forth in a bright ray, but the clouds again collect and conceal it. We no longer have a glimpse of it, and the whole world is veiled in shadow. Yet, the wind blows, and the clouds disperse, or raise themselves aloft; the light beams forth again and again for the inquiring and heaven-turned eye, until at length it gains the victory, and clouds no longer obscure its heavenly image. " Out of darker into light, through the shadows!" is the usual course of the development of the higher life in the soul of man. The moment when the sun has fully arisen in the soul of the sceptic is nevertheless a wonderful one, and to him a miracle.

This we have lately seen in the confessions of one of the highest clergymen of Denmark, the richly-gifted Bishop Mynster. We have seen his bitter doubts, and his spiritual combat of many years, during which time he was the preacher of a Gospel in which he was not a believer, but the beauty of which often transported him; we have seen how the light which at once broke in upon his soul, and made him a believing and enraptured, happy Christian, came to him suddenly, in his solitude, whilst he was reading some passage in " Spinosa," " wholly unconnected with the thoughts which all at once arose in his soul, and made all light and certainty within him."

But all actual miracles are flowers which conceal their roots under the surface of the earth, and burst forth in deep con-nexion with the eternal laws of nature, although our dull human intellect cannot trace them out.

Hertha sought also, sought among the shadows of earth for a God, not merely for her own soul, her own happiness, but for all souls. For this reason, therefore, Yngve's mode of proving to her his existence, produced so powerful an effect upon her mind; and from the same cause, therefore, arose so many new questions, so many new enigmas to be solved. Hertha's earnest spirit, thirsting anew after the truth, would not be satisfied with the half, or the incomplete; would not be put off with any reasoning, the cogency of which she did not acknowledge. Her stern conscientiousness compelled Yngve still more deeply to reflect upon the doctrines which he preached, and her questionings and doubts gave him new problems to solve, and caused him to pass in their examina-tion, more than one sleepless night. That he himself was an honest inquirer, that he would not offer Hertha any solution of the problem of existence, of the soundness of which he himself was not fully convinced, and that he candidly acknowledged his ignorance, or his own doubts, where they occurred, were circumstances which raised him in Hertha's regard more than greater learning would have done. Hence it followed that she had the fullest confidence in his honesty, and she herself was invited to seek with her friend for elucidations of those difficulties which the developement of their minds gave birth to.

Hertha was one of those souls who must see in order to believe; she must see goodness in the being and the ways of God before she could put her trust in them. Until that was the case she could not love him, and he was not *all-sufficient* for her.

Yngve in the mean time saw, with heartfelt joy, the influence which he had obtained, and could obtain, over the soul of his friend. The noble young man's desire of doing good, and of enlightening, was added to the desire of the young philosopher to argue and prove; and when he saw that it would be months, probably, before he was sufficiently recovered to return to his profession, he proposed to himself to go through a course of history which should make apparent to his friend the good providence of God towards man, and which could alone reconcile her to the government of the world and to its governor.

Every time Hertha came, Yngve read to her portions of that work which was becoming of infinite value to himself, and to which she, in her turn, made objections or remarks. Frequently, also, she gladdened him by her cheerful approval. Then were they both very happy. To all her questions regarding the fate of the various nations and peoples of the earth, which seemed opposed to the just and loving providence which Yngve was endeavoring to establish, he had, finally, only one reply, and that was:

"God is love!" And the light which then beamed in his glance gave Hertha a presentiment that this answer really might overspread the whole field of dark questionings, and

the lofty image of Him who first made these words an ever-
lasting proverb on the earth, stood forth all the more exclusively and dominantly in her soul.

The human mind resembles the Swedish Island (Gottland,
the eye of the Baltic), which, according to an old legend,
alternately elevated itself above the surface of the sea, and
alternately sank below it, until its people carried fire upon the
island, after which it remained steadfastly above. So alternately
rises and sinks the uneasy island of the soul seeking for light,
until a fire is kindled in it, a fire which is called—love of God.

In the mean time spring advanced. The birches reddened
in the pasture fields ; their slender leaves put forth ; the star-
lings built their nests, and filled the air with their plaintive
whistling and trilling; the hawthorn bloomed in the meadows;
the lilacs were full of buds; bees murmured, and all the fruit-
trees in the garden were full of blossom. The abundant waters
of the little river danced down the wooded steeps of the
mountain district, where it had its birthplace, and down to the
ever greener meadows amid which lay the parsonage of Solberga. When Yngve was first able to support himself upon
his injured knee, he wandered, leaning on Hertha's arm,
beneath the blossoming trees of the garden, and through
copses of pine and birch, down to the banks of the river.
How extraordinarily weak, and yet how elate he often felt himself! He was impatient at knowing himself an invalid ; he
was enchanted by the touching beauty of nature—a minor-
key pervades the life of the spring in our north, even as pervades the northern folk's song,—he was conscious of a heartfelt gratitude to her upon whose faithful arm he was supported
so firmly and tenderly ; he was made happy by the assistance
she rendered him ; and Hertha——need I tell my lady-readers
that she was happy in rendering him this assistance ?

The first time that he was able to go somewhat farther, she
conducted him to the churchyard, which lay on higher ground,

at some little distance from the parsonage, and to Alma's grave. She had plaited it with white roses and mignonette, and had placed a seat opposite to it. Here, for the first time, Hertha spoke of her beloved sister, and for the first time Yngve felt what a depth of tenderness was concealed in her soul, and that the bitterness of her feelings had its root in the strength of her sympathy for the suffering of others. Yngve repaid her confidence by making her acquainted with his own family circumstances—his mother and her beautiful life. He described her as one of those souls so filled with the love of the Saviour that it became to her like a new nature and a perpetual inspiration, which caused her to speak and to act with a clearness and a straightforwardness which captivated or overcame, as by the power of some beautiful music. He told her of his happy childhood in this mother's home, with several brothers; how she taught him always to act according to his best convictions, and thus to be regardless of consequences. She used often to quote the words of an old hymn:

> Do right; do well in dying;
> And leave the rest to God!

This had early given rise in him to a cheerful and joyous disposition, and a certain freedom from anxiety as regarded the future. He described, also, this mother's person and manners,—described how handsome, how gentle and lovable she was; how unceasingly and quietly she labored for others; seeking to strengthen, to raise up, to comfort; and how the inward peace seemed to beam around her whole being, like the glory of a saint.

The two friends often returned to this place, and to this subject. Yngve sometimes read to Hertha the letters which he received from his mother, now closely occupied at the sick bed of her brother, Yngve's uncle. And the peculiar life and beauty which Yngve had so lovingly described, breathed forth from the letters. Hertha listened to these communications with the mingled feelings of pleasure and pain. Sometimes her eyes filled with sweet tears, as she contemplated this love, this sweet relationship between parent and child. Sometimes she felt a painful sting in her heart at the contemplation of a beauty, a peace from which she was so far apart; and the great admiration and love which Yngve expressed for the feminine type, as represented in his mother, at times gave rise to a sentiment akin to jealousy in her heart.

The proud mind also raised itself at times in opposition and self-defence.

"She has never experienced injustice and severe treatment," said Hertha, on one of these occasions; "she has always experienced love, and then it is an easy thing to be gentle and amiable!"

But she blushed at the tone and the spirit with which these words were uttered, and all the more so when Yngve's serious eye was riveted upon her, as if enquiring what it could be which had now wounded her. She endeavored to avoid it by asking still more of his mother and his family circumstances.

The mother still lived as a widow, in the house of her elder brother, and Yngve was not satisfied with her position there, although she never complained; he knew that she was not happy. He looked forward with longing to the time when he should be able to have a home of his own, and take his mother to live with him. He talked with childish delight of how he would arrange everything for her; how her room should be furnished, simply and elegantly at the same time, as he knew she liked things to be. Yngve was the eldest of his brothers, and the mother had given all that she possessed for the education of her sons, that it might be as complete as possible. She was compelled, therefore, herself to live on very circumscribed means. Yet she felt herself, and all her letters testified to this, rich in her sons and their future. Yngve also spoke of his brothers, whom he cordially loved. They were some years younger than himself, and were only just now able fully to provide for themselves, the one as tutor in a private family, the other as a naval officer.

"Good lads! excellent lads!" Yngve used to call them,

"yet nevertheless they had their faults;" which evidently had often caused their brother uneasiness. He talked about them sometimes in a fatherly kind of tone, which made Hertha one day laughingly ask him, "how much older he was than his brothers?"

This led to the discovery that Yngve and Hertha were nearly of the same age; Hertha only a few months the elder of the two. Yet it seemed to Hertha that she was very old in comparison with Yngve. He was in fact so young in soul. Life and hope in him were in full blossom. Often, indeed, would the youthful flow of his spirits carry him along into playful extravagance. Then he would joke and laugh at everything, and draw caricatures of the ladies and gentlemen of their acquaintance, nay, even of himself and Hertha, which made her smile in spite of herself; and however it might be, even she herself became younger, as it were, during her intercourse with Yngve. Her heart grew brighter, so also did the expression of her countenance. Many remarked that she began to be really good-looking, and it was only Mrs. Uggla who suspected a galloping consumption from the heightened and clearer color of Hertha's cheek.

THE NEW HOME.

Hertha's new home, Kullen, was about two miles from the parsonage. Between the two places lay the consumed portion of the town with its ruins and heaps of rubbish. But at Kullen as well as at Solberga, the garden was full of blossoming trees. A garden in which lilacs and fruit-trees are in full bloom, and around which softly murmur thousands of insects, where every kind of shrub and plant puts forth fresh leaves day by day, has always seemed to us like a poem which must some way or another call forth the poetical in every soul. Yes, for every soul possesses, after all, a spark of the Promethean fire, however crushed down it may be by the rubbish of egotism or every-day life. Truly poetical natures require but a very small portion of this glory of the spring to be powerfully excited. E. G. Geijer enjoyed the whole wealth of nature and of spring in a blossoming cherry-tree outside his window.

Old Mr. Falk, during his town and business life, had almost forgotten how a garden looked. Removed from his usual surroundings, and in a great measure debarred from his usual avocations, which the shattered condition of his health no longer permitted him to attend to, and also in consequence of this enfeebled state of health, rendered more susceptible than formerly to gentler influences, he found himself, as it were, astonished at the beauty which all at once surrounded him, and spoke to him of many subjects with which he had in his early youth been acquainted, but which had since then passed wholly out of sight.

The early summer was this year unusually beautiful. The Director walked in the garden, beneath blossom-laden trees;

he watched the work in the garden as it went forward, and presently began to take part in it; he was especially interested in attending to the trees. Martha and Maria were seized with a perfect passion for gardening; the former planted peas and beans, and laid out asparagus-beds; the latter, flowering-borders. Before long they might be seen working in common with their father, whose temper in the mean time became more cheerful and more amiable. To this contributed, in no small degree, the circumstance of his having, according to his promise, given up with full confidence, the entire domestic economy to Hertha's management. He allowed her a certain sum monthly for this purpose, but interfered no further in any of its concerns. Such an arrangement of domestic affairs cannot be sufficiently recommended, whether the well-being of the man, the woman, or the family itself be considered. The best of men become tiresome when they take upon themselves "Martha's cares and anxieties;" and we have known some clever statesmen who have become intolerable masters of the family because they busied themselves with the management of household details. Arago felt with justice that his veneration for the celebrated La Place was considerably decreased when he heard his wife ask him in an under voice, for "the key of the sugar-box." It stands to reason that we require from women that degree of skill and management which will enable the men to leave these cares in their hands, fully assured that they will be well attended to. On this subject, however, enough has been already preached and dogmatised. But even here, in every case must be allowed some rudimental state before the attainment of the highest degree. No good housekeeper ever became such at one bound. Only concede to a woman a good will, time, and opportunity, and be easy. In nine hundred cases out of a thousand, " she'll do it !"

Hertha was so desirous of rewarding her father's confidence, so solicitous to give him satisfaction, that she soon overcame her natural repugnance to, and even her want of experience in the business of household economy; and never before had the

Director been so satisfied with his meals, and so contented with the management of his family. Besides which, since he had left everything in his daughter's hands, he no longer enquired after every glass which was broken, or every sixpence that was expended, and this saved him many a petty vexation and annoyance by means of which he used formerly to embitter his own life and that of others.

By degrees also a little beauty began to be introduced into the house; and although the Director at first regarded these innovations with suspicion, he became reconciled when he observed that they did not cost him anything. Some of these were ornamental works made by the hands of his daughters; others also were purchased by a portion of the present which her father had given her, and which Hertha thus appropriated to the beautifying of his new home. There was, however, one especial room in the house with a window on the sunny side, and looking into the garden, which Hertha arrang- ed and adorned with peculiar affection! it opened out of her own chamber, and her sisters called it "Hertha's cabinet:" but Hertha had, in her own mind, given it another name.

The house was built of wood, spacious and well finished; and, all honor to stone houses, yet it has always seemed to us that wooden houses are more comfortable, as well as certain- ly warmer and more healthy. Something of the calm and the peace of the forest surrounds us in these the offspring of the forest. They generally assimilate also more to nature and life. Pretty porches project into the gardens or beneath green trees.

It was so at Kullen. The porch opened into the garden, overshadowed by tall trees, whilst trails of fragrant honey- suckle hung luxuriantly around its ornamental trellis-work. Here might be seen, during the long, light summer evening, the Director sitting smoking his pipe, and Aunt Nella near him, with her yarringles busily winding a ravelled skein, whilst she entertained herself and her brother-in-law with stories, to which he listened with more and more attention.

These two had passed their youth together, and it is even said that a mutual affection existed between them, in particular on her side, when her young and more wealthy half-sister returned home from the school at Stockholm, where she had finished her education, and at once gained possession of the heart which Aunt Nella had begun to regard as her own property. But she tenderly loved this sister; and with bitter pain, but without anger or complaint, silently drew back, so that nothing might interfere with her sister's happiness. This was the unknown, but beautiful, romantic episode in Aunt Nella's life; and to it belonged also the unceasingly faithful devotion with which she adhered to her sister, her brother-in-law, and their children. Of her brother-in-law she entertained a dread, mingled with love, which made her, indeed, often suffer under his power, but never blame him. She had been contented with living in his house, like a silent night-lamp, valued and called into requisition only in the hours of night and of darkness. She had seen her sister fade away amid the gloom of an inharmonious marriage, and had watched and wept over her, and sometimes silently thanked God that she herself had not been married; yet, nevertheless, she preserved a regard for her first and her only love, which made her, to a certain degree, blind to her brother-in-law's faults, which she called his " fixed ideas," and bound her to him and his children, as the serf is bound to the house of his lord. The constantly repelled flame of life had, in the mean time, in her own solitary room, kindled the powers of imagination and called forth certain " fixed ideas" in her own mind, which had neither foundation nor reality. In every other respect Aunt Nella was a perfectly honest and prudent person. She had an excellent memory, particularly as regarded the days and the acquaintance of her youth, and, like most elderly people, she was very fond of living those old times over again. As many of these belonged also to the youthful days of the Director himself, Aunt Nella's conversation and reminiscences had an unusual interest for him during the long summer evenings. He regularly longed for tea-time, seven o'clock in the evening, because now, instead of taking his tea, as formerly, alone in his room, he desired to be taken out into the porch, and sent to Aunt Nella, requesting her to let him have "a cup of tea-water." Aunt Nella was not slow in obeying his wishes. Her heart throbbed in her breast, as she, with her yarringles in her hand, hastened out to the porch and seated herself on the green bench, exactly opposite her brother-in-law, who commonly said:

"Well, Aunt, can you tell me about ——" such and such an occurrence, or person, who had figured in the days of their youth. And immediately the little old lady was ready to disentangle the threads of innumerable youthful memories, which, although, it is true, they were in a state of intricate perplexity, yet always, like the knots tied upon the Quipas of the Peruvian Indians, served as points of memory to indicate certain persons and periods. Now, the great lawsuit was the most important of these points, or, more correctly speaking, was a thread which mysteriously ran through them all, and when it became visible, the Director used to grow angry, and say:

"Now then, now then! Are we at that again? Leave all those absurdities, and let us stick to the reality!"

But the great lawsuit was to Aunt Nella the reality of realities, and she could not help it: the mysterious lawsuit, therefore, came up again and again; and when it, by degrees, was placed in new and peculiar points of view, and became mixed up with legal process, in which the Director himself was involved, he began by little and little to listen to the story with a certain degree of curiosity. There might possibly, after all, be something in it.

Aunt Nella felt herself, in the meantime, probably as a night-lamp would feel—if it ever feels at all—which was advanced from a corner in the nursery to the drawing-room, or as a naught—thus 0—which finds the figure 1 set before it.

She felt herself quite important, and remarkable, and happy, to be thus called out every evening and lighted for her dreaded, yet, in reality, always beloved, brother-in-law. She felt herself important to the whole family, and so she was in fact, when she could thus amuse the master of the family; and her histories became more and more animated, and the great lawsuit assumed greater significance and more remarkable form. Thus passed on the summer, and many things in the family had become brighter. Hertha was allowed to employ her time as she liked, and enjoyed this freedom. If her father only saw her at meal-times he was satisfied.

One subject, nevertheless, continued to cause her trouble. It was that her father took no steps for the accomplishment of his promise as regarded her becoming legally independent. She had twice ventured, with a beating heart, to remind him of his promise to her; but she was always put off with a stern reply, either, that she need not trouble herself about it, or by the enquiry, "why she was in such a hurry? If she wanted money she might ask him!"

The emotion and the good-will which had been excited by the events of the fire, and by Alma's death, seemed now to have died away again, and his selfish disposition was once more in the ascendant.

A young woman placed in circumstances such as those of Hertha is very helpless. The nobler, and the more delicate and sensitive are her feelings, the more difficult is her position. There are people who, without any desire to act unjustly, have yet an indescribable difficulty in giving out of their own hands either money or power. We do not condemn them; we know that selfishness and avarice, as well as levity and indolence, have their origin in natural organization, and that to a certain degree they are beyond the power of man.

"Dear D., what am I to do to get rid of this cursed avarice?" asked, more than once, the rich banker B. with a sigh, from his friend and principal bookkeeper. He wished, but he could not free himself from his hereditary sin. Many a human being here on earth advances no further than the wish to do right. It is good, nevertheless, for him to advance so far, and—"that which is impossible to man is possible to God." We therefore condemn the selfish man no more than any other sinner, but we sincerely wish that human life and happiness could become as much as possible wholly independent of either the feelings, the consent, or pleasure of individuals. Swedish women have still, in this respect, much to desire from the laws of their native land.

Hertha would have felt still more acutely her father's breach of faith towards her, had it not been very evident to her that his powers of mind were declining, and that, probably, in this might lie the grounds of his procrastination. She saw with uneasiness that his memory for later events was failing, and that it was difficult for him to understand money affairs. Yet, at the same time, he continued with inflexible obstinacy, the sole management of them, and would communicate with no one on the subject. "Tell me if you want money!" said he a few times, and seemed not to have any idea, or to be able to comprehend how insufficient this was for his daughter's peace or future prospects. She thought with great anxiety of these future prospects, both as regarded herself and her younger sisters, whose welfare she now felt it her duty to guard with motherly care. She looked around her for a helper in need, but the more she looked the more she perceived how infinitely solitary she was; without relation or friend who could give her advice. Circumstances called upon her to be the support of the house and the family, but denied her that which alone could have given her power as such. Neither her freedom nor her property was in her own power, and her whole soul was repugnant to applying to a stranger for counsel, or appealing to the Swedish Court of Justice to compel her own father to give her that freedom which he refused to her. Besides this, she knew the feeling of Courts of justice with regard to the lately agitated question of allowing an unmarried woman to become legally independent at a given age, and this had shaken her faith in their justice.

It was during these distressing circumstances that her soul aroused itself and found peace in its own pure desires, and in the conviction that the governing power of the world was more just than human laws and judgments. The Gospel which

Yngve had revealed to her, began to diffuse its light through her soul. She often thought of the words, "Righteous Father, the world has not known Thee,"—and appealed from her earthly to her Heavenly Father, now her only hope, and continued quietly to fulfil her every-day duties, attentively watching the while for any favorable turn which circumstances might take, in the hope that the moment would come when she could take a decisive step to secure herself and her future.

She began during this time to exercise a more and more beneficial effect upon the education of her young sisters. She endeavored to accustom them to a settled course of daily work, and showed them the ultimate object of this as beyond our earthly life. They must serve God and His kingdom in so doing; that was the principal thing; whether in wealth or in poverty was secondary. The object of life was, in every case, grand and rich in results. She talked with them, moreover, of the Saviour.

Thus talked Hertha; but like the good man, whose spiritual conflict we have lately mentioned, often fascinated by the lofty doctrine which she promulgated, she yet withdrew many a time to her own chamber to shed the bitter tears of doubt and suffering. It often appeared to her as if she consecrated the lamb for sacrifice; and she wept over her sisters, over all the young souls which would be born, live, and slowly die in this hard unrighteous world. Afterwards, she dried her tears and went from her own room, grave, but calm, ready to work, to sustain, to comfort. She concealed the tomb in her own heart, and let the flowers above it send forth their fragrance for others. A certain, singular, lofty, and touching beauty developed itself the while, in her glance, voice, and whole being, together with an increasing power over the souls of others, which she felt, not without pleasure. Her young sisters, in particular, attached themselves to her with an enthusiastic devotion. Her glance, her words, seemed to operate upon them, almost with a magical power.

It was about this time, when Providence brought her

A NEW ACQUAINTANCE.

A FRIEND of mine, a witty lady, said, on one occasion, that she did not compute her life by ordinary years, but by the acquaintances, who became important to the life of her soul. Such a new acquaintance was to her a new-life's year. This mode of computing life's years is to my taste, and I have good reason to adopt it. Did not my youth, properly so-called, commence through a new acquaintance, when the years which are commonly called the youthful, lay a long way behind me !——

Hertha had said the same. " My youth is passed ; is passed forever!" she had exclaimed, but the acquaintance of Yngve Nordin had caused her to feel that she never before that time had known the true youthful-life of the soul, and day by day only increased this consciousness. One day when she, as usual, accompanied by the pastor's wife, visited her patient, they found with him Judge Carlson, whom we have already mentioned as a "noble old man." His white hair ; the unmistakeable expression of earnestness and honesty in the frank, cheerful countenance, which seemed almost without shadows, impressed the beholder favorably at the first moment, and few were they who, on a nearer acquaintance, were not charmed by his gentle humanity, at the same time that they felt a reverence for his integrity and love of truth. Truth was his only passion, and he sate at her feet like a disciple, listening and learning. For this reason he never hesitated to abandon an opinion which he discovered to be faulty, or openly to acknowledge that he did so. People, however, who were afraid of petty consequences, and who loved rather the little, every-day *I* than truth herself, imputed this to him as weakness and vacillation.

12

He had, as well as Yngve, been elected a member of the committee—nay the family, who were to prepare a plan for new dwellings for the working-classes, to be erected in place of those which were burnt down.

They now laid before Hertha and Mrs. Dahl their ground-plans and elevations, and called upon them to become fellow-workers in this family.

"I take it for granted," said Judge Carlson, "that mistresses of families, in Swedish towns, have never been consulted with regard to the construction of the house. I cannot otherwise account for the want of convenience which prevails in the arrangement of dwelling-houses, in particular in the kitchens and domestic offices. In our country, too, where the years may be counted by the winters, how important it is that particular attention should be paid to the comfort and convenience of those within the house, the greater portion of whose life is occupied by the daily business of the necessities of life. On the principal floors, it is true, care is taken to have the drawing and dining-rooms convenient, but the other rooms, those appropriated to the domestics in particular, are placed just how and where they can be; and in smaller houses the mistress of the family has often to look for the kitchen across a court, a lobby, or even on another story. We must have this different; we must contrive some way of having comfort and convenience for the inhabitants within the house; and we must now begin in our own town—you must help us in this!"

These last words were addressed to the two ladies now present.

This proposal chimed in with the subject which was always present in Hertha's soul, and the life, as it were, of her life.

"Thank you," she said, smiling, "that you will permit ladies to give an opinion on a subject which nearly concerns their comfort,—their well-being, it may be said."

There was no bitterness in Hertha's expression, although in the words—she could not help it—there was a secret reproach. The lawyer perceived it, and accepted the challenge in a chivalric manner.

"There is probably no one," replied he mildly, "who would more earnestly wish than I should that ladies were consulted, and their opinions listened to with regard to most of the questions of life. Their natural tact and intuitive perception would make them the best of councillors, especially if they were educated fully to comprehend the subjects which would be likely to come under discussion."

"Which are these subjects?" asked Hertha.

But now a great difference was discovered in the views entertained by Judge Carlson and Hertha. The old lawyer conceded to woman the very highest influence, an influence indeed which would operate upon the whole race, through her action upon domestic life and morals; he would desire to see her developed to her utmost power and extent, for the benefit of home, husband, children, parents, brothers and sisters, and through the domestic circle, for society at large ; but he would not desire to see her education directed to any sphere of action beyond domestic life and its immediate world. He would have public seminaries for her, but only with the intention of developing her for that sphere "which nature evidently and nature's lord, created her for."

They were the views of the old school which he propounded, although with some modifications in a liberal direction, and with an exception in favor of unusually gifted ladies.

Hertha could not be silent; could not listen to a noble-minded man expressing, according to her views, opinions so utterly imperfect, without her spirit raising itself like a northern Amazon on her war-horse to the sound of the war-clarion.

"Can any human judge," said she gravely and without temper, "pronounce judgment on this subject? Has he sate in council with God, and heard the Creator say to woman, 'Thus far shalt thou go and no farther!' Is it not to encroach upon the office of the Supreme Judge, and to circumscribe his kingdom, when human judges will bind with their statutes a being whom He has created in His image; when they inclose her in a small, narrow circle, and say, 'Within this shalt thou breathe think, behold, but not beyond it. It is the will of God!' Oh no, God has not willed it," continued Hertha, whilst a calm but inward fire by degrees kindled her whole being, "God has not willed it to be so. Ask all mankind and light-seeking souls of my sex what the Creator speaks to them within their own consciences, and you will hear something very different. May I speak?"

"Yes, speak!" replied the lawyer, astonished at the young girl's words and expression, at the same time that he was extremely curious to know what she would say: "speak; I will listen and learn!" added he cordially, when she hesitated a moment to express herself.

Hertha resumed: "Thus He speaks to me, and to every soul which seeks for freedom and light: 'Thou art my child; and all that is mine is thine, thy just inheritance and thy share; whether it be liberty, knowledge, art, power, happiness, or whatever else which I have created in the world, and which I gave to thee and thy brother to rule over and have dominion in. Thou art my youngest child, and my last witness among the created beings of the earth. In thy heart have I written my law of love. Go, possess thy portion in my kingdom, in order that thou mayest in all parts of it testify of me, and help thy brother to extend it over the earth.'

"Thus speaks the Father, every day to his daughter. But what does the brother say to the sister? Does he not say, 'I am the first-born. The greater portion of the inheritance belongs to me. Thou must be contented with such portion as I shall leave thee; because I am the strong one, and power and honor and glory are mine. Seek for labor, for light, and for joy in the sphere which I shall point out to thee, and then thou shalt have my support and my favor. But take care not to intrude upon my share, otherwise it will not be well for thee; and thou wilt be going out of thy proper vocation, which is to—amuse and to serve me!'"

Hertha paused; the lawyer said,

"Well, I still recognise the justice of the brother's speech, although it is now, in various countries, becoming considerably softened, more reasonable, more manly, but—let us hear what the sister replies."

"'Yes;' she replies," continued Hertha. "'Brother, God created us both in his image, made us both rulers over the earth, and gave us each other for helpers, that we might together glorify Him on the earth. He did not make thee for my master, and when thou becamest such, the order of the world was destroyed, and Paradise closed against us. We were born as equals on the first morning when everything was yet good; as equals, he has again given us birth on that second day of Creation when the spiritual man is born upon the earth, and has placed us again side by side, as two pilgrims seeking for Eden, and only hand in hand can we again find it. Thou dost not know, I do not know as yet what powers he gives to thee or me;—but give me my paternal inheritance of liberty, my portion of the kingdom of life, and of all which God has given us, and all which is mine will become thine and thy lot, even as mine will be twofold.'"

Again Hertha paused. The lawyer said:

"The sister does not speak amiss *in abstracto*; but now let us come to the practical application of her speech. What would it be, for example, at the present day? What would she ask of her brother?"

"The possibility of an education and independent action such as he enjoys," replied Hertha with earnestness and warmth. "Open to her schools and colleges, which would give her an opportunity of knowing herself and her inborn powers; and afterwards open to her the paths in which she might freely exercise them; otherwise they become both to herself and society a dead and buried talent. Remove all the old barriers and limitations, cast aside cowardly fear; have instead, a large-minded confidence in God, that He can guide and preserve his work. Let the sister as well as the brother ask herself, 'In what way can I serve God and his kingdom on earth?' And let them reply by the free development in his service of the gift, the talent which He has given. Thus together seeking for the Supreme Good, will they not find each other and be inwardly united, as is now very seldom the case? Brother, sister, child of God! Those words ought to become truth on the earth, but they can only become so when the freedom both of brother and sister introduces the fulness and the perfection of both. Do not say, therefore, that is the man's portion and that is the woman's portion, but say, rather, man and woman are two portions of the same humanity, called to serve God, the one as man, the other as woman, according to the gift and the power which He has given."

Hertha was silent; but she had spoken with that enthusiasm which is the result of strong conviction, and which never fails to produce a deep impression upon the hearers. Judge Carlson had attentively listened to her and contemplated her while she spoke, animated by a noble and heartfelt inspiration. When she ceased speaking, he, too, remained silent for a moment, and then said:

"You are the best advocate on this subject which I have ever met with, and I confess that you have placed the subject before me in a new point of view, and it is possible that the one which has hitherto been mine, may be altogether too narrow. In the mean time, however, let us look at the subject a little closer, and I will give you a few cases to consider. You have only as yet placed before us the bright side of the results of emancipation. Let us for a moment contemplate the other side."

The lawyer now advanced many strong instances of this dark side, several of which were drawn from real life, in various countries, and gave various absurd descriptions of emancipated women, all of which have been too often produced, and are too well known, for there to be any necessity of our repeating them here. To this Hertha replied:—

"Have faith in the divine: give it fair play and it will conquer; awaken it, and let God be the guide. The absurdities you have mentioned have been produced from pure contradiction; in the same way that monsters among flowers are produced from deficiency of air and light; they are the offspring of an endeavor which has not found its proper vent. They prove the existence of a life, a longing which deserved a better guidance. Give this, by means of justice and love; awaken the higher consciousness; let the feminine ideal, or rather the human ideal which woman represents, be it what it may, in domestic or civil life, in science, art, mechanics, or in the highest, the religious life, stand clearly forth before the eye of woman in their glowing years, and they will learn to love it; allow them liberty to form themselves according to this type, and beauty will then drive away the ridiculous. The educational abortions of which you speak will vanish as ignes-fatui at sunrise."

The conversation was long continued in this strain, and Hertha, who was all the more inspired, as well by the influence of the subject itself as by the enjoyment of an intellectual combat with an opponent of superior knowledge, noble, far-seeing, and her own equal in love of truth, developed more and more her own inward wealth of larger views, and feeling for the general, although her insight into the particular might not yet be fully clear.

Yngve, at the beginning of the contest, had not, without fear and some uneasiness, heard her keen expression of opinion, but the further she went, the calmer, the more joyous, the prouder he became of his friend, and observed with delight the impression which her words and her manner produced upon the old lawyer. He had begun by supporting Hertha, but afterwards amused himself by jocular remarks, now in favor of the arguments of one side, and now of the other.

The pastor's wife, who probably considered the discussion to be one of those " which did not concern her," went in and out in the mean time, busied in covering a table in the room with a delicious entertainment of the fruits of the season. Hertha now rose to assist her in these good offices. Excited by the conversation, and the part she had taken in it, she perhaps never looked so dignified, and at the same time so gentle and charming, as now when she presented to the gentle·

men the beautiful fruits from the parsonage garden. Yngve watched her, but he said nothing, whilst he listened to the lawyer's admiration of her whom hitherto he had only known by report. Hertha saw approving and loving looks riveted upon her, and she felt herself wonderfully happy.

Who is there, to whom God has given a spark of the eternal fire which they have felt long penned up, burning amid ashes in the depth of the heart, and all at once, owing to some circumstance, or conversation (for a word may be a circumstance), the air reaches it, the light is admitted to it, and it lights up treasures not hitherto known of, and becomes conscious of its own riches?—such will perfectly understand Hertha's feelings at this moment.

They may be easily understood by men of genius and intellect, but scarcely at all by women of the present day, so rare is it for their mental gifts to be made known in an atmosphere worthy of them.. Wherever they exist, they are early enlisted in the service of vanity and drawing-room life, and should they not avail for these purposes—they are either crushed into a bureau-drawer or back again into the soul, even though it should be choked with them.

When Judge Carlson rose up to go, he took Hertha's hand with an expression of heartfelt esteem, and said:

"We have met to-day as combatants, but will you promise me one thing?—If ever you should need a fatherly friend, and think that I could be of service to you, promise that you will call upon me?——"

Hertha pressed his hand between both hers, looked into his clear, benevolent eyes, and said:

"Will you sometimes allow me to talk with you? It will strengthen my faith in justice and the progress of good."

"The progress of good!" exclaimed the old man with the fervor of youth; "that is granted, that is inevitable as the providence of God. We ought not, especially at this time, to doubt of the progress of any emancipation, any truth which is dear to us. We require only patience and—courageous and warm hearts such as—thine, young girl!" And with fatherly tenderness he clasped Hertha to his breast, and impressed a kiss upon her pure brow, as he added: "God give thee light;—enlighten thy sisters!" He then kissed her hand, bowed deeply, and went out.

Hertha, captivated by a feeling, a delicious consciousness, altogether new to her, had allowed her head to rest for a moment on the old man's breast, after which she stood silent, sunk in thought. Yngve looked on the while, not without a certain feeling of jealousy; but when Hertha turned to him beaming with an inward roseate dawn, he could not resist saying:

"How handsome you are, Hertha!"

"Alma also used to say so sometimes," replied Hertha, whilst an expression of melancholy overcast her beaming countenance, "and I confess that I know I can be good-looking to those whom I like, or when I am happy, but sometimes, and with those whom I do not like, I can be excessively ugly."

"I can very well believe that," said Yngve smiling, "although I have never seen it. To me you have always seemed handsome, Hertha. You understand very well that I am not talking about mere external beauty; you know very well that you are not what people commonly call handsome, but I am talking of expression—of the whole being. Just now, when you offered us the fruit, you seemed to me a real Iduna. And my Iduna you are, and will continue to be, my sorrow and wound-healing goddess!"

"But who has very nearly forgotten her patient this evening!" said Hertha, gaily, as she seated herself at a table to prepare the white bandages with which Yngve's knee still required to be bound. The setting sun, which threw its rays into the room, through the quivering leaves of trees, cast a golden lustre over Hertha's hair and hands. Yngve had never before been so conscious of their beauty, and he expressed what he felt. Hertha then looked at him with a grave and almost reproachful glance, as she said:

"Don't talk in that way, Yngve!"

"Why not?" replied he, "if I say only what is true and what I think. May I not say what I think? And you—are you now really candid, Hertha? Can it actually displease you that I think you lovely, and that I say so?"

"No; on the contrary, it pleases me; but this it is which displeases me and—humiliates me; that having hitherto found our pleasure in the holy and the highest, the spiritually pure, we should now sink down into the common and the petty."

"You are too severe, my friend. An innocent joy in the physical beauty of others or of ourselves, if we possess any, is certainly just and even beneficial. God has given us the sense of beauty, and created the beautiful as an expression of His glory. It is also a portal through which we get a glimpse into His heaven."

"Perhaps you are right," continued Hertha, "and yet I abide by what I have just asked. Perhaps it is because I am afraid of my own weakness. I am afraid of becoming covetous of admiration in the usual common way, and that—I will not be. Life, it appears to me, is too earnest and too great for such small endeavors and small pleasures. And if you are my friend, you will not make a compact with them against me, but will help me to despise them. Am I now candid enough, Yngve?"

"You are a—magnificent girl, and I will do all that you wish. That is to say, that I will in certain cases not say what I think. Because it cannot be forbidden to me to think and to like. But you have an easy method in your own hands of preventing me from thinking and talking as I have just done. Let me see your ugliest countenance."

"I don't know whether I can show it you, but I will try. Now I will see in you domination and injustice, as large as life!" And Hertha assumed an expression of defiance and menace. After that she laughed and said, "Now, was I ugly and repulsive enough?"

"Yes and no," replied Yngve. "You were not agreeable; but—I felt as if I would make a compact with you against

that which you might be thus looking upon, and do battle **with it** to the death—even if it were—I myself!"

"Could you? Oh, Yngve, that I shall not forget!" said Hertha, "because now I understand how good you are; and I know that you perfectly understand me!"

Tears filled her eyes; but she hastily dried them as she said:

"But we have now been like a couple of children; and yet we have been so lately discussing such grave subjects. Will you not, before the sun sets, take your evening walk? Let us see the sunset from Alma's grave; and as we go along tell me something about the beautiful old man whose acquaintance I have just made, and whom I like already. I felt my heart expand whilst he was with us. That is a glorious feeling."

The two were soon on their way to the quiet grave, talking the while on subjects which made the heart expand, because they talked of the life and activity of a good man and fellow-citizen.

The churchyard lay on high ground, and, from Alm grave, the view was beautiful across the Klar river, the meadows and farms on its banks, and the wooded region beyond.

Yngve seemed this evening more fatigued with his walk than usual. When Hertha sat down on the green-painted bench by the grave, Yngve also seated himself as usual upon a grave-mound close by, in order conveniently to stretch out his suffering knee. The sun went down in glory above the mirror-bright water; the evening breeze blew softly, but refreshingly, over the resting-place of the departed; the fragrance of the mignonette was wafted pleasantly from the grave. Yngve quietly leaned his head against the knee of his friend. Thus they sate and contemplated the beautiful spectacle before them until its splendor had paled. Neither of them spoke; but to judge from the expression of their glances, Yngve seemed to give himself up with thorough enjoyment to the fulness of the moment by the side of his noble friend, whilst her soul released itself from the life of the present moment to take in a remote prospect, which seemed to present itself more and more clearly to her inward eye, and which caused the fire of her heart to burn higher, and her eyes to beam with a still more beautiful light.

Yngve observed it, but would not disturb her inward contemplation, her soul's inspiration, by any question of his own. He respected her silence, as in the ancient time the silence of the priestess was respected to whom the Divinity spoke.

From this time the eye of Hertha's soul really obtained a clearer vision; her heart a new hope. She often found at the parsonage with Yngve her new friend and acquaintance; and the conversation which was carried on between them, and in which the good pastor sometimes took part, according to his peculiar humor, became, through her leading questions and influence, all the more rich and illustrative.

Frequently when she walked homeward from these conversations, it seemed to her as if her body had wings, and as if she breathed with fresh lungs. Her thoughts developed and arranged themselves in a manner which gave her indescribable pleasure, and which astonished herself. Discords dissolved away before the eternal harmony that broke in upon them.

As she passed through the desolate ruins of the town she felt as if she must break forth into singing.

When she, after such conversation, re-entered her home, new life and the refreshment of new life seemed to enter with her, and there was nothing which did not arrange itself and become brighter under the influence of her enlightening, invigorating, and cheerful disposition.

But we have occupied ourselves long enough with "Hertha's part;" we must also look a little after the others who have a part in our history, as leaves and buds in the life of a plant. As on a fine day one goes out to make visits to one's friends and acquaintances, to ask how they all are, and have a few moments' friendly chat with them about health and sickness, about marriages and deaths, about this and that in the circle in which we live, so will we now go out and make among our old acquaintance in Kungsköping a few—

SHORT VISITS.

No. 1.

PROFESSOR METHODIUS sits at his writing-table surrounded by books and spots of ink, hard at work to weld together by the necessity and power of axioms the links in the chain of the world's thoughts and transactions. In this manner, and "beginning at the beginning," he will axiomatically and incontrovertibly make it apparent how and by what means the whole human race may be improved and rendered happier. "Everything," says the professor, "depends upon the perfection of the system, and on the most accurate adherence to the method, and on not passing over one single item." But the professor had not yet got his system into a proper working state, the screw did not yet rightly hold, nor the cranks move, as he was accustomed to say, but, nevertheless, he sees the moment approaching nearer and nearer, and now, as a beginning, the first sheet of "The History of the Creation of the Earth and of the Human-race, together with their Development, ancient, present, and future," is going to press. With secret pride and authorly joy the Professor writes and re-writes, endeavoring to concoct in the best and most comprehensive manner the grand title of his work—

"The History of the Creation, and Development of the Earth and the Human-race, past, present, and to come."

On the other side of the room sits Mimmi Svanberg, and writes—

"MY DEAR GUSTAF:

"It is a fact that I am the best sister in the world, because I have just now said No to five invitations, and neglected at least twenty-seven commissions for no other reason than to sit down, according to your gracious commands, and amuse you with the gossip of our good town, which you contemptuously and high-treasonably call, instead of Kungsköping, 'Tattle-köping.' But that is too bad of you.

"First, you wish to know 'how papa and I find ourselves.' Thanks for the inquiry. Papa is just now sending to press the first sheet of his great work, the long title of which I can never remember. He—that is to say the author—is happy over this first sheet, and, as usual, good and gentle as an angel. I have a whole swarm of crotchets in my brain, and, among the rest, have to discover how I am to get a dress for Aunt Marianne, neither too coarse nor yet too fine; neither too homely nor yet too grand; neither too old nor yet too young; neither too grave nor yet too gay; neither too cool nor yet too hot; neither checked nor striped, and not too dear; and not too,—I don't know what, but becoming and just what it ought to be. That is easy and amusing, don't you think so? But adieu now to crotchets, and let me have a chat with you about all your 'inclinations and aversions' in Kungsköping. First, of the Corsair of Kungsköping, as you styled the Honorable Mrs. Tupplander, because it is probable that I shall shortly come into feud with her, however unwilling I myself may be to do so. But I cannot calmly see poor Amelia Hård trodden under-foot and ill-used for a by-gone error, which she is endeavoring to retrieve with all her power, and which she is better able to do than most in her circumstances. And if you were here I know I should have a champion in the fight, of which I will now say no more. Mrs. Tupplander has been for some time in a great state of vigilance, going in and going out of houses, large and small, and her reticule is ready to burst, so cram-full is it of all the news she gathers up, whether well-founded or otherwise, and I expect that something uncommon will proceed out of it, at all events a little piratical plunder.

"And now for your 'inclinations,' about which all sorts of

reports are abroad, and which it will require your whole strength of mind to bear properly.

"First, your 'great inclination,' Hertha. She seems strongly inclined to a young man, whose doctor and support she has been ever since the great fire, and it is asserted that these two will some time become one, which I heartily wish may be the case, for they are a handsome and noble couple. If old Falk will only not say No, because he is a young man without property. In the mean time Hertha is become very much better-looking and much happier than she ever was before, and—it is a good thing that you are away on your own concerns in Stockholm.

" Your 'little inclination,' Alina Dufva. Dear brother, take care of yourself; there is an eagle which is hovering over that little dove, and looks as if he wished to carry her off to his nest. And it seems as if Mrs. Uggla would soon not have more than four Miss Dufvas to sorrow for and sigh over.

" Your 'old inclination,' Ingeborg Uggla—I prepare you, my brother, for the fact, that she, perhaps, may not wait till you come and bow before her. Our estimable Dr. Hadermann may, perhaps, stand in your way. I fancy that he is likely to do so. The other day at a party where we were both of us tolerably dull, he seated himself just opposite to me, and began in this strain—

" ' Is not Ingeborg Uggla very much changed of late ?'

" ' How do you mean, doctor ?'

" ' Well, she is now so kind and active for others ; does not sit always prick, pricking over her needlework, sewing at her dress or her finery, as she used to be always doing—she dresses herself simply, and is not always going out as former-ly ; she is not always at parties, is not party-sick, as I call it, but is beginning to be quiet, frugal, and comfortable.'

" ' Do you know,' said I, ' that if many girls are party-sick, it is because their homes are dull and joyless ? and that I think is the case with Ingeborg. The mother is ' pleasure-sick,' and 'marriage-sick,' on her daughter's behalf, and makes her life wretched. But if Ingeborg employed herself a good deal for her toilet, and made up her finery for herself, it was to save her money for other purposes, because she does a good deal of good silently, and has always done so, as long as I have known her.'

" 'Is it possible?' said the doctor, who seemed both astonished and affected. 'I thought,' continued he, 'that she was one of those fine ladies who turned up their noses at poor folks, and at simple creditable folks.'

" 'Then you deceive yourself,' said I; 'Ingeborg is really a fine lady, but she is at the same time a noble-minded creature; she has a warm heart for the suffering, and values nothing so highly as a person of real worth, as for instance—yourself!'

" 'Me!' said the doctor, and became quite crimson; 'it is not possible!'

" I laughed and said, 'Ask her, and then you will hear!' I then related to him several beautiful traits which I knew about Ingeborg. Our good doctor listened attentively and looked quite tender-hearted, but merely said: ' How much one may be mistaken!'

" And now I fancy that these two people, who hitherto out of pure dread have not ventured to approach each other, will come to—understand each other better. You understand me. Ingeborg has, I know, long cherished a sentiment for Dr. Hedermann, which she thought was unparticipated by him, and that made her timid and shy in his presence. I hope that you can bear this discovery with strength of mind. But, my poor brother, what will you say when I now proceed to tell you about your 'fat inclination.' Set a bottle of water by your side, before you read what follows.

" As you know, I like to mix in all our six or seven social circles and coteries of the town, and therefore I was a short time ago at one of the third or fourth rank subscription-balls, which you are very well acquainted with. Alderman-cheesemonger Jönsson's wife and daughters, Adelgunda and Concordia, were there,—all three as fair, fat, and good-tempered as could be wished for, in the race, who you know make much account of being in good condition. I determined, as usual,

tc have a little conversation with Mrs. Jönsson, who amuses
me greatly, and accordingly seated myself beside her during
the dancing and said—

"'They really are very capital these balls, and the price is
so reasonable.'

"'I don't exactly think so,' said Mrs. Jönsson bluntly,
'every ball costs twelve skillings, and in the course of the
evening there are hardly more than four dances, that is three
skillings a dance. That is dear enough, I think. And how
people tear about in the waltz; enough to work all the flesh
off their bones! I am sure that Adelgunda will be quite thin
with all that tearing about.'

" When the waltz was over, Mrs. Jönsson called Adelgunda
to her and they both went into the inner room. I accompanied them, being a little curious, and saw the tender mother
take a large sausage sandwich out of her bag, which Adelgunda must eat standing.

"'You wish,' said I to Mrs. Jonsson, 'to counteract the
effect of the violent exertion of the waltz.'

"'Yes, that is just it,' said she seriously; 'it is not, you
may believe me, so easy to get up again the flesh which people dance off their bones; and especially when they are betrothed,—girls always get thin then.'

"'Betrothed!' exclaimed I. 'Is Adelgunda betrothed?'

"'Yes, believe me, that she is. Did not Mamsell know?
Yes, she is just betrothed to Lieutenant Krongranat. So
now she will have a little title of her own; ay, ay, I thank
you!'

"I was surprised, and offered my congratulations, and looked at Adelgunda, who stood there eating her sausage sandwich, and looked calm, and fat, and fair, and actually quite
splendid.

"'Well, that is excellent,' said I; 'but where then is the
bridegroom?'

"'He is now gone to Stockholm, to buy a few things,' replied Mrs. Jönsson, with a glance full of meaning, half at me
and half at Adelgunda.

13

"' Yes, yes, I understand,' said I; 'I should not wonder if Mamsell Adelgunda grew a little thinner; it must make her a little uneasy to know that her bridegroom is such a long way off as Stockholm.'

"' Oh, there's no danger,' said Adelgunda, with imperturbable calmness.

"' Think if he should not come back!'

"' Oh, there's no danger; he'll come back again safe enough,' said Adelgunda.

"' And when is the wedding to be, if I may ask?'

"' At Martlemass,' replied Mrs. Jönsson; 'I think my geese will be fattened by that time. We shall have a large wedding, because all the relations must be invited, and I don't believe I shall be able to sit with my hands crossed till it's over. And no help can I have from Adelgunda, for I will not let her be fagging about and running the flesh off her bones. No, I would rather be worried to death myself; that is the lot of mothers and the way of the world.'

" You see now, my brother, ' the way of the world,' as far as your inclinations in Kungsköping are concerned, and I can see from this distance what an effect it produces on you; I see how you go to the stove and light—your cigar, and sit down on the sofa to smoke it.

" For punishment thereof you shall now hear a little about our society's affairs, our family-union. It succeeds better than you, Mrs. Uggla, and Co. predicted; nay, indeed, so well that it is a pleasure to behold, and these new family-connexions seem expressly calculated to make people pleasantly acquainted with one another, and to lead to alliances of friendship, and even to some of a warmer kind, as I have just related. And then the visits to the houses of the poor, and the sympathy excited for their circumstances; I tell you, brother, all this produces more good than you can believe; nay, the simple fact of a poor mother or father being able to pour out their troubles, to speak of their prospects and wishes for their children, it is like admitting fresh air into the breasts and the dwellings of those who sit in darkness. Industry, comfort, and hope increase under the friendly countenance of those who are better off in life. And one can sympathise and help in many ways without giving money. The Countess P. is unceasingly active and kind. It is a delight to accompany her on her visits to her district. The Count also is excellent both in word and deed. Our good pastor's wife busies herself about the children and the infant-school without intermission, (she is especially the mother of the motherless,) and labors to obtain for the school a better situation than it now rejoices in. A number of poor mothers come daily to beg that their children may be there taken charge of during the day, that they may be at liberty to go out and work for them. I have been to-day with the pastor's wife to visit the school-room into which the children were received after the great fire. There was a terrific crowd, but all was neat and orderly. A couple of loquacious children related to us the fate of the school after the fire in the following manner :

"'Just when the mistress had ended the morning prayer; that was on Monday, wasn't it?—Ay, it was; for you see, Thursday was the fire, and on Friday everybody's heads were turned, and Saturday was a holiday; so first on Monday the children came here again, then the gentleman came in—he that manages for the house. And he said, the mistress and we all must get ready to pack off that very moment, because the building must begin in a jiffey, spite of burnt-out folks. And then there was a pretty halloo-baloo, as you may believe; and we got ready to start. But just as we were going, the lady talked to the works-director right well, and said it wasn't a bit better than if we'd been burnt out of house and home altogether. And then the director was so good as to pack us all in here altogether, and in that way we are again a school, you see. But you see the worst of all is, that they are such noisy folks that live in the other room, they are burnt-out folks, such a lot of them ! Sometimes we are almost frightened out of our little lives, they are so wicked, and make such a din; all the more since the mistress has fallen sick, with all the hurry and worry; and if it had not been for Mother Amalia, we could not have got through with our lives. But she is such a rare one, she is! and so clever, and teaches us so capital! so—it's regularly jolly, now!'

"It was during dinner-time that we had this talk with the child. But do you know who that 'Mother Amalia' was who went among the children and gave them their food, assembled them to prayers and reading and singing, and instructed them with a firmness and a motherly affection at the same time, which made the children obey her as nature obeys our Lord? This 'Mother Amalia,' whom the children praised so much, yes, she is no other than that same Amalia Hård whom you can remember very well in her gay days, and whose later sorrowful history you also know. The infant-school had been removed, or rather crammed into a room in the house where she lived, and she had taken the sick school-mistress into one of her two rooms, and nursed her whilst she was unable to perform her duties in the school. Beside the cradle of her little boy now sits a little lame girl of nine years old, of cheerful disposition, with bright eyes and the most lovely voice, so that it is a pleasure to hear her sing. Amalia teaches her new songs, which she allows her to sing with the school children. Amalia always had a good heart, even in her giddy, youthful days, and now she shows it, together with abilities, and a desire to do good, which we had never before given her credit for. Love for her child seems to have ennobled her, and developed in her a maternal sentiment even for other children. If Mrs. N. should not recover, as seems probable, because she suffers from chronic affection of the chest, Amalia would probably be engaged as mistress of the school, if there were not an *if*, and especially if Mrs. Tupplander were not in the way. The world is very unjust which makes such a mighty sin of one moment's false step, and pays so little regard to years of fidelity, fulfilment of duty, self-sacrificing love, industry, and to the unquestionable earnestness and power of a wish to do right. Amalia seems now as if born anew, and quite happy in her fresh occupation. If one could but see the end of it. I foresee a regular struggle with our Corsair. The pastor's wife is not

nerself quite satisfied with the affair. But I hope that our
Lord will help us—I mean Amalia, Hertha, and myself.

"Apropos of myself; I am in a fair way of losing my heart.
Can you guess to whom? Why, to no other than to your
friend and the sworn enemy of the ladies'-society, the Protocol
Secretary—N. B. He is so good to our poor folks! and in
that case he may be as angry as he likes with ladies'-socie-
ties.

"Towards me he is particularly gracious (although I turn
to him in all sorts of parish business), the reason of which I
opine to be, that I very often fool him into laughing. He
does everything that I ask of him. I have often remarked, as a
general rule, that what people will not do for the sake of necessity, they will often do either for the sake of a joke or a good
laugh. And in this way your friend N. B. and I have become
very good friends. But you know what I have said, if I
should ever meet with a wealthy man—for I will not be poor
if I can help it, least of all as a married woman—ready to help
and do good—(in a rational sort of way, of course), whom I
can like, and who will have me—and papa along with me, then
—I will not promise for what may happen!

"Now you laugh at me, and I do so too, and go and get
ready papa's supper, and look after seventeen other things,

"But remain for ever, and with my whole heart,
"Your devoted sister,
"Mimmi S."

No. 2.

Mrs. Uggla sits in her arm-chair and reads the newspaper,
sipping every now and then her afternoon coffee. Now she
lays down the newspaper, takes off her spectacles, raises herself a little in her chair, and sighing with a secret satisfaction,
says:

"Such a number of old ladies dead! and three of them my
good friends!—It is a fact though, that the newspapers are
very interesting. One learns so much from them. What,

is that you again, dear Ingeborg?   Cannot I have any peace?"

"Not just now, mamma dear—impossible! I must have fifty little children's blouses cut out by the day after to-morrow; I have not half done them, and if mamma will not help me I shall get into disgrace in my family, and be scolded by Dr. Hedermann. I must now go with Hertha to visit our sick outside the town, and if, dear mamma, you would be so good and go on with the cutting-out while I am away, I shall then get through my undertaking with credit; otherwise I shall not."

"Well, in that case I suppose I must," sighed Mrs. Uggla, rising from her chair; "but it is very wretched with all these schemes, which only give people trouble! Now, where have you put the scissors and stuff? It is quite certain that I ought to have the title of mother in the cutting-out family!"

And so sighing, Mrs. Uggla began her work, half-smiling the while at Ingeborg, who kissed the hand in which she placed the large pair of scissors, and said cheerfully as she went out:

" Only don't be too quick, mamma dear; leave a little for me to do! "

Ingeborg went, and Mrs. Uggla began her work in good earnest. Mrs. Uggla was really both more occupied and less out of spirits than she used to be. Ingeborg knew what portion of the business which occupied the attention of the family-groups was calculated to call forth her mother's interest and sympathy, and this falling, as it were, into her hands, had given a new turn to her thoughts and conversation. The human-being—let naturalists say what they like on the subject—is a ruminant animal. He chews the cud of feelings and thoughts, the bitter as well as the sweet, when he has time for it.

"The human heart," says Luther, "is like a pair of mill-stones. If good corn is placed between them, they grind it into good meal. But if they have no corn to grind, they grind away themselves."

With this true observation we will proceed to our **next visit.**

No. 3.

Two young ladies are walking together on the road that fine evening, towards the end of summer. We recognise Hertha and Ingeborg. Their steps are directed towards the town. The evening sky glows with a warm but tender light; the air is calm, the crickets chirp in the grass. Ingeborg's countenance, brightened by the evening flush, and animated by her walk, is very unlike what it appeared in the ball-room a few months ago. She now looks well, healthy, and cheerful. The two young friends had walked in silence for some time, when Ingeborg said:

"People say so much about a beneficent activity for our distressed fellow-creatures being beautiful, but they never speak of the joy it gives, nor of its beneficent, elevated influence upon those who practise it. And yet it seems to me that this is so great, that it is like the reward of heaven to those who labor in its service. I confess, that for many years I have not felt so well and so cheerful in mind, as I have done during these last months, when I have been obliged to be actively employed for our society. Ah! it is such a good thing to be able to forget one's own poor *I*, and to think about other people, and to work for them; and when one feels that one can be of some little use, can do some little good by one's life and one's work, it elevates the mind. Occupation during the day; walks in the fresh air, on one's visits to the dwellings of the poor, waft away many a germ of disease, both of mind and body. Why, Hertha, should the lives of so many of us be like a stagnant mere, when we have both time and strength to give, and when there is so much, and such countless numbers of people who need them?"

"I have often myself asked that question, Ingeborg," replied Hertha, "but have not yet found an answer. A great deal of fault lies in the way in which society looks at the problem of our life, as well as in our education and position in society. Much also lies in our own apathy, or, more properly speaking, selfishness. A great deal of egotism prevails in our sex; and the feminine I is only too much inclined to see the whole world in the little, narrow circle which it calls its own. Many, too, there are who wish to do otherwise, but dare not. In the mean time the benevolent societies, which are now being established in all Christian countries, are signs of an extended horizon, and a higher and more comprehensive life. The heart begins to expand its world. This is good, and the well-inclined obtain therefrom encouragement and guidance. But I confess that the direction into which it principally extends itself is not sufficient for me. These works of benevolence, as they are called, this activity for the outwardly poor— does not satisfy my soul, nor the requirement of my spirit. I desire an activity for the mind, a service in the service of the spirit. And—no need that it should be less *God's*-service than laboring for the hungry and the naked!"

"Ah, no," said Ingeborg, "the very contrary; the bitterest poverty is that of the spirit; the most tormenting hunger is that of the soul. But not many are able to satisfy it. You who are one of the unusual and strong souls, you may do it, and many, many will bless you for that reason. We all of us need more freedom and a wider future than we possess for the powers which God has given us. But not many of us feel the thirst for knowledge and light which you speak of. The greater number of women, it seems to me, are created to find their most beautiful happiness as wives and as mothers; they do not commonly covet anything higher!"

"But this is a defect, Ingeborg, and a contractedness of mind in them who, being these, aim at nothing higher than being merely happy. And that which beyond everything else appears to me to be the fault of our sex, is precisely this unconsciousness of its highest vocation. Therefore so many of them live, suffer, and enjoy as thoughtless, aimless beings, ruled by circumstances instead of ruling them; requiring everything from another, and living as parasites instead of having life and peace in God, and living as His witnesses and the benefactors of their fellows."

"You speak beautiful and proud words, Hertha!" said Ingeborg, whilst tears filled her eyes, "and it does me good to hear them, although they show me how far I am from the point of view which they assume. And many, like myself, fettered by circumstances, over which they have no control, may be able merely to raise themselves, by feebly fluttering their wings, above them,—nay, many never can raise themselves before they have broken the chain of human life."

"And I too," said Hertha, smiling sorrowfully, "am considerably weaker than my words. I only say what I wish, and what we ought all to be!——"

"What the devil are the girls marching along for?" sounded a harsh voice behind them, and at the same time some one was heard advancing with hasty steps. They turned round and saw Dr. Hedermann, who as soon as he had reached them took off his hat, wiped his forehead, and said:

"I think you must have wings at your feet. Here have I been on the full trot after you for the last quarter of an hour, all the way from the village yonder, in order to catch you. But you ran away as if you were afraid of me. Now confess that you saw me coming, and hastened away because you thought that I was going to the cottages after you, and you were afraid of being scolded by the wicked doctor, who is always finding fault with people, and especially with ladies and their goings-on. Confess! Was it not so?——"

But the young ladies had nothing of that kind to confess, nor did they seem afraid of the wicked doctor, but, on the contrary, glad to see him and to have his company the rest of the way. The three were now soon in the full discussion of their general family affairs, within the society, and of various measures and proceedings with regard to the sanitary management of the poor children. The good doctor and Ingeborg especially agreed on this subject, and while the twilight gathered around them and the stars came forth in the heavens, thoughts also and plans were suggested for the destitute little ones which would brighten their dim future.

Hertha took leave of her friends at her own door, and the doctor accompanied Ingeborg to her own home. But the conversation which had hitherto been carried on so easily, seemed now all at once to be stayed. A certain melancholy silence overcame the doctor, and he answered nothing to an attempt or two made by Ingeborg to renew the conversation. The two became silent; the doctor plucked now and then a little flower from the dewy grass, a blossom of fragrant white clover or a sprig of ladies' bed-straw, and thus they reached the town and Ingeborg's home.

Here the doctor paused.

"Will you not come in and say a word or two to mamma?" said Ingeborg almost beseechingly.

"Not this evening," replied the doctor, decidedly, "but another time, when I will ask you, Miss Ingeborg, something. But—do you like field flowers, Miss Ingeborg?—simple, every-day flowers?"

"Better even than garden flowers."

"Indeed! I could not have believed that; but one makes many mistakes in this world. Well, it is pleasant that you like common flowers; see, here are some. Good night."

And as the doctor gave Ingeborg the little bouquet, he fixed upon her a deep, strangely questioning glance, a glance which went like an arrow to her heart, and awoke there a feeling at once uneasy and delicious. Never before had he looked at her in that way.

Ingeborg found her mother in an unusually excited state of mind. An invitation had arrived to a grand entertainment in the neighborhood, given by the Von X——'s, he being a lord of the bedchamber. "All the *élite* of the town and country would be there," said Mrs. Uggla, "and Baron P—— and Count S——; and, Ingeborg, you must have a new silk for the occasion."

"Now, mamma!" said Ingeborg;" now, when such numbers are without clothes in consequence of the fire. I don't feel as

if I ought now to think about a new ball-dress. Ah, no! but
if mamma loves me, let me rather have the money which
it would cost, and lay it out as I like."

"But, dear Ingeborg, it never will do to go to such a ball
in your old dress, everybody——"

"Then do not let us go," said Ingeborg.

"Not go to the ball?" said Mrs. Uggla with horror.

"No, do not let us go," said Ingeborg, with more decision
than usual; "I know, dear mamma, that you would go
merely for my sake, and I would much rather stay at
home."

"You might just as well be a nun, and go into a convent,"
said Mrs. Uggla, both angry and vexed, "as you have made
up your mind to be an old maid, and live a stupid unnatural
life."

"Is my mother then so tired of me that she wishes to get
rid of me *à tout prix?*" said Ingeborg; "I am very sorry that
you are so tired of me, mamma."

"I am not, indeed, tired of you, my dear child," said the
poor old woman, sighing, "but don't you see, it is for your
own best interest. I know that my temper is bad, (ever since
your father died it has got worse,) and that I cannot make
your home happy, and it is distressing to me to see that you
must wither away in it, and lose your good complexion, and
have nervous headaches, and to hear people wonder that you
don't get married; and I know that you might have made a
good match if you had not been foolish, and if you, like other
girls, would but take a little trouble to please gentlemen."

"Never, never again in that way," replied Ingeborg with
unusual emphasis. "If I cannot win a good husband otherwise than by my dress and my dancing, then let me remain
for ever unmarried. My dear mother, we have hitherto only
thought too much about this matter. Let us now endeavor
not to think of it any more; leave the whole calmly in our
Lord's hand, and think of something else; for example, how
we can make each other happy in our home, and serve God
with the talent that he has given to us. Tell me, mamma, do

you not think that I am looking more healthy, and that I am more cheerful than I used to be?"

"Yes, that you certainly are."

"And the reason, dear mamma, is because I have begun to walk in another path than that of balls and suppers, and have begun to labor for something else than endeavoring to please, which is the hardest labor in the world, especially when people have passed their youthful years. Will you now, mamma, allow me to continue in the way which I have begun, and I then promise that you may be perfectly easy and contented on my account?"

"You do not understand it," returned the mother mournfully, "and I never can be easy and contented until——Ah, you do not know what it is to live a solitary life on small means. But I know it, and therefore I wish you not to experience such a lot; but if you will do so, then I cannot prevent it. You may be an old maid and welcome for me, but it would be much better to go into a convent, because then there would be some credit in it."

And Mrs. Uggla in great warmth went into her bedroom.

"Would to God that we had convents in our country!" sighed Ingeborg silently. "How beautiful and great to be sustained by one common sanctifying spirit; to be elevated by holy songs; to dedicate one's life in affectionate sister-communion to a service not of the world, at peace with one's conscience and with life. But no," continued she, as she glanced upwards to the heavens, bright with stars, "I will not sigh after the impossible, but will ask what God's spirit requires from me in this place and at the present time."

A ray, a point of the light and life which announces the advent of a new day, and which even in northern countries calls forth new life and new creations, stirred the soul of Ingeborg with the freshness of rich anticipation; she recalled to her mind the evening's conversation with Hertha and with the doctor, and she felt clearly that she, too, had a vocation in the present time's work of freedom, and a prospect towards a new and more beautiful life.

A new reliance on the fatherly guidance of God, and an assurance that she had now chosen the right path, the path which He had appointed for her, filled her soul with an unusual joy. Animated by this feeling, she went into her mother's room, embraced her, kissed her, and said:

"Don't be unhappy about me, mamma. All, believe me, will turn out right."

The poor unhappy mother looked astonished at the bright, beaming countenance of her daughter; but when Ingeborg attempted to impart to her the feelings and thoughts which occupied her whole being, she said:

"You are a good girl, Ingeborg; better than your mother. You are perhaps right, but I am one of the old school. I cannot follow you into all your modern theories. We shall see who is right in the long run. God knows best. But you must now act as you think right."

Again in her own room Ingeborg laid the little bouquet of wild flowers on the table by her pillow, and thought pleasantly of a fresh life of labor in the service of humanity, and in the society of noble friends, and every thought became like a fresh fragrance breathing clover-flower on the green field of life. She would have slept well, but for the peculiar glance which Dr. Hedermann gave her at parting, and—what could he mean? asked she of herself. The wicked doctor! it was too late almost for him to give her such a glance now!—if it had been seven years ago;—but now, now, was it possible that —— Such thoughts and questionings prevented her from sleeping.

Neither did Mrs. Uggla sleep. With many sighs, she thought:

"To lose such a splendid chance! but she is a simpleton— and those modern notions! She'll never be married! never be married! Oh ho!"

No. 4.

Mrs. Tupplander is in a state of great excitement; she throws her bag down upon one chair, her cloak on another her bonnet on a third, and exclaims:

"Miss Krusbjörn! Miss Krusbjörn! where can she be? Come, and I'll tell you the news! Here's a pretty piece of scandal! But I don't mean to spread it! I don't mean to lay a cushion under the burden. Such an ungrateful creature! Did you ever hear anything like it, Miss Krusbjörn? Amalia Hård is come back to the town; she has with her a child, and she calls herself Amalia Winter—I suppose on account of her family—and lives in the house where the infant school is, and she now goes and teaches the children. What do you think of that! Such a shameless proceeding! Pretty instruction will she give to the children who has an illegitimate child of her own. And besides that, she receives, late in the evening, visits from a gentleman, who, it is supposed, may be the father of her child; but who he is I cannot make out, though I will know before I've done. Is not that a pretty tale? And our pastor's wife and Mimmi Svanberg can allow such things! But you see whether Hertha has not had some underhand dealings with them, on purpose to get a maintenance for her cousin. For they are cousins, Amalia Hård and she! But if I have any weight with the Directors of the school, there shall soon be an end to such goings on. Is there nobody to be found of a creditable name and of good conduct, who can undertake the management of the infant school during the illness of the mistress? I know of a certainty there is. And such a one, and no other, shall have that place as sure as my name is Karin Tupplander. But now there is a regular intrigue going on in the town. And it comes of that and nothing else, that the engagement between Mr. von Tackjern and Eva Dufva is at an end—positively at an end! The girl has heard some gossip about some dispute or other during the fire—all stupid talk; and so she has

begged and prayed of her parents to consent to her breaking
off her engagement. Now she is trying to become quite
learned, and her parents are afraid of her becoming a blue-
stocking, and therefore they intend to take her abroad for a
time. But if one betrothal is at an end, there are no less
than five others which are in progress! Young people are
thrown so much together by these society-families, that it is
really frightf'l, Miss Krusbjörn! In my time people did not
so easily and freely get acquainted, and for that very reason
modesty and good morals prevailed. My late husband, Miss
Krusbjörn, never once gave me a kiss even during our betrothal, but only tickled my elbow. And therefore he had respect
for me all his days. People did not formerly betrothe themselves so hastily, nor make such a merriment of it as they do
now. A girl turned her tongue seven times in her mouth
before she said Yes! She sate then at her sewing from
morning till night, and danced minuets at balls. She did not
leap and tear about in the waltz as she does now, Miss
Krusbjörn. But, other times other manners! Now there
are no less than two of the Dufvas, who it is said are to be
married to the two brothers Orn; and Hertha Falk, also;
but she ought to be actually betrothed with Lieutenant
Nordin, because she has been his sick nurse all the summer.
At least it is not becoming for people to have such familiar
intercourse if they are not engaged to each other. And that
I shall let my dear Hertha understand; and then I shall get
to know how it stands with the betrothal. Well, well, papa
Falk will have a word or two to say on that matter. But
now I must above all things make out who is the gentleman
who goes of an evening to Amalia Hård. He was with her
twice last week.

"Now listen to me, Miss Krusbjörn; I have promised to
have a coffee party on Sunday afternoon. One must see
one's friends sometimes, and prepare for what one has to do;
and one can always make out such a quantity of puzzling
things when people are thus brought confidentially together.
Let us think how many biscuits and tea-cakes we shall

-equire for about twenty-five or thirty persons. Things are dreadfully dear, Miss Krusbjörn, but still one must see one's friends some time !"

After this visit on the outskirts of life, we will return to its innermost; we will talk about

LOVE.

——miracle of earth and heaven,
'Thou living breath of happiness,
Fresh breeze of the divinest bliss
To life's woe-stricken deserts given,
Thou heart that throbbest through creation,
Of gods and men, thou consolation.—TEGNER

But we mean by this high and glorious love which really deserves to be called

The fresh breeze of divinest bliss
To life's woe-stricken deserts given.

We are not speaking of its many imitations, or of that dwarfish race to which people in a mistake give the name of loves, and who fly about shooting their arrows at random; butterflies which flutter from flower to flower; "Loke's fire," which kindles shavings, burns up quickly and soon goes out. The "house-warming" of which people talk in Norway, the child of habit and sluggishness; the catch-fly which is viscous in the spring, but dries up during the heat of summer; ignes-fatui, which dance upon life's swampy fields, glimmer in the dark, but vanish like vapor at sunrise; all these and many other symbols of love have their prototypes in life, yesterday as to-day; and we will let them live their little life, if they will only keep to the night, and not give themselves out for any more than they really are, not set up any claim to the name of *true love.*

Love is not love,
Which alters when it alteration finds,
Or bends with the remover to remove

14

> Oh, no, it is an ever-fixed mark,
> That looks on tempests, and is never shaken;
> It is the star to every wandering bark,
> Whose worth's unknown, although his height be taken.
> Love's not time's fool, though rosy lips and cheeks
> Within his bending sickle's compass come
> Love alters not with his brief hours and weeks,
> But bears it out even to the edge of doom.*

True love loves the eternal in its object, and the nobler the object the more the sacred flame increases, feeding itself with esteem, approval, admiration, a divine and human joy over the good and the estimable in the beloved, sometimes also a divine compassion over his deficiencies, when at the same time the soul is noble and the desire only after good. Happy thou who lovest a noble object,—yes, even if thou art not beloved in return; thy whole life will be ennobled and enlarged thereby; thou thyself wilt grow by thy love, grow up in heaven, and there be united with thy beloved in the bosom of eternal love. If, however, thou lovest thus, and art thus loved in return by thy beloved!—

Thus did Yngve and Hertha love each other with all their souls' best power. The more intimately they became acquainted, the more pure and inward was the joy which they experienced in each other; the more they felt themselves to be deeply united. But the serious character of their intercourse; the subjects which furnished them with conversation and thought kept in long abeyance the magical enchanting sentiment which the poet calls

The heart which throbs through all creation,

which throughout all nature clothes in wonderful beauty object for object, which makes the sea luminous, gives fragrance to the flower, causes the birds to sing and adorn themselves with the most brilliant plumage, and which makes one human being see in his fellow human being, not an equal but a being

* Shakespeare's Sonnets.

of superhuman charm and superhuman power, whose mere step and voice make the pulses beat with wonderful joy, and whose silent presence even changes the whole existence to a festival.

Yngve and Hertha had begun a league of friendship of the most Spartan-like severity, which should exclude every weaker and commoner feeling. The inexpressible charm in each other's being, the grace, the fascination, awoke love which stole upon them like summer into the bosom of spring, as the sunbeam steals into the folded bud and opens it for a new life. If Hertha in her intercourse with Yngve had always continued to be the proud woman, whose words were keenly caustic, she would still have continued to be an object of esteem and also of admiration, but she would not have become dear to his inmost soul. The affectionate and womanly heart, however, which constituted the very essence of her being, had, during her intercourse with him, more and more revealed itself. The upright and noble disposition, the clear insight into truth which she continually saw in Yngve, the manly gentleness which was the principal trait in his character, had operated upon her, as a calm bright day upon the tumultuous waves of the ocean agitated by the storm of the night. Unconsciously to herself her mind and her language became more and more gentle, her whole demeanor more beautiful and more agreeable, and not unfrequently did the bright, flashing glances express a deep though imprisoned warmth of feeling.

Yngve resigned himself with joy, and with the fulness of his whole heart, to the sentiment which so powerfully and so blessedly began to captivate his soul. Not so Hertha; she resisted the feeling which attracted her towards Yngve. The view which she took of woman's position and life, especially in the north, and the effect of her own peculiar circumstances, had made her suspicious and proud as regarded men in general, and caused her to oppose herself, as it were, to the impression which Yngve made upon her. He was, in fact, a man, and she had said in her heart, "I will not love; I will not give my soul and my happiness into the power of a man!"

And this determination, together with the gloomy background of her own life, which caused her to regard love and its joys as a game for weak souls, a game too mean for the earnestness of human life, gave to her a calmness and a power of self-control much beyond what was in the power of Yngve. She said to herself, "I will be Yngve's friend; I will be to him as an elder sister, and love him as my brother!" But Yngve's amiable image became ever more and more an abiding light in her soul, and accompanied her even in her dreams.

One night it seemed to her that she was floating through space, striving to ascend upwards towards the home of the sun, but a weight as of lead lay upon her breast, she could not breathe, and felt herself sinking downwards towards a black, bottomless abyss, which yawned beneath her. But all at once the weight was lifted from her breast, she breathed more freely, and felt herself sustained as by a new power; more easily and more securely than before she floated upwards towards the world of light, to " Himla the lofty palace, fairer than the sun." At that moment she perceived that she was not alone. A beaming angel with the glow of morning on his beautiful countenance floated towards her, took her hand, and riveted upon her his beaming gaze, and that gaze was— Yngve's.

Another time she again saw herself beneath the verdurous tree of the world; the lofty Nornor sate by the Urda fountain. But the severity which she had formerly seen in their countenances was softened to a maternal earnestness, and she heard them say:

> Hail to the spirits heroic,
> They who have seen;
> They who have honestly striven!
> They shall win victory;
> They shall be welcome;
> Shall drink of the waters of Urda!

She saw the life-renewing fountain leap up,—oh, so clear, so wonderfully clear and glorious! whilst brilliant rainbows encircled its silver-white water-mist. She advanced towards it; and the Nornor filled a golden beaker with water from the fountain and gave her to drink. But just when, with a beating heart, she raised it to her lips, behold it was in the hand of a youth, and the youth seemed beautiful and good as Balder is described in the songs of the Edda; he smiled upon her as he extended to her the beaker, and she recognised in him—Yngve.

Hertha made a sketch of this dream in her diary, and wrote beside it:

"Oh, Yngve, much could I lose, much could I resign, but not my hope of deliverance and my faith in thee!"

Under the influence of these feelings, Yngve and Hertha endeavored, almost involuntarily, to give each other pleasure in a noble way, even in externals. Yngve adopted more and more, both in style and manner, the purity and delicacy which distinguish the true gentleman. This pleased Hertha, and, in reality, it pleased himself. Hertha, on the other hand, although always grave and severe in her taste as regarded dress, yet had a pleasure in wearing the colors which Yngve said became her. Day by day they became more lovely to each other, and more happy, but also more indispensable to each other.

When the year advanced to midsummer, and the Apollo-butterfly, with his large white wings and purple spots, fluttered over the wild-roses, which in such luxuriance adorn our hedges and woods,—when the harvest-crops blossomed and waved fragrantly in the wind, Yngve and Hertha went out together almost every day (he supported on her arm), now along the harvest-fields, where the corn softly whispered, or through the many chambers of the fir-woods, where the sun-beams, as if bashful, stole between the lofty columnar bolls, and the Linnea sent forth its perfume from the moss, which spread soft velvet carpets for the feet of the wanderers; or by the river, which flowed like crystal between its flowery banks; and they conversed on subjects which cause the soul to expand, or they walked silently in the deep and sweet consciousness of their souls' inward communion, whilst they listened to the soughing of the woods, and to the almost spiritual melody of the thrush, and all was at once life and peace.

Only when Hertha remained away for a day, she would find her friend, on her next visit, in an excited state of mind, vexed and irritable, but at the same time amiable, and Hertha then immediately introduced some topic of general interest, that the storm-cloud, which she called "a little selfishness," might be dispersed, and Yngve soon forgot his annoyance.

Sometimes, during their wanderings, Hertha turned Yngve's attention to the beautiful objects of nature, for which she, like most women, possessed a deep feeling, but of which, like the greatest number also, she possessed no scientific knowledge. She inquired from Yngve about the trees and flowers, about stones and insects. Yngve told her their names and their peculiar qualities. He took up the lovely mosses and leaves which grew around them upon the granite hills, and showed her their wonderful formation, and told her of the beautiful colors, and beneficial properties which the Creator had bestowed upon these, the most humble children of nature. He talked to her about the sparks in the stone, and the life in the insect.

"How happy you are, how happy you men are," sighed Hertha, "who are able to learn so much! How fearfully ignorant are women in general on a vast number of subjects, which at the same time lie so near to them, and which might give such rich nourishment to their souls and to their whole being. Thus, for instance, nature—we love it; we live in the midst of it. It has essential resemblances to ourselves, and yet it is foreign to us, and we live amid it like strangers. What do we know, what do we feel of its marvellous wealth, order, and life?"

"Ah!" replied Yngve, "do not say so! you feel, you comprehend much more in the general than we do. We know something about outward distinctions, classes, orders, divisions;

but you comprehend nature in its fulness—its innermost, its divine life."

Hertha shook her head, and said with a smile:

" I might thank you for the compliment, if it did not resemble many other compliments by which men endeavor to compliment us out of those spheres of life where they yet are happy to be themselves able to live. I know, Yngve, that you believe and intend what you say. But if it be true that God gives us the ability in a pre-eminent manner to comprehend the life and the divine in nature, would this ability be diminished by our knowing something more about this life, its arrangement and character, its thoughts, if I may so express myself? Would it become less rich to us, less divine if we were able to study it, to learn to think about it, learn to comprehend it with awakened minds, instead of dreamily losing ourselves in it? Would not nature then really nourish our souls, and we perhaps precisely because of our deeper feeling, and with our sight strengthened by the microscope of science, might be able to make observations, discoveries, which—now are not made, and which, therefore, natural science or human life have not the benefit of. Should we not by that means become acquainted with the actual divine purposes of nature, instead of, as is now commonly the case, our own dull fancies? In my youth I used to look at the rocks, the trees, the grass, and all objects of nature, with unspeakable longing, wishing to know something about their kinds, their life, and their purpose. But the want of knowledge, the want of opportunity to acquire it, has caused nature to be to me as a sealed book, and still to this moment it is to me a tantalising, enticing, and ever retreating wave, rather than a life-giving fountain which I can enjoy, and enjoying, thank the Creator."

" Is it really so ?" said Yngve; " oh, then it ought to be different. You are right, you are perfectly right! And I had not thought correctly on the subject. What egotists we men are, after all; will you begin to-morrow a little course of natural history? I will teach you anything that I know,

It is not much; but it might serve as an entrance-card, and, by the help of good books, you could afterwards go on by yourself. But in the beginning we can study together."

"Thank you, Yngve, you are very kind!" said Hertha, and looked at him with a glance which shone through tears; and then she added, in an undervoice, as if to herself, whilst she glanced over the landscape around them, which was clothed as a bride in all the beauty of a northern midsummer, "I shall yet become better acquainted with thee! Oh, life, after all, is so beautiful!"

These words, from Hertha's lips, gave a feeling of heavenly joy to Yngve's heart, because he heard in them the fulfilment of his heart's wish, which was to reconcile her with life.

And life became more and more beautiful to them whilst they thus lived and learned together, contemplating God's work and wisdom in nature, in history, and, above all, in that history which alone is able fully to explain both the order and disorder of the former. Because Hertha understood more profoundly than Yngve that—

> ——Nature is a fallen angel,
> But in the fallen angel's face shine clearly
> The lofty features of a heavenly lineage,
> And Daphne's heart beneath the bark is throbbing.

They never spoke of love, but they called it forth, they loved it; and its delicious fascination cast a magical light over their life, and all which surrounded them. They walked pure and peaceful in each other's sight, illumined by the eye of God, as were the first loving couple on our earth in the Garden of Paradise.

THE SERPENT.

Hertha said one day to Yngve:

"Yngve, help me to explain this old primeval story: but first I will read it aloud to you; its contradiction has long tormented me."

Hertha read:

"Now the serpent was more subtile than any beast of the field which the Lord God had made. And he said unto the woman, Yea, hath God said, Ye shall not eat of every tree of the garden?

"And the woman said unto the serpent, We may eat of the fruit of the trees of the garden:

"But of the fruit of the tree which is in the midst of the garden, God hath said, Ye shall not eat of it, neither shall ye touch it, lest ye die.

"And the serpent said unto the woman, Ye shall not surely die:

"For God doth know that in the day ye eat thereof, then your eyes shall be opened, and ye shall be as gods, knowing good and evil.

"And when the woman saw that the tree was good for food, and that it was pleasant to the eyes, and a tree to be desired to make one wise, she took of the fruit thereof, and did eat, and gave also unto her husband——"

Here Hertha stopped, looked at Yngve, and said:

"She had, after all, a great spirit, this our first mother, because she sought for knowledge, sought to become as God, even at the risk of losing life and all its daily enjoyments. She obeyed a mighty inspiration."

"But the serpent tempted her," suggested Yngve.

"Yes, so it is written; but now listen to me, Yngve. If knowledge—the 'being made wise'—is a means of attaining perfection, of becoming as God,—and we know of ourselves that it is a necessary means by which we can gain a knowledge of God and his truth,—when then is it said that this knowledge is forbidden? And when the love of knowledge, the desire for a higher consciousness, was the power which drew on Eve, wherefore is she punished, and after her all her daughters—by an exclusion from the tree of knowledge, which taught good and evil, and by the same rule from the tree of life, which gives her permission to live for ever? How irrational is that, how unjust,—at least so it seems to me,—how unreasonable, how severe appear both lawgiver and judge!"

"From the Christian point of view, certainly," replied Yngve, "and when we look at portions of the narrative in detail and literally—taking it for granted that our translation from the original is perfectly faithful. And to me it has always seemed in these parts to bear traces of the darkness which belongs even to the profoundest views of nations during their age of childhood. But the basis of its idea seems to me true, and those detailed portions of the narrative may be explained from this point of view. For in order to become possessed of a full self-consciousness and to be a free agent, the human being must pass through a strong temptation. That is (in consequence of the spiritual-natural-law) for the human being to make of his own I the centre, instead of the true centre—God. Selfishness (as pride and love of pleasure) is the temptation, 'the serpent' which caused the human being to fail in his allegiance to his rightful Lord and Benefactor, and too soon for the sake of his own greatness, to grasp after that which was the forbidden fruit—forbidden only during the period of childhood, when the human being could not digest it. Obedience to, and faith in his highest benefactor, were his first duties. The interdict which the Creator had imposed He could have removed; He could have appointed a time when He, the fountain of all knowledge and wisdom, would have taken the human child by the hand and led it to the tree

of knowledge, and taught it what was good and what was evil.
Knowledge as well as pleasure are forbidden only to the selfish
principle in humanity. Man must attain to them only through
firm obedience and love to God. The fall was this—that the
selfish principle conquered; that the human being became a
god to himself, and sought to obtain the highest, but not by
means of the Highest. The natural and inevitable consequences of the fall are the loss of Paradise, the degradation,
the darkening of the whole human world. The restoration
begins with a new inspiration in the human consciousness—
how bright your eyes are, Hertha!"

"My soul is bright, Yngve. Oh, I see it—I understand it
now,—the powerful impulses of our first mother, the fall, the
long excommunication, and—the restoration, by means of the
new birth, in the soul of the new Eve. I see her sit at the
feet of the Saviour, see her illumined by his glance and guided
by his word, impelled by a new, a higher inspiration, again
approach the tree of knowledge and thence pluck the fruit forbidden no longer, and give it to her friend—her husband.
The last witness of the Creator in the first Creation will come
forth as the last witness of him in the second, bearing witness
to him from the depths of conscience, and through a higher
knowledge, a more spiritual comprehension of life and reality.
Do you not see it as I do, Yngve?"

"I see it is so if—the witness is pure, noble, holy in desires
and inclination. The deeper the insight the higher the knowledge. But the life of the heart is ever the strength of the
woman, and the means of the highest knowledge is pre-
eminently for her a higher love. Don't you think so,
Hertha?"

"Yes, she must love truth, God above everything."

Both were silent. A painful feeling seemed to enter
Yngve's soul, and after a moment he said with a deep and
earnest voice:

"Can any one love God, can a human being understand his
love and how to love him without having first loved—his
fellow? Can you do it—are you unlike me? I never rightly

understood what the love of God is, until I learned to love—a fellow-creature."

Hertha was silent. Yngve regarded her with a tender inquiring gaze, as he continued—

"Could you not, with your whole heart, be able to love a fellow-creature—your equal?"

"Yes," replied Hertha hesitatingly, "but I should be afraid of the selfish—the harrowing effect of such a feeling."

"But if you were loved by some one who, like yourself, loved the highest, should you then be afraid of responding to his feeling, Hertha—would you be afraid of loving—me?"

Hertha grew pale; cast a glance at Yngve, like a flash of lightning which is quickly concealed by cloud, and replied softly—"Yes."

The extraordinary confession in this word fanned to flame the long-cherished fire in Yngve's breast; he seized Hertha's hand, pressed it to his breast, as he exclaimed—

"Beloved, beloved Hertha! Be not afraid of me; love me as I love you! God has given us to each other—I feel that deeply. Oh, you are mine, mine!"

But whilst Yngve thus gazed on Hertha with burning love, her countenance became paler and paler, and when his warm lips rested upon her lips and her eyelids, she whispered with unutterable depth of feeling:

"Oh, Yngve, why would you break the peace between us?"

She felt near fainting. "Give me a glass of water," she said hastily, to remove Yngve and to gain time to collect herself. Yngve rose.

It was not agreeable that the pastor's wife came in at that moment and interrupted the conversation of the lovers. And the delicious melon and other fruits which she brought with her did not prevent Yngve from wishing the good lady at the place where pepper grows, nor yet that Hertha, after a moment's pause, availed herself of her presence to leave the room.

Yngve followed her outside the door, when he said quickly, and with an anxious tenderness, "Hertha, I must see you, must talk with you to-morrow. I shall come to you!"

"Not to-morrow, Yngve," replied Hertha; "to-morrow I shall be prevented from seeing you; but soon, if you wish it."

But there was in Hertha's expression a sadness which Yngve could not understand, and which made him uneasy.

"Have I distressed you?" asked he. "Oh, just bear in mind that I have loved you so tenderly and so long in silence, that I——"

It was not agreeable that the pastor now came and interrupted the declaration; and he saw very plainly that he was not welcome; he exclaimed therefore in a jocular way:

"Oh, oh! You have got something to say to one another which I have no right to hear, I can see! Well, well, I'll go my way, and—when you have need of the old clergyman, you can just let me know, children. I'll come immediately with the book!"

But before he had left the spot, Hertha, with a hasty salutation to both gentlemen, was speeding rapidly away from them.

On her way home she endeavored to read her own soul, to obtain a clear knowledge of her own excited feelings. What had happened to her? That which is of the most common occurrence,—which happens to the most ordinary woman from the most ordinary man; her feelings had awoke under the burning ray of the kiss of the beloved. Was she displeased by his bold advance? No, in reality not. This is never displeasing to a woman on the part of the beloved, when she knows that the fire which burns in it is not that of earth. And Hertha could not be mistaken in the heart-felt reality, the truth of Yngve's feelings. But still she mourned over this their outburst, and the feelings which it awoke in her; mourned as the sylphide mourns when, snared in the magical web, she sees her wings fall off. Although enchanting as the fragrance-laden zephyrs of the tropics, were the feelings which now were kindled in her soul, she still regarded them as a falling away from the pure region in which she had hitherto lived and breathed with Yngve.

"It can never again be between us as it has been!"

thought she with uneasy regret, as she felt that Yngve had obtained a power over her which she did not voluntarily concede to him, and to which she would not willingly submit herself. And then the old serpent of suspicion whispered:

"Perhaps he talked thus; perhaps he behaved thus to the first girl whom he loved, and then—deserted. Perhaps she was, like me, weak; and I foolish, like her!—Yngve has been really inconstant—perhaps guilty—did I not once see an acknowledgment of that in his looks? And I might——Nay, Yngve, you will not find me so easily won. It is not for such sentimental talk, for such selfish love that I have, through the whole of my life, longed and suffered, and now have been graciously gifted by God with light and hope!—No! away with such weakness! away with these selfish feelings and thoughts!"

And Hertha walked with a proud step through the ruins of the consumed town. Then came to her mind the remembrance of Yngve's noble and amiable character; the remembrance of the beautiful devotion which he had shown towards her; of the light which in so many ways he had let in upon her soul; and she was filled with sentiments of unspeakable tenderness and gratitude. And these, in connexion with her pure, moral feelings, soon showed her a way to reconciliation and harmony.

"I will talk openly with him," thought she, "I will open my soul to him, and if he be the Yngve which I believe him, the noble Yngve whom I can love, he will listen to me and understand me, and become clear before himself and before me. I will take his hand and lead him into the most holy sanctuary of life, and let a holy fire consume the burning coals of sensual pleasure from our lips, out of our hearts. I will sanctify both him and myself in the service of the Highest. Thus only, Yngve, can you become mine and I yours."

And Hertha's heart beat again freely and strongly, and her eyes beamed with a fire so pure and so glowing, that a seraph of heaven might have believed it beheld one of its fellows in this wanderer on earth.

"How bright your eyes are! How handsome you are

after all, Hertha!" said the young sisters, who rushed to meet her on her return home.

"I think you are the handsomest creature in the whole world!" said the enthusiastic little Maria, embracing her.

Hertha kissed her sisters and smiled. She now felt herself cheerful and happy.

But when late in the evening she went into her chamber, she found, on the table beside her bed, a letter, at the sight of which an unpleasant sensation involuntarily passed through her. Its contents were as follows, in a handwriting unknown to Hertha :—

"Friends of Hertha F. consider it to be their duty to inform her, that the young man in whose company she is most days, and to whom there is every reason to suppose that she is betrothed, pays in the mean time secret visits to a person of not very good repute, living at No. 3, —— Lane, and who is at the same time considered to be the father of her child. This person calls herself Amalia Winter."

" It is a lie !" said Hertha coldly, as she flung the anony-mous letter on the floor, " a scandalous lie ! Yngve, we have seen each other for six months ; we have opened our souls to each other, promised each other truth and integrity, and you should have been able—no, it is not true !"

And she trampled on the letter with proud scorn and anger. But she was feverish through the night, and did not sleep a wink. The following day she occupied herself busily with the affairs of the family, and was incessantly employed in them. But when twilight came, she put on her bonnet and shawl, and went to Amalia's lodgings.

As she approached the place it was already very dusk ; nevertheless she saw a man going out of the house, who passed down the street in the direction opposite to that from which she came. True it was dusk, and he passed into the twilight like a shadow ; nevertheless the figure, the difficulty with which he walked, supported by a stick, an indescribable but unquestionable feeling, which did not permit of a doubt, told her his name.

THE NAME.

HERTHA entered Amalia's room in a state of feeling which is easier to imagine than to describe. She found her alone, sitting beside the cradle of her child. Amalia was evidently in an excited state of mind, but not alone from suffering, though she appeared to have wept. She rushed towards Hertha with agitated impetuosity, embraced her, and buried for a moment her face on her shoulder.

Hertha released herself softly from her arms, took her head between her hands, and gazed with her deep, earnest eyes into those of her cousin, and said:

" What is the meaning of this, Amalia ? You are excited ; you have been weeping."

" Yes," replied Amalia, turning away and re-seating herself by her child; " yes, but not from sorrow. I have had a pleasure, a comfort ; it will henceforth be better for me— better than I deserve. But do not ask me any questions, Hertha. I cannot, must not say any more !"

" You *must* tell me more, Amalia!" said Hertha, with terrible earnestness ; " you must tell me the name of him who is the father of your child."

" Impossible !" replied Amalia. " Do not ask it from me, Hertha! Everything, everything except this, will I tell you. I have sworn not to reveal it. I should make him unhappy should impede his future success——No, no, never !"

" Answer me," said Hertha in a voice which sounded almost awful, it was so calm, so low, yet at the same time so fearfully imperative ; " is the name—Yngve Nordin ?"

Amalia started up. " My God, Hertha! How, how have you come to know the name? I have never mentioned it to any one; I had sworn to conceal it. I vowed this to him, because—I was more guilty than he. My inexcusable levity was to blame; I seduced him, and not he me; that is the truth—the whole truth. He was weak, but he is not wicked. He will now make amends;—he will provide for his child. Oh, he is in reality noble and good!"

Amalia might have continued talking thus; but Hertha scarcely heard her after the first acknowledgment. The room, the earth, the whole world, swam round as it were. She felt dizzy, and was obliged to seat herself. She sate immoveable, with her head bowed into her hands, and without speaking a word. At length Amalia approached her, asking anxiously:

"Hertha! why are you sitting so? Will you not look at me; nor speak a word to me?—Are you ill?"

"Yes," replied Hertha, rising slowly, "my head feels very strange, and—I must now leave you, Amalia; but you shall soon hear from me. Farewell!"

She was deathly pale, but the deep twilight prevented Amalia from seeing it.

Amalia followed her anxiously. "You will soon be better again," she said.

"I hope so—I trust so."

"And you'll soon come again to me?"

"Soon—as soon as I can."

"And you'll hide the secret—*the name*—as if in the grave."

"As if in the grave," repeated poor Hertha, in a half-suppressed voice, as she left the room.

She was obliged to pause when she reached the stairs. She sate down on one of the steps and rested her head against the wall, and wished for a moment to lose consciousness and life together. People coming up the stairs obliged her to rise. She walked homeward like some one in a frightful dream. An intolerable burden lay upon her breast, and eternal darkness seemed to spread out his black wings over life and the whole world. When she reached the desolated portion of the town she was again compelled to stop. She seated herself on a

15

blackened piece of wall. "Was the extremest truth—the extremest reality—of life and reality, a ruin ? Yngve ! Yngve!"

She reached home ; her young sisters rushed into her arms.

"You have stayed so long!—and it is so dark ! We have been so anxious!"

Hertha kissed her darlings, asked them to leave her alone for a moment, and went into her own room.

Before long she came out again, evidently calmer, in order to join the rest of the family at table. The Director and Aunt Nella were more loquacious and more lively than usual. Hertha, as usual, attended to all at table, ate and drank also a little, but still the young sisters every now and then cast upon her questioning and almost sad glances. They saw that everything was not right, that something out of the common way, that something very sad had happened to her.

When the family separated for the evening, Hertha took her sisters with her into her room, seated herself, and putting an arm round each of them, said—

"Little ones, I must go a journey which will require a week, perhaps two, and you must, in the mean time, manage the house, and see that everything is comfortable for papa and aunt.

"Early in the morning you, Maria, must give this letter to papa, and afterwards you must read the papers to him in my stead. Martha must in the meantime undertake the housekeeping. Here are the keys of the larder, the cellar, and the store-room, and there the housekeeping money for the remainder of the month. Let me see, my little Martha, that you can attend to this as well as you have already begun, as my adjutant. Endeavor that I may be able, on my return, to praise you both. Whatever you can think of as best for the comfort of papa and aunt, that do. You must also think of me, my dear children, and pray God for me, and I will—I will write to you, and tell you the day when I shall return, and perhaps I may be back before you expect. In any case I will write to you."

The young girls began to weep.

"What has happened?" asked they; "you are so pale, Hertha? And your hands are so cold. Something distressing has happened?"

"Yes; but don't ask any more, now. Some time, perhaps, I may be able to tell you—but now, good night, little sisters; good night!"

She clasped them in her arms, kissed them, and desired them to go to their own room. But they clung sorrowfully round her neck.

"Do not forsake us!" besought they, weeping, "we have nobody to cling to and look up to but you. You are our only support, and the only joy we have in the world. Don't leave us!"

"No, no, never!" said Hertha, with decision, "never, with my soul and my heart; and if I go away for a little while, it is only that I may be able all the more calmly to stay with you, my sisters, my darlings!"

But Hertha could not separate herself from them until they had covered her with their caresses and tears.

"Sister?—if there is a word which is pleasant to me to hear—pleasanter than the sweetest music, it is that word, sister!" said on one occasion to me a mother, with two separate families of daughters, whom she had taught to speak that word of love.

Happy the home where the name "sister" is spoken in love and in joy. Heaven's innocence and the communion of angels live and bloom there in sweet images, the growth of an inspiration which, in scarcely any other relationship, is so pure, so free, and so refreshing. No attachment is at the same time so tender and so joyous, so productive of innocent mirth, of fresh, ever-young laughter, and at the same time so affluent of peace, of heartfelt love, as that between sisters.

But unhappy the home where the word "sister" is spoken in bitterness by bitter hearts! There lives the rust which "eats into the heart," and there the intercourse which makes life wormwood, and "embitters the well-springs of earth." Sisters, who live together in this spirit, take courage and separate!

Sisters, who during a heavenly communion afforded me heavenly joys, and bitter sorrow only when Heaven took you from me; beloved sisters, it is of you that I think when I speak of the sweetest and most purifying sentiment in the world, that which binds sister to sister, and enables, through this love, much to be borne and much to be overcome.

When Martha and Maria were together in their little chamber, they gave for a while free vent to their tears, as well as to conjectures which did not afford them any light. Finally, they endeavored to console themselves with thinking what they should do in the house during Hertha's absence, and which would give her pleasure on her return. And these little plans for the future cast a roseate glow over the increasing darkness of evening.

Hertha, on her part, had felt in her sisters' embrace the renewal of a firm resolve to live for them; but for that purpose, precisely for that purpose, must she now leave them for a little time; she felt that she must do it.

Reader! either by thy own means, or by means of another, has a misfortune happened to thee, which thou knowest to be irremediable; which has struck thee with a kind of panic terror, and cast a fearful burden upon thy breast, and taken away, as it were, thy breath, and dimmed thy sight—so that it seems to thee as if thou couldst never more be happy, never more breathe freely—then thou wilt understand what Hertha felt. If thou dost not die of this blow, or become insane,—as sometimes happens,—then will a strange unrest take possession of thee, and thou wilt feel that in order to escape the ravenous beast which threatens to tear thee to pieces,—the night which seems as if it would swallow thee up,—that thou must fly, fly away from the time and the place, away from thyself, if possible,—away from the horrible oppression which weighs upon thee, from *that* which is there, as a corpse, a ghost before thine eyes, and which prevents thee from thinking or feeling aright, by the horror of its silent, sorrowful presence. And if thou so feelest, oh, well for thee if thou canst take wings and fly away from the time and from the place!

It is indeed merely an earthly, physical means; but it is never-theless a little help to obtain breathing room, and to give the soul time and power to reflect upon itself, and upon that which has happened. Travel diverts the mind. The black demon which has eaten into our hearts is lulled to sleep by it. We do not incessantly feel him stabbing and gnawing, and we are able to gain strength to combat with him; yet not alone from travelling and action.

In order to escape from the torturing pang which had over-come her, and to avoid the visits and proximity of Yngve, and to gain time for reflection on the line of conduct which she ought to pursue with regard to him,—in order to endeavor, from her own soul's depths, to obtain some light in the dark-ness which now surrounded herself and him, Hertha felt that she must go away for a time,—whither, was a matter of indifference to her—only away, away from him.

Through the whole night she paced to and fro in her cham-ber, restless and sleepless. Sometimes she stood by the window and looked up to heaven, but without prayer, and almost without thought, except that dark abyss of doubt which had so long lain like a Nidhögg at the root of her soul, and which now again lifted up his head through the covering of flowers which had latterly been placed there. The stars glittered brilliantly and coldly, and darkness overspread the earth.

At daybreak she dressed herself for her journey; took a little travelling-bag which contained some necessary articles of clothing, together with a small sum of money, the gift of her father, and with this in her hand set out on the way to the harbor, which was between one and two miles distant from her home.

Like Rudolph some months before, with the sense of a vast unhappiness in her soul, she walked solitary along the dreary high road to seek for rest somewhere, a long way from home. "Poor Rudolph!" sighed Hertha, involuntarily. She felt a reproach of conscience for having almost forgotten him (al-though she had written to him and he to her more than once since his flight), for the feelings and thoughts which had during the last few weeks engrossed her whole soul; and she suddenly took the resolution of visiting him at Copenhagen.

"I will see him!" thought she; "I can understand him better than formerly, and that will help him to bear his unfortunate life!"

And perhaps also help myself, whispered a low voice in Hertha's soul. There was now an object in her journey beyond herself, and this object shone like a little star on her gloomy path. It gleamed above her in the dark heaven; it lighted and guided her steps.

There is nothing which, for energetic and at the same time truly feminine characters, is so sustaining under their own calamity, or which is endowed with so great a power of compensation, both for soul and mind, as the being able to comfort and support another—above all, a friend. By the thought of this the soul holds itself fast, as by an anchor, while the storm rages and the waves heave aloft, she feels her own danger less;—it may be that she forgets it.

When Hertha reached the harbor she found one of the steam-boats just leaving for the western coast, and its dark column of smoke circling aloft towards the clear blue heaven. As soon as she was on board, the plank was drawn to shore.

THE JOURNEY:

GIANTS AND FAIRIES OF LIGHT.

WHAT a poem is that gigantic work in Sweden, which unites the Baltic with the Cattegat, and which we call the Götha Canal, the "blue ribbon of Sweden;" what a poem, from its history and natural scenery, the grandeur of its design and execution, its great or delightful memories! For three hundred years have the kings of Sweden, from the first Gustavus till the fourteenth Charles, assisted by the genius and the great men of the country, Barsk, Polhem, Swedenborg, Thunborg, Platen, striven for its completion, supported by the arms and the money of the people. Opposed by natural impediments, and by all kinds of difficulties, after great adversities and desolating war, amid internal discords, after great losses, as that of Finland, have the rulers and the nation always anew turned themselves to this internal great work, and have begun together to labor upon it, as if in the common understanding that it was in the internal power and life of the country that the nation beheld their secure support and the hope of their future.

What a poem is now the journey from the town of Birger on the shores of the Maler Lake and the billows of the Baltic Sea to the town of Gustaf Adolph, on the shores of the Cattegat, as we pass on the waters of "the Blue Ribbon" through the interior of the country, where primeval mountains open for us, thundering, their gates, and we are borne up on invisible arms, higher and higher, from plateau to plateau, till we reach at length the uninhabited primeval forest, the bosom of wild mountain lakes then silently break our way through the bosom of the rocks, and are lowered from them into enchanting lakes which we had just seen lying like mirrors far below our feet, set in frames of fertile country gemmed with towers and castles and cottages; then speed on through glorious parks, whose leafy trees familiarly caress us in passing with their green boughs; then emerge into a wide, wild country, in which the giants of nature wrestle, without, however, disturbing or impeding our way—

> Wild waters down the cliffs are thundered;
> Rage the Gold Island's powers unblest,
> But genius comes—the rock is sundered,
> And a ship lies on its breast!—

and thus are we borne by the mighty arms of science into the bosom of the loveliest scenery, and out upon the broad, calm animated waters of the river Gotha; and all this, whilst a whole world of ancient memories and present romance accompanies us on the journey with its vala-song; its battles; its runes, its ancient saga, legend and history; its heroes' graves and landmarks; giant-cauldrons and holy wells; ancient castles, ruins and so-called convents,—with here and there some grand or tragic memory,—or the erections of the present day in factories and forts, splendid gentlemen's seats and small red cottages beneath the shade of fir trees, all in perpetual and ever-varying change; a wonderous runic song, in which the wood-lady and the statesman, the mountain king and the beautiful maiden, the water fairy and the queen, fiction and reality contend for the laurels of poesy by the life-like pictures which they present, the feelings which they awaken.

No point, during the whole journey, is however more remarkable than that of Trollhätta. Thou hast left the heights and the mountain-lakes behind thee, Wettern with its spires and fertile shores; thou art in the great Wenner lake, into which four-and-twenty rivers pour their waters from the provinces and the heights around; thou hast left at a distance the fruitful terraces of Kinnekulle, and beneath the gloomy shadows of Hunne and Halleberg thou advancest into the forests of Westergylln. The waters of Wenner swelled by the four-

and-twenty rivers accompany thee, and cast themselves down
the mountain in the wild, stormy fall of Trollhätta. But thou
art at peace in the forest. Thou art borne silently through
its pine-wood parks upon the granite mountain, and hearest
merely at a distance the thundering contest of the giants of
nature. Thou emergest from the forest just where the foaming force with its powerful blue-green mass of waters, is all
at once changed to the deep broad river, which between
idyllian, flowery, and pleasant shores hastens towards a background of blue-grey, distant, billowy mountains, on to the
sea.

> And poets' songs are in his praise indited,
> And ships and men go with him as he goes,
> As guest by affluent towns he is invited;
> And fertile fields his devious path enclose.
> But they detain him not; he onward hasteth;
> The gilded tower, the fertile meadows by,
> He hasteth ever onward, till he casteth
> Himself into his father's arms to die.
>
> *The River* by TEGNÉR.

How solemn, at the same time earnest and agreeable, is the
scenery of the very spot where this transformation takes place,
and the steamer emerges from the forest-covered mountain by
two arms between green wooded hills, to drop down into the
free waters of the river! What a contrast is this peace with
the wild combat, the fall and the locks hard by, the crags and
the fall of Trollhätta!

Thus, once upon a time, stood here, beautiful and affectionate, *Ogn Alfafoster*, the foster-child of Alferna, when, for
her sake, Starkodder, her giant-lover, wrestled and fought a
mortal fight beside these rocks, with her betrothed husband,
Hergrim. Yet she was not calm, as this scenery, for she
loved not the human warrior who conquered; she loved
Starkodder the giant, and attended him in death.

But we have forgotten ourselves in these memories, and we
now return to the poor traveller, whom we accompanied

hither, and who was scarcely in a state to enjoy the scenes of which we have spoken.

The morning wind blew cold, as the steam-boat worked her way over the dancing waters. Silent and perturbed in mind, Hertha, wrapped in her dark grey woollen shawl, seated herself and watched the heaving waters, the careering clouds, the flying shores, the whirling, beckoning trees, the leaves of which were already tinted with the frosts of the autumnal nights, and which seemed to be wafting to her their farewells. Hour after hour passed on, and Hertha sate thus immoveably. It was as if the pulses of life had stopped under the pressure of a convulsive hand.

By degrees several gentlemen-passengers emerged from their berths below, on deck. They smoked their cigars, spit about, and made the deck filthy. They noticed the lady with the fine figure dressed in black, and her immovability excited their jocular remarks. They called her "the statue," and began to wonder whether she actually were flesh and blood ; whether she had the power of motion, could talk, and so on. A sort of half-gentleman determined to make the attempt of giving life to the statue.

He seated himself beside her, smoking his cigar, every puff from which the wind blew in her face. She turned her head mechanically away.

"Aha !" thought the new Pygmalion, "she can move. Let me now see whether I cannot make her talk !" And he began, between two puffs of cigar-smoke :

"Very—fine weather to-day ;" puff, puff, "but rather cold ;" puff——

No answer from the statue ; not a movement.

Fresh puffs of cigar-smoke, spitting, smoke, puff, and a fresh attempt :

"A very fine view ;—don't you think so ?—Have you any commands ?"

The statue now turned her head and looked at the speaker. He drew back a little, and looked confused, again drew back a little, returned to his cigar, spit, hummed a tune, and

went back to the tobacco-smoking group, to whom he whispered :

"She is certainly mad. She looked at me with such a
glance, I was really frightened. It was a regular Medusa,
hu——"

"A very well-grown Medusa!" said a tall, elderly gentleman, with a connoisseur's glance at Hertha, "and not so ugly
either ; though she is just now in a bad humor ; she might let
one talk to her when she is in a better temper."

Many gentlemen and ladies were now on deck, and the seats
were all occupied. The elderly gentleman seated himself by
Hertha, smoked and spat. After he had continued to do this
for some time, he said a few words to her in an under-tone.
She made no reply ; again he spoke, and this time Hertha
rose and went to another part of the deck. But every place
was occupied, and she remained standing for a moment as if
hesitating. A young man, with a pair of earnest, intellectual
eyes, rose and offered her his seat. She accepted it gratefully.
It was close to an elderly lady, who quickly began to talk to
Hertha, and when a few monosyllabic words gave her the hope
of being listened to, she proceeded to give an account of her
family, the purpose of her journey, her course of life, her
state of health, and all her confinements. She also inquired if
"the lady" were married or unmarried ; desired to know her
name, and informed her that her own name was Tallquist.

Hertha's young protector went below deck, but soon returned, with a little printed tract in his hand, which, with a
polite and kind expression, he offered her. The tall gentleman now stood quite near Hertha, blowing great puffs from
his cigar. The younger stayed also near her, but without a
cigar, and, while he seemed wholly occupied in looking at the
scenery through his glass, he thrust himself between Hertha
and her persecutor. She felt that she had a protector near
her, and a sense of gratitude was, therefore, the first feeling
which she experienced, through the four-and-twenty hours,
which was not painful to her. Apparently listening, but, in
reality, perfectly deaf to the old lady's account of her life, she

sat with her eyes riveted upon the tract which she held in her hand. By degrees some words attracted her eye, and she read as follows, in Danish:

"To be agonised as I am, and still may be, is certainly what no one, humanly speaking, can call desirable; nevertheless, it may be that which, in a much higher state, I may thank God for as the greatest benefit. To be agonised and brought low, even for a noble cause, is, I can very well understand, something which one, humanly speaking, cannot desire, something which one would wish to avoid at almost any price, if, by experience, one were not exalted by the thought, that in a far higher point of view, this extreme of suffering may be regarded as the greatest benefit."

Hertha turned the page and continued to read:

"*April* 11. In torments which a human being has seldom survived; in agonies of mind of eight days' endurance, which were enough to deprive the mind of reason, I am yet sufficiently ——

"My wishes have often been for death, my longings for the grave! my desire that my wishes and my longings might be fulfilled. Yes, O God! if thou wert not Almighty; if thou couldst not all-powerfully compel; if thou wert not love which could move irresistibly; on no other condition, at no other price could I be induced to choose the life which is mine, again to be embittered by its unavoidable consequences, the effect which mankind produces upon me.

"Yet thy love, O God! prompts the thought of daring to love thee, inspires me under the possibility of being all-powerfully compelled—joyfully and gratefully to desire to become that which is the consequence of being loved by thee and of loving thee; a sacrifice offered for a race to whom the ideal is a foolishness, a nothing, to whom the earthly, the temporal, are the only real."

Hertha did not inquire by whom this heart-rending con-fession was made;* but she felt that a combating and suffering

* S. Kirkegaard, in his last "Moment."

heart throbbed here in unison with her own, embittered, bleeding, loving, and still, though as in the midst of the flames, seeking to lay hold upon God; and she felt less solitary in the world.

When the steam-boat reached the locks of Trollhätta and the company on board landed, as is usual, to visit the fall, Hertha mechanically accompanied them.

Before long, however, it seemed to her intolerable to make one of the merry, chattering groups of people, and she dropped behind them all. As she was thus walking solitarily along the footpath, through the wood, she observed that some one was following her; presently he had overtaken and joined her, and Hertha recognised her persecutor of the morning, who now, with an inquisitive and bold glance, seized her hand, as he said:

"Why are you walking here by yourself; you who, nevertheless, seem so charming?"

Hertha snatched away her hand, and looked at the speaker with a glance which made him say:

"Bless me! there's no great harm done; and surely one may speak to a girl without her——"

Hertha looked round impatiently for some of her travelling companions, and just at that moment saw Mrs. Tallquist coming after her, puffing and out of breath, calling:

"Listen, Mamsell! Mamsell! How many locks are there between here and Stockholm? Tallquist and I have laid a wager about it; but I don't know precisely whether I am right; I want to hear what others know about it, and Tallquist is in full chase after me."

"I really cannot tell you," replied Hertha, "but we can very soon find out," added she, anxious to have Mrs. Tallquist's company until she fell in with the remainder of the party; and Mrs. Tallquist had so great a desire to communicate one thing and another to her, that she had no need of asking for her company, especially as Mr. Tallquist now overtook them, still more out of breath, and still more pantingly than his wife, but by no means in so good a humor because of her unexpected escapade after Hertha.

"I only wanted to ask about the locks," said Mrs. Tallquist, "and to know which of us was right."

"The devil take the locks!" growled Mr. Tallquist.

The Tallquists, Hertha, and her unbidden fellow-traveller, soon reached the rest of the company now assembled on the heights above the Hell-falls, and just about to continue their way to the lower locks at Åker.

When at this latter place the company again went on board to continue their journey, Hertha was not with them. The wild thundering falls, the solitary region, the wood-covered mountains around them, the contest between the giant powers of nature and the strong symbolic language in which they seemed to address her, attracted her to them with a congenial power. It seemed good to her to rest here and get rid of the people; to get rid of the familiarity of the intrusive gentleman and the communications of Mrs. Tallquist.

When the steamer burst forward through the locks of Trollhätta on its way into the beautiful river, Hertha was sitting alone on Gull, or Gold Island, with the thundering falls roaring around her, and the words of Kirkegaard in her hand. The deafening thunder of the fall seemed to her a lullaby which would hush to sleep the wild combat in her breast, and for the moment it did so. When evening came, and with it darkness, she went to the Inn, and ordered and obtained for herself a room.

She passed a sleepless night. With the first flush of dawn she went out. She wandered from the falls of Toppö and Gullö, through the wood, and over the rocks, down to the Hell-fall. She stopped for a moment at the Giant's cauldrons in the primeval rock, only to recommence her wandering immediately, from the necessity of allaying the torture of the soul by the weariness of the body, and to gain a moment's forgetfulness of life and suffering—a moment's sleep. But all the more seemed darkness and the horrors of darkness to encompass her soul. Energetic natures are able to suffer a great deal without being crushed or subdued; nevertheless, there is a state in which they have great difficulty in sustaining themselves. It is that in which sleep deserts them and gives them up a prey to dark phantoms which take possession of their souls. Sleeplessness, which converts the four-and-twenty hours into one unbroken day, and compels the dry, hot eyes to stare unchangingly at one single dark point, is the old hag who felled Thor to the ground after he had already wrestled victoriously with gods and giants. Suffering, in its extremest form, causes to us the loss of our higher consciousness, our light and our strength. If any one had asked the restless wanderer by the fall of Trollhätta, at this time, what she was seeking for, she might have replied—"Myself!"

The words of Kirkegaard no longer consoled her. The spirit which spoke to her in them was too much absorbed by the combat, had not yet passed victoriously through it. In the dark tumultuous state of mind in which she then was, she threw the printed tract into the foaming waters. It whirled round for a moment, sank, and vanished from sight. How beautiful to sink thus, to vanish in the cool depths, and forget, and rest ;—the thundering, whirling waters would be heard there no longer !

"Yngve ! Yngve ! How is it possible !" was the dark unceasing thought in Hertha's soul, which lay there as the coil of a serpent. And truth and love, abhorrence and scorn, alternately attempted to unfold it—in vain. Her thoughts began to be confused, and she dreaded insanity.

There stands on Gull Island a solitary blackened pine-tree, which with its crown of wild, distorted branches, hangs over the abyss, as if it would tumble into it, a strange demoniac figure, which calls forth dark thoughts, and seems to be the offspring of such. Did it spring up in the foot-prints of the beautiful giant-bride who once stood there, and hurled herself into the abyss to escape the misery of life ?

The dark figure riveted Hertha's gaze with giant power. It pointed into the abyss below, and seemed to say, "Down there ! down there !" It was a moment when everything appeared dark to her. But there came a caressing breeze and fanned her burning temples, and made a murmur among the pine-trees of the rock.   Hertha seemed to feel the caresses of her young sisters, and to hear their words :

"Do not forsake us !"

And she turned away from the tempting falls, determined to make every possible effort to gain a few hours' sleep, and by that means to clear her mind.   She obtained for herself a soporific draught from the medical man at Trollhätta; but it afforded her no repose, only a trance full of fever-phantasies.

She was in a church at the hour of midnight; the full moon shining solemnly amid dark, threatening clouds, was visible through the chancel window.   Silent human figures sate like shadows in the chancel, and at the farther end stood, against a dark background, a lofty, golden crucifix, which shed a pale gleam of light through the chancel.

The organ pealed, and a voice sang—

"O Lamb of God, which takest away the sins of the world !"

With that, the shadow-like forms advanced to the altar and knelt there.   Hertha, impelled irresistibly, accompanied them, and partook of "the body and blood of Christ," with the rest.

She then turned to leave the church and went to Yngve; she saw him lying in his morning slumber, handsome and smiling, on his bed.   But she awoke him, and said to him with sorrowful earnestness :

"Yngve! thou hast lied before heaven and before me, and thou must now die.   But I have sanctified my lips by the blood which can make thee pure, and I am come to sanctify thee !"

And she bent over him and kissed him.   With that Yngve's red lips grew pale, and a marble rigidity crept over his features and his limbs.   He gazed at her with a reproachful and yet affectionate gaze, until it was set as in stone. She closed his eyelids, and he was dead, and with him all her joy in life.

She saw another world, a wonderful kingdom of death and silence. There was a great city with gates and streets and a market, but of graves, and monuments hewn in stone. Not a tree, not a flower, not a blade of grass was to be seen among them. A starless, steel-grey sky expanded itself over the graves, over the city of the dead, which seemed to expand into infinitude, over the whole earth. Deep twilight rested there, and not a sound, not a tone of life was heard, except a soft soughing which sometimes raised itself, then sank and died away like deep beseeching sighs.

When Hertha's eye became accustomed to the deep twilight which prevailed, she saw human forms by many of the monuments which lay there in prayer, and again and again laid their lips to the walls of the graves. They seemed in the mean time to be expecting something. Hertha also stood by a monument, a single column, which she embraced with her arms and held clasped to her breast, and she very well knew who lay below, and why her warm heart throbbed against the hard stone. Thus passed on many, many years, and many of the supplicating ones by the graves grew weary and left their posts, to return to the cities and the pleasures of life. But Hertha did not grow weary, but stood faithfully with her warm heart beating against the hard granite stone, wishing for the moment when they who are in the graves shall hear the voice of God.

Suddenly a light blazed in the east, and a strong voice cried aloud, "The moment is come!" and the earth trembled and the graves opened. The column which Hertha embraced moved, and she felt that a heart was throbbing against her heart. She held Yngve in her arms, and he opened his eyes; but oh, what a gloomy earnestness in his look as he said—

"Why hast thou woke me—only to lead me to judgment?"

Hertha replied: "I have won thee from judgment, Yngve, won thee, by watching and many prayers. Only canst thou love me? Remember our bond, and speak the truth!"

Yngve's eyes turned away from hers and gazed in another

direction, at a shadowy form which stood near, as if waiting for him, and which bore the features of Amalia. Hertha at this felt her heart contracted by an unspeakable pain, and soon she again saw herself alone, wandering like a shadow among the graves in the kingdom of the dead.

Such, and many more, were the delirious dreams amid which Hertha's soul sought for some point upon which it could rest.

One morning, after a dream kindred to the foregoing, she rose and wandered into the country, in a direction opposite to the fall, the thunder of which now began to be a torment to her. She heard the bells ringing for church, and saw the country people going churchward in their holiday attire, whence she perceived that it was Sunday. She followed them to a little country church, at the outskirts of the forest. It was a simple, but tastefully built stone church, with a spacious chancel, at the far end of which stood a tall, gilded crucifix, which shone out brightly from the dark background. It resembled that which she had seen in her dream. She stood still. The peasants, in the costume of the country, filled the church. The clergyman went to the altar. Hertha could not follow every word which he said, she merely understood that he invited all to come to a holy—a consolatory communion. And when the hymn was sung, " O Lamb of God," and the congregation rose and advanced to the altar, Hertha accompanied them, and bowed her weary head at the foot of the cross.

The peacefulness of the church, the mystical words which were uttered by the priest, the mild, earnest countenances which surrounded her, among which many were elderly, some blind, the sight of the cross, the thought of him whose type it was, all operated forcibly on Hertha's soul; and when the clergyman approached her and looked at her with an astonished and hesitating glance, which she returned by an expression of so much suffering and so earnest a desire, he could not refuse her the holy Communion, to which, however, according to the Swedish ecclesiastical laws, she was not entitled, as her name had not been announced for that purpose, nor had she been present at confession. But he involuntarily obeyed the inspiration of the moment, certain that he had now before him a human being who needed the means of grace. Hertha received them, bowed her head, and—her tears flowed apace.

A lofty and glorious form stepped between her and the beloved but guilty man, who caused her anguish; stepped between her and the whole world, which now vanished from before her eyes. At His heart, at His feet, she laid herself down, her life, her sorrow, her beloved, his sin; his and her own life, everything, in deep and perfect resignation, and she felt herself to be saved. Like the fainting wanderer of the desert, she laid herself down at the margin of the fresh fountain, and drank in new life.

Silent festival! Who can tell the hidden miracles of salvation which, ever since the hour of thy institution, thou hast performed, and still performest. The forms of religion may vary, churches become antiquated and changed, generations come and go, but thou, silent, mystical festival, still remainest, always the same, gathering together the scattered flocks, feeding the souls with the same body and the same blood; and all the mysteries of existence centre in thee and beam forth from thee. Silent, sacred festival, communion of all sects, mystical bond of soul with soul and of all with the ONE; preserver of the life of love, in a world which is poor in love, yet which requireth love; preserver of hope; nurse of the community of heaven, so long as thou art administered in the church, or thence sent out to the chambers of the suffering, so long still lives therein the life and power of Christ; and if I, as well as many others, look with longing towards *a Church of the future* more true and more active than that which now, in our north, rules the consciences of men, it is because they then may more generally, more inwardly, come to thee and partake of thy fulness, silent, holy festival, fountain of life!

When Hertha wandered back through the soughing pine-forest towards the fall, she felt that everything was not lost, that ONE remained immoveable, firm, and steadfast; one whom she might love and look up to, and attach herself to with all her soul and all her might—the Shepherd and the Friend of every soul. The falling waters, the roaring storm, all the disquiet of human life, they had their time and their termination, but He remained for ever. They were the means, not the end, because *He* was there, and she had been made cognisant of his presence, his life. In the world was strife, but in Him she could have peace, that she clearly felt. A calm, lofty, loveful resignation possessed her soul, together with a grateful joy over the change which she experienced, and the experience which was her portion.

Such an experience is of inestimable worth for the whole of life, and gives to the soul a certainty of the being of God, and of his immediate relationship to her, which nothing is evermore able to shake.

And either He lifts the soul up to his heart and lets her taste of the joy which no tongue can express, or bends her to the earth, as the winds the reeds of the shore, so that she is satisfied that He is with her and that He is love. In the deepest winter's night this is her light.

Such were Hertha's thoughts as she went homeward through the solitary wood, and in that light which now shone into her soul all the dark enigmas of life seemed cleared up. Even the confused, distorted image of Yngve became transfigured. Was it not the doctrine which she heard from his lips, and which now she comprehended with a new feeling of its truth? Could he indeed be false—be a liar? Must not all be a lie rather than this be true? Hertha came hastily to the determination to put the question to himself, and let the truth be judge between them. First, however, she must see Rudolph. She now felt herself in a condition to benefit him; and again serene and determined, she resolved on the following day to continue her journey to Copenhagen. She merely required a night's rest. It was now the seventh night since she had slept.

This night she slept deeply and soundly. But the struggle of the soul re-acted on the body, and she awoke in the morning with a terrible headache. She sent for the medical man of the place, and asked from him a copious blood-letting. It was with a sort of bitter pleasure that she watched the blood flow until she nearly fainted. Could she but, with the whole of her blood, have purchased Yngve's freedom from blame! After the blood-letting and a sedative draught, Hertha remained lying comparatively free from pain. Thus she lay for the whole day with her eyes closed, and only now and then a tear which slowly forced its way through her dark eye-lashes down her pale cheeks, made known the silent sorrow of her soul.

Thus was she still lying in the evening, when she heard the door open and some one softly enter the room; but in the belief that it was one of the maid-servants of the house, who had promised to look after her, she continued to lie still with her eyes closed. She then felt a warm kiss impressed upon her hand, which was at the same time bathed with tears. Hertha opened her eyes, and beheld a lovely young girl on her knees, by her bed, watching her with an expression of the most heartfelt love:

"Oh, pardon me! pardon me!" besought at the same time the sweet voice of Eva Dufva, "and don't send me away. I heard that some one, who appeared very ill and out of spirits, lay here, and I wished to know if I could be of any service to her, because I myself also am sorrowful and sick at heart. But now that I recognise you I cannot leave you. Oh, let me remain with you till you are well again. Let me be like a sister to you, or a servant. Who knows, perhaps the insignificant and the weak may be of some little service to the strong. That would be so agreeable to me. I will be so silent, so very silent; but I cannot leave you. It will do me more good to be with you than anything else."

"How did you come here?" asked Hertha, as she caressingly laid her hand on the young girl's neck.

"With my parents," replied Eva; "we are on our way to Copenhagen, where my father has business, and they have allowed me and my sister Marie to accompany them, to divert my mind and to enliven me, as they say. For I have been, and still am, very uneasy in my mind ever since—but I will tell you all about that afterwards; if I only may remain with you. You will dissipate the uncertainty of my mind; you will enable me to become clear as regards myself and what I ought to do; no one can do this if you cannot. Oh, let me stay with you! I would give up everything in Copenhagen, if I might only remain here by your bedside. Sister Marie can go with my parents to Copenhagen."

"Ask your mother to let me speak with her," said Hertha; and Eva, who heard a consent in the words, kissed Hertha's hand passionately, and hastened to her mother.

It was soon arranged between Mrs. Dufva and Hertha, that Eva should remain with the latter until she was sufficiently recovered to be able to cross the Sound, when Eva should accompany her and join her parents in Copenhagen. Hertha had told Mrs. Dufva of her intentions of visiting an invalid relative in that city; and Hertha, although not properly belonging to the circle of their acquaintance, was universally so highly esteemed and respected, that Mrs. Dufva, without demur or deliberation, left Eva under her protection.

Eva Dufva was overjoyed at this arrangement. She was at that age when it is so common for warm-hearted girls to form enthusiastic attachments to persons of their own sex, particularly when these are distinguished by a force of character in which they themselves are deficient, and Eva Dufva had long since felt that attraction towards Hertha which the weak climbing plant feels towards the strong tree, around whose bole it is necessary to entwine itself in order to raise itself to the light.

The little chamber, by the fall of Trollhätta, which during the foregoing four-and-twenty hours had witnessed such gloomy suffering, exhibited this evening a pleasant picture.

It was the pale invalid, who, now evidently convalescent, was sitting raised up in bed, with her rich golden hair thrown back from her temples, and falling in unrestrained masses over the snowy pillows, whilst her eyes, still weak from the effect of fever, rested with motherly affection on the young girl who, kneeling by her bed, held her hand between both hers, now pressing it to her lips, now laying it against her burning cheeks, whilst she poured out her overflowing heart.

Eva related how she, in consequence of Mr. Von Tackjern's behavior at the fire, felt the repugnance which she had always entertained towards a marriage with him so increase, that the thought of it became intolerable to her; and how she had prevailed upon her parents to consent to the engagement between them being broken off. In the meantime, the circum-stances of the family, in consequence of the fire and other losses, became greatly embarrassed. She saw the distress of her parents, and their evident wish that the engagement between their daughter and the wealthy Mr. Von Tackjern should be renewed. He, on his part, had expressed his willingness; he considered her having broken their betrothal as merely a usual "woman's whim," which he was willing to forgive, and proposed that the marriage should at once take place, to obviate the necessity of a second betrothal.

"And now I know what lies before me," continued Eva; "after this journey, which is to 'dissipate my crotchets,' they will urge me to make an end of the thing. My parents will say that 'I can do as I like; that they do not wish to persuade me;' but they will look anxious; I shall read in their looks and their expression what they wish for; I shall see how easy I might make theirs and my sisters' future by my marriage; so that I should be able to please everybody, and make every-body happy except—myself. But is it right in me to regard only my own happiness? To disappoint every one 'just for the sake of my own pleasure?' Is not that wrong and ego-tistical? Ah! I have gone from church to church that I might meet with counsel and light; but they have preached about submission and obedience, which, nevertheless, my heart rebelled against, because I do not know whether, in this case, it is the will of God. If I could only know it! I have prayed to God for light, early and late, and yet—and yet no light has come into my poor mind, and it has put me out of heart, and—sometimes I have felt indifferent about myself and everything else in the world, so that I could have thrown myself away, seeing that God did not trouble himself about me. Ah! that was, after all, a sinful thought, for he has indeed led me hither to you, and you, I know, will teach and enlighten me."

Hertha had allowed the young girl to pour out her whole heart; she then said:

"Have you not sometimes thought that you might become a mother in this marriage?"

"No," replied Eva; "at least I have not liked to dwell on the thought. Hu! no!"

"It is, nevertheless, the only one which could give you light on your way," said Hertha. "If you would choose a father as guide and counsellor for your child, would you choose Mr. Von Tackjern?"

"No!" said Eva with decision. "No: that I never would!"

"Do you think that he might become different; that he might be changed through your influence?"

"Ah!" sighed Eva, "that is what people have said to me, but I do not believe it. He is so much older—so much more worldly-wise—so much stronger of will than I am. I should never have courage to be entirely myself with him; to ask anything from him. I should, if united with him, become less candid, less cheerful than I am now. I fancy even that I might become cunning with him, because I am afraid of him. I would not like to depend upon him; not be his son or his daughter!"

"Then do not become his wife," said Hertha with great decision, as she laid her hand on the young girl's head, "otherwise you will sin against God and against the vocation of *mother*, which He might give you, to watch over the well-being of the children which might be born of this marriage. Ah, Eva! I wonder every day how people in a general way, whether in or out of marriage, can so thoughtlessly bring into existence—that great, bitter, awful existence, of which heaven or hell is the point of exit—children, human beings, with immortal souls, which are capable of so much suffering, so much despair, and which one day may reproach the author of their being for having called them into existence! It is especially to the maternal heart of the woman that the Creator has intrusted the responsibility and the care of the children to which she may give birth; and yet how seldom does she reflect on this when she is about to give herself to a husband! Eva! this is my last word to you on this subject—never marry a man whose daughter you would not like to be!"

"Hertha!" exclaimed Eva, "you have lifted a stone from my heart; you have removed the bandage from my eyes, and I now see everything clearly! Oh, you are right! you are right! and it is God who has led me to you, because——But, Hertha, do not abandon me after this, for I shall stand in need of your support and your advice. My parents are kind—very kind. But they fancy that a girl must either marry or stop at home, occupied by her pretty 'ladies-work,' and that she ought not to undertake anything but the care of her toilet or making calls; and that has never been sufficient for me, and it will become less sufficing after this. There are many of us at home; we are not all needed there, and I must now, of necessity, leave home for a time. If I could only undertake something which would be helpful to my parents and my sisters!—but then I am so ignorant; know a little of many things superficially, but nothing thoroughly. Nevertheless, I would so willingly work—work really hard at anything—if I could only reap some benefit by it, and come out of that state of uncertainty and incompleteness which is at present the state of my mind and the state of my home-life. I go about, as it were, in twilight: I don't know what I am, nor what I may be. I am seeking for myself. I am like a field lying fallow, but which might become fruitful by the hand of the cultivator."

The longer Eva continued thus to speak, the more Hertha's glance beamed on the young girl; she raised her head, assumed once more the expression of self-consciousness, power, and resolve which were peculiar to her, and her earnest gaze penetrated with tender inquiry into the young girl's soul which had thus revealed itself to her.

"I understand you," she said, "and what you say rejoices me. For us women a great deal of the field of life lies fallow, and men would prevent us from bringing it up into cultivation. But a clear and steadfast will is able to break through many impediments. Do you feel in your soul any longings after a larger, more general activity, in any particular direction?"

"No, I do not," replied Eva. "I dread publicity, and fear my own incapacity to work independently. But I should be glad to devote my small activity, my small ability in life, to some object which I felt to be great and noble, worthy of living and laboring for. And I would gladly clasp a poor child to my heart, and live and labor for it. That would make me happy. I should not be afraid of poverty with that child. I should be able to provide a frugal living for it, and for myself. That has been and is my dearest dream for the future. But first I will become a better, clearer, stronger human being than I now am, and therefore let me love you, see you, come to you sometimes, look up to you. It is so beautiful, so glorious, to be able to look up, love, admire!"

"Ah! do not look up to a fellow-creature, your equal!" said Hertha, with a deep and sorrowful earnestness. "You will, in that case, find yourself deceived; look up to God alone! This cannot be too often insisted upon; human beings are weak; the best are imperfect, and true, bitterly true, is our old proverb, 'Trust not in that which another holds for you!'"

There was such a sad earnestness in Hertha's expression, whilst she continued to warn Eva of too much trust in or dependence on another, that Eva was profoundly impressed by it. But she said, still caressingly:

"You will really trust in me and my attachment to you. I know that I could die for you. They who love you once, must love you for ever, and become more earnest and better in consequence. I do not wish,—I am not worthy to know what is the reason of your thinking so ill of mankind; but certainly you have suffered, and suffering darkens the mind, and causes it, perhaps, not always to judge correctly. Forgive me for venturing to talk thus to you, but—I am so very found of you, and it grieves me so sadly that you should feel thus."

And Eva covered Hertha's hand with her kisses and her tears.

In the old Saga of Gudrum, who sate by the corpse of Sigurd, but could not weep like other women, because she " will merely die," it is said how—

> ——the noble
> Earl-daughters,
> Gold-ornamented,
> Sate before Gudrun;
> Each one related
> Her bitterest sorrow,
> That which the sorest
> Her heart had afflicted.

At length the mourner was so far consoled, that she burst into tears and song.

Thus is individual sorrow alleviated by sympathy for another.   Thus also now were the sufferings of the two young women alleviated by the deep sympathy which each felt for the other.

Soon might Eva be seen, with a mind much calmer than of late, gracefully and silently busied, and setting out a little supper for Hertha, and seeming to forget herself in serving her; whilst Hertha allowed herself, with a quiet resignation, to be waited upon, and even received with a smile, bread and a glass of milk from her hand.   And when, later in the evening, Eva read aloud to her, Hertha fixed her eyes on the innocent countenance of the charming girl, as it was lit up by the lamplight, and sank into a dim dream about faith and love upon earth.   During this, she fell into a calm sleep; and after Eva had continued to read for a good half-hour, in order to deepen her sleep still more, she made herself a little bed at the foot of Hertha's, and rested there better than she had done for a long time—the good young girl!

The following day Hertha felt herself very much better. She wrote home to her father and sisters, fixing the day for her return, and the day following, with Eva Dufva crossed the Kattegatt to Copenhagen, where she restored the young girl to her family—not without having formed a close compact with her for the future—and then went to seek out Rudolph.

Well was it that she came to him at this moment! The unfortunate young man, pursued by unspeakable mental disquiet, by the horrible memories of the night of the fire, which seemed more and more strongly to rise up in his soul, was just about to leave the house into which he had been received, and to wander out into the world, without any other object than that of flying from himself.

Hertha did not dissuade him from this purpose; on the contrary, she strengthened him in his intentions of taking a long pedestrian journey, and in concert with the relative who had received him under his protection, laid out for him the route of such a journey, and furnished him with letters which would enable him to find friends and protectors at various places on his way, in case he needed them. This was good for the unhappy young man; but oh, how much more so was her presence, her strengthening, consolatory words, and the thought that she had come to Copenhagen merely for his sake; that he was something to her; that she had an interest about him. Joy and gratitude for this made him as a child in her hands. She, on her part, strengthened by the baptism through which she had so lately passed, talked to the poor son of the twilight with quite another wisdom and quite another power than formerly, comforting and strengthening him at the same time.

When Hertha had, with motherly care, provided the suitable equipment of Rudolph for his journey; after she had seen him, with his knapsack on his back, weeping but still happy, happy by her blessing, set out on his solitary way with his pilgrim-staff in his hand, she, without a single glimpse at the glorious works of art which are possessed by this northern

Athens, turned her face towards her own country and her own home.

Once more there she was received with unspeakable joy by her young sisters, whose tears and endearments made her feel what she was to them. Her father received her with dark and stern looks, but without saying a word, although within himself he cursed and swore at woman's emancipation. But he felt for his eldest daughter a high esteem mingled with fear. He needed her, and was afraid of driving her away. Aunt Nella, who was utterly confounded and perplexed by Hertha's inexplicable journey and return, said a good deal about "Hertha's wild ideas," and muttered still more about their probable deplorable result, whilst she occupied herself with the interesting tangled skeins which she was getting ready for a great weaving which was to be done in the family.

The young sisters had a great deal to say about Yngve Nordin; how he had come to Kullen the very day that Hertha set off; how he was extremely annoyed by hearing of her sudden absence, and made many anxious inquiries about her, to which they could only give sorrowful and unsatisfactory answers. He had since then been there many times to learn if there were any tidings of her, and, finally, he had left a note for her. In this Hertha found only these words:

"Hertha, what is the meaning of this? I have a right to demand an explanation.   YNGVE."

Why did Hertha press these words with a convulsive energy to her heart? It was because their frank spirit, challenging as it were her suspicion, conveyed to her soul, as with the speed of lightning, the conviction that they were written by an innocent and injured person, by one who in the candor of innocence demanded satisfaction. Oh, that it might be so—that she had been mistaken! But how was it possible, credible?—Dark enigma, how can it be solved?

ST. BRITA'S SUMMER.

Not enchanting, as the North American Indian-summer, but yet tender, charming, and beautiful, is that time in Sweden which we call St. Brigitta's summer, or "the Britt-summer." It commences at the same time as the American after-summer, but it closes much earlier; its life is like a beautiful smile, which for a moment illumines a gloomy countenance.

Already are housed the harvests of our fields, and night-frosts and heavy rains, sometimes snow-flakes, have chased away the beauty of the meadows and the leafy trees; flowers have drooped their heads, and leaves become withered; when, at the commencement of October, occurs a time of bright sunshine and calm weather; when the Swedish landscape all at once presents a beaming autumnal splendor, with its many-colored leafage, its brilliant bunches of fruit, the wild-service, and the mountain-ash; its gorgeous sun-flowers, its whortle-berries in the heath, and its beautiful birds, circling about in the tree-tops, and, like the novice, putting on their most glorious attire, just at the moment when they are about to take leave of the beauty of life, and go into their wintry graves.

The northern saint, who sename-day occurs at this season, and whose inward warmth was such that she, during the severest winter, lay upon the earthen floor of the unwarmed convent-cell of Wadstena, and was not conscious of cold, was scarcely less remarkable than is this summer in the midst of the chill, autumnal life of November.

The wild-service and rowan-trees which grew round the parsonage of Solberga, were bright with crimson bunches of fruit, and flocks of gay silk-tails were circling around them, in the brilliant sunshine of a fine morning in the Britt-summer. The parsonage itself, bright and clean as hands could make it, had altogether a holiday appearance, just as if its inhabitants were preparing for a festival. Fresh-gathered juniper twigs were strewn on the floor of the entrance and dining-room; the sun shone gaily through the bright window-panes upon the white tables and fresh flowers.

The pastor's wife had an incredible amount of things to do, she had set all her maid-servants to work, and might be seen herself, with her great bunch of keys, going from garret to cellar, from larder to dairy, from one press to another in the house, looking out table linen and silver and china.

Just at the very time when she was absorbed in the linen-press, in the agonies of choosing among several table-cloths, between the large rose and the little rose, the traveller and the star-patterns, the pastor came into the room and exclaimed:

"Well, my little old woman, it is no use trying to have a moment's conversation with you to-day, is it? It is really terrible to think what a great deal you have to do, and how much trouble these 'schemes and machinations,' as Mrs. Uggla would call them, cause you."

"What's that?" said good little Mrs. Dahl, cheerfully, "trouble! Don't you know that such trouble as this is my greatest delight, especially when it is for the benefit of the Infant School? And the object, and the occupation which it gives—may God bless them! They are my life and my pleasure, and without them I should not like to live. To-day I have been bustling about in the house like a flame of fire, ever since four o'clock this morning, and everything to-day has gone on so well, and fallen out as I wanted it, just as if it were under the control of some good angel. The dough has risen so beautifully that it is quite a pleasure to see it; and—you don't know what a nice present I have had this morning!"

"I guess—a haunch of venison!"

"A haunch of venison? You are not very far wrong!

something quite as good as that: three hares and a woodcock! You know we must cook tnem for the feast."

"Three hares! a leap for every hare, and a kiss for the woodcock!" exclaimed the pastor, delighted; "I thought I smelt something uncommonly good in the kitchen. But, harkye now, could we not give the sexton's family one of these hares?"

"That we'll see in the morning, father dear, that is to say, if there happens to be a hare left after our evening-feast. You must bear in mind that we shall have about thirty people. But, as for that, we might ask the sextons to come and eat a bit of the roast; and—(I think I'll take the little rose; it's true that it is somewhat worn, but nobody will see it by candle-light), and the old women in the poor-house shall each have her loaf for Sunday."

"You are an excellent woman, and a rare housewife," said the pastor, with all his heart.

"Ah! there is indeed some skill required in being a house-wife, with no more means than I have. Do you know, my old fellow, that I have actually thanked God this very day because I was not rich, for in that case I should not know and feel as I do now, what a pleasure there is in planning, and scheming, and working, so that one's small means may be sufficient for all, and a little to spare! And when I have labored the whole week, and then at the end find that I have a little over, which I can give away, without detriment to the family, to some poor body or other, is it not a pleasant feeling? It is, indeed! Besides, there is a fresh life both for body and soul in these occupations which the rich never can experience. And when I, during the day, go about and look into the farm-yard, or the larder, or the garden; and thence over the fields, and see how green they are growing, or how the harvest ripens, or up to the sky, and see that it is bright as to-day, or that blue openings through the clouds are glancing towards me like friendly eyes, then I think that the earth is so beautiful, God so good, and life so glorious, that I am—ready to cry!"

" Cry ?" said the pastor, astonished, " why cry ?"

" Why, for this reason, because I have not anything or any one about me that could feel as I do ; for this reason, that I am—childless ! Think if I had eight or nine daughters, or at least half-a-dozen, to bustle about with, to teach how to work and to enjoy, as I do, how amusing it would be for them and for me ! And for me, who am just now beginning to grow old, and really have need of some one in the house in whom I can trust, because servant-girls are but servant-girls, and one cannot leave them to themselves. I sometimes think that I certainly shall have daughters in heaven, seeing that that happiness has been denied to me on earth."

" But in heaven, my old woman, people bustle about neither with work, nor servant-maids, but they——"

" Nay, my dear fellow," interrupted she, " don't talk to me about your heaven, in which people are either to stand or sit with palms in their hands, and sing psalms both day and night, and do nothing else besides ! Because I tell you that into such a heaven I do not wish to go, even though you yourself were there. I should not continue long sitting there with palms in my hands, and I am very certain, too, that our Lord would not desire such an unnecessary thing, either of me or anybody else ! No, to work, to strive, to go ever onward, to have much to do, and much to care for, that must I have there, as well as here, if I am to thrive at all. And don't you tell me that our Lord has no other ways of employing me and everybody else who wishes to serve him, than by sitting with palms in their hands, and singing psalms. He has enough in his great household, both larders and gardens, to look after— they may be spiritual, such as Swedenborg talks of—and poor souls who need to be fed from them. I desire nothing better than to serve our Lord, but he must set me to some real work, and not to hold palms in my hands. And if he is as good as I believe him to be, he will give me some daughters to educate and teach as his maid-servants, for then first will the kingdom of heaven become a true heaven to me !—(No, after all, I'll take the large rose, the little rose has too many holes in it !)"

17

"Listen, mother," said the pastor, "you talk as often about these daughters as about the kingdom of heaven. Why should we not have such on earth, if we can? We can afford it, and we have room enough since we came here, and I am quite convinced that it would be amusing and good for us to have a couple of young girls in the family, whom we could become attached to, and who would attach themselves to us. Perhaps our Lord has denied us any children of our own in order that we might be all the more willing to adopt those of others, who do not need them. If you like, let us, the sooner the better, take one or two daughters into the house."

The pastor's wife now remained sitting with the large rose-patterned table-cloth on her knee, looking at her husband with an expression which evidently showed that his words had gone to her heart.

At length, she said:

"If you only knew how often I have thought of the very same thing! But, hitherto, I have not seen any young girls whom I would really with my whole heart wish to call mine, and take into my house. But now I actually do know a couple of young sisters to whom I feel that I really could become as a mother, and whom you, of a certainty, would also become fond of."

"Who are they? who are they? I'll go directly and hunt them up."

"They are Eva Dufva and her sister Marie. They are both nice girls, and would become really clever and excellent women if they found their right place and fell into right hands. The mother is a splendid creature, but she does everything in the house herself, and leaves to her daughters nothing but trifles, and such occupations as can neither fill up their minds nor yet their time. Besides, there are many daughters in that family, and the Dufvas' affairs are in an anxious state, so that I fancy they would be relieved if a couple of the girls were adopted into a family as its own children. And besides, Eva requires to go away from home and out of the way of that engagement which I like her for

having broken off. She requires to be removed out of the
way of all temptation and over-persuasion to its renewal. She
requires a new and a fresh sphere of activity, and that she
would have here. Marie is only a child, but she is an angel-
child, and has been fond of you ever since she read for
confirmation with you, so that I should have been quite
jealous if I had not been so pleased. I have a presentiment
that both those girls would be delighted to come to us, if
only their parents would consent. But what do you say
about it?"

"I say that it might have been planned in Heaven, so good
does it appear to me. I think that the parents will be quite
agreeable. And as far as the girls are concerned, I mean to
set about it without delay, and tell them that if they do not
spring at once into our arms, and call us father and mother,
we will have nothing to do with them."

"Softly, softly, my dear old man; don't be in too great a
hurry, else you will frighten them. Besides, we must say
that the thing is an experiment for a year or two, that we
may see how we get on together, and so on."

"That is a matter of course; but they will get on well with
us, and we with them, of that I am convinced. The girls are
coming here to-day with their mother, are they not? This
very day the proposal must be made, and, if possible, the
matter arranged."

"I have had an impression all morning," said the pastor's
wife, "that something out of the common way was going to
happen to-day—something good."

"God grant it!" said the pastor. "I, on the contrary,
have had, this very day, great anxiety about that poor lad,
Yngve. Ever since that witch-girl, Hertha—whom I should
really like to have in the confessional, and give a sound talking
to under four eyes—set off in that inexplicable and unaccount-
able way on her journey, without saying a word to anybody,
never has he been like himself, as you yourself know. He
neither eats, nor sleeps, nor reads, but goes and pines away in
grief and in anguish, which sometimes seems like contrition.

I cannot understand the affair. He will not say anything. But I have seen him wring his hands till they have cracked again, and strike his forehead, or strike the table with his clenched fist, as if he were in a towering rage. And then between-whiles he sits gloomy and dark, beating his brains about something, whilst I have seen fever flush his cheeks, and his eyes flash angrily. I wish with all my heart that Count P. would carry him off with him to France before she —the witch—comes back. It would serve her right, and perhaps be the only salvation for him."

"Yes, but she is come back, and will probably be here to-day."

"What do you say?" exclaimed the pastor, disturbed, "and why did you not tell me before?"

"Because I did not know till this morning that she returned last evening to Kullen. And I have now sent a messenger to her with a note, inviting her to join us and the other members of the Brother and Sister Societies here to-day; and I told her that it would be best for her to come, if she wished yet once more to see her patient, because he was going abroad for the establishment of his health, according to the advice of the physician; and that Count P. had invited him to accompany him to France next week."

"You have done all that this very morning?" inquired the pastor, amazed. "Of a certainty you are a remarkable woman —sometimes. And I must go at once and tell this news to the poor lad."

"Wait! wait! If he were to know that she is come home, nothing would prevent him from rushing off to her; and that would never do, weak as he is, and with his lame knee. He would be breaking a blood-vessel or some mischief; he has already, twice this week, spit blood. No, that will never do!"

"Well, then, I shall myself go to her, and speak a little of my mind to her—the witch!" said the pastor vehemently.

"Wait, my old man; I expect my messenger back every moment."

"Wait, and wait, and wait: but I cannot wait," said the pastor impatiently. "Who knows when your messenger will be back again? I myself am the best messenger. Besides, I want to see the girl, and, if possible, get to the bottom of this business. And if she is not as much worn away and changed, as he, Yngve, and does not look as unhappy, if she put on her proud demeanor, then—God have mercy on her!"

And with these words the little pastor was outside the door, and soon in full career towards the town.

"Those men!" sighed the pastor's wife, and shook her head, "they always will have their own way. There he goes now, hurrying along, and will get warm, and then chilled, and—if he had only waited a quarter of an hour—but now I may as well lock up my press, and I had better take out both the large and the little rose; very likely there will be more guests than I have calculated upon; and, besides, the children will want some napkins—the mended ones are good enough for them. But now I will go and look after Yngve and spice his breakfast with my good anticipations. He had better not hear more at present."

All this was spoken half aloud by our pastor's little wife, who, like many elderly ladies, had acquired the habit of muttering to herself.

She had no little to do that day, our good lady of the parsonage; for, as we are already aware, there was going to be a great feast there that day. The whole of the United Benevolent Societies were to meet at the parsonage; and afterwards, all the poor children of the Infant School, the greater number of whom belonged to the families who suffered by the fire. The children were, one and all, to receive a complete suit of warm clothing for the approaching winter, (and there were still a few little blouses, shirts, and pinafores to finish, which were to be done this afternoon,) and the entertainment was to close with a dance. As regarded the refreshments, several of the ladies were each to contribute a portion, so that any want of eatables was a thing not to be thought of. An entertainment on this plan was given twice a year at the parsonage; and many of the participators of the feast took care that it was not very costly to the minister and his wife. Its spiritual portion, cheerfulness, or its cheering power, came as a matter of course; and it was a saying in the place, that people enjoyed themselves nowhere so thoroughly as at the pastor's. Besides, people found there that which is no longer so commonly met with, old mead and old-fashioned cordiality.

When our little pastor returned, it was with an expression very different to that with which he went away.

"I understand nothing about the whole story," said he, "but it is more serious than I imagined. And not a word, not even half a word can I get out of her in explanation. In the mean time, I have a note from her for Yngve. As to your messenger, my little woman, I met him on the way to Kullen, as I was returning thence. He had only some half-dozen errands to do by the way, and——"

"Ah, what? Half-a-dozen! He had only four or five,—but she is coming here to-day, is she not?"

"Either six or seven;—yes, she is coming, but whether it will be a pleasure for anybody, God alone knows."

"How so? Did she look stiff or proud, as she can look sometimes?"

"No, not a bit of it, and it is better that she did not; but as pale as marble, as if there were no blood in her body, and an expression as if she were going to death or judgment. I, who had gone to her determined to give her a very grave curtain-lecture, I declare I stood before her like a school-boy who has forgotten his lesson, and is ready to cry. But I tried to look savage, and said, 'Yngve is ill,—will soon set out on a long journey,—come and talk with him.' On which she replied, quite mildly, but with a sort of death-like immovability, and with colorless lips, 'I will come.'

"'To-day?' said I. 'To-day,' replied she, 'and—be so good as to give Yngve this,' and she handed me this note, which was ready written.

"I looked sharply at her, and asked her if she had nothing

more to say. She replied, 'Nothing more at present! but—I will come!'

"'Well then, in God's name welcome!' said I, and turned round to go my way. Never before did I feel so awkward, and in such a strange state of mind."

"Ah, if she only comes, everything will then get right again," suggested the pastor's wife. "I don't understand the matter any better than you do, but of this I'm sure, that, one way or another, this will be a lucky day; the bread is incomparably good ; everything has gone on well in the kitchen, and I feel as excited, and at the same time in such a holiday state of mind, just as if——"

"You were going to have a couple of daughters in the house," interrupted the pastor, "and it will be so; but—now I must go to Yngve. May this note only not make him madder than before."

Yngve seized it with passionate earnestness, the little white note on which he recognised Hertha's handwriting. He broke the seal, and read these words in silence :

"Yngve,

"Meet me to-day, at five o'clock in the afternoon, by Alma's grave. I wish to speak to you there.

"Hertha."

"She is come, she is come then, at last!" exclaimed Yngve, with enthusiastic delight. "I shall then see her, hear her, talk with her. My God, I thank thee! By the grave. Yes, there. And even if she comes to me with death, I shall thank her. Oh, Hertha! Hertha! Thou dost not know ; thou dost not understand "—and Yngve bowed his head into his hands and wept.

"Poor youth, poor lad!" sighed the pastor, silently, as he wiped his own eyes. "It is horrible to be so desperately in love : I was in love quite enough with my Elsa, but never in this wise!" And in order to avoid questions which he in part could not, and in part feared to, answer, the pastor hastened to leave the room, as he said, "He had a child to baptize," thus leaving Yngve to read and re-read the few words which this little note contained.

Again alone, he pressed it to his heart, to his feverish lips, and gave himself up to that pathetic folly, which is to the lover—be his name what it may, Yngve Nordin, Napoleon, or Palmerston—wisdom and the supremest life; that is to say when they are beloved.

We now leave the pastor to his baptizing; the pastor's wife to her manifold occupations; and accompany Yngve to—

THE MEETING BY THE GRAVE.

It was a wooded church-yard planted with thick-branched maple and lime-trees, to which Yngve betook himself, and where he had already spent many happy hours, at the side of his beloved. It was exactly a fitting place for a solemn meeting.

The sun of the Britt-summer day shone still warm above the trees, which also were bright with their varied tints of gold and fire-color. And whether it might be or not, that the heart of nature was stirred by secret sympathy with the silent disquiet of the young man's heart, it too seemed to be waiting for something upon whose word or look depended life or death. Sudden gusts of wind, which moaned through and swayed uneasily the branches of the trees, and chased the clouds across the hitherto clear sky, alternated with pauses of death-like stillness, when the lightest footfall might be heard, and when tree and flower, and waving grass, stood still as if listening. Then again the wind rose and the trees murmured, as if agitated by sighs, and the leaves fell over the graves ; and the wind was warm as the wind of the tropics, as the sweet, the bitter disquiet of love ; and again it became hushed and still, and all things seemed to wait.

Yngve stood by Alma's grave, with a strongly beating heart, awaiting her who could give him life or death ; so it felt to that agitated young heart, the emotions of which had, by expectation and suffering, been excited to the highest pitch. Already he waited five minutes beyond the appointed time ; think, if she should not come.

Yngve leaned against an old tree, shaded his eyes from the blinding light of the sun, and stood listening during a moment of death-like calm ; he knew that he should recognise the sound of her steps. Just then a genial breath of air fanned his countenance; the tree murmured, and something said to Yngve, "she is there!"

He raised his eyes, and *she* stood actually before him, but so changed, so pale, so solemnly earnest, that she might have been but newly arisen from the grave, with the last, heavy dream of human life upon her soul.

He involuntarily extended his arms towards her. And she—the strong, proud girl—was obliged to support herself by the seat at the grave, because her knees trembled beneath her weight. Yngve's emaciated countenance bore evidence of the amount of his suffering, but in its pure expression, now, as it were, transfigured by the glowing light of the sun, was no consciousness of criminality. The two contemplated each other in silence; which he was the first to break.

"Hertha!" said he, "you too have suffered; I see that!"

"Yes," replied she, "and you——," she thought of adding, "have been the cause of it," but she could not do so. The longer, the more closely her glance questioned the countenance of Yngve, the stronger appeared to her the impossibility, the heavenly conviction that he could not be guilty, and she exclaimed—"No, no, you are not false;—no, you have not acted deceitfully;—no, I see by the expression of your countenance, that you are incapable of such guilt. Oh, my God; I will rather die at this moment than be deceived in this belief!—Yngve! you are not the—you cannot be—the lover of Amalia, the father of her child!"

"You are right; I am not!" replied Yngve, calmly.

"I believe you, I believe you, and I thank God!" exclaimed Hertha, with clasped hands. "But tell me—why did she mention—Yngve Nordin?"

"Because," replied Yngve, "that is the name of my youngest brother, as well as my own. All the three brothers are called Yngve, but with the addition of another name; the brother of whom you speak is called Alfred Yngve; I, Yngve Frey."

"Oh, I understand—understand all now!" resumed Hertha,

greatly affected—"it is he then who is guilty, and you—you are Yngve Frey (Free!)——Why, why did I not know this before? A great deal of suffering might have been spared!"

"Why did I not know until a few days ago that Amalia was your near relative? You never mentioned her to me, nor she you. I only received my brother's confidence a few weeks ago, and had no right to betray his secret before—circumstances, such as have now occurred, render it a duty in me to do so."

"Oh, Yngve! and I have believed you guilty! How shall I ever forgive myself!"

"Hertha!—give me the right to obliterate this memory; give me your hand—become my wife; henceforward let all be clear, let there be no concealments between us—at least, if this be the only thing which has sundered us!"

"Not the only thing; hear me—now or never must all be said. Yngve, I have been told that you were fickle; that you loved another woman before you loved me. Answer me! Is there no woman who, more than me, has a title to your fidelity; no child which has a right to demand from you the name and the protection of its father?"

And Hertha's voice faltered not; but she herself was deathly pale, and her countenance had resumed its solemn, almost severe, gravity.

Well for Yngve that he needed not, as she expected, to evade her eye; that he could fearlessly look her in the face, as he replied:

"Give me your hand, mine is free, and no such responsibility rests upon my heart. I have loved before I loved you, yes, but from the overflowing life of youth, and not from the fulness of the soul. I might have erred, have fallen, if my mother had not stood like a good angel by my side. When she saw my tendency to be carried away by the feelings of the moment, she talked openly with me, showed me the danger of being thus led away, and convinced me by examples out of every-day life, of the misery or the burdensomeness of those connections which shun the light, and impose duties or responsibilities upon us which oppressively or re-proachfully accompany us through life. She made me feel it to be a beautiful and noble object to preserve myself worthy of a pure woman's love. And how I have thanked her, not now alone, but ever since I knew you!"

"Is it then really so?" exclaimed Hertha in a transport of calm certainty, for Yngve's manly and fresh explanation had dismissed every shadow of doubt from her soul; "you are then really and truly the man whom I sometimes dreamt you to be, *my* Yngve, Yngve Frey! and I may be proud of loving you and of being loved by you! Oh, Yngve, this is certainly a heavenly delight! whether we are separated by man, or by fate."

"No," interrupted Yngve solemnly, "that shall not be! 'What God hath joined together let not man put asunder,' and you are now mine before His sight. Become the same also before man; become my bride, and in a short time my wife; give me the right to watch over——"

"Hush, hush, beloved!" interrupted Hertha. "Let us not now talk about the future, not now! Let us rest at this moment, it is complete in itself—perfect. You are over-excit-ed, my Yngve, by the disquiet of many days; I am wearied by the conflict and the agony of this time. Seat yourself at my side; let me hold your hand. How handsome you are, Yngve! how noble and good you are! The sun loves you, it smiles upon you; God's spirit embraces us; the trees, as it were, clap their hands above us: the flowers caress your feet because you are Yngve Frey! They spring from the grave, from the heart of Alma, which has obtained new life through my happiness. How beautiful life is, Yngve, *my* Yngve! how great and glorious it is to live—to love!"

Thus spoke Hertha, with calm but rapturous emotion, as she beamed upon him glances in comparison with the bright-ness and fire of which the glow of the sun was faint. That force of expression which was Hertha's characteristic, and which gave to her countenance a captivating interest, was

now transfigured to beauty of no ordinary kind. Yngve
could only contemplate her with joy-bewildered eyes, while
he drank in her words as an elixir of life. When they ceased,
it was because they were sealed with a kiss,

"As warm as life, as faithful as death,"

whilst heart throbbed quickly and strongly against heart.

It was not the feeble soul's oblivion of all except the transport of the moment; not the ardent rapture of passion; it
was the clear consciousness of an eternal union, a deathless
love, which here bound two loving hearts together.

But a thrill, as of an electric shock, hastily passed through
Hertha. The air swayed around them, and in the same
moment was heard the loud tolling of the bell. The church
bells tolled; the chiming for the dead commenced. A little
troop of people dressed in black slowly advanced from the
churchyard gate toward an open grave.

Now the procession paused. The chiming bells ceased, and
the monotonous voice of the clergyman was heard for a
moment, together with the restless soughing of the trees;
then came the heavy fall of the three shovelfuls of mould on
the coffin in the grave, accompanied by the words:

"Dust thou art, and unto dust shalt thou return. Our
Saviour Jesus Christ shall wake thee up at the last day!
Let us pray!"

After which the usual prayer was spoken by the clergyman:

"Man that is born of woman is of few days, and full of
trouble. He cometh forth like a flower, and is cut down; he
fleeth also as a shadow, and continueth not!"

Yngve pressed Hertha's hand closer to his heart and said:

"Love is stronger than death!"

"Yes," replied Hertha, "I believe it; I know it."

"Be mine in life and death," returned Yngve.

"I am so!" replied Hertha; "but I have still something
to say to you before—how beautiful is that song, Yngve! how

it seems to sanctify the sleep of the grave—only it is too sad. Joyful songs, Yngve, ought to be sung by graves; songs which unite night with day, time with eternity; songs about the future and its anticipations; songs about the beginning and the completion. But you are pale, Yngve, and the evening is growing chill; the sun has set; let us go home :— support yourself on my arm, as you used to do, my Yngve!"

At that moment the chimes began again to play; and one of the men separating himself from the funeral procession, hastily approached them.

It was the little pastor, who, uneasy at the long conversation of the lovers by the grave, now came to look after them. They offered him their hands, and their beaming looks told him still more than their words, that all was clear, all was right between them.

"Well, then, the Lord be praised!" said the pastor. "You need not, however, sit here the whole night, but come with me, like good children, else mother at home there won't be pleased either with me or with you. And the visitors will be wondering and asking. Come, children, come along with me."

Yngve and Hertha accompanied their friend, whilst the funeral procession dispersed in various directions, though the funeral chimes would yet continue for some time.

"Who has been buried this evening?" asked Yngve.

"A young man, such as you, and who was only lately betrothed," replied the pastor sorrowfully.

The three walked in silence to the parsonage.

MERRIMENT AND DANCING.

In the parsonage of Solberga all was life and cheerfulness. People drank coffee and dipped in their biscuits; they sewed, talked, joked, and laughed. The gentlemen would help the ladies in making the blouses and pinafores; but they made mistakes, and turned the little garments upside down, sewed in the sleeves wrong, either purposely or by accident; received instruction, were scolded and also praised, sometimes, when now and then they showed themselves willing to become " clever with their needle," or to serve as sewing-cushions for a moment or two, which office, to speak the truth, they performed very indifferently. In the mean time these occupations gave occasion to a great deal of merry contention, and through all one little garment after another was finished, exhibited, praised, and criticised, with or without justice, and then raised aloft, that is to say, put on the top of the little pile of clothes which was arranged for every child, upon a large table.

Mimmi Svanberg levied a contribution on all the young men of the place in these words:

" Cousin, I shall compel you to give me a twelve-skilling piece," or, " My dear Mr. M. N., will you give me a twelve-skilling piece?" And there was not a cousin, nor a Mr. M. N., nor even a Mr. N. B., who did not give her his little silver twelve-skilling, as cheerfully as it was asked, well knowing that it was given for a good work.

After that little collection, Mimmi Svanberg became the life and soul of the sewing society, whilst she now here, and now there, contrived between one person and another, to knit the threads which she held in her soft hands, and which were always knit to somebody's advantage. Here it was a young governess who wanted a situation in a family; there a family who were in want of a governess; here an old couple who were willing to adopt a child; there a little child who needed to be adopted; here a shawl which required selling; and there a lady who wanted to buy a shawl; and here old aunts and young cousins who wanted advice; and Mimmi Svanberg must do all this and find counsel for all these. Mimmi had really enough to do.

Then the children came, received their new clothes, and began to sing their songs; little Mina led them with her clear voice; and after that followed dancing—first with the children, and afterwards among the company themselves.

Some of our readers may have experienced how an entertainment which immediately follows or is connected with some work of love in which the company to be entertained have taken common part, is animated by a more than usually good and cheerful spirit. The heart enters, as it were, into the dance, and the feet receive wings therefrom. Seldom had the gay Swedish folk-dances, " Väfva-Vallmar" and the " Nigarpolska," which comprehended both old and young, been danced with more animation, nor amid more hearty merriment, than this evening after the clothing of the children at the parsonage. Every now and then, also, the pastor's wife refreshed them with her home-brewed, foaming mead. And no hearts, this evening, were more joyful than hers and her husband's, for they had obtained a daughter in the house named Eva Dufva, who accepted the invitation of the good couple, as Noah's restless dove the twig of the olive-tree, which afforded her a resting-place above the swelling waves, the dreaded deluge.

When the dancing commenced, Hertha left the company to return home, and Yngve accompanied her.

CONVERSATION BY THE WAY.

THE full moon had risen, and now, alternately concealed by clouds, which an unsteady but not ungenial wind chased across the heavens, and now shining forth brightly from between them, lighted the lovers on their way.

Yngve was again supported on Hertha's arm, and both walked silently, feeling how momentous was the approaching decisive moment.

Yngve, however, soon broke the silence.

"We must soon separate, Hertha," said he, "I must leave you. In a few days, as you know, I must go abroad for the winter, in order fully to establish my health, that I may be able next spring to return to my former employment, to all which is dear to me, my native land, my mother, and—oh, let me add, my bride! Unless you agree to this, unless you decide our fate, I cannot take the journey with calmness; and besides that, the thought that I must preserve my health, not for my own sake, but for yours, will be more beneficial to me than all the watering-places in the world. You know, because I have told you so, that I have not much property, but I am without debts, and my prospects, in the career which I have adopted, give me the hope of soon obtaining an independence, both for me and mine. You know my heart, you know how I love you, Hertha—why then many words?—can you not love me? cannot you trust yourself to me with your whole heart and with your whole soul, have faith in me, as I in you? then—I will ask nothing from you. You have demanded an undivided heart. I ask, I demand nothing less from you!"

"Then, now hear my confession, Yngve!" replied Hertha, "and after that you yourself shall decide upon our future! you are not my first love, Yngve!—although I have not loved any man before you. Mine has been a joyless childhood and youth; my first impressions of life were bitter, my first impressions of home and marriage were that distress of mind and anguish which are the results of domestic dissensions, of my mother's tears and hysterical cries of unhappiness. These produced in me an early disgust of marriage, and I made a vow with myself, many a time, of late years, that no child of mine should, amid deceitful caresses, be brought up to quaff that bitter wormwood draught called Life. I saw noble and gentle women oppressed; heard their silent sighs; saw them become pale and sink into the grave, after a life without joy and without purpose, and, in proportion as my hatred to the oppressor grew, grew also an infinite compassion, an ardent love for all oppressed souls, which I might very well call my first love, and I vowed to myself to live for them, and never to give my heart and my hand to a husband. But you came, Yngve; I learned to love you, and through you I began to have faith in man's justice, in man's magnanimity. That was much, but you gave me more; you gave me faith in God, by the knowledge of his ways, by the insight into his revelation; oh! I have to thank you for very, very much!"

"Is it then only gratitude?" said Yngve; "is it no more than this which binds you to me? in that case, Hertha, we may easily part, because——"

"No," interrupted she, "ah, no! and you cannot wish for more than my heart gives you, in the first place involuntarily, I acknowledge it; but afterwards of free will and cheerfully, since I have come to know you fully; and yet, nevertheless, I cannot help dreading marriage, even with you, because I dread its consequences; dread the becoming a mother; dread, in particular, being the mother of a daughter! How is it, Yngve, that woman, the whole world over, is commended, as daughter, wife, mother, sister, friend, nurse, comforter,—yet, at the same time, among all people, how common it is to regard the birth of a daughter with indifference, or dissatisfaction, nay, even with pity? Is it not from this cause that woman's lot on earth is an inferior one; that she is not entitled, as men are, by the laws of the land, to freedom, independent action, or to seek for happiness in her own way? that she is destined to be depreciated and to suffer much? And here, in our native land especially, how gloomy is her path; how circumscribed her portion! how is the whole of her life crushed down by unjust laws, and the pleasure of men! No, no! I cannot be the mother of a daughter!"

Yngve now replied, with as much tenderness and feeling as if he were speaking to a sick person:

"I understand you, my beloved. But you are too much affected by your gloomy impressions, and not yet accustomed to contemplate brighter scenes. But have faith in God, then —how can you do otherwise than hope in the extension of his kingdom, his justice and love on the earth? Our laws, with regard to the freedom of woman and her future, may be changed; yes, they must be changed; if not, our nation must abandon its share in the real elevation and advance of free nations. It cannot possibly be long before all nations discover the true means of their moral ennobling, and before the stream of spiritual emancipation, which is permeating the world, will also elevate and liberate our nation by means of its most vital laws and institutions. I cannot doubt of it when I think what Swedish women were and are for their native land, even under laws so narrow-minded as ours are with regard to them; I cannot doubt of it in presence of a woman such as you. And you, and I, and all good citizens will labor to speed forward the advent of that day."

Hertha looked up, whilst her eyes beamed with a sort of bitter joy. "Yes," said she, "I will combat for that object, even though it should debar me for ever from the more delicious joys of life. Yes, I will remain faithful to my first love!"

"How? what do you mean?" asked Yngve, astonished.

"Let us rest a moment here, Yngve; you must be tired with walking, and these walls," they were now among the ruins, "afford us convenient resting-places; we can tal'· better here."

Yngve seated himself upon a fallen wall and gazed with excited attention at Hertha, who continued standing opposite to him, as she rested her arm upon another blackened wall; the moon brightly illumined her expressive countenance and noble figure. She continued in a grave and gentle voice:

"Is there no higher object for man and woman than marriage, than that of building for themselves a little nest and then living happily with each other, and with their offspring, like animals, or savages who approximate to animals? I will not blame such as do not seek any object higher than this in life; but God has not permitted me to find it all-sufficing. Were it so, I should be disloyal to my first love; I should have lived and suffered in vain. Yngve! I love you with my whole heart, and yet I cannot, I will not live alone for your happiness and my own,—in that case I should not deserve to live."

"Strange girl! For what then will you live?"

"To liberate my captive sisters," replied Hertha, with fervor and earnestness, "to liberate those souls whose longings and sufferings God has given me to feel and to understand; as far as my ability and my little sphere on earth extend, to break the fetters which bind them, to inspire them with the desire which inspires me; to give them the hope which has become mine, since I have become acquainted with you, Yngve, and through you with the Lord of freedom and love. I am not too sanguine in my hopes, as you are; I know, Yngve, that such men as you and Judge Carlson are rare in the world, and I fear that it will yet be long before our Swedish legislators will concede to woman the right of unrestricted human and social freedom and development; long before they will throw open to the daughters of Sweden those educational institutions which would give them an opportunity of acquiring knowledge and self-reliance; in a word, before they will do for them that which they have done for the sons of our country. Besides, I know that I am only a mean woman, not having arrived at years of maturity in the eye of the land, without the right to control my own property, or my own actions; ignorant of many things which it is important for me to know; but I feel within myself a will, and latterly a light, which may place me in a condition to work towards a coming deliverance.

"I have of late often had a vision which will grow clearer and clearer to my eye, until it becomes the light and object of my life. I see—myself, in lofty, light school-rooms, surrounded by young women, and conversing with them of their souls' inner voice, and of God's voice in it, of the most important object of life and of society, of the vast importance of every individual life, every individual gift, and their consequent connection with it; of their value as members of a divine community on earth as in heaven, of their highest duty and highest right. I would found an institution of education, a higher school, where they shall not learn French or German, or music or drawing—all those can be learned elsewhere —but where young girls, out of whatever class of society they may be, which have awoke to a consciousness of a higher want and for whom the spiritual cell in which they have lived has become too limited, may acquire the true knowledge of themselves and of their vocation, as members of society; may teach themselves to reflect and to answer the questions, 'What am I? what can I do? what ought I to do?'

"I would impart to these young human souls an insight into their own souls, and into life, which shall teach them to understand their own position and calling in it; I would open their ears to hear the voice of God, dedicate their desires to the obedient fulfilment of its bidding. One and all should follow their own individual course, but all tending to one common object; the freedom of the one should operate for the freedom of all. Prayer and labor should be our tools; our watchword, 'Freedom in God through Christ.'* And a day will come,

---

* If any think that Hertha here propounded erroneous doctrine, we would take the liberty of recalling to their memory the following texts, among many others to the same purport:—

"For ye are all the children of God by faith in Christ Jesus."

There is neither male nor female: for ye are all one in Christ Jesus."

Galat. chap. iii. 26 23

Yngve, when the voices from this little flock of enfranchised and enlightened souls will arise and reach the ear of him who sits upon the throne of our native land,—will reach the assembly of legislators, not as the cry of emancipation for women, feeble and inharmonious, but as a strong, harmonious, accordant choir; and then they must listen, then they must understand, and then, perhaps, they will act according to justice and truth.

"I perhaps may not live to see this day, but I may prepare its advent; see the rosy tints of its dawn ascend in young combating breasts, on pure foreheads, and then—I shall die contented.

"Many things in my plan are still immature and indistinct. But I know that it will clear itself up, and that I shall mature myself for it. Neither do I know the time nor the hour when I may be able to set it in operation, but I feel within me that it will come. And in the mean time I will prepare myself for it, will endeavor to acquire the knowledge in which I am deficient; will endeavor to become acquainted with such persons as might be able to assist me, either by counsel or by action, although I shall rely not alone on such aid—because how seldom do we find that people will reach forth a helping hand towards the accomplishment of a good work, which is peculiar and out of the common everyday track? Every one who devotes himself to such a work must be prepared to stand alone, unsupported—often perhaps to be abused and counteracted. But this gives me very little concern. *One*, I know, there is in heaven who will understand me, and one also on earth—you, my Yngve! And now I ask you, my Yngve, can you, will you extend to me your hand as a *helper* in my undertaking, and enter into my work; can my love become your love, my friends your friends, my life's object yours?"

"You open to me a fore-court of the kingdom of heaven," exclaimed Yngve, "and ask whether I will enter into it? Yes,

"As many as are led by the spirit of God, are the sons (children) of God;"
"And if children, then heirs; heirs of God, and joint heirs with Christ."
Rom. chap. viii. 14, 17.
"All things are yours."—1 *Cor.* chap iii. 21.

Hertha, yes! that I will, with all my heart and all my soul! Neither do I see that my occupation as engineer can prevent me from actively participating in a labor of higher importance than all plans of advancement in time and space. Yes, I know that it is precisely by means of such an intellectual activity that my life's endeavors, my soul's desires will find their full purpose and accomplishment. Only you must promise me one thing; for I also have my conditions, beloved!"

"What are they, Yngve?"

"That you will allow youths as well as young girls to attend your classes, your lectures! Of special branches of study, abstract philosophy, we can obtain sufficient knowledge in our academies and colleges, but not a living view of life, of society, and of ourselves; this can be given best by a womanly soul, such as yours! Therefore—let youths also attend your classes, Hertha!"

"Any one whom you may introduce to me, Yngve, shall be welcome to me as a brother."

"Good! we are then agreed on this. Give me your hand, my bride, my wife—my helper in labor and pleasure, in joy and sorrow, in life and death!"

In reply Hertha extended her arms and clasped her friend in a faithful, warm embrace.

The evening wind fluttered around them, and scattered them with ashes and dust from the ruins around them. They felt it not. They had built for themselves a home and a house not made with hands, one which would stand when their hands had become powerless, and in which they might dwell when their hearts had ceased to throb on earth against each other, as they did now. That they knew, and were happy, nay blessed! The joy of heaven united itself with that of earth in their pure bosoms.

"Let us now go to your father," said Yngve; "everything must be said and done this very evening. In order to bear the thought of a long separation from you I must know that in the spring I may return and claim you as my wife."

Hertha sorrowfully shook her head; and now began to

prepare him for the difficulties, nay, even the opposition which, in all probability, they would have to encounter from her father. They might expect long delay, possibly refusal. They must arm themselves with patience.

Yngve would not listen to this, he was impatient and irritated by the thought that a woman such as Hertha, of matured age, and with her own independent property, should not be allowed to decide her own choice or her own future.

"It is irrational; it is not to be thought of," said he, "that your father will refuse it to you!"

But the certainty which Hertha possessed, that this was not only possible, but even probable, communicated itself by degrees to Yngve, and depressed him. The certainty of their hearts' inward union, and the thought of the bond which they had formed, was not sufficient to sustain his joyous state of mind at this moment, when in addition the approaching separation hung like a heavy cloud over his heaven.

The remainder of the way was passed in silence. As they passed Kullen, Yngve said:

"I have a request to make of you, Hertha. I have had by degrees all my little store of books sent to me at the Solberga. Will you take charge of them, and let my books talk to you of me whilst I am far away?"

"You could not give me a more precious gift, Yngve," said Hertha, "excepting one, which I will beg of you!"

"Of me!" exclaimed Yngve, joyfully surprised, "what—what can I give *you*?"

Never had Hertha's voice been so melodious, as now when with humility and heartfelt emotion she said:

"Your influence with your mother; that she will consent to come and be a mother in my home, a mother to me and my young sisters. She shall find there daughterly respect and love. I have spoken with my father on the subject, and he sees it in the same light as I do. Our home needs a good and prudent mistress, my young sisters an experienced and motherly oversight, and I the leisure, in dependence upon this, to prepare myself for my future undertaking. Thus, as I, through you, became acquainted with your mother, I feel that I shall love her; that she will be a good angel in my home and—for me, who will learn from her that gentleness in woman which you, Yngve, value so highly. And there is in my home a room within mine, with a window towards the setting sun, a pleasant little room, which it will delight me to arrange according to your mother's taste, and which I long since destined for her. Pray of her, Yngve, to come and take possession of it, and call it hers; it will make me very happy! Will you, Yngve?"

"I know not how to thank you?" said Yngve, deeply affected; "but I understand you, and I will write to my mother."

Now they were at Kullen, and entered the house with an uneasy presentiment as to the reception which they might meet,—little dreaming, however, that they would meet and be met by

THE GREAT LAW-SUIT.

At the moment when Yngve and Hertha entered the hall, Aunt Nella came rushing in from her own room with her large portfolio under her arm, her eyes wide open, and with altogether a most bewildered appearance.

"Yes," said she, addressing Hertha in a passionate and reproachful tone, "you are come in time to accompany your father to prison, unless I can save him and us all! Ay, now it is all plain enough; now we shall see what comes of it."

And so saying, Aunt Nella began hastily to ascend the stairs with the great portfolio in her arms, incessantly talking the while of "enemies," and "prison," and "law-suit," and "I very well knew that it would come, that I did! But I shall be as good as they! I shall show them my papers. They shall see, they shall see, they shall see——"

Greatly amazed, Yngve and Hertha followed Aunt Nella's steps to the dining-room, where the door of the Director's room which adjoined it, stood open. Within Hertha saw lights burning, and her father pale with anger, standing before two gentlemen, who were strangers to her. They seemed to have brought a written document, which now lay on a table between them and the Director, and upon which he, from time to time, cast angry glances.

"I will continue my suit against you as long as I live!" said he in a voice tremulous with anger.

"As you please, Mr. Director," said one of the gentlemen with calm politeness; "but the longer you do so, the more you will lose. The verdict of the Court——"

"The Court!" screamed Aunt Nella, as she stormed in

with her great portfolio, "the Court must first hear what I have to say, and see my papers!"

And before the astonished eyes of the two gentlemen Aunt Nella held up the big portfolio, as she continued, "And if it comes to freeing my brother-in-law and myself from the talons of the law, and from prison, means will not be wanting ; see here! and see here !"

And Aunt Nella, from out of the confusion of letters, scraps cut out of newspapers, and patterns for embroidery, drew forth several small pieces of paper, which soon fixed the attention of the gentlemen. These small pieces of paper were actual scrip, some for several hundreds, and others thousands of rix-dollars, and the amount of which, when all added together, showed a total value of about ten thousand rix-dollars.

The two gentlemen had evidently begun with the suspicion that, "the old woman must be crazy!" but afterwards it seemed to be that, "the old woman might perhaps be wiser than people imagined."

Aunt Nella continued: "My enemies have long persecuted me in secret, but now when their malice is revealed, and they seek to drag in my brother-in-law also, it is my duty to place in his hands those means which may free both him and myself."

Aunt Nella said this with pathos, and not without dignity. But the Director, who wished to make an end of this scene, said shortly :

"Keep your money, sister-in-law ; I have no need of it ; but I thank you for your good intention. Gentlemen, we have, I believe, nothing more to say to each other. I have received your summons, and shall appear before the Court. Good-bye."

The two gentlemen bowed coldly to the Director, and with half a smile to Aunt Nella.

The Director again fixed upon her astonished and deferential regards. They said evidently, "This from Aunt Nella! Who would have expected such a thing of her ? Ten thousand rix-dollars! The *Nought* (Nolla) is of more value than I imagined."

Aunt Nella, who saw the astonishment and read the thoughts of the Director, sunned herself, in the expression of his glances, without rightly comprehending that they had reference to the *nought*, which he had formerly considered as her only value. The excitement which had so lately given him strength, died away on the departure of the gentlemen, and he sank down in his arm-chair with a deep sigh and almost fainting.

Hertha went up to her father, as she said:

"Father, I am here. Will you not tell me what it is that has so disturbed you? Cannot I be of some use? cannot I help in some way?"

"And I," said Yngve, also going forward and taking the Director's hand, "cannot I be of some service to you? Let— oh, let me serve you as your son and as Hertha's husband! My whole life shall prove how highly I value this happiness!"

Exactly as a wall of rock raises itself against a rushing flood, and dams up its course, so now rose up the Director, and gazed at the two with looks of astonishment, which became all the more rigid and severe as he exclaimed in broken sentences:

"Thank you—thank you—for the offer of so much help; but—I believe myself not altogether incapable of helping myself, of managing my own affairs. I do not feel as yet any need of support—I feel myself as strong and as clear as I ever did. And as regards your offer to my daughter, Lieutenant, I am astonished that she did not prepare me for it, as, according to my ideas, it was her duty to do—and I am—in consequence—not prepared with an answer. My duty, as father and guardian, forbids me to give my daughter to the first man that asks her, and of whom I know nothing at all; and— no disrespect to you, Lieutenant, but I think that the time for your proposal might have been better chosen."

"If so," replied Yngve, calmly, and with cordiality, "then permit me to return some other and more suitable time, which you may yourself appoint, and when I may give you all the information regarding myself, which you have a right to demand."

There was something so good in Yngve's expression, his manners were so pleasing, and at the same time so easy and cordial, that sooner or later he won upon all with whom he came in contact.

Even the Director could not resist their influence, and bowed his head as a silent assent to the young man's entreaty. When, therefore, Yngve mentioned his approaching journey, and requested that an opportunity for this much-desired interview might be granted on an early day, the Director replied: " To-morrow evening at six o'clock."

When Yngve had taken his departure, the Director broke out violently against his daughter, upbraiding her severely for not having prepared him for Yngve's offer.

" Don't tell me," said he, " that you were not prepared for it yourself. An old maid like you knows only too well when a man means to make her an offer, and it is in that case her duty to prepare her father beforehand. Besides, you know that I am no friend to surprises."

To Aunt Nella the Director said:

" I do not really need your money at this time, sister-in-law, but you ought not to let this scrip lie carelessly among all sorts of loose papers; it will be best for me to take charge of it for you, and I will take care that you have your interest regularly. I can place it to better account than you can. And if I should have occasion to borrow your money, you know that you have good security for it with me."

" It is the savings of forty years, brother-in-law," said Aunt Nella, and began to cry, affected at the thoughts of herself.

" Yes, which you were able to make in my family for the most part," said the Director, " and whilst you there lived free of cost, and had no need to spend anything. But in any case it is very beautiful, very beautiful of you, sister-in-law, and I esteem you very much for your prudence and circumspection,

and for the proof of friendship which you have given me to-
day. I shall not forget it! I shall regard all yours as if it
were my own, and take just the same care of it."

And so saying, the Director laid Aunt Nella's scrip in his
pocket-book, and after that pressed and shook her hand, as he
said half-jokingly:

"Only think of a little creature like you being worth ten
thousand rix-dollars! Who could have thought it?"

Aunt Nella curtseyed and smiled, and was happy in the
commendation and the friendliness of her brother-in-law. On
her way down to her own room, however, it seemed as if the
portfolio had become considerably lighter, nor could she avoid
a certain uneasy feeling in this consciousness; but then, again,
she thought how her and her brother-in-law's interests would
henceforth become one, both in the great law-suit and out of
it; and in this way Aunt Nella seemed to be magnanimously
sacrificing herself like a real heroine of romance (and Aunt
Nella was—I know not whether I have mentioned it before or
not—in secret a great novel-reader); and she foresaw that an
hour would come in the course of the great law-suit, when
her noble conduct would be made known, and openly acknowledged in some kind of protocol, because that was the way in
which things happened in the histories of heroines of romance.
Poor Aunt Nella!

In the mean time she enjoyed the pleasure of being regarded by her brother-in-law, after this evening, with quite
other eyes than formerly; he considered her evidently no
longer a single cypher, but four cyphers with a one standing
before them.

A MOMENT.

In our northern folk-songs there commonly occurs between the minor key of the beginning and the end, an interval of a few bars in the major key which, in the most delicious manner, soothe the ear and touch the feelings, in which the soul seems to cast a bright glance, rich in promise, into a future affluent in spring and love. The evening on which Yngve, according to the appointment of the Director, again found himself at Kullen, resembled such a major key in the life of the lovers.

The Director, who seemed to have taken his resolution with regard to Yngve, received him with politeness, and, without any repulsive coldness, allowed him to explain his prospects, and then replied that he wished to become better acquainted with him; wished him a more important position in society, as well as more certain prospects of an independent income before he could consent to his marriage with Hertha. Hertha, it was true, possessed some property from her mother, but not as much as people generally believed; and not sufficient of itself for the maintenance of a family. It was the Director's duty, therefore, as her father and guardian, to watch over her future prospects. The future alone could decide the issue of Yngve's wishes with regard to Hertha, but he might openly plead his own cause with her, and in the mean time would be welcome to the house of Hertha's father.

All this was reasonable enough, and was more than Yngve expected after the scene of the preceding evening. He therefore thanked the Director cordially, and expressed his hope that before long he might be able to satisfy his reasonable demands, and offer to Hertha a position in life secure from pecuniary difficulties. Yngve also contrived to create an interest in the mind of tne Director for the undertakings in which he was interested, and in which his future prospects were involved. He produced altogether so agreeable an impression upon the Director, that he received from him an invitation to stay to supper.

Such an event as a young man being invited to stay to supper, had not occurred for many a long year, never since the time when Alma's lover visited with them.

The dining-room at Kullen exhibited this evening an unusually agreeable aspect. The large fire of pine-logs, which crackled and flamed merrily, threw a joyous light upon the father of the family, who sate in a comfortable corner, smoking his pipe and talking with Yngve about the various schemes for railroads and water conveyances in Sweden and other countries : upon little Aunt Nella, who sate by the fire busily winding off her yarn, and muttering to herself with an unusually pleased expression; on the supper-table, which was spread and adorned with flowers by Martha and Maria ; and lastly on Hertha, who came and went, as she silently attended to her household duties. She appeared to Yngve, this while, so noble and beautiful, that he sometimes became quite absorbed, and forgot that it was needful to answer the questions of the Director about railroads, or else he replied wholly at random. For instance, when questioned about a certain branch of railway, he answered like one in a dream, " an actual Iduna! " and as to the direction of another railroad, he replied with warmth, " to all eternity! "

The director looked at him in astonishment, but when he observed the direction of his eyes, he smiled, puffed the smoke from his tobacco-pipe, and did not seem offended. They had scarcely ever seen the Director so civil and so kind to any one before. How happy the sight of this made Hertha, and the pleasant anticipations for the future which it gave rise to, both in her breast and that of Yngve, may easily be conceived.

The evening meal became, under these circumstances, one of the most joyous which had ever been partaken of in that home. When it was ended the Director spoke to Yngve about his mother, and now made her, through her son, that offer of a place in his family, which Hertha had prepared him for. Yngve perceived that the Director regarded this matter as an affair which would be advantageous to the family, and he silently commended her consideration.

Before they separated Hertha led her friend into the room which she had prepared and arranged for his mother.

"See, Yngve," said she, "your book-case shall stand there, and here in this easy chair your mother shall sit, and I here, beside her, when we read together your books and your letters. Here, at this writing-table, will your mother, and—I also sometimes—write to you."

Hertha wished, in this moment of separation, to leave upon Yngve's mind the impression of her close connection with his mother, and of the life she would lead in her new home. She wished that he, in memory, should see them together.

Yngve was at the same time so affected, and rendered so happy by all that had taken place, that when he took leave of Hertha's sisters, he pressed them to his heart with an earnest tenderness that at once astonished and affected them; he kissed Aunt Nella's hand and then her cheek, which caused her to make such a start of pleasurable surprise, as broke her yarn-thread; for she discovered, all at once, a great resemblance between Yngve and one of the ball-room admirers of her young days, and she began to puzzle her brain about some secret intrigue in connection with this circumstance. Yngve was disposed to clasp the Director and the whole family in his embrace, but the distant though polite demeanor of the former checked any extraordinary demonstration as regarded him. Nevertheless, when Yngve, with an expression of filial reverence and gratitude in his frank and handsome countenance, yet once more shook his hand at parting, the Director accompanied him to the door, and said, with undisguised good-will:

"I wish you all success and a happy return. You are still quite young, and while the Patriarch Jacob could wait seven years, and again seven years, for his betrothed, it ought not to

19

appear long to you to wait a year or two for one who is dear to you. Time flies fast."

Hertha, this evening, kissed her father's hand, as she had not kissed it since the time when she looked up to him in blind obedience and **love**.

SEVEN YEARS:

THE PATRIARCHAL RELATIONSHIP.

WE read in the history of the Patriarch Jacob, that the seven years which he served for Rachel " seemed to him but a few days, for the love he had to her." And I knew a Swedish girl who devoted herself for ten years to wait upon her blind and necessitous father, and who, although she was young and blooming when she entered upon this service, and was pale and withered when it was ended (at her father's decease), yet who found not those ten years to be either long or oppressive. The reason of this was, that affection had been the impelling principle, had sustained the soul, given wings to time, had made even weariness dear, and changed life into a beautiful pastime.

How different must it be when the service is for those whom we cannot love, or when force or injustice enchain the free soul to a lot which it has not chosen! how oppressive the days then become; how interminable the years; how gloomy the heart, life, the future, Providence—everything!

We will pass with light and hasty steps over those years of Hertha's history which we have now to describe, and only by a few touches delineate their lights and shadows.

Half a year after the parting which we have described in the foregoing chapter, Yngve returned to Sweden, his health re-established, and full of earnestness, hope, and activity. Two years afterwards he was advanced to a position in his profession which gave him the certain prospect of a modest competency for the future, and he now renewed his request to Hertha's father for his consent to their union. The Director replied that he did not consider Yngve's prospects as yet sufficiently established. Besides which, his health, he said, was such that he could neither dispense with his daughter's care at home, nor yet could he look into the state of her property. He considered it best, therefore, that the lovers should yet wait for a year or two.

It was now, that Hertha for the first time broke the bonds of silence, which long custom and inherent reverence for the patriarchal guardianship had imposed upon her. She spoke seriously and plainly with her father, reminded him of all his promises, told him of her own human right to dispose of her own person, her own property, and to determine her own future. She appealed to him in the name of justice and of reason; but, ah! her father, in his favor, could oppose against her the decisions of the law, " the Paternal Statutes." After he had listened to her with an almost scornful calmness, he proved to her out of the Statute-book itself, that she possessed no right at all over her own property, over herself, or her future, otherwise than in as far as her father would consider it. She was " a minor" in the eye of the law, and was bound to guide herself entirely according to the will of her guardian. His promises to her—he could not remember having made any. If he had ever made any promises, it could only be on condition of his fulfilling them in case he found it right to do so, but that nobody, either by force or otherwise, should compel him to do anything which he was not willing to do of himself. He was not one who would allow himself to be compelled. He had now spoken his mind, and there was an end of it, and people knew what they had to do.

Hertha did not this time give way to the proud feeling which rose up within her. She besought her father to listen to the voice of reason; she reminded him, with tears, of Alma's last prayer. Nor did she now even demand, she only prayed on her knees before him—for her freedom, for her human right, which if her father would not grant her from a sense of justice, would he not do so out of kindness and mercy?

But the Director at this moment was excited beyond himself. "Did she wish to kill him?" he asked, "or to drive him mad? Could she not wait a year or two? More he did not ask for." And he ended by appealing to her affection as a daughter. "She ought to obey her father. He knew better than she did what would contribute to her welfare. He did not like sentimental scenes. He knew what he would have, and have it he would, and there was an end."

Reader, if thou hast ever prayed for something which was right and reasonable; prayed earnestly, put thy whole soul into thy prayer; humbled thyself, renounced thyself in order, through love and sacrifice, to obtain—thy right, and yet hast been denied, then perhaps wilt thou be able to understand Hertha's feelings as she arose from her humble position at her father's knee. Pale, rigid, with a gloomy expression of eye, and with a dark presentiment in her soul, she rose slowly and left the room without saying a word. But her soul was in a state of tumult.

She was calmer, but gloomily resolute, when on the afternoon of the same day she related the result of her conversation with her father to Yngve and Judge Carlson, who came on purpose to hear it.

Both were exceedingly angry, and advised her to appeal to the courts of justice, and let them decide between her and her unreasonable father. Without doubt they would decide in her favor.

"I believe so too," said Hertha: "but one thing is certain, and that is, that I shall never appeal to them to obtain my rights against my father."

"Then you do not love me," exclaimed Yngve, reproachfully; "you will let me die of Tantalus-agony rather than consent to a bold but rational procedure. You do not understand my affection for you—you cannot have the same for me. You are afraid of your father—afraid of the world's judgment of you,—I am nothing to you—my life and my happiness are nothing to you."

Hertha fixed upon Yngve a look of unspeakable reproachful anguish, but she said not a word.

"I honor your delicacy of feeling, your sense of filial duty," said Judge Carlson, "but these may be carried too far. Reflect that you sacrifice both your own and another's future for egotistical perversity, for unbounded obstinacy. And you have already mentioned to me your anxiety about your father's affairs, and his ability to manage them—reflect, therefore, that you are probably sacrificing not only your own, but your sisters' property, which is in his hands,—as well as their future prospects."

Hertha bowed her head into her hands and sat for a moment silent. When she again raised her countenance it was bathed in tears.

"Oh, my friends," said she, "do not be angry with me. I cannot do otherwise; my conscience forbids me. Because my father is an unreasonable father, must I be an unnatural daughter? Must I rise up against him who gave me life, and embitter his life?—cast a shadow upon him through the whole kingdom—reveal his weakness or his injustice? No; I will not merit the reproach of having acted unworthily as a daughter. I should in that case consider myself unworthy of being one day a mother. No; I will not appear publicly as an accuser of my father. Rather let Yngve and me wait patiently—die, if so it must be. I will do all that lies in my power, all that can be done by the performance of duty, by persuasion—and perhaps a time may come when my father's heart will not be so closed against me as now; but never, never will I through force and compulsion deserve his hatred, his curse. And if you can accuse me for this, Yngve, you are no longer the noble, the right-minded Yngve whom I loved."

"But your sisters?" resumed the lawyer.

"Show me," said Hertha, "a way of securing their future prospects, without giving a death-blow to our father's respectability, and to his life, perhaps, by my laying before the monarch and the nation my suspicions of his stewardship of our property. Can you show me any other way? Do our laws afford no other means?"

Both Carlson and Yngve were silent. Hertha rose up.

"Give me your hands," said she, "you cannot disapprove of my feelings. Support me rather in the severe time of trial which is at hand, Yngve!"—Hertha's glance spoke what no words could express, the suffering which she endured on his account.

He understood her looks, and replied by clasping her to his heart.

"Forgive me!" whispered he; "never more shall you hear a reproachful word from me."

Yngve's resolution was, however, taken at this moment. He would separate himself for a time both from Hertha and his native land, and accept a professional offer which had been made to him abroad, and which afforded him more advantageous prospects than he had at present in Sweden. For it was to him unendurable to live near Hertha under the constraint which his half-engagement to her and her own wishes imposed. And he was right. Hertha did not love Yngve as he loved her. No woman can fully understand the passion which glows in the whole being of the enamored young man, nor can she participate it. She loves equally as much, often more, or better than he, but in quite another manner.

Carlson contemplated the two young friends with deep sympathy, and Hertha with real admiration, because he perfectly understood her.

"Remember your promise," said he to her at the close of this interview, "to make use of me whenever you may want the help of a fatherly friend, of one who would be a father to you, and—would to God that I were so!"

Yngve set off soon afterwards with one of his young friends to Piedmont, whither his new engagement called him. Judge Carlson removed to his magisterial district. Hertha remained alone in her father's house.

The Director's health improved somewhat during the following year, in the course of which he received various flattering public marks of honor. He had made himself known and esteemed as a clever and unflinching servant of the government, and therefore the order of the Knight of the North Star was conferred upon him with the title of Chief Director, and his name was changed to that of Falkenhjelm, which name was borne by an elder branch of the same family. He was spoken of in general as a "substantial old fellow," a "close man," a "prudent man," a "clever old gentleman," and so on, and regarded as a man of great practical understanding, as well as substantial wealth. Meantime the mysterious law-suit proceeded, regarding which Aunt Nella continued in profound silence, to give significant looks and put on an important air, but about which, from fear of her brother-in-law's displeasure, she never dared to speak aloud, and about which he himself never spoke, excepting to the lawyer to whom he had intrusted his cause, and with whom he had long and mysterious conferences. This law-suit and these conferences had evidently a great influence upon the Director's temper, which in consequence became more and more gloomy and irascible, in spite of the light which was cast from the sun of royal favor over his civil services. Hertha, who sometimes doubted the justice of her suspicions regarding her father's mismanagement of the family property, became nevertheless uneasy at the repeated proofs which occurred of his failing memory and impaired powers of mind, but still she could not even here attain to full certainty.

There occurred at this time in her life, one of those long states of twilight, which are so general in the lives of women in the north, especially in Sweden ; states of twilight during which every object is involved in shadows, and when one can only act or work inasmuch as the little flame one lights can enable one to see ; states which wonderfully remind us of the Scandinavian "Hades," that wonderful world of mist, full of rain-clouds, and shapeless magical forms, and clammy, poisonous rivers.

But there are two kinds of twilight, that of evening, and that of the morning. The former deepens into night ; the latter brightens into day. Weak or melancholy temperaments belong to the former, but energetic souls, and those also in which the strength of God's love has kindled its elevating flame, are—yes, even if the whole of their earthly life continues in twilight—they are the children of the rosy morning, and their souls and their labors are tinged by its celestial glow.

We need not say to which of these two classes Hertha belonged: Her energetic soul, the light which came to her from the friend who reconciled her to life; faith in a superintending, fatherly providence, which never deserted her, since she had so evidently perceived its guidance in her heart, in her life; the purity and beauty of her connection with Yngve; the conviction that she had acted according to the highest dictates of duty and conscience—all these helped her to overcome the bitterness which unjust power awoke within her, helped her also during the unhappy continuance of twilight in her life and home, to kindle a light which did not merely enlighten herself but others also,—nay, indeed almost every one who came within her sphere of life.

Towards her father she continued to be an obedient and careful daughter, even when she was obliged to give up all hope of finding in him a fatherly support in any respect. Love him she could not, neither show him the love, the sweet, affectionate attention which love only can inspire. And although he received all that he demanded; punctuality, obedience, order in everything which concerned him,—he complained not unfrequently to his faithful, old servant of his eldest daughter's obstinacy, want of affection, and insubordination towards him. She was, he said, of an inflexible character, who would not take the pains to please her father, or make him happy; she was stubborn, irreconcilable, unforgiving, selfish, and so on.

Oh, thou fool! Thou desirest love and reconciliation, but thou thyself exhibitest the opposite; thou complainest of coldness and want of feeling in look and manner, and thou thyself art the cause of this by thy own behavior, thou thyself doing nothing to call forth kindly feelings. She of whom thou complainest may have treasures of love and tenderness in her heart, but thou wilt never experience them, and thou wilt never be able to see a true glance from those eyes, because thou hast excluded from thee the sunlight of those eyes, by thy unworthiness, thy severity; thou hast built up a granite wall between that eye and thine own. Thou fool! which seest the mote in thy neighbor's eye and perceivest not the beam which is in thine own, accuse thyself, and become different to what thou art! That soul is cold, thou sayest. What if she be merely true and honest towards herself and thee? Better, nobler is it that she show herself as she is, than that she should dissemble an affection, act a lie by appearing agreeable to thee, when she neither does nor can feel so. Esteem and love will not come at call. They must be won.

Attachment to Yngve's gentle mother, as well as to her young sisters, were the light in Hertha's domestic life, and by degrees a fresh light dawned in that active employment, of which we have spoken, and which gave new life to her soul.

During the three years which Hertha devoted to those preparatory studies which she herself considered absolutely necessary, before bringing into operation the educational institute which it was her intention to establish, she was fortunate enough to become acquainted with two men of more than ordinary knowledge and elevation of mind. They had become attached to her as brothers, and imparted to her the wealth of their own large views and practical knowledge, than which nothing could be more valuable to her, whilst they themselves were, in a high degree, benefited by the noble spirit and life of this extraordinary young woman. Hertha came to experience that which she, who now traces the history of her life, also has experienced, and which will ever live in her grateful memory as one of her most precious human experiences, that however unfavorable the laws and spirit of society may be to the full development of woman, yet that it seldom, if ever happened, that a woman, gifted with any unusual powers of mind or gifts of genius, does not sooner or later find manly friends who faithfully offer their hands to help her to attain the object towards which her natural gifts prompt her.

It is another question whether this extension of help can ever become sufficient, whether it does not always come too late, or is of necessity too partial to admit of her full development. "No one," wrote Mozart, on one occasion, to a dilettante music-composer, "can ever, after all, become a master, who has not already from childhood had experience of the master's ' *donnerwetter*' and the discipline of the school." Certain it is, that technical certainty, clear insight into means and purposes as well as the application of our own powers, are not obtained without early, sure guidance, long practice and trial. Helpless deficiency adheres even to genius which has been long left to guide itself in the wide world by its own will.

Hertha, with deep sorrow, soon discovered all this; discovered with what helpless deficiency she would have to combat in herself, before she could accomplish her purpose. Her courageous spirit, however, admonished her steadfastly to persevere towards the object which she had set before herself. " There are subjects, after all," said she to herself, " on which I can give instructions to young light-seeking souls, better than even the most learned men."

In the mean time it soon became evident to her that, in order to render her plan effective, it must be carried out in a form more in accordance with the views and the point of sight from which the circle in which she moved looked at things. To accomplish even this, her position in the family, as regarded money and her father's peculiar temper, compelled her to endeavor, by her own labor, to obtain the means of putting her plans in execution.

Many of our young readers have doubtless wondered already why Hertha did not endeavor, by means of authorship, to acquire this needful independence. But Hertha knew that she was not possessed of the necessary gifts for this purpose; she did not write as a matter of choice; she talked better than she wrote. Action and life were the springs of her inspiration; it was when in living contact with other souls that her own soul felt and extended its wings. Besides—but we will let her speak for herself in some of the entries in her diary:

" *May 1st*, 18—. I have determined to commence a week-day school, or *Pension*, as it is called, where young girls shall be taught everything which is considered especially necessary for them in this world ; that is to say, languages, history, geography, needlework, drawing, music, etc.; all of which are unquestionably good ; and this school will aid me in carrying out my plan for the other higher school, devoted to the exercises of the soul and the powers of mind ; but which I think of styling 'Practices in Language and Conversation,' in order not to awaken any 'uneasiness in the camp,' or any suspicion of any schemes of emancipation. The week-day school, in which I shall be assisted by a male and female teacher, will assemble every day. The higher, holiday-school, for the practice of language and conversation, only twice in the week; and only voluntary or select pupils shall be admitted to it. The entrance to the former school shall be by payment; to the latter only by Love to the Eternal.

"In the mean time I must have some money to provide a store of books and materials for the week-day school, and for this I must go to my father. I shall beg him to let me have the small sum of interest due upon my maternal inheritance. I will only ask for that which is my own, and as a means of providing a future competence ; nevertheless, I have a bitter presentiment that I shall be refused. But I must make the attempt. Alas, that the making of a reasonable request to a father should be felt as a something dreadful ! "

"*May 3rd.* My presentiment was right. I received a negative reply. 'Such were unnecessary establishments,' he said, ' and served only to make girls full of pretension, unpractical, and useless at home,' etc. etc. ' There was, besides, already a girls' school in the town, and that was more than enough. Another could not support itself.' 'It was the duty of a guardian,' he said, ' to see that the minor's property was not misapplied, but that, on the contrary, it was augmented by the interest being added to the principal, and that such duty he would fulfil, so long as it lay in his power.' 'I could do just as I liked about the school, but I must not look to him for any money.'

"I have now written, therefore, to Judge Carlson, and asked him for a loan. It is very repugnant to my feelings to do so, but it is my only resource. I shall see whether he will keep his promise.

"'Cannot you grind?' I, on one occasion, heard a witty, elderly lady say, with a cunning smile, to another, who complained that she could not get her husband to perform a promise which he had given her. And there is, I know, a certain *grinding* in the house, a perpetual recurrence of reminding, bothering, worrying, which, with the addition of black looks, tears, or cold, cutting words and looks, is able to overcome the stoutest resistance, and give such as are clever in this art an incalculable power of obtaining whatever they wish for. But another thing I know also, and that is, that I neither can nor will avail myself of such ways and means. The royal way of love and truth is the only one which I will take. And the society or the house in which the object is attained less easily by this means than by subterranean or crooked ways, has something wrong in it."

"*May* 10th. May the noble Judge Carlson forgive me for having, for one moment, doubted of his chivalrous spirit : may he forgive me for not having entirely relied upon his friendship and his promise! He has now, both by word and deed, proved himself my friend. Father in heaven! this is Thy work, and thy bringing about! Henceforth I will alone look up to Thee for help and counsel ; alone follow Thy guidance! Thou wilt stand by me. And now, henceforward—henceforward prayer and work!"

In the autumn of the same year Hertha wrote :

"*November* 1st. My week-day school flourishes greatly; more pupils offer themselves than I expected. It gives me a great deal of work, and not of the kind which I love! I cannot begin my holiday-school till the new year."

Early in the year we accordingly find the following entry in Hertha's Diary :

"*January* 18th. I have begun my lessons in language and conversation with some of the elder girls, by the reading of

Sophocles' Antigone; that glorious woman, who, faithful both by word and deed to the law of conscience and duty, defies the strong command of the tyrant, the slavish usages of society, her sister's timid counsel, and even the prayers of her beloved, and stands fast in death, appealing to

> The law infallible; unwritten law supreme,

which,

> From to-day dates not, nor yet from yesterday; but
> From eternity, the moment known to no man;

She who, with all youth and womanhood's deep feeling of the glory of life, and natural horror of the fearful death which she knew lay before her, if she persisted in the defiance of injustice, yet still persevered, still stood firm, and although, in her last moment, half doubting even the justice of the Gods, doubted not the voice of truth in the depth of her own conscience, but in entire self-consciousness accused her father's city, because she had to suffer and die for having—

> Held that as sacred which in truth is sacred.

"This glorious image of the heroine of conscience, may lead my young girls to understand more fully the ideal of the Christian woman, not merely (as is now so common) one-sided in humility, which so easily becomes slavish, but also in heroism.

"I read this tragedy of Sophocles in the German translation for the sake of the language, and we afterwards conversed on what we had read. I have encouraged the young people to write down their thoughts on this subject before our next meeting. It will exercise them in thinking on topics which give strength to the moral being."

"*March* 1*st*. We have finished the reading of Antigone, and I am pleased with the result of this experiment. Among the ten young girls who attend my holiday-school, are some who have received a lasting impression from this reading; all have in some degree become elevated by it, and their inward sight has become clearer.

"*Aurora*, whose character and natural gifts impel her to a strong demonstration of her feelings, and who certainly will sometime be distinguished (if she can develope herself) as an artist or a poetess, has learned from Antigone to disregard minor inspirations and petty conquests. She will allow herself to be inspired alone by the Sun.

"*Eva* and *Maria*, those Egeria-natures, who would rather live concealed in the sacred grove from which they whisper the pure teachings of wisdom into the listener's ear, have learned from Antigone faith in and dependence upon themselves or upon the inner voice, which reveals itself during the intercourse with God.

"*Martha*, the prosaic and practical nature, has learned that with her more earthly gifts and power she also may become a servant of the Highest."

Here follows a description of the talents and dispositions of many other young girls; but as it would not greatly interest the reader, we pass it over, and introduce two later entries in the diary, by which it will be seen how Hertha's plan arranged itself, and cleared up before her mind's eye.

In May she wrote as follows :—

"We shall now undertake exercises in the French and English languages, the purport of which shall be the contemplation of the womanly Christian consciousness in relation to a certain given mission or vocation in society, through peculiar gifts or calling. The biography of noble and distinguished women, either celebrated or known but of few, will serve as the text for our contemplation.

"The consciousness of thought ought to be a living observation and will. Biography is excellent for this purpose.

"This will be preparatory to Conversations on Society We will contemplate in their mutual relationship, families, communities, states, arts, sciences, and finally the Church, as the mother, under whose protection these various limbs grow into one body and one soul in the kingdom of God—the highest community, in which every natural gift is ennobled to a gift of mercy. The most noble heroes of family-love, of social-love (that is of humanity), of art and science, will enlighten us in our endeavor to understand the importance of each in life, and in the extension of the kingdom of God on earth.

"The conversation on Society will lead us to its innermost life and guiding power—Religion. Read: General history of Religion; the biography of the various founders of Religion. The relationship of natural religion, so called, to revealed; its light, its darkness, its insufficiency to solve the enigma of existence, to answer the requirements and the questionings of the human heart. The doctrines of the Christian religion: God in Christ. The history of Jesus Christ.

"The ideal and the reality of society. The Christian work of redemption in the soul and in the world.

"Woman's part in the work; her peculiar vocation and position in society. Her character, her duties, her rights. Her vocation as MOTHER, or nurse, or whatever else she may be. Her power as such influential. Without Egeria no Numa.

"Woman in Sweden. Her position, past and present. Swedish women in the history of their country. The future of the Swedish woman, and her influence on the future of Sweden.

"My young girls must learn to think highly of their native land, highly of their own mission, but not, therefore, highly of themselves. They must ever look above themselves, who are to grow continually.

"Read the Vala-Song. Its last prediction, the renewal of the heavens, the education of the new human race, 'born of the morning dew,' in the sacred grove, can only be accomplished by the second Eve, the woman born anew in God.

"Natural history, in its more profound relationship to human life, must also become a subject for the Conversation-lessons of the holiday school, when—Yngve comes home, and can teach and help me to initiate the young girls into its sanctuary."

"*June.*—Intercourse with these young souls is like a refreshing vernal breeze to my soul; it is beautiful to see the light of dawn in them, and to anticipate a fuller day in their life!

"If I could surround them with noble and beautiful objects in the holiday-school, their consecration to the high and the holy would be powerfully promoted. We shall see! I sometimes think of fitting up the orangery,* which is now quite empty, as a room—such as I see in my waking dreams. A statue of the northern goddess of youth, Iduna, stands in the centre,—around, on pedestals, busts of the heroes of humanity; at the farther end the statue of Christ, after Thorwaldsen, the best which I have yet seen; for the rest a few good pictures, and beautiful plants; and amid all these the young human souls who will here advance in the worship and service of the Divine! Oh, if it could only be so! Even the Christian temple has a gate which is called 'the Beautiful!'"

"*July.*—The summer is glorious this year. I take my young girls out in the woods and the fields; it is refreshing to both soul and body. We botanise together, and I talk with them of their relationship with nature, and of the life of nature, 'the sighs of the animal creation,' and its explanation in a 'new heaven and a new earth.' Read with them beneath the great ash-trees, our deep-thoughted northern legends, of the Neck, the Hill-people, &c., from the Swedish Sagas.

"Our Conversation-lessons have, during these beautiful evenings, been held in the open air. There we have read the Northern Mythology, and have contemplated the truth in its scenes and symbols. In the evening the girls danced on the grass, and it was a delight to see fresh, life-enjoying youth, thus rejoice in and beautify nature. All educational institutions for girls ought to be in the country.

---

* A large room with lofty windows, which extended from one end of the house at Kullen.

"I have written to Yngve about my schools, and my future plans regarding them. His letters always strengthen and encourage me, but they distress me at the same time, because he is evidently not happy, although he never complains. Oh, Yngve! neither do I repose upon roses!"

Towards the close of the year we find this entry:

"I am very weary after many sleepless nights spent in preparation for the examination of the week-day pupils, winding up the accounts of the year, &c., together with the fear, the conviction that little or no profit will accrue to me, after paying off the loan and other expenses. My holiday-school will have to wait a long time for the beautiful hall.

"Yngve, Yngve! my soul cries after thee. I can dispense with marriage, but not with thy presence, thy sympathy; not with the joy of seeing thee, of attending to thy happiness, my friend, brother, HUSBAND before God! Something within my soul tells me that thou standest in need of me, of my care, my love. It is midnight, all are sleeping around me,—my heart wakes, and thinks, Yngve, of thee!"

"*New Year's Day.* A letter from Yngve, and in it a bill of exchange. Yngve says that he will pay for his mother's board in my father's house. But so much, Yngve! much more than —but I understand thee, and am no longer proud towards thee. I will do as thou wishest, Yngve, with regard to the beautiful hall,—the Iduna-hall, as it shall henceforth be called, —and a couple of youths shall be admitted to its school in memory of thee.

"I have also had a letter from Rudolph to-day, and a small sum of money 'for the sufferers by the fire,' writes he. Poor Rudolph!"

In the following autumn Hertha wrote:

"My holiday-school begins to be celebrated, Yngve, and is visited by some distinguished ladies and men of great intellect, who take an interest in it. It pleases me on account of my young girls, to whom it is beneficial to listen to the thoughts and conversation of the visitors. Yet it is a restraint on their cheerfulness, and for this reason I receive these large parties but once a week.   Besides curiosity attracts many to the Iduna-hall, who have no fresh, life-giving fruits to communicate.   And, let it be as it may, the young ones and I are happier by ourselves.   The bashful Eva, my thoughtful, quiet Maria, and Aurora, overflowing with life, as she is, are never quite themselves excepting at such times.   Aurora has yet to acquire ease and tact, but she has unusual powers both of head and heart; she is the only one of my young girls who betrays genius.   The youths were uncertain and bashful at the commencement, but they are beginning now to exhibit themselves in a beautiful light, and they seem to be happy amongst us.   I feel for them, as for the girls, a maternal tenderness, and it is delightful to me to see their confidence in me.

" A few days ago a young man called on me, who had once been my protector when I stood in need of one.   He now wished for the situation of tutor in my week-day-school, and I was fortunate enough to be able to give it to him; for this school also must be extended to receive all the pupils which are offered.   Olof E. is a young man of noble character, and will be a support to the day-school and a welcome participator in our evening conversations.

" Last evening the Conversation in the Iduna-hall was unusually animated, I might say brilliant.   It was my great reception evening, and I proposed 'The Right Comprehension of Liberty of Conscience' as the subject of conversation.   The handsome Mrs. N. spoke in a manner which astonished me and animated all.   Ingeborg Hedermann expressed liberal and excellent sentiments.   The young were silent; but I saw beaming glances from the eyes of several.   Judge Carlson was present, and spoke judiciously and nobly on the subject of liberty of conscience with reference to religion.   I carefully kept the conversation to the general subject, avoiding all reference to the circumstances of our country. Such reference will come of itself."

Hertha's diary during the following three years exhibits an increasing development, both of her own mind and her plans.

In the spring of 18—, she wrote:

"Yngve! if I could now conduct thee into the Iduna-hall—for now it is complete—show thee the statue of our noble, grave, and yet mild Scandinavian goddess of youth, surrounded by laurels and blossoming roses, and the yet more elevated one of Him, who stands with extended arms inviting the whole human race to his redeeming embrace; and, ranged around, busts of noble and wise men, who glance forth from between evergreen trees—thou wouldst then rejoice, my Yngve, because this is thy and my joint work. A handsome collection of books, thy books among the rest, and some good pictures, complete the ornament of the hall. It is beautiful, and cheerful, and rich in instruction; a fitting home for young, pure, and upward-striving souls. Oh, if I could only, beyond everything else, see thee, Yngve, among the flock of young creatures that assemble around me; hear thee speak to them and teach them, as thou in former times taughtest me! When will that hour come?

"Wilt thou know me again, my Yngve? I am much aged, and I grow rapidly older each day that I spend in the week-day-school, and by every sleepless night which it costs me. Nevertheless I take care of my outward being as I never did in my youth. In those days I was too proud to wish to please by my physical *I*, and too unhappy in my own soul to trouble myself about my body. Now I take care of it, and adorn it that I may please—my pupils; that I may produce such an impression upon them as is no way at variance with the purpose of my holiday-school in the Iduna-hall; I desire, even I, to produce a beautiful, or at least an ennobling impression; and for this purpose I consult my own taste and my mirror, as well as silently an—absent friend: fashion, on the contrary, I regard very little, being only careful not very much to offend against it. Every person who has a decided individuality of character, which is stamped upon the exterior, ought to dress as much as possible in conformity with it.

"My young friends flatter me : call me beautiful; and if I do sometimes appear so, it is because the brightness of their glances and of their youthful souls is reflected back upon me."

It was inevitable, but that Hertha's conversations and other " schemes " and " undertakings," as Mrs. Uggla termed them, would call forth many kinds of opinion, and sometimes not very favorable ones, in Kungsköping and its neighborhood. The meetings in the Iduna-hall were regarded by many with suspicion ; there was no use in them, people said, and they were afraid of the new and unsettled opinions which were there propounded ; afraid of the young people being led away by great thoughts of themselves, pretensions, and so on. But the enthusiastic devotion of the young people themselves towards their maternal instructor and friend, carried her triumphantly through every attempt to depreciate her influence, and every doubt of her sound and salutary teachings. And when fathers and mothers saw their young daughters develope themselves, not merely in outward grace and the ability to acquire knowledge, but also in nobility and sweetness of character, under Hertha's guidence, they permitted them to follow it still further. Many parents also candidly acknowledged her merits with regard to their children. As far as the children themselves were concerned, they looked up to Hertha as to a being of higher order. She stood amongst them like the fruitful mother-tree of the Banana above a group of young offshoots which spring up at its feet. Every one of the disciples called her by her name, and addressed her as *thou ;* her relationship to each individual was of a deep personal kind ; her keen but warmly affectionate glance rested on all of them with a fostering power. At the same time she was never fondling and weak, her maternal tenderness was of much higher character.

———

"I have now seen 'the Sibyl,'" wrote a young man, when describing her, "and have also been present at some of her 'Conversations.' She is a Christian Vala; her inspirations breathe forth a sentiment kindred to that of every nobly beating heart. I confess that I did not, in the first instance, meet her without a prejudice, and that I went rather in a critical spirit than willing to learn. But she has conquered me by the effect produced by her soul's attitude, if I may so speak, with regard to the highest truth. Her beaming eyes, her simple but imposing demeanor, her voice, her gestures, her silence, her words. Thus, her whole being has produced upon me an uneffaceable impression, and has awoke in me a love to the true and the noble, which will henceforth guide me through the world's twilight, or ignes fatui. She must produce an elevating effect upon every one who is not in soul a dwarf or a mole. She is not handsome, but still there is a picturesque beauty in her noble bearing, her simple but dignified costume, and I—should have fallen in love with her if I had dared."

"You wish to know something about her appearance, her dress, her manners, &c.," wrote one of Hertha's elder pupils to one of her friends. "She dresses generally in snow-white muslin, made up to the throat, and which, entirely without starch, falls in soft rich folds around her beautiful figure,—sometimes also she wears agate-colored silk,—a black mantle, of velvet in winter, and lace in summer, is worn on the shoulders; with a small white lace collar round the neck. Her rich, gold-colored hair, which grows naturally in soft wavy masses, is turned back from the temples, showing the beautiful growth and the etherially branching veins; so that the glorious countenance, with those wonderfully beaming eyes, is presented freely and clearly. The hair simply platted behind, is fastened low on the neck, as we see in antique busts. She wears neither rings nor bracelets, for her hands and arms need them not, nor any ornament whatever, not even a flower.

Frequently however will she gather from the flowers in the hall and adorn our heads with them, for she loves to see us well and tastefully dressed, according to our age; but she cannot bear to see us wearing fine jewelry, or colors which do not harmonize with each other, and any fault in taste or arrangement she always notices. She wishes that the outward human being should express the harmony of the soul; but not according to old 'ma bonne's' notions that we should be all 'one like another,' but that every one should endeavor to be entirely herself, in a nobler manner, 'as God has willed it.' And I confess that I take more pains to please her in my exterior, than I ever did to please any man. She herself attracts us by her own demeanor towards the noble and the beautiful, so that not many words are required to awaken in us a yearning after the same. It comes with her to us, as of itself, in the Iduna-hall. She looks so stately, and, if I may so say, highborn, that one, at the beginning, feels oneself quite small beside her; one shrinks as it were, but when she begins to speak, when she looks on us, then there is in her something so tender and maternal, that one is raised up by it, and one seems, as it were, to begin to grow;—and that one does really, at least in aspiration, after the good and the true, and in desire to attain them. There are times when I feel a longing to lay my head on her knee, and let her see my whole soul so that she may enlighten it, and lift it upwards!"

"Life and its purposes seem so great in the light wherewith she enlightens them, and yet nevertheless the smallest thing, of natural endowment, disposition, or action, acquires a significance and value in this light. The whole of life becomes clear to us in her glance. Many persons consider her to be stern. But I and all my young friends, are profoundly acquainted with her goodness. To many of us she is more than a mother, taking care of our bodies, as of our souls, our health, our future, our happiness. Her sisters almost worship her!"

It was thus that the young regarded her. We have already seen the state of Hertha's own soul whilst she, developing herself so beautifully, labored for others. Unhappy she was not, yet neither was she happy.

The week-day-school was a continual strain upon her mind, and was by no means a satisfactory labor. The parents were often stupid and unreasonable, and either could not or would not understand what was best in the education of their children. And besides this, she had incessantly to combat with the small worries of every-day life. Within herself too, she struggled, and not always successfully, against the bitterness which her father's want of integrity towards her, awoke in her soul, together with his increasing parsimony in the house. But more than all, she suffered from the unspeakable tenderness and anxiety which she felt for Yngve, as his letters betrayed more and more the cruel want which he felt of her and of a home, and as it became more and more evident to her that his health was suffering in consequence.

He wrote less frequently, and a certain painful depression was often perceptible in his letters, however rich they might otherwise be in the life of affection and thought.

It was an understood thing between the two friends, that if any change took place in the mind of the Chief Director with respect to themselves, Hertha should lose no time in making it known to Yngve, and that he should then immediately return. But year after year had gone on and no change had occurred which would justify Hertha in recalling Yngve. Seven years had thus passed since the day when they plighted to each other their faith in life and in death, and had been obliged to part, and Hertha was now no longer young.

At this time came another of these letters from Yngve, which, without uttering a complaint, nevertheless caused Hertha to press her hand upon her heart, as if she felt there an agonising pain, whilst the tears slowly filled those sorrowful eyes, which seemed to gaze into distance. After this letter she sate down and wrote :

"Yngve, come home ! Come home, beloved friend ! I cannot bear any longer to be separated from you, to see you suffer and to experience in myself, because you suffer, feelings which are like pangs of conscience. For I see, Yngve, though you do not say so, that you are ill, both soul and body. Oh! come back, and let me once more be your physician; it will make me also young again, and God will once more bless what you once called my 'power of healing.'

"I have nothing new to tell you, as regards my home; everything remains unaltered as far as my father is concerned; or if either looks darker, more impossible, because his temper is evidently more morose of late,—but still, still I say, ' Yngve, come home !' A presentiment, an inexplicable presentiment, a trembling but delicious presentiment tells me that we soon, soon shall be united to part no more. This life is short, and ——— come back, beloved Yngve! Your mother prays for this with your

" HERTHA."

To this summons Yngve replied by fixing the time for his return; the exact day he could only state on his return to Sweden. In about six weeks he would be there.

From the moment that Hertha with certainty could look forward to Yngve's return, a quiet peace and joy settled down in her soul. During the spring-life which the thought of this gave birth to in her whole being, a new youth, as it were, blossomed within her. The beautiful form, which had seemed somewhat to stoop and become attenuated, resumed its rounded contour; everything about her seemed to become brighter,— even the temper of her father, who, now that his daughter no .onger needed money from him, but almost entirely furnished the house-keeping funds from her own means, ceased to interfere with her private affairs.

Yngve's gentle mother, whose increasing weakness evidently showed that she was not long for this world, revived anew in the prospect of her beloved son's return, and she had now no other wish than to live to see him united to Hertha, the daughter of her heart.

Whilst Hertha's home exhibits this cheerful aspect, and she herself awaits Yngve's return with a throbbing heart, and assisted by her young sisters arranges everything in the house as beautifully and charmingly as possible for his welcome, we will give ourselves a moment's repose, and inquire after old friends and acquaintances at Kungsköping, and see what changes seven years have made amongst them.

The last time, that we and our readers made a round of calls in Kungsköping, they may remember that we found Ingeborg Uggla and Doctor Hedermann together, and he (the wicked Dr.) caused her a sleepless night pondering about "the question" which he had to ask her.

As we have an especial little friendship for Ingeborg we will betake ourselves first to her in our round of inquiries at Kungsköping.

TALK UNDER AN UMBRELLA.

QUESTIONS ABOUT A——DROMEDARY.

AFTER the evening's conversations which we have already related in our "short visits," Dr. Hedermann remained absent from Ingeborg's home for several days. She began to fancy that he had forgotten her, and the question which he wished to ask, and this grieved her more than she was willing to confess even to herself. She was therefore glad to dissipate her uneasy feelings by active employment. And this she found daily in the so-called "Children's Dormitory," which had been instituted by the doctor immediately after the fire, and placed under Ingeborg's charge. Thither went Ingeborg daily, whilst her mother sighed over all those new-fashioned undertakings which converted young ladies into servant maids, "and prevented all good matches" in the world.

One day Ingeborg went to her "Children's Dormitory" without observing that the sky looked threatening and cloudy, and therefore without an umbrella. When she reached the children's home, it began both to rain and snow. She ordered a fire to be lighted, and let the small creatures gather round it. She took up a little weeping child, which probably missed its own mother's loving care, and walked up and down the room with it, softly rocking it in her arms; and on her warm bosom it soon was hushed.

The fire burned and crackled cheerfully; the little children chattered and played merrily on the floor in its blaze, and the little fellow slept sweetly, resting his head on Ingeborg's breast. The cheerful comfort of the time stole into her heart. She felt with joy what it was which would help her to overcome all its disquietude; silently thanked God, and clasped with still deeper feeling the little slumberer more closely in her arms.

"Childless, and yet a mother," whispered she to herself; and whilst tears, not of pain, fell upon the sleeping little one, she softly sang—words which the moment and her own feelings improvised—

> Though I without husband or children may live,
>   A mother I still may be,
> For the friend of all children, the Saviour, may give
>   His friendless, poor children to me!

Thus sang Ingeborg softly to herself, casting every now and then an inquiring glance at the window, against which pattered the down-pouring rain, and remembering that she had not brought an umbrella with her, and that her mother would soon be expecting her home to dinner. But her uneasiness was soon relieved, for, as good luck had it, she saw Dr. Hedermann coming up the street with a large umbrella, and presently both he and the umbrella were in the room. The children set up a shout of joy, sprang forward to meet him, and clung round his knees. He gave a friendly recognition to Ingeborg, set his umbrella down in a corner, and seated himself before the fire, whilst, with evident enjoyment, he permitted the children to climb his knees, his arms, his shoulders, and there perform every kind of evolution. Of Ingeborg he took no further notice, nor said a word to her.

But when, after having laid the little one from her arms upon the bed, and had some conversation with the woman who had the charge of the establishment, she was ready to go home, the doctor hastily shook himself free of his young swarm, with a good-natured slap right and left, and rising up, let them all tumble helter-skelter around him. He then took up his great umbrella, and, without a word, followed Ingeborg out.

Away went both through the pelting rain, and the doctor held his umbrella over Ingeborg.

" I am afraid that you will be wet on my account, Dr. He-dermann," said Ingeborg, casting an uneasy glance at the doctor's wet left shoulder.

The doctor made no answer, nor yet altered the position of the umbrella, and Ingeborg, with a beating heart, had a presentiment that the important question was coming. At length he spoke and said:

" I have a question to put to you, Miss Ingeborg, but—will you give me a true, honest answer ?"

" Yes, certainly, as far as I can," replied Ingeborg, with an anxiety which was evident in her voice.

" Very well," continued he gravely. " Tell me, then, is it true that you—laughed at me and turned me into ridicule with your young friends ?"

After a pause, Ingeborg replied : " Yes—it is true—but—it was many years ago."

" Is it true," continued the doctor as before, " that you called me a dromedary or a camel ? I don't remember which of the two animals ?"

" Yes, it is true," again said Ingeborg, with burning cheeks and eyes full of tears ; " but, Dr. Hedermann, it was not out of malice, but from thoughtless, girlish gaiety, called forth by a something peculiar in your carriage and manner when you first came to the town. If you only knew how often, since then, I have been ashamed of that stupid talk, such as young girls often indulge in, merely for the sake of a little laughter, or to say something which they think is amusing, how I have repented of it, you would forgive me, and not think ill of me, nor consider me ungrateful, because I then—did not know you—did not——"

Ingeborg could not finish what she would say, because of her tears.

" I don't think very badly of you," said the doctor, in a low voice ; " I think it was very natural that a young, pretty, and indulged girl should consider a great shaggy figure like me laughable, and——"

" But " interrupted Ingeborg earnestly, " I was then a

thoughtless, worldly child, and could not judge of people, could not understand——" Again poor Ingeborg was unable to proceed.

"I believe you," said the doctor, "and now—now we are changed, judge differently—eh?"

"Yes, very differently!" was all Ingeborg could reply.

"I believe you," said he again, "and I thank you, Miss Ingeborg, for having so candidly answered my questions. And now we are at your home, and you must go and dress for the great ball at X. this evening."

"No, we are not going there; my mother has consented to let us stay at home."

"Then you will be at home this evening?"

"Yes."

"Will you see anybody?"

"If any friend comes he will be welcome."

"Do you regard me as a friend?"

"Yes, one of the best; especially since you have asked me this question."

"Indeed! Well, but—if I had yet another question to ask you? But I will reserve that till evening."

"And you are no longer angry with me; you don't believe me any longer to be one of those 'fine false souls,' unworthy, ungrateful——"

"I'll tell you what I think of you—in the evening," said he, and left Ingeborg with a look which betrayed neither anger nor yet an unforgiving spirit.

ANOTHER QUESTION.

In the evening, the very same evening on which the great ball was given, to which Ingeborg and her mother were invited, Mrs. Uggla sat in her small, handsomely furnished drawing-room, shaking herself in her arm-chair, with her snuff-box in her hand, and a most mournful expression of countenance, contemplating her daughter, who sat at a little work-table, busy hemming coarse towels. The coarse work contrasted with the delicate white hand which flew over it in the rapid movement of the needle, with the elegant needlewoman herself, and the room in which she sate, which was splendidly furnished with the addition of many small needless articles of luxury, and of which the temperature was almost too warm whilst it agreeably breathed forth the fragrance of " Eau de Portugal," which Mrs. Uggla kept near her in a scent-bottle.

Mrs. Uggla sate and looked at her daughter, sighed and took snuff, and thought of the extraordinary times in which we live, which make young ladies of good family, like maid-servants, and let them hem coarse towels instead of doing elegant embroidery and beautiful work, and which now caused Ingeborg to sit there with red eyes, making no figure at all, instead of, like the other young ladies of the town, looking brilliant in their ball-dresses, ready for the great ball at X. Mrs. Uggla sighed deeply, looked at Ingeborg, and thought; " she'll never make a good match! It is all over for that, now !'

At that very moment a ring was heard at the door.

" Who can that be ?" said Mrs. Uggla, annoyed, "it must be some beggar or other "

But it was Dr. Hedermann, one of the persons whom Mrs. Uggla liked best to see in the world, but who was never accustomed to visit her at this time of day. When she had expressed her astonishment and delight at this visit, the doctor said :—

"I found it was so excessively stupid to sit at home by myself, that I thought I would come here and see whether I could have any supper with you. But if you will have me you must let me have pancakes for supper."

There are people who are always welcome ; and if Mrs. Uggla had received a grand present, she could hardly have been better pleased than by this request of the doctor, because Mrs. Uggla had at the bottom a true Swedish house-wife's heart, and to this nothing is more welcome, nothing gives greater delight, than to entertain a friend. She therefore rose up with unusual alacrity to give orders for supper, and to have pancakes baked.

Dr. Hedermann seated himself opposite Ingeborg, and asked her to lay aside her work, saying in a voice which betrayed deep emotion :

"You answered my question so honestly this morning, Miss Ingeborg, that it gives me courage to come forward with another, which may seem foolhardy enough,—but still, in any case, I am certain that you will give me an honest and true answer."

Ingeborg felt unable either to answer or to look up. But when the doctor seemed to be waiting for her reply, she said :—

"Well ? The question ?"

"Can you like me ?"

Ingeborg let fall her work and looked at him with her clear, honest eyes, and as she replied :

"Yes, that I can."

"Fancy me, as——your husband ?"

"Yes," said Ingeborg, as before.

"Is it possible——is it actually possible ?" said the doctor, astonished and affected; "but I must believe it when you——

nay the deuce.—I shall say *thou*, ever after this—when thou tellest me so, and lookest at me with those eyes, and my blessed, sweet Ingeborg, I would tell thee how happy it makes me, but—hang me!—I can't do it!" And the doctor took Ingeborg's hand and pressed it to his lips, to his tearful eyes, and held it between his two great hands, as he continued:

"Look you, child, it is a wonderful thing, a very wonderful thing that such a great, rough sort of fellow as I am, should yet always have taken a fancy to fine ladies, should have liked their society, and have had pleasure in the elegances with which they surround themselves, and yet which I myself would not give a pinch of snuff for, when I look at the thing for itself. But now that has been my weakness, and whenever I have thought of a wife, I have looked about for a woman as delicate as a real pearl, set in gold, but yet at the same time a true human being in heart and deed, who could put up with the rough as well as preserve the smooth in life. I became several years ago in love with such a pearl set in gold, I loved her almost to adoration. She allowed herself to be worshipped by me, then made a fool of me behind my back, with another lover as fine and false as she was. When I first discovered this, I became ill, then angry, afterwards bitter, and afraid of elegant, fine ladies; I suspected them altogether of being false, and became an enemy to them—excepting when I became their physician. And when I fell in love with you, Miss Ingeborg, pretty nearly fifteen years ago, I revenged myself on your and on my own weakness by finding fault with you, until the time when you had that affection of the eyes; then I saw a something in the depth of those eyes, a something which affected me, and made me tender-hearted. I fancied that I saw there an angel with imprisoned wings, glancing forth with heavenly serenity from the mists which sought to dim its countenance. I did not believe what I had seen, did not believe my own feelings, until the reality of your life convinced me that you were the woman whom I sought, fine as a true

21

pearl set in gold, and at the same time a real human being in heart and in deed, an angel in goodness, a noble, truthful woman ; and the only thing that I now wonder at is, that I actually have found such a one, and that such a woman can actually take a fancy to and like me !"

" Oh Dr. Hedermann !"

" Call me David, and say thou to me, or I will run away !"

" If thou didst but know," resumed Ingeborg, with quiet tears, " how much more wonderful it seems to me that thou canst like me, who was so deceitful, so full of faults, and besides no longer young."

" Young enough for me," said the doctor. " Thou art ten years younger than I am, and a thousand times more lovely in my eyes now than before. And it is to me most difficult to comprehend how thou really canst like me !"

" But do you then believe me still to be a thoughtless, giddy girl ?" said Ingeborg, cheerfully ; " let me then tell you how you—I beg pardon, thou didst convert me. When I had that sad affection of the eyes, which threatened to produce blindness, and thou wast my physician, I was so deeply affected by thy kindness, thy care for me ; and when I owed the restoration of my sight to thee, I saw in thy eyes that which I never forgot. Thy conversation, thy example, thy whole life became beacons to me and helped me by degrees to free myself from the fetters wherewith custom, and my good mother's mistaken tenderness, had bound me to the mere emptiness of life. I never loved it ; I hungered and thirsted after something better, but knew not what, until thou showedst me the way. Since then I have silently followed thee as far as I was able, but without any hope of being able to overtake thee, often made unhappy by thy bitterness and mistrust of me, but yet more happy in the new duties which thou hast pointed out to me in a life for others, than I had ever before been for a moment, whilst I lived merely for myself."

" And thou art not afraid of a life of labor with me, Ingeborg ? For will not conceal from thee, that I regard myself as one of our Lord's humble stewards on earth, and all that I have obtained from him of spiritual or physical good, I must employ in his service; I do not like spending money in dinners and expensive wines, and such unnecessaries, but desire to live a simple, frugal life, as one of our father's laborers on earth. Art thou not afraid of this, Ingeborg? Thou art not accustomed to it."

"I shall soon become so, if thou consider me worthy to share it with thee."

"And thou canst fully trust thyself to me?—I am snappish and odd sometimes—very queer-tempered,—say cutting things —wilt thou not be afraid of me?"

"If I am so, I shall tell thee."

"But if I get angry, unreasonable?"

"Then I shall try to break thee of it.

"Well said, Ingeborg! Thanks for the promise. Thy courteousness and gentleness will be my correctors. I will put myself under their teaching.

"Now look," continued the doctor, suddenly assuming a humorous gaiety, "when a dromedary or camel will take his driver upon his back, he falls down on his knees before him, as I do, and the other places himself on his shoulder, thus, and takes the bridle in his hand, and then the obedient dromedary rises, and is guided by that hand, even though it be the weak hand of a woman, and he carries her to the Herberg, through the desert of the world, thus."

And so saying, Dr. Hedermann lifted Ingeborg upon his shoulder, and marched with her along the room.

No wonder that Mrs. Uggla, who at that moment entered and beheld this extraordinary "undertaking," believed that the doctor was gone mad, and was very near falling into a fit from sheer terror. But when she saw Ingeborg's calm and smiling countenance, she stood stock-still with the door in her hand, whilst the doctor exclaimed gaily to her:

"We are only rehearsing a scheme which we have agreed upon carrying out through the whole of our lives. I am a sort of dromedary which has undertaken to carry Ingeborg through the desert journey, and Ingeborg will be my gracious leader and governor, yet with the proviso that Ingeborg's mother gives us her blessing on our way."

"Let me descend, my dromedary," said Ingeborg, "my mother does not understand the joke."

"Then we will explain it to her in earnest!" said the doctor as he obeyed Ingeborg, and turning to her mother, explained what had taken place, besought Ingeborg's hand and her mother's blessing with such cordial feeling, that Mrs. Uggla, both affected and astonished, had neither words nor opportunity to express the many doubts which she felt with regard to the match, nor yet her amazement at the way in which it had been brought about. Mrs. Uggla really had never thought of Dr. Hedermann as her son-in-law, and she considered him, in fact, not altogether *comme il faut*, as her daughter's husband. But she had too much respect for him and his medical skill to let this be observed.

"But he is not a nobleman!" said she, sighing, to Ingeborg, when they were alone.

"But he is an honorable man and the best of men !" said Ingeborg, "and mamma's daughter will be happy with him."

"And he is a wealthy man—lives in his own house—the towns-people will say that Ingeborg has made a good match," sighed Mrs. Uggla, *in petto*, with a sense of consolation.

She was one of the old school, the good lady, and firmly adhered to the old style.

A WEDDING AT KUNGSKÖPING.

WHAT THE TOWNS-PEOPLE SAID.

DR. HEDERMANN so hurried on the publication of the banns and the marriage, that in one month after the evening we have just described he led his own Ingeborg into his own house as his wife, and he made Ingeborg's mother such handsome presents on this occasion, that she almost forgot to sigh because he was not a nobleman. But then, on the other hand, he .played her, on that very wedding-day, such a trick as she never forgot and hardly ever forgave him. For, instead of following the old Swedish custom, not the most agreeable, according to our fancy, but which, in Mrs. Uggla's family, had always been the ceremonial usage at weddings, just at the very time when the bride ought to have vanished in a mysterious manner from the little company, and when Mrs. Uggla was giving significant hints to Ingeborg on the subject, what should the doctor do, but take it into his head to play the part of dromedary, snatch up his bride, place her on his shoulder, and carry her off before the eyes of all!

Ingeborg's cheerful and consoling words to her mother, "We shall soon come and see you again, mamma!" had very little consolation in them, as she beheld Ingeborg placed in a covered carriage, wrapped up in a cloak of the doctor's, who then stepped into the carriage, and away it drove rapidly with them—nobody knew where!

Mrs. Uggla would have distressed herself horribly at this sort of abduction, had not Mimmi Svanberg, who was present at the wedding, and had been admitted into the plot, com-forted her somewhat by the assurance that this mode of procedure was modern and universally practised in England and America, and would soon be the fashion in this country also. Mimmi Svanberg laughed so heartily at the whole thing, and talked so about the story of Pluto and Proserpine, that Mrs. Uggla really began to think that the affair was not so terrible after all, and was ready to smile at Mimmi's joke, and promised not to trouble herself at all as to what the Kungsköping people might say about the matter.

The Kungsköping people were not very well pleased with the wedding, which was carried on so quietly and silently that they had hardly time to know anything about it before it was all over, and the doctor had gone off with his wife. And when the new-married couple after a few weeks' absence returned to the town, and instead of paying visits or sending out great invitations, as the Kungsköping people had calculated upon, continued to live wholly in stillness and quietness, occupying themselves with the poor and the sick of the town, rather than with its well-to-do inhabitants, the people of Kungsköping began to grumble, and say all kinds of things about " meanness," and want of " knowledge of life," and that the " doctor was a tyrant to his wife, and that she would be very glad to see people if she dared;" and in short, it is impossible to say what other extraordinary reports might not have been circulated by the townsfolks, with their corsair Mrs. Tupplander at their head, about the new-married couple, " who did not behave like other people;" if they had not been driven out of their heads by another wedding, which was more in accordance with the honor of Kungsköping and the respectability of its inhabitants. This was the wedding of Adelgunda Jönson and Lieutenant Krongranat.

Mrs. Jönson, who was now fully entitled to call her daughter " her ladyship," spared nothing to make the wedding worthy of her daughter's new rank and her own family's respectability.

Long before, and long after the wedding, the people of Kungsköping talked with admiration of the wealth and the solid luxury which was expended on this occasion. Never before in Kungsköping had so many tables been seen so richly covered with silver, and with so many dishes, so much " fatted calf" and roast goose. And seldom among wedding-guests had been seen before so great a number of jolly, fat, and, to all appearance, substantial and well-to-do people. The queen of the feast, Mrs. Jönson, shone like a sun of warmth and gladness; Adelgunda in her splendid silk dress, covered with lace, was as fair, and round, and plump, as her tender mother could desire, and was greatly admired by all the crowds, who flocked thither from far and near, to " see the bride."

The wedding-feast lasted for five hours, healths were drunk, and verses, composed by a Kungsköping poet, recited; very beautiful poems they were said to be, but the following three lines only have reached us—

> She is a turtle fair and true,
> He is so brave, so faithful too,
> And both to love pay homage due.

And long after the wedding the standing topic of conversation at every coffee party in the town, was her new " ladyship," and all her new clothes, trinkets, furniture, &c.; and even the wedding-dishes and arrangements were all cooked over again by the tongues of the town, and served up again with variations and remarks. Seldom did any wedding make a greater stir. Mrs. Tupplander only shook her head about it, and said there was far too much of it—far too much; and that it was not becoming to make such an ado about a wedding, when the bride, " her new ladyship," was in fact only a cheesemonger's daughter.

But after this speech became known in the Jönson family, Mrs. Tupplander never again, as she had always done, received the present of a fat goose at Michaelmas from Mrs. Jönson.

The people of Kungsköping had soon many brides and weddings to talk about, and one and another in the town began to suspect that the great fire, which burned down so many houses, had also kindled the hearts of the young people;

because never, in the memory of man, had there been so many marriages within one twelve months in Kungsköping, as in that which succeeded the great fire.   Many also, besides Mrs. Tupplander, attributed to the family-unions, and the acquaintance which young people made one with another at its family committees, and the mutual working together which was the result, a considerable share in the kindling up of these real unions.   And perhaps they were not altogether wrong in their reasoning.

In social life, as it generally exists, young people meet those of the other sex only in social circles, or at balls, where they are only able to see and become acquainted with each other in the most external manner, and with many people the mere outward is not the best part of them.   Vanity-fairs are the principal scenes of their meeting.   What wonder then that they so seldom approximate in a cordial and earnest manner? What wonder that marriage becomes, especially among the educated classes, more and more rare, in proportion to the many who are able, and perhaps who would wish to marry? When a winter-season at Stockholm is over, people hear two or at most three marriages spoken of as the result of it, when at the same time many hundreds of young people have fluttered about with each other at balls and other social pleasures.

If the intercourse of social life were more noble, natural, and simple, if young men and women could meet and become acquainted with each other, during their occupation, at their work-places, in academies, or in Christian societies, formed for useful and good social purposes, they would then be attracted to each other by the interest of a common worthy purpose, by noble emulation, by friendly mutual aid; they would then become acquainted with each other, not merely by the external, but above all by the inner man, by heart, will, and ability. Then certainly many more and much happier marriages would be contracted than is the case under existing circumstances, and those half or criminal connections, which at present people the world with so sorrowfully increasing a number of illegitimate children, would, of a certainty, be greatly decreased.

The true love would then have fair-play against the false. Whereas the latter only is favored by our artificial social life.

We do not know whether the people of Kungsköping said so or not, but we know that Dr. Hedermann and his wife, as well as the sensible Mimmi Svanberg, would not contradict these ideas, founded on many observations made behind the scenes, by a participator in the world's drama of life.

But we will now return to our Kungsköping, to relate an occurrence which took place there, during the time of Yngve's visit to his native land, after his first short absence abroad, and before his second long and sorrowful one.

It will, however, be best introduced by the account of

A CONTESTED ELECTION.

THE directors of the Kungsköping Infant-School are assembled, both gentlemen and ladies.

"No, that shall not be," exclaimed Mrs. Tupplander with a shrill voice ; "no, I will never give my vote in her favor. The woman who has had an illegitimate child is not a fit person to be the Superintendent of the Infant-School. How would it look? A pretty example would hers be for others to follow! That I know of a certainty."

"But," said Mimmi Svanberg mildly, "when she now sets so good an example of maternal tenderness, fulfilment of duty, industry, and many good qualities."

"What's the use of it?" screamed Mrs. Tupplander, "when she has an illegitimate child, which proves beyond everything how virtuous she has been. No, far better take Miss Von Schaf, who has no blemish on her reputation, or Mrs. Meritander, who has brought up seven children herself, and is, in every respect, a meritorious person."

"But," said the pastor's wife, "Miss Von Schaf is a weak woman, who has no authority, would command no respect, and Mrs. Meritander is too sharp-tempered and severe, her own children are not the best proof of her ability for the instruction of children. Of the three who are proposed for this situation, it seems to me, that Amalia is incalculably the best fitted for the purpose, although I concede that it is an annoying circumstance that she is not free from blame. But she has conducted herself in an exemplary way for several years, and has during Mrs. N.'s long illness, now for two years, attended both to her and the infant-school in a manner which is really admirable."

"But then she has a blemished reputation," shrieked Mrs.

Tupplander; "that is the case neither with Miss Von Schaf nor Mrs. Meritander. Who knows Amalia Hård's merits? Very few; but everybody knows that she has an illegitimate child, which she has the shameless—the peculiarity, I will say, of not concealing, but always keeping with her."

"But she never goes into society," remarked a voice: it was that of Hertha.

"What does it matter," replied Mrs. Tupplander, "whether she is out or in? It is quite sufficient that she has her child with her, and that it is illegitimate. She shall never have my support. It will be a discredit to the whole school. One must pay some attention to what people think and say: one must have some regard to chastity and good morals. What would the world say?"

Many of the directors took Mrs. Tupplander's view of the case, and the debate began to be hot and stormy, when Yngve Nordin requested attention to a few words which he had to say.

"Allow me to inquire, are we not all agreed that Amalia Hård is, both by her own wishes and ability, and especially by her motherly disposition towards the children, the most suitable of the three candidates for the situation of teacher in the school?"

Many voices assented to this.

"Very well," continued Yngve; "then let our object be the greatest benefit of the children, and let us take the best instructress for them, and leave the world to say what it likes."

"But that's nothing to the purpose," continued Mrs. Tupplander in her shrill tone. "She has, as the mother of an illegitimate child, no right, no claim to the place, and—what must she be called; what sort of name can she have?"

"Call her *Mother!*" said Hertha's melodious grave voice· "she has suffered enough and endured enough to deserve the being called so with esteem; and I know that she wishes not to be called by any other name than *Mother Amalia*, as she is already called by all the school children. Before God no child is illegitimate; and it ought not to be called so by man. Let us all, who have not forfeited the world's casual esteem by a casual error, unite in giving to Amalia that support and reparation which she deserves from her later conduct; let us, instead of rejecting her and her child, do them justice, and assist them in becoming respectable."

"I put no cushions under crime—not I!" again exclaimed Mrs. Tupplander, and shook herself from right to left; "but I vote for Mrs. Meritander!"

Yngve Nordin, who seemed assiduous in calling forth the free expression of dissimilar opinion among the directors, again spoke:

"If it be especially the rank of *Mrs.*, as a married woman, in which Amalia Hård is deficient, I am warranted in making known to the directors, that she will in a couple of weeks be legally entitled to this rank. To-morrow the bans will be published in the Town Church of her marriage with the man who is father of her child."

There was on this announcement a general silence of astonishment. Mrs. Tupplander, quite beside herself with surprise, remained sitting with her lips apart and her eyes wide open, staring at Yngve, who continued:

"Pecuniary circumstances will compel him for some years to remain abroad, where he has been fortunate enough to obtain a lucrative employment. In the mean time it is his wish to give his betrothed and his child that reparation which a name can give, until he is able to return and fulfil his duty as husband and father. In the mean time his wife can conduct the infant-school."

"Who—who is he? if I may ask?" exclaimed Mrs. Tupplander, beside herself with curiosity.

"That," said Yngve Nordin, "will be published in the morning from the pulpit; and any one who goes to church may learn it. But let us now return to the business of the meeting—the election of a mistress."

The debate was resumed, but now with increased advantage for Amalia, and finally she was elected, though by a small majority, because Mrs. Meritander had various friends among the directors, who wished to help her and her children to "a living." Mrs. Tupplander, very red and very angry, withdrew her name as one of the directors of the infant-school; nor was any protest made against her doing so, nor any regret expressed.

ANOTHER WEDDING.

SILENT as love's whisper of pardon for past errors was the wedding which united Amalia Hård with Yngve's brother. They were married in her room by the well-known little pastor: Yngve and Hertha alone were present. Such was Amalia's wish.

After the ceremony was ended, a mother bent over her sleeping child and whispered: "My child! my child! sleep now peacefully; sleep sweetly; no one henceforth will call thee illegitimate! God has forgiven thy mother!"

"And thy father also!" said a low manly voice, and with that Yngve's brother laid his hand on the boy's head.

When Amalia rose from her knees she was clasped in Hertha's sisterly embrace. After that Amalia's husband led her up to Yngve, saying, "Let us both thank him, who taught me my duty towards thee and our child, and who rendered it possible for me henceforth to raise you up."

Yngve's brother was also a handsome young man, but of a weaker character than his elder, manlier brother.

"Let us now eat and drink on the affair!" said the little pastor cheerfully, "because there cannot be a real Swedish wedding without both eating and drinking; and it does not do to hurry over marriages as those mad people, the English and the Americans, do; just get the ring on the bride's finger, then into a carriage, and drive away to the world's end. No: let us follow our forefathers' jog-trot manners; they never forgot, on any suitable occasion, both to eat and to drink; and, therefore, do you now follow me to the bridal feast!"

And with that the pastor went out, down stairs, and led the little company into the school-room, which they found sanded and strewn with fir-twigs, and in the middle a well-covered table, at which Mimmi Svanberg and the pastor's wife were very busy.

This was a surprise for Amalia and Hertha. But there is no need for us to say how agreeable was the entertainment, spiced as it was with good-will and cordiality.

On the afternoon of the same day, Yngve departed with his younger brother, the former to be re-called by Hertha whenever she could give him the hope of a favorable turn in their affairs, as regarded the future.

The people of Kungsköping, who in our story occupy the place of chorus in the Greek drama, made many edifying and moral reflections upon this marriage, which upon the whole was approved of, as quite in order, although Mrs. Uggla and many other good souls shook their heads as to its future prospects. Amalia in the mean time rose in the regards and favor of the town, and Mrs. Tupplander's enmity was stranded upon her good conduct and the steadfastness of her friends.

With respect to our other friends and acquaintances in Kungsköping during the last seven years, we may state that Mimmi Svanberg continued to be the councillor and the helper of all in the town, whence she was called by various of her friends, " the town-councillor." We see her always active; now with a myrtle crown for a bride; now present at a funeral; now making a collection for a cripple who needed the water-cure; now with a little bundle of coffee and sugar and fine bread under her cloak, hastening forth in the twilight to take a little joy into a poor home; or at a great ball amid joke and earnest, enticing people to help one another, without their being aware of it. Always cheerful, always kind, spinning a multitude of threads of mercy, on purpose to catch somebody in them, she seemed to be always devising some new joyous mode of obliging people, and showing how happy any one may be by so doing.

Many wondered how Mimmi Svanberg, with only small means herself, could yet have the opportunity of doing so much for others.

"My means," said she on one occasion, with a smile in reply to such a remark, "are human hearts, and our Lord's help."

And after all, these ought to be the surest funds. But one must first put trust in them.

Eva Dufva blossomed as a rose at the parsonage, embraced with unspeakable love by her adopted parents, dividing the day between healthy domestic duties under the guidance of the pastor's wife, and affectionate attention to her new parents, "for," wrote Mrs. Dahl to one of her friends, "when the evening comes and I go into my comfortable chamber to rest after the labor of the day, a pair of small arms are thrown around my neck, and a sweet rosy mouth whispers into my ears caressingly a pleasant name, and I feel myself a mother, and know that life is rich and delightful. I have never been so happy, especially now that I have Maria with me."

The good, active pastor's wife had actually now the happiness of having two daughters in the house, " and that is something," said she, happy in having two, but still longing after more. She was, besides this, always endeavoring after a better locale for the infant-school, but she always met with a multitude of difficulties, which were the more to be lamented, because the number of children in the school continually increased after Mother Amalia had the management, and after the little singer Mina, with the clear voice, and the clear, pious eyes, taught the children such delightful songs.

In the mean time the town was rebuilt, and the family-unions extended and flourished thereby, knitting up relationship between the wealthy and the poor; knitting up here and there among its members a real union in marriage, or a bond of friendship, such as might satisfy the warm heart's need. Such was the friendship which grew up between the Countess P. and Mimmi Svanberg, beautifying the lives of both, and continuing even when the latter was married—but of this somewhat later.

Professor Methodius had not yet been able to get his system

into operation, and the first sheet of his great work had been set up by the printer no less than seven times.

The Protocol Secretary, N. B., had not yet finished his book against ladies-societies. Rumor began to say that he himself was in a fair way to enter into a private ladies' society—that he was intending to get married!

But wilt thou see, friendly reader, at the end of these seven years (and as a consolation for all the bitter and caustic things which have been said in this book against matrimony), a really happy married couple, then look into the home of Dr. Hedermann and his Ingeborg. She always busy, domestic, ready alike for rough or for smooth—he, happy to sit beside her with a son and daughter on his knees, and gazing with a love which borders upon reverence on his gentle wife, whose "camel" or " dromedary" he every now and then does himself the honor to become, either when Ingeborg is not strong, or not in a condition to walk far.

" But what does it matter ?" says she; " I am really so happy, after all!"

She is her husband's help, not only at home, but also in his life, as a good citizen, in her oversight of poor children, and of the doctor's excellent institutions for them.

Mrs. Uggla, who cannot any longer sigh over the seven Miss Dufvas and their future, as at this time four are married, two are adopted at the parsonage, and the parents have now only one left at home, whom they would not part with at any price,—Mrs. Uggla, who sees her daughter happy and in the best possible circumstances, almost worshipped by the best of husbands, whose only fault is that of being sometimes " rather queer," does not rightly know what she, at the present time, has to sigh about. She has begun therefore to trouble herself about all the children which Ingeborg may probably have, and to sigh over the future, especially if they should be daughters.

All the people of Kungsköping had a great deal to say about Hertha's educational institution, and especially about the evening Conversations of which we have already spoken ; but in the mean time, she acquired more and more consequence in the town, and people became generally agreed in the opinion that the week-day school was excellent, and that the Conversation-lessons might be very useful as practice in foreign languages. The young people of the town regarded Hertha as a sort of Sibyl to whom they silently or openly propounded all important questions. They asked themselves, " What would Hertha say ?"

And now we will return to

HERTHA'S HOME.

HERTHA'S home was prepared as for a festival; the clear blue sky of midsummer and its blazing sun which " came forth like a bridegroom from his chamber, and rejoiced himself as a hero to run his course, glanced in through the open windows of the Iduna-hall; brilliant butterflies fluttered in upon the wings of fresh warm summer breezes, to salute the lilacs and lilies of the valley, which exhaled and diffused fragrance around the beautiful image of the goddess of youth. It is a glorious midsummer morning.

Do you see that tall and noble woman, who in snow-white attire stands in the beautiful room as its priestess? The breeze plays with the light, black-lace mantle, which falls from her shoulders, and caresses with a rejoicing breath a countenance, which, though no longer young, is nevertheless possessed of beauty—of a peculiar picturesque beauty. The eyes and forehead, especially, are unusually full of expression, whilst the bitter expression of the mouth is softened at this moment by a quiet, melancholy smile. It is Hertha, and Hertha expects Yngve home. This day, this very morning he is expected. And as Freya, of old, took an oath of everything in nature that it should not hurt her beloved son, so seemed Hertha at this moment to conjure them all to join with her in welcoming Yngve, her friend, her soul's bridegroom, and to beautify his return home. She looked on the beautiful plants, on the statues, on all which make the Iduna-hall a temple for the soul, on the butterflies, and up to the clear blue sky, with a new love, because Yngve would soon see them in this room, and she, as it were, admonished them to be more beautiful than ever to receive him, for all that was hers was his also. Many, many things on earth at the same time circumscribed her joy and her hope, but her soul at this moment, rising above every oppressive fetter, ascended in a song of thanksgiving to the Father in heaven for all that she had won and for the wealth of this moment on earth. As a strong tree raises itself again after the storm and lifts its head aloft and spreads out anew its branches as a shelter for the birds of heaven, so did Hertha raise herself after the conflict of so many years, full of thanksgiving, of power and will to comfort and to bless.

Her young sisters entered attired in their best; they also expected Yngve with eager yearning; for it would make Hertha so happy.

"How handsome you are to-day," said they, embracing her; "you look like a bride and like a priestess at the same time."

"Hush, hush, flatterers!" said Hertha, clasping them in her arms, "you must not spoil me. Where is our little mother?"

It was thus that Yngve's mother was spoken of by the daughters of the house.

She too entered from her room, not unlike a happy shadow, so pale, but yet at the same time so full of delicious joy, in so soon being able to see her beloved son.

Breakfast was set out in the Iduna-hall, in the midst of lilacs and deliciously fragrant lilies of the valley. The table was covered with the most exquisite delicacies which a country life affords; nothing was wanting to complete the whole but the warm morning beverage,—this waited for Yngve's arrival. Everything seemed to wait for Yngve.

That was in the morning at Hertha's home.

At this very time, a scene of quite another character was witnessed at about three English miles' distance. A steamboat was seen burning on lake Wener. It was making way towards the nearest land. The shore towards which the steamer was advancing was covered with forest, uninhabited and wild. The peasants of the neighborhood lay as yet sunk in their Sabbath morning sleep, and such few as had become aware of the fatal mischance, were a long time in getting the boats of the shore in action. The occurrence of any accident to a steamboat is so rare in Sweden, that people are just as little prepared for it as they would be for an explosion of the moon.

It was one of the canal-steamers on its way from Götheborg through the country, which had this morning taken fire. The passengers, who had been woke out of their sleep by the outbursting of the flames, found themselves, as they rushed on deck, enveloped in fire. The boats on board were found to be unfit for service, but the land was near at hand; they were making rapid way towards it, and all still hoped. Suddenly, however, it struck; the engine ceased to work, and the fire increased on all sides. They were not many fathoms from land, but the water around the vessel was too deep for any to get to shore, excepting such as could swim. An awful and heart-rending confusion prevailed, amid which pale mothers besought men to save their children.

One of the men sprang upon one of the paddle-boxes, and cried aloud: "All here who can swim, do as I do!"

And with these words he threw himself into the water; then turning towards the vessel, he called to a young mother, who stood by the gunwale with her child on her arm, "Jump overboard! I will catch you, and swim with you and your child to land. Don't be afraid!"

She followed his injunction, just as the flames caught her dress, and he swam with her to the shore. Another young man followed his example at the same moment, and yet two others. These four brave men swam to and from the vessel, saving all who could not save themselves. The first young man, who was the most energetic and the best swimmer of all, rescued in this manner no less than fourteen persons, mostly women and children His cordial manners and great courage

—the animated glances of his unusually fine eyes—his coolness and skill—all contributed to give him the confidence of every one; the chief hope of all seemed to be centred in him. The work of rescue had been carried forward so rapidly and so successfully, that not a single life was lost, either among the passengers or the steamer's company, nor yet even injured; and although they were compelled to see from the shore the vessel burn to the water's edge, and many had to deplore the loss of their property, yet the predominating feeling at this moment was that of having been rescued from a terrible sudden death, and of gratitude towards the brave men who had saved them.

One of these saviors, however, the most active of them, did not hear the thanks which were given to him. He lay, a little apart from the throng, upon the mossy turf of the forest, and a clear stream of blood poured from his mouth over the moss and the ling. His cheeks, lately crimsoned as by the flush of fever, now were ashy pale, and those beautiful eyes were closed as in the sleep of death. Silent and terrified, the lately saved throng gathered around; the women weeping, because he was dying from the efforts he had made on behalf of themselves and their children. Yet an attentive observer might have remarked, from his sunken cheeks, that death had long before begun its work in him and undermined his health. Still, however, he is beautiful, as he lies there with his well-developed chest, bared to the wind, and the drenched, rich, dark-brown hair thrown back from the pure forehead. The dark pine-trees extended quietly over him their waving branches, as if they would shelter him from the hot beams of the sun.

" Who is he?" asked all aloud, or in an undertone. "His dress looks like that of a foreigner, but his speech and his countenance, with its good, manly expression, are Swedish."

" My brother! my brother!" exclaimed a voice of deep anguish, and a young man pressed through the crowd, flung himself upon the ground beside the apparently dying man, and laid his ear to his heart. He again sprang up and exclaimed: "Take care of him! Let nobody remove him from this place before I return!"

And with these words he rushed through the forest in the direction of Kungsköping.

The remainder stood irresolute round the pale young man. Grateful hands wiped the blood from his lips, and bathed his temples with water from the cold forest-sprin ș. He lay quite still with closed eyes, and they knew not whether he was alive or dead; they could not perceive that he breathed. But to remove him they dared not. In the mean time the greater number of the people began to proceed to the town, because they could thence send help, and besides, each one had to care for himself and his to find lodgings, dry clothes, etc. On the other hand, the peasants of the surrounding district collected and formed a close circle around the young man, who seemed to have bled to death, or to contemplate the vessel which lay upon the mirror-like lake, with extinguished engine-fires, but still burning hull.

They talked about Yngve.

"He is certainly dead," said one. "He ought not to lie here," said another. "He ought to be carried to the town, to the doctor," said a third.

"Do not touch him!" cried one of the women whom he had saved, and who faithfully kept watch by his side: "the effusion of blood would begin afresh, and he would die by the way. We must wait; of a certainty some one will soon come to him from the town." And she related to the astonished listening people the noble achievements of the stranger that morning.

They waited in silence; the sun ascended higher in the heavens, and penetrated the thick forest with his beams. It grew very hot. The throng talked together in a low voice:

"What a pity for the young man!" said one woman; "he looks just like one of God's angels!"

"A brave fellow!" said an old peasant, "and one of the gentlefolks, too. It would be a good thing to have many such in the country if the enemy came."

The sun rose higher and higher, and the pine-tree branches no longer sheltered the dying man from its fiery rays. "We cannot stay here the whole day," said the peasants; "we must go home, but we will first carry him into the nearest cottage."

"Wait!" still besought the faithful watcher; "wait a little while longer! Some one will soon come."

Some one came. A tall lady, clad in white, came through the wood with rapid steps; she was followed by men with a softly-cushioned bier. The crowd hastily opened at sight of her calm commanding presence, and made way for her. She knelt by the side of the unconscious man, laid her hand upon his heart, and then her ear to his mouth. She then smiled and looked up:

"He still breathes! he lives!"

She made a sign to the men with the bier; she herself raised Yngve's head upon her arm, and carefully, with the help of the men, placed him gently upon it.

"Friends!" said she, addressing some of the crowd, "go on before us and clear the way through the wood, so that nothing may impede us. No one who serves this man to-day shall fail to be well rewarded by me!"

Willingly, but silently, they obeyed Hertha's command. She was known and respected throughout the country; she was well known in the dwellings of the distressed; and, besides that, every one felt deep sympathy for the young man whose noble actions that very day they knew.

"Now, gently, step for step, through the forest to the town," said Hertha. And on went the procession of men, women, and children, dressed in the Sabbath and holiday attire of the country, and soon opened a way through the forest. Close beside Yngve's pillow walked, watchfully, two women—she whom he had so lately saved, and she whom he loved so deeply, and who now turned aside everything which might touch his face—ah! dearer to her now, as it lay in the shadow of death, than it ever had been in the full glory of life. When the procession emerged from the forest into the blaze of the sun, these two ladies held over the head of the slumberer leafy branches which they had broken off for that purpose; and thus they reached

HERTHA'S HOME.

IN THE EVENING.

THE bridegroom is in the house of the bride, but the wedding——that is a long way off! Farther off it seems now, than it ever did before, for Yngve seems at the point of death; yet he lives; great is the power of love, great also sometimes is the power of the physician's art. The physician is sent for, and in the mean time Hertha is alone with Yngve. She kissed his mouth, his eyes, his cheek; she kissed his cold hand. Who can now deny her that? She can now permit herself to do so, for he will, indeed, soon die. The angels in heaven could not have given kisses of purer or more unselfish love. Never had she kissed the life-warm young man with a love like that with which she now kissed those cold and lifeless lips!

And those kisses of Hertha's have awoke Yngve from his death-slumber. He fixes his eyes upon her; he inhales new life from her glances. He raises himself. He soon rests his head upon her shoulder, and he whispers words of love and joy at seeing her again. But Hertha lays her finger upon his lips, he must not talk now. Soon comes the physician to see what he can do.

Dr. Hedermann is here; he gives the patient a composing draught, which is administered by Hertha's hand. Perfect rest is prescribed. Hertha alone may be near Yngve. He cannot bear her from his presence; he follows her with his eyes; he seems to live in her sight. In the course of a few hours his pulse has become stronger; he gazes intelligibly around him, he can sit up; he would talk even, if he might be permitted. But Hertha allows it not. The physician warns of great danger, but still gives hope. Yngve may possibly live.

Oh, how softly Hertha moves around him, and strengthens and consoles him silently by her presence, her own soul's fulness and strength. Yngve's mother cannot do as much for him now, because her own physical weakness has overcome her soul's strength, and she cannot look at him without tears.

But Hertha has not this day shed a tear. It is now no time for weeping.

The doctor has ordered a warm foot-bath for Yngve in order to draw the blood from the chest. It is prepared for him in the evening twilight, and mingled with beneficial and fragrant spices. In the hour of twilight Yngve sat and enjoyed its luxury. He asked not now whose are the soft hands which bathe his feet. He closes his eyes and dreams himself back to the time when he was a child in his mother's home and her hands tended him. They would gladly do it now, but they have become too feeble, and it is not the mother, but she, who regards herself as his wife, who laves his feet and calls the warmth of life down into the stiffened limbs. Yngve had closed his eyes, leaning back among the pillows of the easy chair; Hertha believed that he slumbered, and when she saw in his still handsome but emaciated countenance the ravages of suffering and hope long deferred, her tears fell for the first time that day. They fell upon Yngve's feet which she held in her lap, and she let down her rich and beautiful hair, and dried them with it. Yngve had often reproached Hertha for not being able to love as he loved, for not understanding what love was, and she had sometimes thought that there was justice in his reproach; but now she felt that there was not.

At night Hertha sat watching by Yngve's bed; he slept, but uneasily, and often awoke as if terrified by fearful dreams, but at the first glance of that faithful friend, he smiled and was calm. During the stillness of the night Hertha prepared herself for the morrow's combat with her father.

FATHER AND DAUGHTER

YET ONCE MORE.

EARLY in the morning Hertha entered her father's room.
She saw, by his threatening and angry countenance, the
tempest which awaited her. But she was now in that state of
mind when the soul takes no heed of fear, and feels a determination and a power in its will which assures it of victory.
Therefore is she so calm, so composed in her demeanor, glance,
and voice. The strength lies in the depth of the will.

The Chief-Director was deceived by this, and began with a
stern voice :

" What liberty is this which you are taking in my house ?
How dared you, without asking my permission, to bring a
stranger hither ? Are you, or am I, master of this house ?"

" You, my father !" replied Hertha. " But Yngve is in his
mother's room ; is her guest, not mine."

The old man knew not for a moment what to say to this,
but continued to look at his daughter with an angry expression, and then said :

" At all events, I ought to have been asked, been consulted
with——I ought indeed to have a voice in my own house !"

" Father," said Hertha, with sad earnestness, " you are
right, I might have asked your permission, have consulted
with you, but—you have made me afraid of you, and the fear
of strife, and the fear of your refusing me my prayer, prevented my coming to you yesterday, because I must have my
own way as regards Yngve. But to-day—to-day I have come
to talk with you, to ask your consent to what I propose, to
what must be done."

"*Must*," repeated the Chief-Director, astonished, "what is it that must be done?"

Hertha continued as before: "Yngve is dying. The most watchful tenderness can alone, by any possibility, save him. I wish to marry him, that I may have the right to attend upon him as his wife."

The Chief Director looked at her with an immoveable gaze, and seemed to be turning over in his mind the means of opposition.

"Father," resumed Hertha, "for more than seven years I have waited for the freedom which you promised me on one occasion, and which I consider as my right, that of disposing of my own person and my own future; I have waited for your consent; I have bowed myself to your will. I cannot do it any longer. The life of another is at stake. I have taken my resolution. Do not drive me to extremes. You may deny me my freedom, forbid me to become Yngve's wife, but nothing in this world shall henceforth prevent me from remaining with Yngve, and being his faithful attendant, even though I should forfeit my reputation by doing so?"

"Do you threaten? do you defy me? will you compel me?" out burst the Director, beside himself with rage. "You intend perhaps to cite me before a Court of Justice; to drag your father into a court of law!"

"Never!" returned Hertha, pale and calm as before, "but I warn you, my father; I tell you what will be the consequence if you forbid me to fulfil my duty to my betrothed. Do not do this, my father, and fear nothing from me. Everything in your family will remain just as it was before. I shall demand nothing from you as my guardian, excepting what you yourself may think well to give. Yngve and I possess sufficient means for the present time. If he recover we shall want nothing. Have no fear of us, my father, and give your consent to that which I ask. Otherwise I shall, with Yngve, seek another home than yours."

"Do you promise," said the Chief-Director, gloomily, "to be satisfied with such a statement of your mother's inheritance

as I shall render; will you promise that on your own, and
your future husband's account?"

"I promise, my father! You know that you may depend
upon me!"

"Are you prepared, you and your future husband, to give
me a written engagement to that effect?"

"Yes."

"Well then, send for the clergyman when you like. Only,
I will have no bridal ceremonies, no company invited; that I
will be excused; do you hear?"

"Yes; and there is no need of invitations. Bridal ceremonies would not be seemly at a dying-bed. I thank you, my
father!"

Thus separated, for this time, father and daughter.

THE WEDDING.

AGAIN we see the Iduna-hall.   A small, silent company is assembled there, in the midst of which is a man still young, though he evidently has not long to live, for "roses of the grave" bloom upon his sunken cheeks, and the fine eyes are bright with a supernatural radiance. This was the bridegroom. All seemed to wait. Anon a door was opened, and accompanied by her maidens and beautiful from the expression of nobility and earnestness, entered the pale but stately bride, with the myrtle crown on her golden hair.

Here in the circle of their nearest connections, were united Yngve and Hertha, by the warm-hearted little pastor, who was so deeply affected by the scene, that he was scarcely able to read the marriage ceremony, but from that very cause spoke with still deeper emphasis the benediction on the new-married pair, who seemed to be united rather for death than life.

And yet they looked more happy, nay more blessed, these two, than bridal couples do in general.

Mimmi Svanberg is present at the marriage, and by her lively loquacity introduces a little gaiety into the seriousness of the solemnity. It is the Chief Director in particular whom she devotes herself to enliven, and she actually succeeds in calling up now and then a smile on his morose countenance. Hertha and Yngve are all-sufficient to each other. Yngve is better this evening than he has been since his return. The fulness and the importance of the time seem to have given him a renewed life. But his affectionate wife watches over him and will not allow him to give himself up to the augmented excitement of the moment, without soon recalling him from the company to stillness and silence with her. Thus, as in former years, she again supported him on her faithful arm.

A SUNBEAM.

MAN—"he cometh like a flower, and is cut down; he fleeth also as a shadow, and continueth not."

These words often sounded in Hertha's memory during the days which succeeded, and when she saw Yngve decline more and more in strength, more and more bend towards the grave.

But God in his love often permits his servant to beautify for days and months the pilgrimage of a beloved being towards "The second light." This was Hertha's privilege.

Yngve seemed, especially during the few weeks after his return home, to revive, as it were, and acquire new strength. The presence of Hertha and his mother, their care and affection, the peacefulness and pleasantness with which Hertha surrounded him, all operated most beneficially upon him. Two rooms on the other side of the Iduna-hall were fitted up especially for him—for the house was spacious and contained much more room than the family required, and the Chief-Director himself made no objection to his daughter's ordering and arranging everything as she pleased in the house when he saw that Yngve's residence there increased, instead of diminishing, the family income.

Yngve passed daily a few hours in the Iduna-hall. The influence of the summer, the wholesome diet which was supplied, produced a feeling of physical well-being, such as he had not experienced for a long time. He began himself to have faith in his restoration to health.

"How can I be otherwise than well, here with you?" said he frequently to Hertha; "you seem to possess a health-giving power."

Towards autumn, however, the daily fever returned with augmented force. In order to devote herself to Yngve,

Hertha was obliged to leave the week-day-school in a great measure to the care of her sister Maria and Olof E. But she still continued her holiday-school; and its Conversation-lessons constituted one of Yngve's greatest enjoyments. But he only took part in them by speaking merely now and then a word. If his interest in any subject under discussion induced him to do more, or if he became animated in conversation, an affectionate, and at the same time beseeching and commanding glance from Hertha forbad it. Sometimes with affectionate pleasantry she would present him with an occupation better suited to his strength, by placing before him a basket filled with fresh flowers and fruits of the season, which it was always a pleasure for Yngve to distribute among the young people, and it was beautiful to see the little flock of life-enjoying youth surrounding Yngve's chair with looks of reverence and love.

Hertha looked on with an expression in which tender joy contended with sorrow. For she could not disguise from herself that the hand which now so kindly distributed fruits and flowers, and then pressed hers so warmly—that this feverish hand would before long lie stiff and cold in the grave. At this thought a dagger seemed to pierce her heart, and she repressed with difficulty a convulsive sigh. Yet she did repress it.

When winter came, with its clear days and fresh snow, and the bulfinch sang in the trees, glistening with crystals of ice, again Yngve's strength revived, and with it his hope of life. He so thoroughly enjoyed the glorious winter of his native land, and all those home-comforts which few countries possess in equal measure with our own rural homes. He was now able sometimes to sit with his father-in-law over his evening pipe by the crackling pine-log fire, and the Chief Director was never unfriendly towards Yngve, and appeared always glad to see him. Yngve sometimes even playfully assisted Aunt Nella to entangle her skein, under pretence of bringing it into order; in a word, he was now occasionally the life-enjoying Yngve of former days. But it was only the blazing-up of the lamp before it became extinguished for ever. Towards spring his strength visibly and rapidly declined, and an unusual depression at times took hold upon his mind. Hertha saw that "a struggle was going forward in his soul." She understood it, because she herself was passing through a silent conflict, and that for his sake. And they conquered together. Yngve submitted himself to his doom in loving obedience, and seemed thenceforward only more fully to enjoy all which that beautiful life had still to offer him—above all, Hertha's love. The weaker he became, the more he loved to have her sitting by his side, and to rest his head upon her shoulder.

Thus they sate one day towards the close of May, when the fruit trees opened their blossoms to the warm sun, and the soft vernal wind, entering through the open windows of the Iduna-hall, sported with the leaves of the plants which stood there. Yngve enjoyed these delicious vernal breezes. A branch of newly-opened apple-blossom lay on Hertha's lap, and his hand played with it as he admired its beauty.

The contrast between ever-flourishing and blossoming nature and the dying man was great, and Hertha, otherwise so watchful over herself, could not prevent her tears from falling. One fell on Yngve's hand; he raised it to his lips and said:

"How beautiful, my Hertha! to know that Nature is blood of our blood, flesh of our flesh, and life of our life; that it will rise again and be transfigured with us beyond the grave, through Him who has life in Himself!—a new Heaven is not without a new Earth! Iduna and her fruits are imperishable truth! Iduna is an immortal thought!"

Hertha could not answer, but she knew that he understood her thoughts, and that he who reconciled her to life will now reconcile her to death by his death. She bowed her head to his, and kissed his forehead. It felt so extraordinarily damp and cold.

"How are you, my Yngve?" whispered she.

"Well!" he replied; "very well, just now!" And he seemed to sink into a soft slumber.

Hertha embraced him supportingly. His head sunk to her breast, and seemed heavy; she no longer heard him breathe.

23

She thus sat immoveably, and her sisters entering, found her sitting almost as rigid, almost as cold as him whom she held in her arms clasped to her bosom.

The three bore Yngve silently to his room, and laid him on his bed. He slept—slept deeply—and the kisses of his wife could not wake him more.

THE ANGEL OF DEATH.

Ye sons of Adam of frail earth's shaping,
  Crumbling again into the same!
Ye are mine; ye are Death's; there is no escaping
  Since sin into the world first came.
      I stand in the east,
      And the western clime;
      And a thousand voices
      Ye guests of Time
I bring ye, the Lord of Heaven's commands,
From air and fire, from seas and lands.

Ye plan and build as the small bird buildeth
  Her nest in the summer's verdant bower;
She singeth in joy, and the forest shieldeth
  The home of her love one little hour;
      But where is the wild bird,
      And where are her halls,
      When the tempest raves
      And the strong tree falls?

WE frequently see a family stand for a great number of years, unmoved by the changes or tempests of time, and growing in calm security, when suddenly a storm comes, which, within a few months or weeks, carries off its members or changes its circumstances, so that it is, as it were, obliterated from the earth, and is mentioned there no more. It is the Angel of Death which has gone forth thither. Such are occasionally the devastations of a tempest, which in a few hours mows down, like corn, both the old and the young trees of the forest, which had otherwise stood unremoved for years.

Such a dispensation of Providence swept over Hertha's family. After Yngve's decease one death followed another in rapid succession. First died Yngve's mother, or, more correctly speaking, peacefully went to sleep a few days after her son's departure, thankful and rejoicing to be able to follow him. Very shortly the Chief Director had an attack of apoplexy, in consequence of the violent agitation of mind caused by the then position of the great lawsuit, in which he was compelled to pay down a large sum of money. He recovered, it is true, in some measure; but paralysed in the lower limbs, and after a severe struggle with death, because he would not die, but live, and continue as formerly alone to govern the pecuniary affairs of the family without taking counsel with any one. He felt himself, so he declared, as strong and capable, as regarded his powers of mind, as he ever had been, and he felt convinced that he should perfectly recover his health, and live many years. He took after his grandfather, he said, who had lived to be a hundred years of age. With this prospect before him he concentrated all his attention and all his care still more exclusively upon himself, seeming to consider his restoration to health as the only important thing in the world. Nevertheless he was not altogether regardless of the anxious charge which his daughters had in him, and he attached himself especially to Hertha, with a kind of childish confidence; and she, from the hour in which she saw in this despotic father, a weak, ailing child, felt once more that she could love him—could watch over him with love. She thanked God for this renewed sentiment of filial affection, and took little thought of all the weary watching and wearing anxiety of mind which, together with her own heart's silent sorrow, more and more undermined her strength. And though her father occasionally acknowledged her devoted affection, and appeared contented if he only saw her in his room, he still merely thought of her with regard to himself, and his selfishness seemed only to increase as his powers decreased. One day, towards the close of summer, a wasp had flown into his chamber, and they sought to drive it out through the window.

"Let it be!" said he impatiently, "it won't sting *me!*"

A few hours after he was dead.

Hertha's apprehensions as to the state of her father's affairs proved, on his death, only to be too well founded. The Chief Director died a ruined man. The maternal inheritance of his daughters, Aunt Nella's forty years' savings, and his own property, had all been swallowed up by the great lawsuit, which was still going on at his death, and which he probably still hoped in his last moments to win. During a slight delirium, which came on a few hours before his death, he talked incessantly of carrying his cause before the supreme court. And he did so—but before a much higher tribunal than he had thought of.

Poor little Aunt Nella did not long survive the death of her brother-in-law, and the result of the great lawsuit. During the last few days of her life she was incessantly searching among the papers of the large portfolio, and talking to herself about the mislaid documents and the lost lawsuit. And thus also her confused but innocent soul appeared before the Supreme tribunal, where she had no cause to dread a severe verdict. Anna, the faithful old servant of the family, soon followed her master.

Hertha, left alone in her home, with her sisters, was now possessed of nothing, excepting what she herself had acquired by her own labor, and the small sum of money which was left her by Yngve.

"We are now poor!" said she to her sisters, as she clasped them in her arms; "but we are able to work; we can earn our bread in the sweat of our brows and never complain, but on the contrary thank God. It will give us strength. Promise me, never to say a word in accusation of our father!"

Hertha wrote in her Diary at this time as follows:—

"Yngve is gone, and with him all joy on earth. Work remains. And now—to work! Work for daily bread, for the dear sisters' future, and for that calling which God has given me. I shall not lay down my pilgrim's staff so long as this hand is able to hold it. But—I feel it already tremble. God! be my stay and strengthen me, for the sake of my motherless ones!"

Without a complaint for that which was past, Hertha turned with earnest zeal to the object which would henceforward alone support her and her sisters, as well as render their future secure.

But during the efforts which this required, and in consequence of the consuming agony of mind through which she had passed, she soon became convinced, beyond a doubt, that she would not long be able to devote herself to her peculiar calling, and that her career would be cut short.

There is a malady which seizes upon women much more frequently than men, and especially on those who have been stricken by some sudden sorrow, or who have been, as it is said, worn out by a painfully laborious life. As an insidious parasite of the tropics seizes upon the glorious Ceiba-tree, fixes itself in its soft bark, and grows, serpent-like, twining itself round its stem and branches, sucking up its sap, until it lives upon a—corpse, such is this malady; it commonly first seizes upon those parts of the body which are most beautiful and tender; those out of which the fountains of life well forth, and thence extends its secret poison to the whole system.

The name of this malady is not mentioned without a shudder, because it is known to belong to the incurable; and that severe suffering accompanies it.

Hertha was aware of her condition; and knowing it to be her duty to live and to work for her sisters, and for the great object of her life's endeavors, besides the natural horror which she had of the disease whose symptoms she believed she recognised in herself, she consulted Dr. Hedermann.

He called her malady a " heart-complaint," but warned her of its consequences, and prescribed what physicians always prescribe, in such cases, rest from fatiguing labor; as well as bathing and the water-cure. Hertha thanked him; besought him not to betray her confidence on this subject; and he left her without any idea that what he had prescribed for her, was precisely that which her necessities prevented her making use of. But she would not allow such a confession to pass her pale lips.

She told no one; she allowed no one to have an idea of the truth as regarded herself. With a calm, steady mien she arose, and summoned all her powers to fulfil the duties of each passing day, and left the future in the hand of God, in whose fatherly guidance she had firm trust—to whose inspiration she incessantly listened. With ever watchful and warm kindness, and with eloquent lips, she stood among the young who gathered around her; she revived all who came to her for counsel or consolation with frankness and sympathy, and none had any idea of the Nidhögg which gnawed at the root of her tree of life. Sometimes a deep sigh would force itself from her breast, which many fancied when they heard it to be a sound of lamentation, but the sigh and the lamentation were so speedily repressed, as to be scarcely observable. She went out commonly for an hour each day, accompanied by one of her pupils, for the benefit of fresh air. Sometimes it happened, on these occasions, that she would suddenly pause, and stand for a moment perfectly silent. This was when she felt a faintness come on. Afterwards she would smile kindly and resume her walk and her conversation. Before long, however, the progress of the destroyer became evident to all in the emaciated form, and she was no longer able to conceal from those who loved her, that the angel of Death was at her heart.

ALL-HALLOWS'-REST

Is the term applied, in some of the Swedish provinces, to a season which occurs generally at the commencement of November, with All-Hallows' Eve. It may be, a few days, or perhaps a week at most, of perfectly, almost wonderfully calm weather, which succeeds the October storms. The lakes lie, like dark agate, at the feet of the mossy primeval mountains, reflecting them and the dark green forests, and every object, however minute, on their shores, in their calm, mirror-like surface, with the most perfect fidelity. Not a breath of air stirs; not a bird twitters; heaven is veiled, everything seems to rest and wait—the whole of Nature expresses a grand resignation, as it prepares itself to meet its fate, to enter its winterly grave. Still ascends, fresh and soft, the fragrance of earth, from the forests and the leaf-clad primeval mountains; but yet a little time, and it reposes stiff and cold beneath the white, enveloping shroud. It knows it, and waits in—" the calm of All-hallows."

We may perceive something resembling this calm, during the latter periods of Hertha's history; yet, at the same time, something more. Man, the lord of nature, does not, like nature, yield to fate only in passive submission; he meets it, he bows himself before it, in the living consciousness of the purpose of his change, and even at the approach of winter, prepares himself for the life of the new spring. It is his glorious privilege. This was deeply acknowledged by Hertha; and it gave a fresh trait of nobility to her not ordinary exterior, and endowed her with a new power over the minds of others. And if her calmness was frequently disturbed, and dark shadows at times fell over her peace, yet the fault of this lay less in herself than in the world with which her honest soul had still to combat.

They who saw her during the few months which preceded her decease, were for the most part greatly struck by her appearance and manners. One of these thus describes a visit paid to her.

"I waited alone for a short time in the Iduna-hall, whilst I was announced, and occupied myself in contemplating its beautiful statues and blossoming plants. I had not seen Hertha for many years, not since the time when I had considered her a proud and somewhat disagreeable girl, evidently out of harmony with herself and the world.

"Presently the door of the hall opened, and a noble figure, but wasted with early sickness, entered, supported on a staff with a white ivory head; in this form I had difficulty in recognising the Hertha of former years. The ambitious and sometimes contemptuous character of her expression, which had formerly rather offended my self-love, was no longer observable. There was something perfectly frank and friendly in the smile with which she advanced to meet me. She seemed to be above all the petty feelings and thoughts of this world. It was in the beaming eyes and the noble, arched forehead, that I was best able to recognise the former Hertha, yet these now bore an expression of quiet power and serenity which formerly was foreign to them. Every feature, every line of her countenance seemed to me to speak of a rich inward history. The strongly developed nostrils had no longer their somewhat arrogant expression, and all bitterness seemed changed to quiet melancholy. But above all this, and over the whole countenance, beamed those splendid eyes with their transfiguring light. The hair which was put back from the temples allowed their singularly beautiful outline to be seen, whilst a simple white, cambric kerchief, or veil, fell softly, shadowing as it were the head, and around the sunken cheeks. Hertha, as she now is, might serve as a model for a Sibyl, or for the Prophetess Vala, if the expression of patient power and of a deep maternal tenderness did not render her rather the type of the Maccabean woman, 'the mother of the Martyrs.'

"I was so affected by the sight of this noble ruin, of the formerly stately woman, that I could scarcely restrain my tears. But she spoke so calmly and kindly to me that I soon became calmer, and listened with indescribable pleasure to her conversation, rich as it was in life's experience, and so filled with great thoughts for the future. She is severe in her demands from our sex, precisely because she estimates its vocation so highly. She spoke of her pupils with great tenderness, and in particular praised most highly two young under-teachers in the school. The old bitter expression, both in voice and countenance, returned, however, when she spoke of the false views which parents take with regard to their daughters' education, and of the impediments which our laws place in the way of the development of young women. But the bitterness again disappeared before the trust and hope in the future.

"She was unable to receive my daughters into her school, because she foresaw that she must shortly discontinue it, on account of her health, which will not permit her much longer to give the necessary attention to it. This subject however she touched but lightly. I have been told that the physicians consider it improbable that she will live over the year, and I left her with the sorrowful feeling that I should see and hear her no more. I shall never forget the light in her glance, nor the affection which I saw beam from the eyes of the young, as I accompanied her into the school-room. All seemed to know that she soon would be taken from them, and it was plain to see, both from her looks and their eyes, how painful this parting would be."

In the meantime, what was the state of that soul whose silent conflict and innermost longing no one knew but God and the friend who was no longer on earth? We will obtain our answer from entries in her diary.

SELECTIONS FROM HERTHA'S DIARY.

"IT is now more than three years since I wrote anything about myself. After Yngve's departure, I lost, in some respects, interest in myself, and my time and thoughts were occupied in working to live. Now again I write in order to employ myself, for I have now leisure. Upon the cliffs of Marstrand, with the great sea roaring around me, I enjoy a little season of rest, for the first time during many years. How beautiful, how delightful it is, for a little while to have nothing more to do than the flowers and the trees; to bathe in the sunshine and be caressed by the winds. Yet I should not have come hither on my own account, because the soft air of " the Madeira of Sweden" cannot benefit me, even if it can do me any good, but my sister Maria requires sea-bathing; her white lips and cheeks attest sufficiently that she suffers from the disease so common to young girls whose employment is sedentary, and who are devoted to teaching. Ah! this life and labor is not proper for her, because she does not like it; but in what other way, excepting this, can she earn her living? I look around for her, but I can see nothing. She was not formed to struggle with poverty and want. Martha can go through this conflict much better. But will not the occupation which alone offers to her, that of housekeeper, drag down her upward-striving mind, and chain it to the petty, to the common, drag down her soul? And what is her future?

" Sweden! thou bringest up thy young daughters too much in the spirit of the step-mother, and this will be avenged upon thy sons and daughters to the third and fourth generation.

" *August 1st.* I accomplish this day my forty-first year. But I feel myself still young. I fancy I could now first rightly begin to live for others, if only I had the time. Fresh feelings, new thoughts, come up with the fresh breezes from the sea; and views open vast as infinite space. Could I develope—could I impart all that dawns within me; but it cannot be on earth; for I must shortly die. And I do not wish to live when I can no longer work. I wish not as a profitless burden to consume the little that I may have to leave to my sisters, my beloved care-takers. Maria is benefited by the sea-bathing, the fresh country-life, and I am also able to go out with her in boat-excursions among the rocks.

"How fresh, and at the same time peculiarly Swedish, is the character of this scenery. The stranger sees only, in the first instance, naked grey cliffs, in the midst of the roaring waves; everywhere rocky islands and reefs. He approaches them, and as if by magic, they open themselves, and reveal in the bosom of the rocks, charming groves and gardens, in which tall white lilies bloom, and ivy and wild honeysuckles clamber around the mossy granite. The vegetation is splendid in the little valleys at the foot of the mountains; and from every point the visitor gazes out over the restless blue sea, and breathes its refreshing but soft air. Oh, this sea, how many thoughts it awakens—thoughts, which here on earth I shall never be able to work out.

"*August 7th.* Is it the disease which gains ground, or is it this want of occupation which does not agree with me?—but my sleeplessness increases, and bitter thoughts and feelings which I cannot bear, and from which I beseech of God to deliver me, have again awoke. The sight of my sisters even awakes them, for what is to become of them when I am gone? My fatherly friend, Judge Carlson, is also gone. My sisters have no friend in the world, no support. Both are well gifted, but not extraordinary young women; they are extraordinary only in their nobility of mind and their self-sacrificing love. How different would have been their lot if they had been early accustomed to exercise their powers in a noble independence, in an atmosphere of freedom, and if the property which—silence! silence, bitter thought, silence.

"God—all good Father, it is not thee whom my voice accuses, for thou hast declared woman to be free, and hast endowed her with manifold good gifts, and hast created the earth rich and beautiful. The bonds which thou hast laid upon her are those of love, are those of His spirit. Oh, how willingly do I bow myself before Thy laws. But before human statutes, which bind what Thou hast unbound, which close up the paths which Thou hast made open, which limit, which impoverish, which mete out the liberty which Thou hast given to all, which clip the wings of conscience and power that souls may be kept in the dust—before these statutes I will never bow myself through all eternity, no! and again no! And those human beings who maintain them, who cry peace where there is no peace—'They know not what they do! Father, take this bitterness out of my heart, and give me thy peace, before I die!'

"*August* 10*th*. The venomous serpent will not give way, and this is a sign to me that I must to my home, that I may work, work for others while it is yet day. This will give me peace. I shall leave Maria in charge of Ingeborg Hedermann and return home with my Martha.

"*Iduna-hall, September.* Again in my home with my accustomed surroundings, in my school, and I am better, calmer. There is, in the activity of the mind for others, a powerful, salutary influence. It is one of the renovating fruits of Iduna.

"*October.* But I shall not much longer be able to work. I must give up my week-day school. My last moments must be devoted to my holiday-school. Dr. Hedermann assures me that I shall not live over the winter. Thank God! I need not consume the little that I would leave to my sisters by a long illness.

"I had yet much to say to them and my other young friends, but I must now concentrate all in one central point, in 'the one thing necessary,' for their well-being, their life. I will impress upon their hearts, or more correctly speaking their consciences, as forcibly as I myself feel it, their eternal destination, their *responsibility as human beings*, and fellow-members of a community, embracing the whole human race, to unite it though Christ in God, with his heavenly community of free sanctified spiritual beings. And therefore be thou alone our teacher during the remaining time, thou good Shepherd of Souls! and may thy greatness and those views which thou openest into human life, nature, eternity, a new heaven and a new earth, obliterate everything small and circumscribed, and separate all selfishness from the young, so that they may understand thy exhortation and thy love.

"Then I shall die contented. Some one more fortunate than I may accomplish the work which I begun, but nevertheless the work is begun, and I see around me a little flock which will combat for a better future in the name of truth and conscience."

In the spring her Diary contains the following :—

"*April.* Dr. Hedermann has deceived both himself and me. I still live, and may perhaps have long to live in this state. My sisters! my sisters! Is it I who shall make you poor? I shall be obliged to sell the drawing-room furniture and my silk dresses to pay the rent. I would so gladly have left them, Maria and Martha, to you my most tender nurses! Father! let me not live to become a burden to them, to impoverish them.

"*In May.* I have not for a long time had a dream worth relating. But my last night's dream was beautiful. I yet once more saw the three Nornor, the stern, motherly three, whom I had often before beheld in my dreams; they appeared to come forth out of a gloomy forest, and beckoned me onward, as they again withdrew within its shadow. I obeyed their call, but not without a shudder, for the forest was very dark, and a cold wind struck upon my breast. But when I had entered, it opened its long columnar aisles, and the lofty pine-tree stems gave forth a delicious fragrance. In the depth of the temple of nature I saw, not the Nornor, but two figures who seemed like shadows; but they advanced towards me, and ever as they came nearer, they assumed distinct form, color, and radiant beauty. I recognised them. They were Alma and Yngve; they smiled and beckoned, and—I awoke with a throbbing heart, and with joy I perceived the significance of the dream.

"*August.* My Iduna, all my beloved statues, my library, my pictures are—sold to a rich man, who will convert them into ornaments for his villa. I have been compelled to sell them, that I may not lessen the small, necessary capital which I have set aside for my sisters. I endeavor to bear it with indifference, but it wrings my heart. Had I been able to retain my property, or had I lived long enough, I would have instituted in the Iduna-hall an Industrial School for girls and boys, and placed my clever Martha at its head, but—this plan of the future must be buried like many another. Well, well! So must it be, 'Naked was I born into the world, and naked must I return out of it!' But yet for one more evening before the Iduna-hall is empty and desolate will I see my young sisters around me, the children of my soul, will talk with them—yet once more—for the last time."

He who a couple of weeks later had seen the festive assembly in the Iduna-hall, one beautiful September afternoon, would not have had a presentiment that the silent, sorrowful guest, whose image the Egyptians had ever present at their festive entertainment as a "*memento mori*," Death, also was present on this occasion, was here the secret guest, so beautiful was the guise under which he was concealed; so bright, so gay seemed the picture of life which was here lit up by the kindly beams of a bright autumn sun. There in its light might be seen a company of festally attired young girls, all in simple white, all with real flowers in their hair, and in the midst of this group of young, graceful creatures—many of whom were beautiful, whilst the countenances of all beamed at this moment with an inward light which made all seem lovely—sate in her arm-chair, a tall and noble female figure, she also attired in white, and one hand grasping a staff with a white ivory head, on which she supported herself, as with clear, beaming glances, and an expression of unspeakable motherly kindness, she looked around her upon the young girls, and spoke to them. True, her countenance was emaciated, and as it were furrowed by suffering, but something was yet there greater than suffering, something which prevailed above its traces with a wonderful touch and daybreak, as it were, of beauty, and gave to it a light, a life, a transfiguration such as no artist, excepting the soul, can conjure up in the human countenance. She still carried her head nobly, and the expression of motherly love was blended in her eye with that of the inspired teacher. Those young girls profoundly recognised it. Delighted and humble, full of devoted affection, they clung around her, and kissed her hands and her dress, and although she did not usually like or allow of caresses, she permitted them on this occasion.

She did not wish the young to have any idea that the purport of this festival was that of leave-taking, but there was a something about it which seemed to tell them its object, and which gave to their minds a profound and solemn impression. Two of these young girls belonged to the highest class of society, other two were daughters of handicraft-workers; the greater number belonged to the middle class; they were all pupils of the Holiday School. At the feet of Iduna stood a table covered with flowers, tastefully arranged in vases of the antique form, and with a rich profusion of the fruits of the season. Hertha was wheeled forward in her arm-chair (the young girls were all emulous of this service) to the table; and here she partook of a meal with her young disciples, after having, in the name of all, thanked the giver of all good gifts, for these His gifts. Hertha had not for a long time felt herself so free from pain, or so generally strong. The animation of the moment restored color to her cheeks; her young pupils gazed at her with joy, and believed that she would be restored to life; that she would be regiven to them, and tears of joy glistened in many eyes. Whilst she, as hostess, distributed with liberal hand the most beautiful of the fruits to her young friends, she turned the conversation to the cultivation of fruit, to the vocation of man as the ennobler of nature, and as usual she endeavored to awaken the thoughts of the young to that portion of the labor which belonged especially to woman, inducing them to express their own sentiments on this subject, and, as ever, giving her own guiding, living thoughts on the subject. She referred to the womanly influence partly by means of a developed sense of beauty, partly also, practical, by means of garden-cultivation. She referred to the beautiful myth of Iduna and her apples, as a symbol of woman's relationship to nature and mankind. The Garden of Eden gleamed forth, as it were, in her representation of the earthly garden.

Olof E., the only young man present at the festival, read, according to Hertha's programme, a short treatise on " Man as the ennobler of nature." This young man took a clear view of his subject, for which he had a profound feeling, and his thoughts accorded in every respect with Hertha's. Nevertheless he was not now listened to with the attention which he deserved. The young people, it was evident, would, at this moment, rather listen to Hertha alone.

When the cheerful meal was ended, she again collected them around her, as was her custom in the hours of conversation, and requested their attention to what she had to say to them; and no one can describe the profound attention with which their glances, their souls hung, as it were, on the lips of their beloved instructress, whom they would now hear for the last time. The feeble and sometimes broken voice, the supernatural glance of her eye, all told them this.

For the first time she now related to them portions of her own life's history; avoiding the mere outward, but speaking of the inner; of her soul's conflict, yearning, seeking, and despair until her meeting with Yngve. She spoke of him— oh! with what expression, with what tones she spoke of him, of how by his integrity, his goodness, his profound knowledge, he gave peace and light to her soul, and reconciled her to life.

24

She then spoke of the covenant into which they had entered on behalf of those whose sufferings and desires she understood better than most, because she had herself experienced them; she spoke of the plans which they had laid for its accomplishment.

"It became my lot," continued Hertha, "to carry out alone that which we had planned together, and therefore it has been imperfectly and only partially done. Ah! I am myself only a fragment of the human being, of the teacher which I might have been for you if——but the state of tutelage in which my youth was held, my long twilight, and still later my grief for the loss of my departed friend, have diminished my power, have bowed me so early. Love for you, my children, has supported me; still I have not been to you what I might have been, what I wished to be. Let your youthful powers, your earnest wishes, compensate for my deficiencies, and attend at this moment to my words as to those of a dying friend! Enter resolutely into God's service, as laborers in his vineyard; this will give you strength to bear much, to overcome much, to give up much, and yet never to feel yourselves forsaken or poor. Gifts are manifold, and employments in this world are manifold, but 'the Lord is One,' as the Apostle says, and in all these we can serve the one. The world is great; God is greater; and all that is in the world is his, and created for his glory. The sun in the firmament and the least flower in the meadow alike testify of Him. Thus must you young women, also, testify of Him, but in a higher significance. Do you know why I invited you this day to come to me, attired as for a festival? It is because I am pleased to see you so, and that I may impress it upon your hearts, to stand forth, with the best and the most beautiful which you have received from God, as witnesses of Him and his truth. Dedicate all those gifts, both outward and inward, which commonly belong to youth, and which so often minister to vanity, dedicate them to Him, the Supreme! Become his servants in beauty and in truth. Scorn to serve anything lower. Elevate, ennoble, the meanest object of earth by consecrating it to his service. Fear not, if it be necessary, to stand forth as the witnesses to his truth in the world; but do it nobly as beings guided by his inspiration. God has permitted his latest work on earth to retain—even after the fall—a perpetual memory of her first love and yearning towards Him and his revelation. Guard this yearning towards Him as your most sacred inheritance; and listen to God's voice in it;—obey its promptings; let not the sacred fire be extinguished on the altar of your hearts; otherwise it will become extinguished in the communities of earth. Let it burn ever more clearly, ever higher, stronger for all that is noble, good, right, true, divine; then will it penetrate, warm, and elevate all the generations of the earth.

"Show yourselves, both by word and deed, by the whole of your conduct in life, worthy of the freedom, the self-responsibility, which you have a right to demand from the laws of your country, and—it will be conceded to you or your successors. Force conviction on all, but do it through your own worthiness.

"Look around you in the world without fear, with no timid or limited glance, and then ask, 'What is it that God requires of me?' Ask honestly; and according to the answer He gives—that do, that become. But ask, like Mary, sitting at the feet of Christ. Avoid pride, and not the less, false humility and slavish subjection to the opinion of the world. Cultivate esteem for yourself, as a witness of eternal truth on earth. Oh, young women! your vocation is great, your future glorious in the service of the Most Holy. Devote yourselves to this with sacred earnestness, resolutely, courageously, humbly, but steadfastly, and—everything else will be given you, through Him. You may, in the beginning, encounter opposition, mistrust, ridicule, scorn, and hard judgment from many people, but persevere patiently; do not suffer anything or any one to deprive you of your hope in the future, your faith in the Redeemer! They will conquer and you with them, for yourself and for numbers!—But I must make an end;—I shall soon leave you; God calls me hence! Let me carry hence with me the hope of your fidelity to your highest vocation, and—I shall die contented, because—I shall not then have lived in vain!"

She ceased to speak. The fever-flush crimsoned her cheeks, and her bright eyes glanced with solemn earnestness around her, inquiringly and searchingly, on the young people who surrounded her. They all arose and approached her; one after the other, knelt before her, and laid their heads on her knees. She let fall her staff, and with both her feeble hands raised each of these youthful heads, gazed into their tearful eyes, and blessed them with her looks, kissed their foreheads, and gave to each one a few words of love and a parting gift.

"Farewell! We shall meet again!" were the last words she whispered, as she finally took leave of them by a glance and wave of her hand.

After this evening Hertha admitted no one to her privacy excepting her sisters, her young friend Olof E., and her physician, so great were her sufferings. She passed her days and nights sitting in her easy chair, with but few hours of sleep, and almost unable to take food. It was a pleasure to her to be read to, in particular those portions of the Holy Scriptures in which large views of the word's emancipation were enunciated. She then raised her head; her eyes were again bright as of old, whilst they gazed, as they had so often done before, into the distance, beholding, as it were, some great and glorious vision. Her intellect remained clear, and the expression of her countenance retained its serenity, excepting in those few moments when it was darkened by suffering or some bitter memory. To the very last she occupied herself, from time to time, with writing; noting down various things which she was no longer able to impart to her young disciples by word of mouth, and often also made entries in her Diary.

A few days before her death she wrote as follows:—

"Thank God, it will soon be all over with me! I need be here no longer a burden to my friends. In the other state I may, perhaps, watch over and work for them as a Guardian Angel. They who circumscribe our private history, our relationships

of friendship merely to our time on earth, have not understood
all that the Gospel can teach us.

"My sight becomes dim; my hand trembles;—but my
mind, my heart, are still young! Alma! Yngve! I come to
you with a soul full of love and athirst for knowledge, that I
may with you, or through you—if I am but worthy of it—
behold the glory of God."

Shortly before her death Hertha again wrote in her Diary,
as if to dissipate uneasy and disturbing thoughts—

"Frequently in my youth, under an impression of my own
righteousness, I was severe and unsparing in my judgment of
others, and spoke with harshness whatever I regarded as right
and true. I have done the same within these last days. A
distant relative, who lost his property through my father,
wrote to me, 'All your misfortunes might have been avoided
if you had in time compelled your father to render you an
account of your inherited property, and had availed yourself
of the means which our Swedish laws provide to obtain your
liberty. Then you might have married Yngve, he would have
lived; you would not, as now, have killed yourself with work,
and your sisters would have been well provided for or established in life. Everything would then have been different.
Do not let us throw the blame upon laws and upon circumstances, of that which is the consequence of our own indeci-
sion or fear of the world's judgment.'

"These words have wounded me deeply. Have I really
been the cause of all this?—have I erred so much? Yngve,
is it I who have dug thy early grave? My sisters, is it I who
have destroyed your future? I cannot see. I cannot clearly
understand things now. Disease has weakened me. The
shadows of death encompass me. Oh, this is a bitter cup!
God be merciful to me!"

The following words, without date, are written with a
steadier hand, but in much larger characters, as by one half-
blind:

"I have wished to do right; I have obeyed the command

of God and my own conscience. If I erred in so doing, if in fulfilling one duty I neglected others, then—the fault is my own. I could not do otherwise, and—I have been the greatest sufferer. Before God I stand justified, because of my honest intentions, but—

"My country! thou whom I loved so much, whom I wished to serve with my whole soul and my whole strength, but who didst lightly esteem my soul and my strength, thou whom I nevertheless bless for the good thou gavest me; towards whose honorable future I still look amid the shadows of death, to thee I confide my motherless ones. Be to them a tenderer mother than thou hast been to me. Give to them, for the sake of thine own future, give to all thy daughters, that which thou hast denied to me; Freedom; a Future; a Home for the Life of the Soul. For myself I desire nothing more. My pilgrim's staff is laid down: my pilgrimage is ended;

> I lift my hands confidingly
> Up to God's holy hill!

KUNGSKÖPING PEOPLE.

NEVER had any person's illness and last moments caused so universal an interest and sympathy throughout the whole social circles of Kungsköping, as those of Hertha. But there were very few of the better families of the town of which a daughter or other relative had not been educated at her school, and who had not to thank her for having given them a higher and more beautiful conception of life.

When she was gone, they sung her praises in chorus, and fine poems, warm from the inspiration of the heart, were composed in her honor. During her long sickness all kinds of things were sent to her which it was thought would please or comfort her, nor would greater gifts have been withheld if Hertha by one word would have allowed it. But her inborn pride forbade this. She only besought from her nearest friends that they would be kind to her sisters when she was dead. And was it piety towards her memory, or the effect of that heavenly guardianship, which Hertha sometimes pleased herself with the idea of being able to afford her sisters, when she was gone, but certain it is that people were kind to them, and that a propitious star seemed to rule their lives. Already before Hertha's death had Olof E—— and Hertha's sister, Maria, become sincerely and devotedly attached to each other, and now when we take our leave of them, we see Olof E—— promoted to a situation which enables him to offer his hand and a safe position in life to his gentle Maria. Martha, it is said, is nominated to the superintendence of an Industrial School, which some of the Kungsköping people have instituted in memory of Hertha, for young girls, and for which they repurchased the statues which she had destined for it. The spirit of life and of love for a higher development, which she had awoke, survived her, and still lives in the town.

Hence it is that the good pastor's wife lived to see the fulfilment of her wishes for the Infant-school. Who became the teacher after Amalia left the town to join her husband at some other place, we know not. After Marie Dufva's marriage, the pastor and his wife obtained a new daughter for their house, and they are yet wishing for another. The good couple have still room in their house and room in their hearts.

Mimmi Svanberg still continued her manifold activity as "town councillor" in the town, even after she was married to a wealthy man of the place. Her protégée, the bright-eyed, but lame little singer, Mina, is appointed singing-mistress in the Infant-school, and divides, her innocent cheerful life between this and her now much happier mother's home (one of the good works of the Family Union), and never, on the face of the earth, did a lame being more resemble a singing-bird, in life and disposition.

Mrs. Tupplander continues to give coffee-parties; to contend against the principles of this age " without rule or morality," and bitterly complains that Miss Krusbjörn is more and more infected by them, and actually defends them.

Professor Methodius still has not brought his system into operation, nor has Protocol-secretary N.B. written his book against Ladies' Societies. He has, however, done much better; he has become a member of a private lady's society— he is married to Mimmi Svanberg.

Mrs. Uggla, who can no longer sigh over the seven Miss Dufvas, nor her own daughter Ingeborg's many daughters, inasmuch as she has only one and two sons, nor yet sigh over her daughter's fate, has now taken it upon herself to sigh over the five Miss Hoppenstedts and the seven Miss Ugglas (her relations) and *their* uncertain prospects.

In conclusion, we will speak of two persons in whom Hertha

had great interest, and with whom she was in constant intercourse while she lived, though we have but little to say of them.

Rudolph—"poor Rudolph," as Hertha used to call him, continued his pedestrian pilgrimage for several years. Every now and then Hertha received a letter from him in which was a small sum of money "for the sufferers by the fire." After Hertha's death all intelligence of him ceased, and it is probable that he did not long survive her. By his letters it was evident that he found neither rest nor repose on earth, but was continually pursued by the memory of the terrible night of the fire, as well as by a voice which seemed to call to him "hence! hence!" But he also heard another voice which caused him to raise his head and his eyes upwards, and which repeated, "thither! thither!" A voice which whispered of a God greater than our own heart, one who knows all things and with whom there is much forgiveness. And as there are human comets which in the course of their eccentric career are seen for a little time above our horizon and then never more return, but may be attracted by other planetary systems, and in their orbit find order and rest, so are there also among mankind nebulosities which never during their earthly lifetime are able to fashion themselves to a decided nucleus; and even for these we look confidingly to Him who can and will perfect all His work. He has placed the one human being as a sun to the other, and thus we see Rudolph, the poor "son of the twilight," through his connexion with Hertha, advancing on his way to light and life.

Eva Dufva lived, Egeria-like, concealed in the sacred grove, where she, through influence, rather than by words, imparted a beautiful doctrine of life's wisdom to all who came near her. Long may she blossom at the Parsonage, pretty and fresh as a rose, and, though in time withering and growing old as other roses, still will she retain an imperishable fragrance of youth in her quiet, active life as daughter, friend, and mother to fatherless little ones. She will never marry; her only passion in this world was Hertha.

THE END.

www.ingramcontent.com/pod-product-compliance
Lightning Source LLC
Chambersburg PA
CBHW021710110726
47902CB00005B/1134